10670489

BITTERSWEET

A Novel Based on a True Story

by Sheila Banks

BITTERSWEET

A Novel Based on a True Story

by Sheila Banks

Sweet Earth Flying Press

Bittersweet
Copyright 2010 Sheila Banks

Published by Sweet Earth Flying press LLC
508 Tawny Oaks Place
El Paso, Texas 79912

Book jacket and book design by Antonio Castro Graphic Design Studio

All rights reserved. No part of this publication may be reproduced, stored in
a retrieval system, or transmitted, in any form or by any means, electronic,
mechanical, photocopying, recording, or otherwise, without the prior
permission of Sweet Earth Flying Press LLC

Library of Congress Control Number: 2001012345

ISBN: 978-0-9790987-3-4

Printed in the United States of America

Cover photograph: Laura Mae Cosey
Photograph courtesy of Sheila, Vincent and Richard Banks

This is a work of fiction. Names, characters, businesses, places, events and incidents are either the product of the author's imagination or used in a fictitious manner. Any resemblance to actual persons, living or dead, or actual events is purely coincidental.

*This is for you, Mama. The beautiful Laura Mae.
Thank you for loving me so much. I love and miss you
every minute of every day.*

*And for Sondra Banfield Dailey. Thank you for believing in me
and my story from the very beginning.*

I hope you two lovely ladies have met in Heaven.

CONTENTS

PROLOGUE
Watts 1965

Ellie arrived just as rabid looters hurled the Molotov cocktail through the storefront window of her shop. It was too late. Brown plastic faces and appendages blown to pieces like bodies in a war zone, swirled through the air in a hellish blizzard of glass, metal and wood. The arms and legs landed at awkward angles, their fashionable mini-dresses and bell-bottomed hip huggers that Ellie had been so proud of, now just smoldering shards of fabric. A single head bounced off the charred broken glass of the display window, before landing on concrete, and rolling to just inches from Ellie's feet; its frozen painted smile still in place.

"What the hell are you *doing?*" she screamed frantically, lunging at the perpetrators. *Had everyone lost their damn minds?*

"Get that old white bitch!" one of the looters barked.

"Stop! Leave her alone!" Faith screamed, catching up to her grandmother. "Nana!" As Faith reached for Ellie, she was violently flung against a wall.

Hands grabbed Ellie, throwing her to the ground, where she was kicked, punched, beaten and spat on repeatedly by the manic mob of angry young black men.

"Nana! Get off her! She's my grandmother! Get off her, dammit!" Faith, mustering strength she didn't even know she had, was up and fiercely elbowing her way through the bedlam. She shoved the riotous attackers out of the way.

"Get the hell away from her! Nana!" Faith sobbed, kneeling on the ground next to Ellie. She gently lifted her grandmother's bleeding head into her lap. "I'm here, Nana. I'm here. Stay with me, please. Please, Nana. Oh, God!"

Ellie's assailants froze momentarily, puzzled looks colliding with the senseless rage on their faces; stupefied by the brown girl, this Negro girl, taking up for the old white woman.

Carol witnessed it all, horrified. She joined Faith and Ellie on the sidewalk. "I've called for an ambulance, Faith. And, the police are already here. Oh, Ellie. Ellie." Carol's stricken face was streaked with tears. As was Faith's, who jerked her face upwards, glaring at the perpetrators with piercing eyes that forced a smidgeon of reluctant shame.

Her words dripped with aberrant loathing. "She's *black*, you cowardly sons-of-bitches. She's as black as *you* are, you *fucking ungrateful, dumb-ass low-lifes!*"

Ellie's beautiful face was now grotesque – bruised, cut and distorted. She opened her eyes, wild and blazing; calling out in a little girl's voice for her "Papa" to please help her.

LeBeau, Louisiana
Spring 1919

"My Mama say you ain't nothin' but a whole lotta yellow gon' to waste!" spat Sprite Number One, angelic in her robin's egg blue Sunday best, but riled by the devil himself to beat the be-jeezus out of this uppity heifer. Skinny-ass hussy always thinkin' she cute and smarter than everybody else.

"Take it back 'fore I snatch you bald!" snarled Sprite Number Two, also in angelic eyelet disguise, and wasting no more time on words. She was gonna whup this gal's ass. Simone had been taunting her and ridin' her like white-on-rice since they was but six years old, and enough was enough!

Twig-like cinnamon and cream arms and legs sliced the thick, sweet air of a sultry Sunday afternoon in the sleepy Louisiana parish of LeBeau. The spiciness of barely audible Zydeco hummed in the background, perfect theme music for the vista of lush, verdant forest and swampland, punctuated with giant Cypress trees, whose ancient gnarled roots rose 5 and 6 feet above the ground.

LeBeau was a world away . . . yet only a few miles from bustling, elegantly sassy New Orleans. There was an undeniable but denied line of demarcation between the classes – the whites and the stylish *Gens de Couleur Libres* in the city, and the poor who worked for them as domestics – or as crawfish fishermen, farmers or common laborers. The inhabitants – a beautiful array of humanity – were black, white, and the deliciously blended Creoles.

"Get *off* her, Simone! Get on up from there, Ellie! Come on 'fore Mama and Papa *kill* you for fightin' again!" screamed 10-year-old Nora, grabbing blindly to catch hold to any flailing limb in the tumbling tangle of 12-year-old girls.

Less than a hundred yards away, the wedding celebration of

Ellie's older sister, Beth, continued. Friends and family laughed, danced, ate and drank in the front yard of the Coursey family home. Children of all ages ran and played, taking full advantage of the joviality of the day and their elders' uncharacteristic lightheartedness. The parents of the bride, Sam and Callie, stood at the edge of the crowd, holding each other, bouncing in place to the music and beaming with pride at their Beth, as she playfully shoved wedding cake into the mouth of her new husband, Beau LaCroix. Beth, dressed in a simple but pretty white, gauzy tea-length wedding dress meticulously and lovingly sewn by her Mama, was a gorgeous combination of the beautiful cocoa-colored Callie and her white father Sam, who was raised from birth as Creole by his adoptive parents.

Callie, nearly 9 months pregnant with their sixth child, didn't look much older than 16 year-old Beth. Unless you looked at her hands. The stumpy nails, swollen knuckles and prematurely worn, wrinkling skin were decades older than Callie's 34 years. She kept her hands oiled up as best she could, but no amount of lubrication could mask the wear and tear on skin and nails in constant contact with water and ferocious cleaning agents like Borax and Listner's Fumigator that could eat through dirt and damn near anything else; the necessary ingredients for scrubbing and disinfecting other folks' floors, kitchens, baths and clothes.

Like most colored women born in the late 1800's, Callie had no formal education. She could, however, read and write to a degree; do figures and was dazzlingly skilled with a needle and thread. Nonetheless, as was the reality for most women with a similar upbringing who wanted to earn extra money, one of the limited choices for employment outside the home was domestic work. So, as soon as her children were old enough to go to school and care for themselves somewhat independently, Callie cleaned the homes of the wealthy and took in sewing on the side to help Sam save enough money to eventually move their family to Oklahoma. That was the dream. The land of milk and honey – and oil.

"Our Beth is almost as beautiful as you were on the day we got married," Sam whispered into his Callie's ear, kissing it and her cheek before resting his chin on the top of her head and wrapping his arms around her just a bit tighter. Callie glanced upward at Sam, who she had loved since they were barely more than babies. It was mutual love at first sight. How Sam adored this woman with whom he'd made a pact to share their lives before they were even old enough to *think* about keeping company. Even at seven years old when he first laid eyes on Callie, he'd thought she was the most enchantingly lovely human being he'd ever seen – maybe even an angel. Giant, dancing brown eyes set against the most glorious smooth skin of almost the exact same color; with masses of heavy, shiny black hair. And, she had the sweetest, funniest manner. Ten years later, they were betrothed. Callie lit up his world each and every day of their lives – just by being *in* his.

Sam Coursey was a good man; a man who had chosen the courageous – but difficult – path over the easy one. Born white into inconvenient circumstances for the underage heiress and her married lover; he was given up as an infant and raised by a large, loving Creole family. No questions were ever asked. In those days, if a child needed caring for, folks just took him or her in. Miranda Coursey – the maid of the girl's family - and her husband, Girard, opened their hearts and home to the unwanted bastard child. Seamlessly and quietly. Sam grew up with a brother and two sisters. That was the identity Sam knew, embraced and lived. He was teased, sometimes good naturedly and sometimes cruelly, for most of his life.

From the time Miranda brought baby Sam home, there were the requisite whispers by neighbors at the outdoor shopping stalls, front porches, the general store and, of course at the high temple of all gossip, especially that which was most scandalous – Church.

"Humph! You know that ain't his baby!"

"Whose baby?"

"Girard Coursey!"

"Ain't no way that's Miranda's baby, neither."

"Those others started out light; but not *that* white. This one is almost see-through."

"Mm-hmm. Unless *this* time, there was a white man in the woodpile, instead of a nigger." Now, that remark drew chuckles and guffaws all around.

"I didn't even know she was in the family way, did you?"

"Naw, but you cain't tell most times no ways," one of the gossips offered almost in Miranda's defense.

And so it went. For years.

Because he "stood out" among his brown siblings with his white skin, pointy nose, skinny lips and stick-straight hair, Sam and his brother Paul had to whup their share of ass coming up. Neither ever started a fight. But, they finished plenty. The Brothers Coursey gained respect from never backing down from one; and unfailingly sticking together.

Sam was tall, handsome, honest and hard-working. Teasing aside, he was generally well-liked by most. To white folks, he was treated as just another light skinned colored man; the coloreds eventually got used to him and, for the most part, accepted Sam as one of their own. Sam drove a taxi in New Orleans for a living. First, the kind pulled by horses; then those new, shiny horseless carriages. He and Callie rode into the city together before dawn every morning. But, it wouldn't be for much longer. All of their sacrifices – especially his Callie's – would be worth it. As soon as their new baby was born, Sam intended to fulfill their dream of a new life in a wonderful, new place. A much better life in which he envisioned giving Callie everything her heart desired.

During the wedding festivities, Callie's and Sam's handsome, curly-headed, caramel-kissed 17 year-old twins, Joe and Jake, were busy pursuing their individual interests. Joe was practicing sweet-talking the young female guests at the wedding. Sam had guessed correctly that Jake was involved in a heated game of craps in a secluded area behind the house. Much to Jake's chagrin, the area was no secret to his Papa. Sam, who like most fathers was a lot slicker than his son gave him credit for, busted up the hustle and confiscated the flask of moonshine making the rounds among the young gamblers just as Jake was about to take a swig. But, where were Ellie and Nora?

Just then, Sam and Callie's petites jeunes filles bounded through a curtain of dancing revelers. Although two years apart, Ellie and Nora were near mirror-reflections of each other. A chocolate and vanilla version of the same perfect face, delicate features and hazel eyes. And, there was no mistaking who their Daddy was. They looked just like Sam. However, their mother's beauty softened what might have been sharp noses and gave more sensual fullness to their mouths. Both wore waist-length ribboned braids – Ellie's honey colored and streaked with marigold; Nora's luxurious raven.

"For heaven's sake, look at the two of you," Callie gently admonished, smoothing hack the stray hairs that had escaped both heads during the scuffle and brushing debris off the cream eyelet dresses she had made for each of the girls for the wedding.

"You been fightin' again, little Miss Ellie?" she queried, one brow raised, eying her middle daughter lovingly *and* knowingly. "Hmm? Both of y'all look as though you've been rolling around on the ground, instead of being perfect little ladies at your sister's wedding reception."

"We was just playin', Mama," Ellie offered cheerfully, crossing her fingers behind her back.

"Yeah, Mama. The weddin's pretty and all," Nora chimed in. "We just felt like playin' hide and seek with Simone. Guess we got a little carried away. Sorry."

Sam leaned down and took a little hand in each of his. "No harm done. How about a dance with your old Papa?" He turned to Callie with a wink and a smile from ear to ear. "You don't mind me taking off with these two beautiful young ladies, do you, Darlin'?"

The girls had actually *started out* by playing. In what surely must have been an unfortunate case of getting caught up in the occasion, Stanley Du Bois had made the grave mistake of trying to kiss Ellie while they bounced up and down to the music. Ellie pushed him down, signaled Nora with "the look" and they both took off running towards her special place – her "root house." The root house was a smoothed-out cavity carved by nature inside the above-ground roots of Ellie's favorite Cypress tree at the far end of the family's property. It was the perfect hide-out, just big enough for two little girls and their treasures.

Before Simone, finding herself bored at the reception, showed up to lure them out by taunting her nemesis, Ellie; Ellie and Nora had been engrossed in one of their more serious discussions, inspired by the events of the day - but a continuation of an on-going debate.

"Beth is a damn fool is all I can say," Ellie declared. "Even if she *does* get to move to Texas."

"Why she gotta be a damn fool, Ellie? Ain't nothin' wrong with fallin' in love and getting' hitched. Mama did it!" Nora protested.

"Ain't nothin' wrong with it if you don't mind spittin' out a bunch of babies and being stuck cleanin' *his* house and other folks houses, too! Humph! I'd sooner chew off my paws than marry some stupid boy."

"You just get your silly old notions from those silly old magazines Mama brings home with her from them ladies' houses she cleans – and there ain't nothin' wrong with that, neither. Mama's just helping Papa save money so we can all move to Oklahoma where they's oil and lots of everything for everybody. And, we're going to have everything we ever wanted. So there, Miss Know-It-All," Nora shot back.

"Who wants to go to stupid old Oklahoma? Not me! I'm gonna see the *entire* world and gonna have the best of everything! You'll see! People will be cleaning *my* house. Just wait and see!"

"Okay, Smarty Pants. We *will* see!" Nora held her ground, desperately hoping to have the last word. For once. Even though Ellie sometimes totally exasperated her, at the same time, Nora adored her free-spirited sister and admired – was maybe even in awe of – Ellie's big dreams.

Then, here come Simone, bored and itchin' to pick a fight.

"Callie"

"I wonder if Beth and Beau have made it to Austin yet?" Callie asked wistfully to no one in particular. She, Joe – one of the twins, Ellie and Nora sat around the smoothly worn pine dining table in their modest, but comfortable clapboard home. Callie and Ellie, who had grown into a very talented apprentice seamstress, were stitching by hand; each working on different sections of a beautifully elaborate gown spread on one side of the table. Nora worked on a doll's dress made of the same emerald satin fabric, while Joe struggled with arithmetic problems.

The previous day had been perfect. Beth was happy; she and Beau obviously adored each other, even though both Callie and Sam felt as though she was a tad young to be getting hitched. There was plenty of food and drink; and everyone had a good time. The heavens had even gotten into the act. Just as family and friends joyfully gathered to throw rice and blessings at the new couple, the sky morphed from sunlit gold into an endless mural of deepest coral and gradations of crimson, slashed with rich plums and the exquisite lapis blue that man has never quite been able to accurately recreate on any canvas. With that magnificent celestial backdrop, Beth and Beau rode off in their horse-drawn wagon, which carried them and everything they owned in the world.

"Well, little Miss Ellie, I do believe you are turning into a might fine seamstress. This stitching is beautiful." Ellie beamed. Nora's little brow furrowed with extra determination, a signal not lost on their mother. Callie lovingly turned her attention to her youngest daughter. "And, you, ma petite chou-chou, what a lovely frock for your dolly. With your sewing talents, you too, will soon be creating elegant grown-up gowns."

With that, Ellie jumped up, swooping the jade froth off the table. She held the dress against herself and began to twirl around the room with it, dancing to a playful made-up-on-the-spot ditty, *"Elegant Ellie ever-*

after, after, after. Elegant Ellie ever-after, that will be me! Just you wait and see! Just wait and seee-eeee!" Ellie then grabbed her sister's hand, drawing Nora into her joyful fantasy dance. Delighted by her daughters' exuberance, Callie chuckled and clapped her hands in beat to Ellie's happy little tune. The three Coursey "women" were laughing and having a grand time.

None of this fun, however, sat too well with Joe. He was, after all, outnumbered by women here – instead of being outside with the men folk, where, of course, his 17 year-old self thought he *should* be – and he *was*, after all – trying to concentrate on something serious. *And*, Jake was nowhere to be found to help even out the numbers.

Callie caught her son's somewhat "fed up with all these womenfolk" look out of the corner of her eye. "Girls, girls, we are disturbing Joseph, who is obviously concentrating on something very important. We're sorry, darlin'," she apologized half-seriously for the commotion. Then, with genuine concern, asked, "How are you coming along with your figures?"

"I don't know what I'm ever going to use this for. This problem involves both long division and multiplication," Joe grudgingly shared, frustrated.

No sooner did he get the words out of his mouth than Ellie brightly spit out the answer. "Boy, are you stupid! That's so easy I could figure it out in my sleep, and *I* only finished the fifth grade – while *you* are finishing high school! Humph! Dummy," Ellie teased.

"Eleanor Marie Coursey, you will *not* speak to your brother that way! Apologize to him right now," her mother scolded.

"You ain't got to take up for me with *her*, Mama. I don't pay her no mind anyway. All those stupid highfalutin dreams of hers. Think she so much smarter than everybody else. Well, guess what, Ellie? You just a girl and you ain't never goin' to do nothin' but womanly work anyway – not important stuff like men do. So whatever little bit of schoolin' you got was just wasted, Miss Fancy Pants!"

Callie rose from her chair – no easy feat - walked over to Joe, kissed him and sat down gingerly in the chair next to him, rubbing her belly. She understood, but wasn't amused. She turned to Ellie. "We all know and appreciate how smart you are, Eleanor."

Uh-oh, Mama called me Eleanor again, so she really means business. I sure hope I don't get a whuppin', Ellie thought.

"So there is no need to show off," Callie continued. "And there is never the need to ever speak that way to your brother or anyone else, for that matter. Do I make myself clear?"

"Yes, Mama," Ellie answered, her head lowered. She hated to upset or disappoint her Mama. Especially now.

Callie then turned back to her son. "And you, young man. You and I both know that you would have figured out that problem eventually. Ellie's just faster at arithmetic, that's all; and she was just being an annoying little sister. Being good at numbers, or sewing or building things or what*ever* - we all have our gifts the good Lord gave us. Can't none of us, though, be an expert at everything. None of us. Don't work that way.

But, you also need to remember that nobody's dreams are *ever* stupid. Dreams are what give us the strength to get up ev'ry mornin' and live this life." Then, looking deeply into Joe's eyes, she asked, "Do you consider my caring for and making a home for you, your papa, brother and sisters all these years not important? After all, ain't I 'just a girl,' too?"

On the front porch, Sam and his brother, Paul, half-heartedly pulled and puffed on their pipes. Both men were tense.

"So, they's movin' up from Thibodaux. How soon?" Paul asked, staring blankly into the creeping darkness; already knowing the answer.

"Not sure. But, we got to be on guard at all times. Their poison is spreading through Louisiana like greased lightnin' and you can't trust no one!" Sam whispered in an urgent voice. He was detailing the movement of the Ku Klux Klan in Louisiana, moving towards LeBeau, casting a much wider net than before. It wasn't the first time Sam had used the color of his skin to blend in at a Klan meeting and spy on the sinister goings-on. Then, just as anonymously, he slid out to return home; two or three days' ride away, and report back with the information.

"Most folks know by now, thanks to you. Know to stay close to home. Don't be wandering off nowheres."

"Jake should have been home by sundown," Sam murmured,

pacing. "Despite the pleadin', preachin' and the lickins', that boy is hard-headed and favors hangin' out in town doin' everything he ain't got no business doin' – cock fights, gamblin', drinkin'. It ain't safe for a young colored man wandering 'round out there, coming home after dark. Especially a hothead like my son. Can't nothin' seem to tame the trouble that boy's bound and determined to find and jump in the middle of. C'mon, Paul, I'm gonna look for him."

Paul grabbed his brother's arm. "I'll admit Jake's a handful, but chances are, Jake's gonna come runnin' up them steps any minute. The one you *needs* to be keepin' yo eye on is *Ellie*."

Paul's voice dripped with venom as he related that while burning crosses, lynching and terrorizing were still the sports of choice for these henchmen of the devil, they had cultivated a quieter evil. Every once in a blue moon, the occasional young Klansman had been known to cowardly swoop down on an isolated bayou family like a circling vulture and simply steal an unmarried daughter – beautiful young colored and Creole girls, especially the lightest ones. Sometimes they kept the girls and young women as illegal common-law wives; sometimes they enslaved them or tortured them and God knows what else. Never to be seen or heard from again. Often the predator has watched his prey at a distance for years; maybe even watched her as she grew up; his appetite steadily sharpened by elder hatemongers, the role models – fathers, grandfathers, uncles, older brothers.

"You know the stories as well as I do, brother! You know we can't trust *no one*," Paul pressed with sadness and disgust.

Sam wearily laid his free hand on his brother's shoulder. "I know, Paul. I know. 'Cause more often than not, the vermin live right amongst us."

Heavyhearted, Sam shook his head and admitted to his brother that it has long worried him sick that his beautiful, spirited child fears nothin' and nobody, "even though she's only 12 years-old and ain't no bigger than a bar of soap after a week's washin'." But it's Jake he's most troubled about. Sam was convinced Ellie was safe because she stayed close to home; but Jake and Joe walked to and from school every day, five miles each way. Paul agreed, but cautioned Sam not to take lightly the threat that might exist for Ellie or even little Nora, because Sam *is* gone everyday, making a living driving his cab.

Just then, Jake sprinted through the darkness and up the steps to the porch, stopping in his tracks when he spotted his father and his uncle waiting for him.

"Where you been, son?" Sam asked, trying to appear calm as he re-lit his pipe; even though the sheer relief at seeing his boy collided with the anger of Jake's recklessness to inspire unsteadiness in his hands.

"Hey, Papa. Hey, Uncle Paul. Uh, see, I was just messin' around with some of the fellas and lost track of – " Jake tried to stumble through, but his father cut him off, dropping his pipe and grabbing Jake firmly by the shoulders, shaking him.

"Boy, don't you know how dangerous it is for a young colored man to be out here after sundown? Especially now, with them damn nightriders movin' closer in." Jake's eyes widened.

"Yeah, the Klan. And, you got alcohol on your breath, too? You know you lose your damn mind when you been drinkin.' Get in the house, now!"

"But, Papa - "

"Don't 'but, papa' me, boy! There ain't nothin' you can say! What the hell you tryin' to do? Get yourself killed? You know good and damn well it *ain't-safe-for-a-young-colored-man-in-this-world!*" Sam's terror for his son was getting the best of him. And, Jake was just lit up enough to mouth off.

"*What*, Papa? What you 'spect me to do? Spend my life hidin' instead of livin'? What you know about bein' a colored man in this world, anyway? Huh?" Jake regretted the words as soon as they flew out of his mouth. Sam released his son's shoulders, then slapped him hard across the face. They were both taken aback.

The blow knocked Jake sober and he was immediately filled with remorse. "Papa, I - " he started.

"Just get in the house, boy," Sam cut him off, but he couldn't look at his son. "Just get in the house and stay there. Ain't you got some lessons to finish?"

Jake nodded, saying nothing more, and headed inside. Paul placed a sympathetic hand on his brother's shoulder.

"I love him so much, you know," Sam half-whispered in a sad monotone. "He and his mother and brother and sisters are my life, Paul. I would do anything to keep them safe. Anything."

———

Just a few days later, during early evening when the crickets, frogs and night birds had just begun their serenade, the men again paced the porch. All of them – Sam, Paul, Jake and Joe. Nora sat on the steps, cradling her rag doll. She was too young to be inside with her sister and her two Aunties, Papa's sisters, Lucille and Agnes, as they took care of her mother. Callie's intermittent tortured screams from inside shattered the soothing sounds of the night.

Inside Callie and Sam's bedroom, Ellie, who was old enough to assist in the delivery, held her mother's hand and wiped the sweat from her face during the excruciating labor. She wanted so much to take away some of Mama's pain. *Dear God, please take away my Mama's hurtin' and please let this be the last baby,* Ellie prayed.

Agnes stood by with fresh white towels, her brow furrowed with worry. Lucille was LeBeau's unofficial midwife. Sam had fetched her early that morning when Callie's water had broken. The labor was difficult; Callie's waves of contractions were so powerful they lifted her body off the bed. When she was sufficiently effaced, Lucille finally had to reach in and re-position the baby for delivery; it was breech. After what seemed like an eternity of screams and straining, Callie's eyes rolled to the back of her head, following Lucille's last bark to "push!"

Somehow, Ellie instinctively knew something terrible was happening. Her heart was both caught in her throat and threatening to explode right through her chest. Her Aunt Agnes tried to hurry her out of the room while Lucille tended to Callie, but Ellie shrugged her off, grabbing her mother in stricken desperation, clinging to her, as though trying to keep Callie's spirit from leaving her body, tearfully pleading, "Mama, no-ooooo!"

"Unspeakable"

God and His angels were surely celebrating the homecoming of their beloved Callie; but in *this* world of fragile human beings, even the skies over LeBeau seemed to mourn the loss of Callie and her stillborn baby girl. It was a miserable, sunless, rainy morning; the kind of ubiquitous, drizzly rain that seeps through clothing and into the pores, chilling to the bone; even though it was spring. Thirty or so family, friends and neighbors gathered to listen to the priest's routine Catholic ritual for the dead, which provided no comfort at all.

Jake and Joe tried hard to remain stalwart, to be *men* – but their hearts were broken – so the reluctant tears flowed. Not even a deluge could camouflage them, so the men-children huddled close to their father and sisters. Sam had sent a telegram to Beth, but had not yet received confirmation that she had even gotten the sad news. Sam, Ellie and Nora were themselves choked with unbearable pain. Sam was lost. How could this be? What would he do without his love? The long, wiry body now bent over, a weeping willow where a proud oak had always stood. His eyes were red, swollen and disbelieving; *how could God be so cruel?* Ellie and Nora clung to their father and futilely wiped tears that just wouldn't stop. They cried for Mama to come back. Please.

———

Unnatural, that's what it is. And, mean and just not right. That's what it is; all these people in our house actin' like the world is just normal; like this is just any other old day. What's wrong with them? Ellie's mind screamed as she crouched under the dining table. Folks was just talking and stuffin' they faces like they was never gonna eat again in life. Every now and then, someone smiled; even laughed. *What was wrong with them?* Didn't they know her Mama was gone and never comin' back?

As tradition would have it, the crowd had assembled back at

the Coursey home for a repast after the service. Sympathetic friends, neighbors and relatives loaded the family's home with the only tangible comfort they could offer – love in the guise of their very best dishes – blood sausage etoufees, gumbos, rice and beans, breads, cakes and pies.

Ellie was too young to understand the emotional balm such a loving human distraction could spread over crushed hearts. Even if the diversion of food offerings and human connecting were only thin-layered and temporary. Nora, of course, didn't understand either, and reverted back to her baby self, hanging on to Sam's right leg with one arm and her doll with the other. The twins chose to retreat to the front porch. Pretend escapism.

"Come on, Baby. Let Auntie fix you a plate," Agnes cooed soothingly, trying to coax her niece out from under the table, hidden by the folds of the intricate lace tablecloth, handmade by Callie, as were so many other appointments throughout their home. Ellie buried her head deeper into her chest and hugged her arms tighter around her knees, not wanting to look at what her brothers had long-ago dubbed "Aunt Agnes' magical cockeye." It was just a lazy eye, but the boys convinced themselves and their sisters that it gave their aunt the supernatural ability to find them wherever they might be or whatever mischief they had gotten into.

Agnes and Lucille stepped into the roles of unofficial hostesses for the requisite gathering, an effort to take some of the pressure off their brother. They both loved Callie more like a little sister than a sister-in-law; and they loved Callie's and Sam's babies like their own. Callie had no other immediate living family to speak of – save a handful of cousins – so, Agnes and Lucille took care of everything.

After a few more moments, Ellie realized Aunt Agnes was not going to go away, so she crawled out from under the table. Still not being able to accept any salve for the raw, jagged hole in her chest, however, she refused to be comforted - shrugging off arms that tried to hug her and turned her head at the offered plates of sustenance, trying not to vomit the churning emptiness in her belly. There were no more tears. Instead, Ellie's eyes were glassy, almost transfixed as she just stared into space.

Well-meaning guests took turns offering their condolences to Sam. "I didn't reach Beth in time," Sam said to no one in particular, speaking in a low, lifeless monotone. "I don't even know if they got to Texas, yet." "Oh, Sweet Jesus, this is going to kill her," Sam broke down, choking his words out through the sobs. "Her beautiful mother was dancing at her wedding just a few days ago. And, now she's gone – how am I going to tell my Beth? How?"

Lucille and Agnes, devastated by their younger brother's sorrow – which they knew was hundreds of times worse than their own – both tried to wrap their arms around Sam. Lucille knelt at his feet, trying to look into his eyes to speak to him; trying to *will* him to have faith that what now looked so dark would one day indeed brighten. Agnes held on to Sam's weary head to keep it from falling, lovingly wiping at the tears that continued to stream. Little Nora stood by witnessing the sadness, terrified that maybe she was going to lose her Papa, too. Ellie only stared.

"It's going to be okay, baby. I promise one day it *is* going to be okay," Agnes insisted, struggling to convince herself as well as Sam.

"No, Agnes, it's not! It's never going to be okay. God, I wish I was lyin' in that tomb with her. I don't know how to live without Callie." The sobs wracked Sam's body.

"You hush, now. Just hush. That's grief talking; not you."

"It *is* me. You were both there. I – I couldn't even hold my new daughter in my arms; couldn't even look at her little body. Oh God, I actually blamed her, blamed that poor little dead baby for taking Callie away from me!"

"No, Sam, no. Stop it! You were in shock," Agnes nearly screamed. Lucille tried to speak, but was too overwhelmed with emotion – her own, Sam's and his children's. Callie was their rock. Praying for strength, she eventually found her voice.

"You listen to me *good*, Sam Coursey!" The intensity of Lucille's resonance startled both Sam and Agnes to involuntary attention. "Bite your tongue! You know Callie would never want to hear you say anything like that. That girl loved you all her life, ever since she was – what – six or seven? From the first time she laid eyes on you. She loved the children.

She loved your life together. And, Callie's love is still *with* you, boy! Don't you feel it? Shame on you if you don't, s'all I can say.

You got four children still at home depending on you – especially Nora and Ellie, who are just little girls. And, Beth, who will *always* need her Papa."

By now, most of the guests had stopped in their tracks, hanging on to Lucille's every word. Lucille had unknowingly taken on the demeanor of their mother, Miranda, a compact but mighty firecracker of a woman in her day. When Miranda used her "Coursey women" voice, which crescendoed into a deceptively deep and booming preacher's vociferation when making her point, folks listened. "You got to respect that love and that life you and Callie shared," Lucille continued, nearly shaking with passion and determination to get through to her brother. "You got to draw strength from that love now to go on with your life and be the wonderful father you have always been. You *owe* it to Callie! And, to your children! And, to yourself!"

"Ellie?" Nora turned around. She wanted to go outside, but she didn't want to go alone. "Ellie?" Nora weaved through the crowd in the small house looking and calling for her sister. She ran out on the front porch. "Y'all seen Ellie?" she asked her brothers, her eyes anxiously sweeping the porch and frontyard.

Jake shook his head. "Naw," Joe sniffled, hands in his pockets, failing at feigning aloofness.

Nora wasted no time running back into the house to pull at Sam. "Papa, I can't find Ellie," she whispered.

No one noticed the little girl when she slipped out of the house. Ellie darted right past Joe and Jake, themselves so caught up in their own grief, they never saw her. Ellie had to run. She ran deep into the thick, marshy woods. She thought that if she ran fast enough maybe the bayou would just swallow her up and she could join Mama in Heaven.

Ellie ran until she couldn't run anymore, finding herself at the entrance of a familiar sight in an unfamiliar setting – a new, perfect secret hiding place. One she had never visited before. She had no idea how far she had run, but the smooth, dry "cave" in the gnarled, hollowed out

Cypress tree in the swamp called out to Ellie, offering refuge. Here she was safe and could cry for Mama where no one could see or hear her. Ellie crawled in, exhausted; and unleashed a woeful, animal-like wail.

She curled up into a ball and rocked herself for hours, her body wracked with sobbing; until she wore her little self out and fell into a deep, protective slumber.

Ellie's cries, however, were both seen and heard. The pusillanimous witnesses to her misery seldom slithered out into the light of day. So, they waited.

It was almost dark outside when Ellie woke up, the scariest time of day in the forest; but she wasn't afraid. Even though she didn't know exactly where she was, she would just run back home the way she came. Papa would be worried; so she had to hurry.

The instant Ellie stepped out of her sanctuary, she was swallowed and swooped up in itchy, sweltering darkness. She was upside down and couldn't breathe. Had the bayou indeed sucked her into its innards? If so, *where was Mama? Where was God? Couldn't breathe*. Then, there was nothing.

Ellie awoke to the stench of suffocatingly powerful body odor and the unmistakable reek of outhouse waste; mingled with the sickening stink of putrid food, stale tobacco and alcohol. She threw up.

She had no idea what time of day it was, or even *what* day. Ellie lay on a filthy threadbare cot with a rope knotted around her neck and tied to some post in the raggedy one-room shanty. *Had she died and gone to hell?* her panicked mind screamed.

"Well, looky who done come back to life." That's when she finally spotted them in a darkened corner of the claustrophobic shack. Two nasty, grimy white men in overalls. *Or, were they the demons in the stories she'd always been told, who resided in hell with the devil?*

One of them shuffled over to the cot and sat next to her. He must have noticed the vomit and roughly wiped at her mouth with a dirty rag he pulled from his pocket. Then, amazingly, he attempted to slobber all over her mouth in what passed for kissing in his perverted behavioral repertoire. Ellie turned her head in disbelief and disgust. The monster slapped her almost unconscious. "Who 'da hell do ya think you are?" he snarled, baring rotted, brown teeth. "You ain't nothin' but a dog, *our* dog, a little mongrel bitch we picked up. And like any good mutt, you gon' to do what yo' massa say!"

Ellie's mind and breathing were racing with the terrifying realization of the nightmare she was in the midst of. *Mama, Papa, help me!* Monster number two shoved Monster number one out of the way, kicking off his overalls and drawers. "Move out the way, Crowbow," he slurred. "Yassuh, and this massa say this mutt's gonna make him feel real good," he spat.

"Jes' wait yo' turn, Lizard," the one named Crowbow slobbered in response, shoving the Lizard monster and resuming his claimed space over Ellie.

Ellie's arms were free, so she lunged at him with all her might. The monster seemed to enjoy the struggle. "Ooooh whee, we got us a wild dog here! Here, doggie. Here, you little mongrel bitch," he called as though really speaking to a dog. Then, he punched her.

Ellie closed her eyes in pain and prayed for God to please send her Papa to help her as the monster ripped off the pretty bloomers her Mama had made for her. The monsters took turns ripping into and violating every orifice in Ellie's 12-year-old little girl body. Viciously raping her. Sodomizing her. Over and over again. Mercifully, Ellie was barely conscious and had the miraculous sensation that she was no longer in her body; she had somehow floated out. *They could not touch her.* When the vile brutalization finally ceased, one of the monsters decided to urinate on the tiny, battered figure; soaking her from head to toe with piss. "She ain't nothin' but a piece of shit anyway," he grunted, sounding every bit like the animal he was.

Day had turned into night and into day again. Sam, Paul, Joe, Jake and a small army of their neighbors continued their search for Ellie, armed with shotguns and dogs whose snouts could sniff out everything from steak to sweat; leaving no Cypress tree cave, bush or blade of grass unturned. They were ready for Klansmen or any other evil they might encounter. Sam, hoarse from screaming his daughter's name, was almost manic in his despair. He blamed himself for being selfish and weak; for being so paralyzed by his own grief over the loss of Callie, he didn't even notice his baby that morning; any of his babies. He was *their father*, for God's sake, and had nearly been oblivious to how much his children were in pain. Jake and Joe were also sick with guilt, berating themselves. How could they have let Ellie slip past them without either of them seeing her?

None of the Coursey men took any comfort in being told, "It's not your fault. All of you had the right to mourn – still do." And, "Everybody grieves differently." Or, "Don't worry. We'll find her. Ellie's just headstrong and wanted to be off by herself for a spell."

After a night of the most heinous depravity any human being could commit against another, and after fully exploiting every sin of gluttony; the monsters pathetically passed out in a drunken stupor.

Sometime during the night, they had tied Ellie's hands as well. There was water in one tin dish on the dirt floor and scraps of food in another. So, if she wanted to drink or eat, she would have to crawl on the ground like a dog to get to either. But, if she wanted to reach either, she would choke herself with the rope tied around her neck.

Ellie worked steadily at her constraints, almost rubbing her fingers and wrists raw. Her resolute spirit had taken over. There was no way she would allow the monsters to win. They would not kill her. They would not break her. She would outsmart them. She would show them.

Being the beasts that they were, the monsters snored and grunted like pigs as Ellie continued to work. Her tenacity paid off as she managed to slip out of the ropes on her wrists; then quickly freed herself from the noose around her neck. She glanced at the monsters, then at a shotgun propped against the door; then back at the monsters again. Even though the unfamiliar poisonous fumes of rage and hatred now saturated every fiber of her being, Ellie decided against killing the vermin; instead, she quietly limped toward the door and out into the early morning light.

The search party was exhausted, sweat-soaked and increasingly terrified for Ellie with every passing moment; but, there was no way in hell they were going to abandon their hunt for the child. The light of the new day would help. Then, hearing someone – or something –

approaching, everyone in the group snapped to attention and froze in place; primed to attack.

A battered, raggedy little figure stumbled through the tangle of trees and brush. Ellie dragged herself a few more steps towards the group, then simply stopped; staring straight ahead blankly, as if not seeing them at all.

That fraction of an instant felt like eternity. Everyone – even Sam - was speechless, gawking at the little girl in disbelief. *She was alive, Thank God!* But, grateful relief at seeing Ellie alive collided with the sickeningly revolting realization of the defilement and torture the child must have endured. Blood and grime were caked up and down her arms, legs and what was left of the dress she had worn to her mother's funeral the morning before. Ellie's beautiful face was almost unrecognizable – dirty, covered with bruises; her left jaw and cheek grotesquely distended. Her little mouth was quadrupled in size and encrusted with blood. One eye was black and blue and nearly swollen shut. Her long, golden brown hair was wild and matted with filth.

With tears of both gratitude and crippling sorrow filling his eyes, Sam approached his daughter gingerly, as though he were afraid he was going to further injure her or frighten her. He knelt down in front of Ellie and gently took her into his arms. Ellie never even blinked; falling into her father's arms like a rag doll. He carefully cradled and lifted his baby girl; thanking God over and again that Ellie was alive; whispering over and again how so very sorry he was that Papa wasn't there to protect her, begging repeatedly for her forgiveness. Waves of emotion – the kind of body-wracking, face-soaking remorse that such men habitually kept under wraps – also overcame the rest of the ragtag group, which silently accompanied Sam and Ellie back through the woods and swampland. Each soul bent under the weight of the knowledge that not one of them had been able to protect this one little girl.

At home, bathed, bandaged and safely nestled in her nice clean bed, Ellie slept at last; unaware of the activity and conversations around her. Nora curled up protectively next to her sister. The adults assumed she was asleep as well.

"Physically, she will eventually recover." Dr. Kennard treaded carefully with Sam. They stepped outside the bedroom and closed the door. The rest of the family paced the parlor downstairs.

"She has two broken ribs, but miraculously, there doesn't seem to be any internal bleeding. The cuts, swelling and bruising should all subside within a couple of weeks, with little or no scarring. However," he continued carefully, "There was extensive bleeding from both her vaginal area and her rectal canal. Sam, I'm sorry, but the bleeding and tearing indicate that Ellie's body is severely traumatized from repeated forced entries."

Sam nodded, his face drained and deeply etched with worry and sadness; his shoulders visibly sloped under the weight of the world.

"We can't know for sure, but depending on how extensive the damage is, I just don't know at this time whether or not Ellie will ever be able to have children of her own. You should also be aware that there may very well be long-term scars that we cannot see physically."

"How soon will she be able to travel?"

It seemed that hours had passed since Sam walked Dr. Kennard to the door. Sam, his siblings and his boys sat in the parlor area, leaving the little girls to what they all hoped was blessed sleep. They stared. Silent. Only the rhythmic tic-tock of the handed-down-through-the-family grandfather clock punctuated the pained hush.

"What you doin', Sam?" Paul asked as his brother broke the motionless stalemate, padding quietly to his gun cabinet.

"What's it look like?" Sam answered in a voice none of them recognized. "I'm gonna go find the bastards who did this to my little girl and I'm gon' first blow off any parts they mistakenly *think* makes 'em men. Then, after they's wishin' they was dead; I'm gonna grant that wish and blow their damn brains out."

"*Who*, Sam? Who? Com bien? How many? How you know who done this? That poor chile upstairs can't even talk. Can't tell us nothing. What you gon' do? Shoot every cracker you come across? And, *where they at*? Y'all didn't find Ellie nowhere near here! How many of them raggedy-ass shanties between here and New Orleans you gon' hit before you got who done this?" Lucille exploded; emotions raw, like those of everyone else in the room.

"Before they kill *you*, that is," Agnes chimed in sadly.

"I'm goin' too, Papa," Joe shot up out of his chair.

"And, y'all ain't goin' without me," Jake added, popping up from his spot on the floor. "I'm gon' kill whoever did this to Ellie!"

"You goin' too, right, Paul?" Agnes continued. "I mean, there's always strength in numbers. Four of y'all against God knows how many of them Klan vermin. But, maybe y'all can pick up a few more brave men along the way."

"Agnes," Lucille interrupted.

"No, let me finish. Go on. Be men. Protect your family. That's what men folk do. And, it is brave. And, the natural reaction when someone you love so much has been beaten and tortured – and God knows *what* else – the way that poor baby was! Mon Dieu! I want to string 'em up myself – rip that so-called goddamn manhood off and stuff it all down their throats! But, whose going to protect those little girls up there after y'all are gone? Which shouldn't take too long, 'cause whoever did this terrible thing got support. They just like rats or hornets or roaches. You see one and you know they's a whole damn nest of them somewhere nearby. Damn sheet-wearing, night-riding, cowardly devils hidin' out; ready to pounce. And, y'all ain't even sure who they are? So go ahead. What's four more funerals to this family?"

"Dust Bowl Veracity"

Many months have come and gone, since I wandered from my home in those Oklahoma hills where I was born. Ohhh-hhh, way down yonder in the "Injun" nation, I ride my pony on the reservation in those Oklahoma hills where I was bo-ornnn. Way down yonder in the "Injun" nation, a cowgirl's life is my occupation, in those Oklahoma hills I do belong. Nora crooned in her best practiced Oklahoma twang, perched contentedly on the refurbished, painted white-with-green-trim metal front porch swing with Ellie, snapping string beans for dinner. Heck, her singing sounded better than the old scratchy version by Johnny Lee Will and the Texas Playboys on the radio!

And, the song was far superior to the reality.

Nora's 13-year-old heart didn't know she really favored this particular tune because its lyrics were the only tangible resemblance to the romantic fantasy of Oklahoma. The Courseys were not the only family who migrated to the Sooner State for its spurious promises of Utopia.

Sam had packed up his family after that terrible night three years before. A better life for their children is what he and Callie had always wanted; dreamed of; worked towards. Callie somehow spoke to the deepest parts of Sam's heart as he contemplated the gun cabinet in the corner of the hallway that night. She planted the sobering truth that there was no way their sons would have stayed behind. Sam would have been leading them all on a suicide mission.

The Coursey family had joined thousands of colored families who trekked to the red, dusty plains and clay hills of Oklahoma from the oppression in southern states like Louisiana, Tennessee, the Carolinas, Mississippi, Alabama, Georgia and Florida; seeking greener opportunity pastures in mixed-race towns like Boley, Beggs, Bristow, Sapulpa, Okmulgee, Langston and Muskogee. Before they settled voluntarily, Blacks were brought to what was then a territory as both slaves and freedmen in the early 1800's. The slaves were owned by white explorers, as well as Indians displaced by the federal government. Those slaves and freedmen populated settlements which sprouted into towns.

For those who had their hearts set on big-city living, just north of the Coursey's adopted home of Okmulgee was Tulsa. Home to Greenwood, or "the Black Wall Street of America," as it was commonly called. Pine Street to the North, Archer Street and the Frisco tracks to the South, Cincinnati Street on the West, and Lansing Street on the East. And, it was fine alright; a 35 square block area of near-heaven. Mostly colored prosperity (which also included a whole new gorgeous breed of humanity resulting from intermarriage between blacks and Indians) – homes, dozens of businesses, doctors, lawyers, realtors, schools, churches, concert halls, silent movie houses, funeral parlors, ice cream parlors, billiard halls, a newspaper, restaurants, a hospital, a bank, post office, libraries, hotels, and stores and shops of all kinds – and yes, brothels - all Black-owned.

Until the previous spring. May 31 and June 1, 1921.

Tuesday, May 31, had started out as a sparkling, especially clean, sweet-smelling blue and gold spring morning. The kind that makes you vault out of bed, just happy to be alive on such a glorious gift of a day. Joe and Jake had graduated high school and were at work, finding solid jobs at Ball Brothers Glass Factory, which employed many – if not most - of the men in Okmulgee. The girls had accompanied Sam on the always-looked-forward-to rare trip to Tulsa. They had purchased supplies for Sam's fish market, which he successfully ran out of the back of his truck on the side of the road in front of their home; along with dry goods and luxury items not to be found in Okmulgee, like dainty and delicious pastel petit fours, which were almost too pretty to eat; handsome fabrics, some of which came all the way from Paris; and even the occasional *Crisis* Magazine from the NAACP, or any of those other fancy magazines Sam knew Ellie had so devoured when Callie had brought them home for her back in LeBeau. He thought maybe, just maybe the magazines and whatever magical content they held for Ellie would bring his little girl back to life.

Just before heading back to Okmulgee, they stopped to visit with the Monteighs, cousins from Louisiana who had moved to Tulsa just before the turn of the century with their two young boys and only three bags, bulging with everything the family possessed in the world. John and Mamie had depleted their meager life savings from toiling in Louisiana to start their printing company from the ground up in Greenwood. Now, after more than twenty years, Monteigh & Sons Printing Company was a thriving business. As its name included "& Sons," John and Mamie proudly turned it over to their now-grown boys, Eddie and Ollie. It was the elder Monteighs' turn to enjoy the fruits of their years of laboring – blessed rest and relaxation; a beautiful, thriving, well-educated family, including grandchildren; their lovely home, church community and joyfully welcoming friends and kin as guests.

"Oh, my, how these young ladies have grown," Cousin Mamie exclaimed over Ellie and Nora. "Sam, they are so beautiful!"

"Thank you, Cousin Mamie," Nora answered before her father could speak. Ellie said nothing, having not uttered a word in two years. Instead of looking *at* Mamie, it was as though she peered right *through* the older woman with the flawless cocoa skin and the long salt and pepper braid fashioned into a stylish chignon at the nape of her neck. *Mama. She looks almost like Mama*, flashed through Ellie's mind; then back she escaped into a world that only she occupied.

"Come. Come. Rest yourselves right here in the sitting room before you get back on the road," Cousin John interjected kindly, knowing part of the story, and feeling for Ellie, her sister and their father. His voice was so loving, it was almost musical. "You all are family. Make yourselves at home. Yes, yes. Mamie, dear, I'll bet our cousins would love some of that lemonade and those sugar cookies you just took out of the oven." One could either dance to Cousin John's voice or snuggle up safely in its melodious warmth.

"Why, thank you, John. That would be just fine." Sam appreciated the respite and the loving link to his Callie. He eased Ellie and Nora onto one of the elegant, doily-covered divans, and then settled himself in one of the creamy brocade wingback chairs.

The afternoon passed pleasantly and quickly. Mamie and John also had a special surprise that kept both girls happily occupied, even Ellie. A basket full of love: fluffy, yippy puppies. Their "Buster," an adorable stray of questionable pedigree that had just appeared on their front porch sometime back, turned out to be a girl that gave birth to a healthy litter of five under the backstairs a few weeks prior. Just old enough now to be weaned from their mother.

With Sam's permission, Nora and Ellie took one of the pups home. Flippo was shiny black with a white diamond spot crowning the top of his little head. Once out of the basket, the frisky little fellow plopped himself right at Ellie's feet; then flipped over on his back as wobbly-legged puppies tend to do. Nora thought she saw a spark of delight in her sister's eye and knew this baby boy was *the one*. Sam saw it too. For the briefest, sweetest moment, a glimmer of light replaced the sadness and emptiness that had resided in his child's eyes ever since the incident.

Until they arrived, Oklahoma's migratory colored population was largely unaware that not only was the state no panacea of racial harmony, but lynching Negroes had been used by whites as a way to control the coloreds – keeping them in their place as much as possible – by infusing fear in them. Worse, lynching also became sport, a form of depraved entertainment for entire white families. Grab a good spot to watch the life drain out of a man or woman. Sometimes, even a child.

For the most part, Black towns became tenuous shelters against the violent bigotry. But, Greenwood, it was thought, was surely a near-impenetrable fortress.

Later that night of May 31, 1921, at the end of that perfect spring day, long after Sam, Ellie and Nora were nestled safely in their tiny, cozy home; Mamie and John Monteigh were brutally murdered. Each shot in the back of the head as they knelt in prayer in their bedroom. Buster and her babies, sensing evil - maybe even *smelling* its presence – whimpered; were discovered and slaughtered. The Monteigh home was then looted for its valuables and burned to the ground.

Hundreds lost their lives that abominable night, which bled

well into the next day. Any sun that might have been present on June 1st was obliterated by the nefarious smoke of devastation that rose from the Greenwood area, creeping from the smoldering ashes of thousands of once proudly-maintained homes and thriving businesses. Black folks called it the "Tulsa Race Riot of 1921." White folks called it "Negro unrest." Whatever its moniker, it was a massacre. A holocaust of an entire community. At the hands of the surrounding community, "neighbors" – including local city officials, police officers, civic leaders and the manpower of the federal government. Those sworn to protect and defend.

Some said the riot was the inevitability of less-educated, less-prosperous white folks who simply couldn't stand it anymore. Niggahs having so much. That the "elevator incident" was just the fuse, the *excuse* they needed to destroy and put niggahs – those disgusting, sub-human, animal *darkies* - in their place. The good ole' American way. Which, in actuality, only mirrored centuries of man's inhumanity to man because of hatred, greed, jealousy, and a delusional, self-proclaimed sense of entitled superiority. Sometimes, even in the name of God.

All the 19 year-old boy did was trip on an uneven elevator floor when the door opened in the Drexel building in downtown Tulsa. He was a shoeshine man and went into the building to use the colored-only restroom. In trying to catch his balance, it was Dick Rowland's misfortune to accidentally touch the handbag of the other passenger already on the car – a 17 year old white girl, Sarah Page. A mere two years younger than he.

Sarah, like all little white girls, had been raised with the delusional belief that she and all of white womanhood were in constant peril of being ravaged by all Negro men – filthy beasts who surely came out of the womb coveting white womanhood's delicate paleness, which, of course, automatically equaled irresistible beauty and desire.

Attempting to save herself and her honor from the "assault," Sarah screamed, which sent the startled young man running out of the elevator and the building. She then shared her tale of the virtue-threatening attack with police; and Dick Rowland was thrown into jail.

That was all the provocation needed to raise the ire of the

resident Klan, headed by local government and civic leaders. Within hours, the plan was laid to haul Rowland out of jail and rig him up for a lynching. News of the elevator incident, the jailing and the impending lynching also moved quickly through the Greenwood grapevine.

Even though the sheriff assured everyone in shouting distance that Dick Rowland was safe in jail, that evening, a group of nearly 100 skeptical Greenwood residents, many of them World War I veterans, traveled to the courthouse anyway. A mob of at least 5,000 white men was already there, rabid and demanding that the sheriff turn over "the boy" to them. After a hostile attempt by one of the blood-thirsty white vigilantes to disarm one of the black men, a shot rang out. Tulsa's worst bloodbath since the Civil War ensued.

The black men fought valiantly; but, they were out-numbered and out-armed by the white rioters. Practically foaming at the mouth for absolute destruction, the whites invaded Greenwood, firing on and butchering innocent black men, women – and children – their dead, often-charred bodies thrown like trash into the back of trucks; arms and legs sticking out through the slats. The insurgents were assisted in their pillage by National Guardsmen using standard-issue, 30-caliber 1906 Smithfield rifles, as well as semi-automatic machine guns given to them by the Tulsa Police Department. Throughout the immoral free-for-all, black women and girls were raped at random by the vile, inhuman invaders. Thousands of homes and hundreds of businesses were ransacked and torched as the hate-fueled infestation made its hellish way through. Airplanes dropped nitroglycerin and dynamite to ensure the destruction of every building standing in the 35-block Greenwood enclave. An estimated 300 blacks and whites lost their lives in the carnage.

Exceptions exist for every rule; and legions of compassionate, right-minded white Tulsa residents hid and fed black families in their basements, churches and businesses during the melee and for weeks afterwards.

Post riot, *authorities* rounded up and herded more than 6,000 homeless Greenwood residents into settlement centers – or concentration camps – for their own "protection." For months, all blacks were required to wear green tags around their necks when they left the camp; tags which had to be signed by a white employer. Those who dared to venture out onto the Tulsa streets without tags were subject to arrest.

Some out of an allegiance to their accustomed way of life, some out of the goodness of their hearts, thousands of whites combed the human warehouses looking for "Aunt Susie" or "Minnie", "Uncle Ben" or good, ole' "Crow" – their maids, laundresses, cooks, porters or com-mon laborers.

When news of the genocide and the senseless execution of John and Marie reached Sam and the children, he set out for Tulsa. Alone. Few knew Sam in the city, so he was free to search – as just another white man – for Eddie and Ollie Monteigh and their families. It took him two heart-wrenching days of searching through and questioning barely living, breathing human carnage; but, he found all the surviving Monteighs and brought them back to Okmulgee. They were enraged, battered and almost paralyzed with sadness over the senseless loss of John, Mamie and the life the Monteigh family had built in Greenwood – but they were not broken.

Now, one year after the riots, life was returning to a remote semblance of normalcy. Even though word had it that the Phoenix of Greenwood was slowly rising from the ashes, Eddie and Ollie knew it would never be the same, and chose to rebuild Monteigh & Sons Printing right in downtown Okmulgee. After staying with the Courseys for six months, they were able to build and move into new houses. A little smaller than the ones in Tulsa... but home.

Nora happily belted out her song, snapping her beans, glancing at Ellie every now and then for any hint of reaction. She would give anything to have her high-spirited, adventurous sister back. Ellie sat next to her, just as silent, sad and empty as she had been for three years now, limp little legs hanging off the swing; hands folded neatly in her lap. Staring at nothing. Then, like a furry, shiny-black 20 pound ball of energy, a fully-grown Flippo bounded up the stairs and into the tiny space between Nora and Ellie on the swing, knocking the tin bowl of green beans into the air; beans flying everywhere.

"Oh, Flippo. You are such a funny boy," Ellie suddenly laughed, hugging Flippo as he happily wiggled in her lap, covering her face with doggie kisses.

"PAPA!" a startled and disbelieving Nora screamed at the top of her lungs. "PAPA! Come quick! Hurry!"

"Nora, what in God's name are you screaming - " Sam bellowed, hurtling through the screen door before he stopped in his tracks. Ellie, his beautiful Ellie, was *back*! Giggling and happily playing with her dog.

"Silly puppy," Ellie playfully admonished Flippo, scratching him behind the ears and kissing his head. "That's what you are, a silly puppy, making such a mess." She looked up at her startled father's face, mouth agape; tears of absolute joy sparkling in his eyes. "Hi, Papa. What's the matter?"

"Back"

"Stop! You done lost your mind, boy? Put me down, Joe!" Ellie squealed, laughing so hard she could hardly get the words out. Joe and Jake took turns hugging their little sister and twirling her around. The twins had just stepped into the yard, coming home from work and laid eyes on the same bright, lively girl they had always known. Papa and Nora were already squeezing Ellie to death and showering her with kisses.

"Sweet Jesus! Ellie, you're back!" Jake yelled.

"Ellie?" Joe almost whispered; then hurtled up all the stairs in one leap. The ecstatic whooping and hollering commenced in earnest, with the entire family overwhelmed with joyous emotion.

Confounding thing was, as much as she loved her family and enjoyed the attention, Ellie couldn't figure what all the commotion was about. *Back*, everyone kept saying. *Back from where?*

Mercifully, Ellie had no recollection of the hours she really was gone after her mother's funeral. The dark night of torture and brutality she'd suffered didn't exist for her. And even though she had merely moved through only the most basic motions of living over the last three years – eating, sleeping, bathing and dressing – she knew everything about the Coursey family's life in Oklahoma; even though she seemingly simply silently stared at nothing.

Usually pleasant and routine suppertime at the Coursey household turned into a grand celebration that evening. Sam's gumbo was consistently superb; but Nora whipped up a peach and raspberry cobbler for dessert and the boys – young men of 20 now – churned homemade vanilla ice cream to top it off. It wasn't even Sunday! The tinny radio tinkled the latest big band tunes; Jake and Joe took turns trading off their little sisters as dance partners. Sam's heart was overflowing with gratitude and happiness he hadn't truly felt in years. He'd get telegrams off to Beth, Paul, Agnes and Lucille first thing in the morning with the good news. Their Ellie was back to her self... and *Praise be to God*, she didn't remember.

"Papa, why didn't you fetch Marie to join us for dinner?" Ellie asked in between mouthfuls.

"Marie?" It was still going to take Sam and the others some getting used to Ellie actually *knowing* about most areas of their lives, even though she hadn't actively participated. Apparently, she had *observed*. Everything. Marie Lyons was the pretty, French-speaking Black-Creek-Creole woman who had been helping Sam at the fish market.

"Yes, Papa, why not?" Nora chimed in. "Marie is so nice. She taught me how to make one braid. And, it's okay with me if she has eyes for you, Papa."

"Yeah, goo-goo eyes," chuckled Ellie, enjoying teasing their Papa, who could not control the crimson sneaking up his face. "It's okay, Papa. We like her. It's fine with us if you have a lady friend."

"Well, it's a mighty fine thing that you two jeunes filles like her, because she thinks you're the cat's meow, too. And, we've been so busy this evening – " Sam searched for his words carefully, not wanting to upset the applecart of Ellie's miraculous recovery. "I reckon I was just too pre-occupied to think much about it. No time to go get her, anyhow."

"If we had one of those telephones, you could have just rung her up," Joe snuck into the conversation.

"Yeah," Jake chimed in. "They got one at Ball Brothers, Papa. We should try it. You can have an operator just ring up whoever you want to talk to in just minutes."

"I know. I know. Your Papa may be old, but I still read. Businesses like Ball Brothers and cities like Oklahoma City and Tulsa have the connections, the wiring needed for that telephone contraption. Hardly anywhere in Okmulgee has those connections yet. We're just a nice, little town that don't need no new-fangled telephones; and I like it that way."

Ellie rolled her eyes.

The gesture didn't get past Nora. "Oh yes. Miss Ellie is back alright. You ain't got to start rolling your eyes already, Gal. Your uppity thinking ain't gone nowhere; that's for sure."

Ellie stuck out her tongue at her sister.

"Girls!" Sam gently warned.

"Joe and Jake are right, Papa. The telephone is one of them modern miracles; and I think we oughta have one. Why, we could ring up Bethie in Texas and everybody in Louisiana like magic! We would be connected with the rest of the whole wide world! Humph! Might even feel like we wasn't living in this one-horse town." Ellie the dreamer and adventurer was still present.

"Ah, there she is. My little girl with the big ideas," Sam sighed happily. No, there was nothing wrong with his Ellie's wanderlust spirit. "I'm not disagreeing with you, Ellie. But, we ain't getting' no telephone 'til the area has the proper wiring for that talking box. And, it's probably too dang expensive. We're not rich, you know."

"So much for the land of milk and honey," Jake muttered under his breath, but not so low that Nora didn't pick up on it.

"Well, I know why we're not rich; and why most folk in Okmulgee aren't rich from the oil that was discovered in Oklahoma." Nora was thrilled for an opportunity to show off *her* knowledge. Especially now that her beloved Ellie was back. Ellie was always the smart one, even though she only finished the fifth grade. Nora adored Ellie and held no envy in her heart towards her sister; she was just happy to know that she was smart, too! She also loved her school, where she was in the 8th grade with other brown and red children.

"Mrs. Henry says that after Oklahoma became a state in 1907, the government got rid of the Indian territory where her family – which is Creek and Creole and black, like Marie's – and lots of Indian nations like the Cherokee, Seminole, Choctaw and Chickasaw lived. Then, all the Indians was forced to spread out and settle on tiny little reservations or in little towns like Okmulgee. That way, only the government and the other white people here in Oklahoma were the only ones to get rich."

"Then hell's bells," Jake retorted, half-joking, half being a horse's ass. "Why don't we have some of that oil money? After all, Papa is white." Nora, Joe and Ellie stared at Jake incredulously. It had forever been an unspoken rule in the Coursey household that any mention of Sam's birth parentage was *never* uttered. Jake regretted the words as soon as they left his mouth and he instantly apologized to his father.

Sam spoke deliberately, carefully choosing his words. "I was reared and loved by Miranda and Girard Coursey. I was raised as, and have proudly lived my entire life as a Creole or colored man or whatever word you would like to use to describe me, son. But not white."

Joe attempted to lighten the atmosphere. "You know, Ellie, there's a fellow at work who has asked about you. Sounds like he's kinda sweet on you, if you ask me. Name's Brady Renault. Too old for you, 'course – same age as me and Jake – but he's seen you at Church and must be blind or something, 'cause he thinks you're real pretty." Joe and Jake guffawed in true obnoxious big brother style, as if Ellie had been with them in all ways over the last three years. That, of course, was as it should be.

Regarding the subject of Mr. Brady Renault, however, there was no rise whatsoever from a disinterested Ellie; but the newly boy-crazy Nora giggled while Sam just shook his head and finished his supper. *Lawd have mercy.*

6

"Sunday Face"

"She never talks to any boys."

"She's stuck up and just think she's cute 'cause she's light, bright and damn near white!"

"I heard she's one of those queer girls who like other girls. Old as she is and no beau! Never!"

"And, I cain't stand the way the heifer talks. All proper like she's some damn queen or somethin'!"

Such were the not-so-Christian post-Mass whispers about Ellie as the expanding Coursey family made their way through the lingering congregation slowly streaming out of Uganda Martyrs Catholic Church in the heart of Okmulgee one sticky summer Sunday morning. The air was choking with sweat and *Evening In Paris Eau de Toilette*, which all the women bought from the same five and dime.

Ellie, linking arms with Nora, was followed out by their father and his new wife, Marie, and Jake and Joe with their wives and babies. How life had changed for them all. Joe and Jake were honest-to-God grown men with their own homes now and were taking care of their own families. Nora, 16, beautiful and long-legged as a colt and a very typical teenaged girl, was able to continue her education and attended Okmulgee's one high school – a luxury Ellie had missed out on. But, Ellie attracted most of the gossip because she kept to herself – the deadliest of sins. Aside from her family and tight, small circle of friends, Ellie refused to conform to life in what she considered to be not much more than a dustier version of LeBeau.

Instead of the soda fountain that most of the other young people of Okmulgee frequented, the local library was Ellie's haunt of choice. Ever a voracious reader, Ellie devoured every book and periodical she could get her hands on. She got lost in the language of William Shakespeare's plays and was mesmerized by F. Scott Fitzgerald's, The Great Gatsby, and the fanciful poetry of the unconventional Edna St. Vincent Millay. But, her favorite works were the richly soulful and racially conscious writings by the jewels in the crown of the Harlem Renaissance – James Weldon Johnson, Langston Hughes, Claude McKay, Jean Toomer, Zora Neale Hurston and Alaine Locke. That lifelong love of reading educated the girl who only made it to the fifth grade.

Sometimes, when no one else was around, Ellie would read passages from a select volume aloud. Over and again. Words she didn't know how to pronounce, she looked up in the library's dictionary. That practice, along with paying close attention to the handful of radio announcers, taught Ellie correct grammar and enunciation. She didn't want either the Louisiana or Oklahoma dialects. So, she worked on it. However, when it suited the situation, the comfort level of the company around her – or when she just plain forgot – Ellie could slip right back into her old, familiar way of speaking; dropping "g's," deleting syllables and ignoring proper verb tenses.

Ellie was also socking away nearly every penny she earned as a seamstress in *Miss Lulu's Cleaners and Fine Tailoring* shop in downtown Okmulgee. Saving enough to eventually fulfill her lifelong goal of moving to Paris and apprenticing at one of the grand Parisian houses of fashion design. *God willing and the creek don't rise*, she would maybe even study at the feet of the great Coco Chanel herself! A more immediate fantasy was about the day she would actually be able to afford and anoint her body with her idol's own famous, exclusive fragrance, *Chanel No. 5* Parfum. Until that day, there was no way she would ever be caught dead in that disgustingly pedestrian *Evening In Paris* toilet water, for God's sake! So, for now, Ellie settled for the nice, clean smell that came with soap and water and Jergens lotion. After establishing herself in Paris, she would then travel throughout Europe and the rest of the world. *That* was the plan.

Because of word-of-mouth and because she was a living advertisement of her stylish and meticulous work, Ellie enjoyed a steady stream of regular customers. She gave them what they wanted. Even though not all women could pull off Ellie's chic, un-Oklahoma-looking outfits with the same panache as she, Ellie enthusiastically pinned, draped, cut and sewed; ultimately making all of her ladies feel beautiful.

Ellie's time was otherwise spent, so she shared few typical interests of other young women her age – boys, dance marathons featuring the Charleston, the Shimmy and the Black Bottom (which were really a more popular phenomenon in white, Northern big cities), courting, marriage, babies and the latest gossip. Ellie's peer imposed "punishment" for eschewing that which was the norm, was to be a frequent and favorite target of the latter.

Today at Mass, Ellie's polished cotton candy-pink sheath, piped in white lace and belted at her tiny waist (a direct slap in the face to the current, drop-waisted flapper style that was all the rage), showed off her slender curves and was perfect for the heat. The white bag, shoes and cloche (Ellie's one nod to the fashion trend of the so-called "roaring 20's") that daintily capped her lustrous golden brown hair, now caught and coiled prettily at the nape of her neck, completed the ensemble. Also, on the opposite fashion spectrum of most of the other young women around her, Ellie had totally eschewed the popular "bob" of the day, choosing to keep her hair long – though waved and elegantly pinned. Her creamy skin was sun-kissed, although it never tanned to the degree Ellie would have liked.

She was simply drop-dead gorgeous, which, coupled with her choice of how she spent her time, also earned the green-eyed ire and raised eyebrows of most of the so-called good Catholic girls and women at Uganda Martyrs' Sunday Mass.

"You know she crazy. Think she too good for Okmulgee," the whispered post-Church-service cattiness continued.

"She won't even give the time of day to Brady Renault, and even my Mama says he's so fine 'his ass would make a Sunday face' for that picture star, Rudolf Valentino."

As if on cue, Brady Renault materialized from behind a tree, inadvertently startling Ellie, who jumped, squeezing Nora's arm. Ellie's siblings were thoroughly amused. Sam was not. Neither was Ellie.

By anyone's standards, Brady *was* what you would call a *pretty boy*. Beautiful, in fact. Perfectly proportioned, chiseled features with a mouth that screamed "taste me;" and unfairly long, thick black lashes that matched his thick, shiny black curls. And, unlike the skinny, "pretty" movie star to whom he was often compared – Rudy Valentino – Brady possessed lean, taught, rippling brown muscles which all the girls adored, and which were all but hidden under the white cotton shirt that stuck to his upper body like white-on-rice in the moist, sweltering Oklahoma summer heat.

Uncharacteristically stumbling over his words, Brady pulled himself up, swallowed and turned to Sam to ask if he could keep company with Ellie. Everyone – except Sam, Brady and Ellie – was amused.

Ellie shot invisible daggers at Brady *and* at her father while Brady seemed to hold his breath in anxious anticipation of Sam's answer. Sam just grunted and shepherded his family on.

Brady Renault had used his looks to his advantage most of his life. He even bragged to his friends that given just 30 seconds, he could wet the bloomers of any female in his presence – young, old and everything in between. Guaranteed. All he had to do was look into a woman's eyes while saying damn near *anything* to her and flash what he believed to be his second-greatest God-given gift – his mesmerizing smile. It worked every time – whether he wanted it to or not.

Except with Ellie Coursey.

She was the most exquisite and elusive creature Brady had ever laid eyes on. And, he knew he *had* to *have* her. Somehow, though, Little Miss Ellie seemed immune to his charms. The challenge of her stubbornness and her apparent disinterest only excited Brady even more, stiffening his member to the point of explosion every time he thought about it or looked her way. That delicious as-yet-unsatisfied jones sharpened his prurient determination to have her. She was, in his estimation, the only woman he had ever encountered who even came close to deserving him; maybe even having his babies. Yeah, Brady licked his lips just *thinking* about spreading open those gams and hitting that poontang. *No, Doll Face didn't stand a chance*, Brady chuckled to himself.

Brady knew he had to be careful, though. He didn't want to chance scaring her off, so he deliberately waited it out, carefully calculating his time – and his next move.

ᴥ CHAPTER ᴥ

7

"Okra Soup Slick"

An entire month passed before Brady decided it was time. He had gone to church that morning, carefully cleaning even underneath his fingernails when he had taken his bath that Saturday night. After Mass, he glided by the Coursey family with only a polite, acknowledging nod.

Several hours later, Brady sauntered up the Coursey home stairs. Sam answered the door.

"Good evening, Mr. Renault. May I help you?"

"Yes, sir. Good evening Mr. Coursey, sir. I hope I am not interrupting your Sunday evening meal, sir. I mean I was wondering if – um, I was hoping to speak with Ellie, sir. Please, sir. I mean, if that's alright, sir," *Dammit.* Brady stumbled all over himself; wanting to kick himself in the ass for sounding like . . . such an ordinary suitor!

Ellie and Brady silently rocked on the front porch swing just as twilight seamlessly traded places with the daylight, with only the swing's gentle creaking and the singing of the crickets breaking the stillness.

Brady was biding his time, turning over in his mind the most appropriate line to use. Ellie beat him to the punch.

"Mr. Renault, I would have liked to have had at least *some* say in who I choose to keep company with IF I were even interested in keeping company with anyone at all! Which, by the way, I am not!"

"Well, Miss Coursey, I would have asked for your permission first before I showed up on your doorstep if you would have ever spoken to me instead of giving me the cold shoulder every time I even looked in your direction!"

A stalemate.

"So, Miss Ellie, I suppose I should ask you now if I have your permission to stay or if you would rather just give me the bum's rush?"

Ellie pondered his statement-not-quite-a-question and decided to take her time answering. She folded her arms and casually examined Brady out of the corners of her eyes. *Humph!* She might not have been well-versed in the ways of the opposite sex and courting, but she knew this one was used to getting what he wanted when he wanted it. Ellie couldn't imagine why, but for some reason, she felt a strange satisfying pleasure in Mr. Renault's apparent discomfort as she made him wait for her reply.

When she rose slowly from the swing, Brady stood up, too. Ellie leisurely walked to the edge of the concrete porch and lowered herself to the top step. "Here, Flippo. Here, Boy," she called to her still energetic and ever-ready-to-play puppy dog. She scratched Flippo behind the ears, and then decided to put Brady out of his misery. "Very well, Mr. Renault. You can stay. *This* time. But, only for a few minutes," she offered with a semi-smirk.

From inside the house, Sam had to shoo Nora away from the sitting room window, ordering her to stop spying on her sister. Nora giggled and ran off. Skipped out, really. She was tickled that Ellie was finally talking to a boy; and not just *any* boy. Every girl in Okmulgee thought that dreamy Brady Renault was the bee's knees. And, Nora couldn't *wait* to hear all the details.

Curiosity, though, got the best of Sam; and, he took his youngest daughter's place at the window, trying to inconspicuously peek out the curtain with one hand; holding his pipe in the other. But, only for a few moments. Marie padded into the room and gently chided her husband for being just as nosy as Nora. "Come away now, Sam. Let's leave the young people to themselves. Ellie will be just fine. That Brady Renault seems to be a very nice young man. I think they look lovely together, don't you?"

"Maybe," Sam grumbled. "But, as far as I'm concerned, Brady Renault is a little too slick for my taste – as slick as okra soup."

Ellie found herself enjoying Brady's company, *in spite of* herself . . . and his reputation. Brady was funny, charming as hell, attentive, acted like a real gentleman and hadn't even tried to kiss her – although he did test the waters by taking Ellie's hand in his as they walked along the river on their fourth one-on-one rendezvous in what was beginning to look like a bonafide courtship. Most importantly, Brady shared her views on the world and also seemed to crave life outside of Okmulgee. The same dreams and goals. Travel. Adventure. Experiencing all the living and wonder that the world had to offer. He wanted to see it all; taste it all; just like she did. Or, at least, that's what he told her every chance he got.

Even though part of Ellie was still kicking and screaming against any kind of involvement with any man (The danger, of course, was the possibility that it could lead to marriage, which was pretty much synonymous with imprisonment to Ellie); the other part of her thought that maybe God had truly smiled upon her and blessed her with a true *kindred spirit*. If such a thing were indeed possible.

Brady gave Ellie exactly what she wanted and told her exactly what she wanted to hear. They frequented the picture show at the tiny colored theater on Fifth Street, the hub of the colored business district in downtown Okmulgee. (Black and Red people in Okmulgee were also allowed to sit in the designated colored balcony of the larger white theater. But, most, like Ellie and Brady, opted not to.) They then passionately analyzed every character and the more reasonable or worldly approach the hero or heroine should have taken. Ellie and Brady laughed and screamed on the Ferris wheel at the county fair, built to be a near dead-ringer replica of the famous ride at the 1904 St. Louis World's Fair. Brady even convinced Ellie to accompany him to Okmulgee's Red Light District's most infamous honky-tonk, the LowDown - where they Charlestoned, Quickstepped and Shimmied for hours. Loving the "adventure" of it all, Ellie threw back her first shot of forbidden bootleg moonshine. She had a ball. *So this is what my wild and crazy brother Jake has always snuck off to do all these years,* she reflected, slightly but happily inebriated for the first time in her life. Ellie had no idea that Jake and Brady spent many an evening at the Lowdown and countless other juke joints and dives from Okmulgee to Tulsa, doing a whole lot more than dancing and drinking.

The budding couple enjoyed private picnics; thrilled at scandalous, secret skinny-dipping (neither undressed or dressed in front of the other, of course); lay on the grass, watching and describing the clouds during daylight; counted the stars, identifying constellations at night. Brady both actively participated and appeared to hang on to Ellie's every word. Together, they also shared Ellie's favorite thing to do in the world – lying on her stomach and devouring the contents of her cherished magazine collection. Some of them were ancient, yellowed from age and dog-eared from years of constant re-reading. Some were brand new and lovingly handled as the treasures they were to Ellie: *National Geographic*, *Harper's Bazaar* (hawked as "the style resource for the well-dressed woman and the well-dressed mind"), *Ladies Home Journal* and *Vogue*.

"When I was a little girl, my Mama used to bring these home for me from the fancy houses she used to clean in New Orleans," Ellie reminisced. The recollections were equal parts sweet and painful. A lump formed in her throat and Ellie fought back prickly, hot tears as she reverently stroked the magazines' covers, remembering Callie. "Now, I read them at the library or Papa sometimes buys them for me when he goes to Tulsa."

"Well, I can't say I've ever seen a ladies' magazine before," Brady admitted. "Except for the Sears & Roebuck catalogue. If you can count that. Awww, but I love this one here, *National Geographic*. Yes sir, that's the one. All them far-away places. Exotic. That's what they call it."

"Yes, and I want to visit them all, from jungles to ice caps. Couldn't you just get lost in the stories and pictures for hours?" Ellie perked up, all of her fire and enthusiasm bubbling back up through her words, eyes and expression as she gingerly picked up a copy of her most venerated publication of all – *The Crisis: A Record of the Darker Race*, the publication of the National Association for the Advancement of Colored People. Ellie clutched the book to her chest.

"Important things are happening in the rest of the world, Brady. And, I want to be a part of it. Like the Harlem Renaissance in New York City." She spoke in whispered, yet urgently excited tones. Brady's face drew a blank.

"The Harlem Renaissance! Only the most important artistic and intellectual movement for colored people ever! It's – how can I put it? It's a – a celebration of Black life and our culture; like artists and writers and great thinkers with views that are so *brilliant*, they are probably scaring white folks to death! Can you *imagine*? You know any time colored folks talk about freedom or independent thought, white people think it's 'radical.'"

Brady didn't know what the hell Ellie was going on and on about and stared at her as though she were speaking some kind of foreign language; but he couldn't help being mesmerized by the passion in her words. Her unshakable resolve that there really *was* another way to live. It made her that much more desirable to him.

"Jeez Louise, Brady. You have *got* to read the amazing stories and commentary in here. The writers really make you think! Mark my words – they are going to change conditions for our race; I just *know* it! Gifted and accomplished Negro scholars who know how to express themselves on paper – like W.E.B. Du Bois, Langston Hughes, Jean Toomer and Alain Locke. My heroes. And, there are colored women writers, too. Zora Neale Hurston and Nella Larsen are my favorites!"

"Then, why ain't you planning to run off to New York, Gal, instead of all the way to Paris?"

Ellie misinterpreted Brady's question as encouragement. "Well, sir. That is actually part of my plan. You have to go to New York anyway to set sail for Europe. So, yes. I'm gonna take the bus to Harlem, U.S.A. and soak up some of that culture. But, Harlem is still *here*, you know? I want to go to Paris to study dress design. To admire the great masterpieces. Stroll along the Champs-Elysees. Sip coffee at the sidewalk cafes. More than anything, though, I think I want to know what it *feels* like to be welcomed at those museums and cafes, restaurants and hotels. Where my race don't matter." Ellie's growing vision felt so real in her mind, she sat up. Okmulgee had disappeared. "just like Josephine Baker," she declared.

"Who?" Brady asked, breaking Ellie's Parisian reverie.

"Josephine Baker! Didn't you ever read about her in the newspaper?" Ellie picked up and started leafing through her *The Crisis Magazine*. "She's a colored girl not much older than me. I just read a story about her not too long ago. Now where was it?"

Brady placed his hand on Ellie's, stopping her search. "That's just fine, Ellie. I can read about this Josephine another time. But, what's so special about her?"

"Well, I know that she is a glamorous showgirl from St. Louis. Started performing vaudeville when she was just 12 or 13. And, like I said, colored people are treated like everybody else in Europe. So, she went to New York for a little while; then decided to move to Paris where she can sing and dance wherever she wants. Do whatever she wants. Go wherever she wants. And, she's but 19 years old and doesn't have any more education than I have. Isn't that grand? I'll bet that Josephine Baker is going to be a big international star one day. Sure hope I'll meet her when I get to Paris."

Over the next few weeks, Brady's and Ellie's private tête-à-têtes became anticipated rituals for them both. More thoughtful. And, increasingly romantic. Ellie trusted Brady more and more, giving away a little bit more of herself at each encounter. Brady looked at her as though she hung the sun, the moon and the stars. At first, the glances, attention and listening were just part and parcel of his plan of conquest; but, one day he realized he actually felt something more. Ellie felt something more, too. More than she wanted to because *this* was *not* part of her plan.

"Know what?" Brady quietly asked during one of their many simple evening walks.

"No, what?" Ellie responded, still walking. Brady stopped. He reached out and grabbed Ellie's arm as she strode past, pulling her back to him. She averted her eyes, but he gently took her face and forced her to look at him. Brady carefully studied every beautiful feature, which made Ellie exceedingly uncomfortable. Her strongest impulse was to run.

Oh Lord, was he going to kiss her?

Ellie had certainly read about kissing in books and stories; and had seen it dozens of times on the silver screen. But, she had never herself been kissed. She had thought about it. Remotely. She and Nora – mostly Nora - talked and giggled about kissing, but, even though she was 18 years-old, Ellie hadn't "gone steady with" or been courted by anyone. Until now. It had just never happened and she didn't know what to expect.

"I think," Brady continued in a low, breathy voice. "I think it is incredible that I have found someone who shares the very same dreams I have always had; someone who wants the same things. Adventure and seeing as much of this world as I can before I leave it." Ellie's hazel eyes sparkled in the moonlight and grew even bigger with astonishment and disbelief.

Brady laughed in the same low voice, keeping his eyes on Ellie's, lowering them to her perfect, pouty mouth and back again. "Doll, you are the most beautiful and most exciting girl I have ever met. I didn't even know girls like you existed; especially not here in Oklahoma. Together, baby, we can – I *know* we can – set the world on its ear!"

Brady lowered his face to hers, covering her mouth with his. First a few light, sweet tastes. Then he claimed more, opening her lips with his cool yet hot; rough yet soft; wet, urgent tongue. Ellie hadn't expected anything other than lips and tried to pull away. But Brady tightened one arm around her waist and held the other hand firmly behind her head, keeping her exactly where he wanted her. After a moment or two, Ellie was kissing Brady back and experienced the strangest sensations. It was as though an internal heat was rising from the bottom of her feet to the top of her head, making her feel nearly faint. Almost as though she were melting. Then, butterflies took residence in her belly. And down *there*. Delicious, fluttering butterflies.

After what seemed like an eternity, which could have lasted even longer as far as Ellie was concerned, they pulled apart.

"So, what's Ellie short for anyway?"

"Eleanor, but, as long as I can remember, everybody has always called me Ellie. My Papa used to say that Eleanor was way too big a name for such a little girl."

"Well, your Papa was right." Brady tightened his arms around her, pressing his forehead to hers. "Ellie is much better suited for you because it is pretty and smart and lively. Saucy – just like you are."

They strolled, hand-in-hand, to a nearby bench and just sat quietly for a few moments, breathing in the night air's cool sweetness.

"Can I ask you another question?" Brady ventured.

Ellie nodded.

"Speaking of your Daddy – er, your Papa, I was just wondering. Is he just a light-skinned colored man or is he white? Just curious, that's all. If it's none of my beeswax, just tell me."

Ellie contemplated his question for a minute. "Well, this is in strictest confidence, Brady Renault, because Papa doesn't like to talk about it. But, I think the account of his birth and childhood is kind of romantic. And, it proves how much my grandparents loved him. I don't even know if Papa *knows* we know. Mama told the story to me and Nora and my older sister, Beth, when we were little bitty girls."

Even though it went unspoken, Ellie loved to dramatically call her father's story a tale of tragic love that wasn't meant to be, and ultimate triumph. "It happened a really long time ago; some time in the mid or late 1880's, but, people didn't keep very good records back then, so we don't have an exact year. Not like today," Ellie prefaced.

Sam Coursey was born to a wealthy French entrepreneur in New Orleans and the "innocent" young daughter of his American business partner. There was, however, a scandalous fly in the affair's ointment. The dashing Monsieur Philippe Jacquard was married and la petite chou-chou who found herself with child was from one of New Orleans' oldest, upper crust, white families. The young woman's family practically kept her captive for the entire pregnancy, hidden away on the 4th floor of their sprawling maison. Miranda Coursey, the Creole housekeeper, cared for the girl as part of her regular duties. Mamu Miranda and Papu Girard (which is what Ellie, her siblings and their cousins had called their grandparents) *then happily and quietly took the baby as soon as he was born; Mamu Miranda having delivered him herself. She and Papu Girard took him into the bosom of their family and raised him as their own; along with their other children. No questions asked. But, Mamu stopped working for the wealthy family right after the young mother gave birth.*

"That baby, Sam Coursey, grew up to be the best man I know," Ellie continued proudly. My Papa is a good man, a brave man who loves, and has been loved by his family – unconditionally – his entire life. I think he really hates white people, though, and certainly doesn't trust them; which is why he doesn't want to be associated with them. Sometimes though, he *had* to be white. Like a few years ago, it was the only way he could rescue our cousins from those concentration camps after the Tulsa race riots. My auntie told me he used to even sometimes sit in on Klan meetings back in Louisiana, so he could warn everyone about what they were up to."

"So, he's only white when he needs to be," Brady nodded in acknowledgment and understanding.

"Know what, though?" Ellie asked dreamily.

"No. What?"

"Well, I don't much care for white folks neither. Most of the ones I've met are mean as hornets, strange in their ways and uppity. Like they were born better'n everybody else in this world; just because they're white. With all the commotion and hell they raise over nothin', I just don't get it.

But, even so, I can't help wondering if I take after that married scoundrel, Monsieur Philippe Jacquard. He *was* an international businessman. I got a real head for figures. And, he was from France; maybe Nice; maybe Paris. Maybe that's why I have always felt such a strong yearning to go there. Maybe 'cause he is my blood Grandpapa, even though I don't know him from Adam and probably will never even lay eyes on him. Maybe, just maybe there's some of him in me."

The two sat silently for a few minutes longer, each lost in their own thoughts. Then, Brady started speaking a mile a minute.

"Ellie, I'm just gonna come on out and *say* this. I love you. I love you more than I honestly thought I could love anybody. And, well, I was wondering what you think your Papa might say if I asked him for your hand in marriage?"

Ellie was completely taken off guard. And horrified. She liked kissing Brady and all. And, yes, she had feelings for him. But marriage? She leaped up, flustered, but tried to remain composed. "My Papa? Well, thank you very much, Brady, for clueing me in first, but I don't care *what* my father would say because marriage is *not* a part of my plans. *As you know good and well!*"

She stormed off, ran back up the path a few feet; then stopped and looked back. "Okay. I admit that maybe I love you, too. But, that doesn't mean I want to *marry* you! Haven't you heard a *word* I've said these last few weeks!?" With that, she was off. Brady had gotten caught up in the moment, but he expected Ellie's rejection. It just hardened his resolve and his manhood. A wild one, that gal. But, he knew he was the one to tame her.

"Gilded Cages"

"Oh, Mrs. Renau-alt," Brady seductively sing-songed, pouring two glasses of champagne in the attractive, but modest bedroom in the home he purchased for him and Ellie. "Come on out of the bathroom, Baby. Your loving husband is waiting for you!"

Inside the bathroom, Ellie was breathtaking in a beautiful white gown and peignoir, which were as provocative as anyone dared to be in the 1920's. Brady had ordered a bottle of her coveted Chanel No. 5 as a wedding present. He told her it was a little preview of Paris, which they would both move to . . . just not as soon as Ellie wanted. But, soon. He promised.

Ellie reveled in sparingly spritzing the intoxicating, expensive perfume at her pulse points; but her lovely face was panic-stricken. It broke Ellie's heart that her Mama hadn't been here on this all-important day to advise her and comfort her. But her stepmother, Marie, stepped in as best she could. And, Beth, bless her, had taken the train to Oklahoma from Texas to be with Ellie, leaving Beau and the kids at home. Ellie took another moment and a deep breath, closed her eyes, then turned around and opened the door to make her grand entrance for her new husband.

Ellie was a vision. As much as he had wanted to, Brady hadn't even attempted necking with Ellie or taking a peek at more than she wanted to show him during their courtship. Now, after all that waiting, he could barely contain himself. Let alone shut his mouth, which was hanging open at the sight of her.

Ellie almost gasped when she laid eyes on her husband, sprawled across the bed in all his jaw-dropping, bare-chested glory. *Now* she understood the bloomer-wetting rumors. Brady *was* magnificent to look at.

He offered his bride a glass. They toasted each other and sipped. "Good girl," Brady cooed. "This is a magic elixir that will help you relax a little bit. I'll take over the rest in that department," he half-laughed in his low, throaty voice. Fortunately, the delicate champagne saucer was shallow; so Ellie was able to consume its bubbly contents in just a couple of swallows.

The wedding night ritual began. Ellie knew she loved the kissing and was happy to keep at that for a while. The passion in their kissing, though, increased quickly – lips, eyes, necks, chests – with each genuinely admiring the beauty of the other. Ellie's temperature was rising a little higher and she relaxed a little more. She resisted at first when Brady slipped the straps of her gown off her shoulders. But then, his hot, wet kisses on those shoulders, skillfully moving down to suckle her lovely, firm, young breasts with pinky beige nipples now at full attention; ignited new liquid heat in Ellie.

Under the sheets, Brady pushed the hem of Ellie's gown above her waist. He didn't have time or patience at that point to take it off completely. He then deftly removed her lacy drawers and began stroking her inner thighs, moving up to the prize. He couldn't contain himself any longer and mounted Ellie to make his move.

Ellie, writhing with newly unbridled pleasure one moment; *froze* the next. Her face transformed from amorous to terrified in a split second; and her voice from a purr to a panicked "Stop!"

Brady, too, transformed – from a smooth operator to an insensitive bungler. Under the circumstances, Ellie hoped for and expected her loving husband to likely be a little disappointed, maybe hurt – but certainly understanding and patient. Not Brady. He reacted instead like a hormonally crazed teenaged boy who was stopped in mid-action. He was livid.

"What the hell's the matter with you, Gal? You actin' as jumpy as frog legs hitting the frying pan!"

Ellie was hyperventilating. "Stay away from me! Don't you touch me!" She was almost screaming, hysterical; backing up and clutching the sheets against her to cover herself.

Confused and totally unsympathetic, Brady threw up his hands as if surrendering, and backed off. "OK, Ellie. Ellie, what's wrong? What did I do? Did I hurt you?"

Ellie was slowly calming down; her breathing was returning to normal and she seemed to be coming back to reality. *Lord have mercy, what did I do to Brady and why?* "Brady. Oh my God. I am so sorry. I don't know what came over me. I swear I don't." Brady sat on the edge of the bed and looked over his shoulder at Ellie, silent; not knowing what to think or feel.

"I do love you, Brady. Please - could you please be a bit patient with me?" she pleaded. She got up and slipped her arms around him, resting her head on his shoulder. "And, this is, after all, the first time I've ever been with a man. Can we try it again?"

Brady dimmed the light, took Ellie into his arms and picked up where they left off. Ellie winced in pain when Brady penetrated just seconds later. Within a couple of minutes, Brady exploded with satisfaction. He rolled off his new wife and pecked her on the cheek. *Now that's more like it*, he thought. *Even if Ellie had just laid there like a damn log. She'll get used to it. Ahhhh.*

Thank God it's over, Ellie told herself as Brady dismounted. Had he looked at her face before he rolled over to go to sleep, he would have seen pained endurance where happiness should have been. Had he looked at her face after he barely planted a passionless kiss on her cheek, he might have seen the silent tears pooling in her eyes.

Nora and Ellie visited in Ellie's sunny, tiny – but well-appointed with the most modern appliances – kitchen. Ellie had made the crisp white curtains at the windows, which matched her starched white apron trimmed in red with a big red apple appliquéd on one side. She made it, too, as well as the simple, un-Ellie-like dress underneath.

"More lemonade?" Ellie offered her sister. Nora, now looking more like a stunning young woman than a teenager, her black hair in a popular marceled style; sat at the kitchen table staring at Ellie.

Ellie, her free-spirited, adventurous sister, Ellie, had been domesticated.

It was as though Ellie was having some kind of out-of-body experience like a couple of those you-know-they-must-be-really-close-to-God ladies at the Baptist church down the street from Uganda Martyrs. (Nothing so exciting as falling out or being in a Holy Ghost trance ever happened during Mass at Uganda Martyrs. Catholics never seemed to get that kind of close to God.) This unfamiliar Ellie chattered on about how Brady took her all the way to Sapulpa for special fabric for their sitting room curtains and how she now receives the Sears & Roebuck catalog and the *Ladies Home Journal* in the mail, instead of getting them second hand.

Nora played with her glass, and watched her sister in disbelief. She wasn't sure what to say to *this* Ellie. "That's swell, Ellie. Do you also take the *National Geographic* or those other ones you always loved so much – that colored magazine with all the writers, *Crisis,* or the really fancy one, *Vogue?*"

Ellie joined Nora at the table and soberly answered, "No." She continued, as if reciting by rote. "Nora, dear, all of us have to release childhood fantasies at some point. I am a grown woman now. Married and everything. And, so, that means I have to be realistic. Right? And, well, my reality is being married to Brady – the best looking and hardest-working man who ever lived."

"Jiminy Christmas, Ellie! What has happened to you? It's *me* you're talking to!"

Ellie stared for a moment at Nora as if seeing her for the first time. Then, she sat at the table and grabbed her sister's hands in her own.

"Oh my God, Nora. What have I gotten myself into?" Ellie asked, eyes wide, somehow snapping out of her homemaker stupor. "I am bored out of my brains. Okmulgee isn't any different than LeBeau – except the heat is drier and the houses are closer together. And – marriage is every bit the prison I thought it would be and Brady is my jailer!"

"Oh Ellie," Nora sympathized.

Ellie rested her head on their clasped hands and closed her eyes as tightly as she could, as though trying to somehow *will* herself free again. Physically and mentally. "Nora, I swear to you that I am trying my best to like being married. Honest! But, I want to have my *own* money. Like I used to! Brady, though, won't let me do any outside sewing or tailoring because he doesn't want his wife to work."

"Oh, my dear Ellie, I know. But, isn't it kind of a trade-off thing when people get married?" Nora asked in her weak attempt to try and help. What else could she *say*?

"No, Nora, no! That is *not* how it was supposed to be. Not with Brady! He seems to have forgotten about our dreams and our plans to travel, and he changes the subject whenever I bring it up. And, he gets kind of mean about it."

"What do you mean by *mean*?"

Ellie ignored the question. "The worst part," Ellie continued, confiding in a desperate whisper, "is the wifely duty part. I love Brady – but I hate 'it.' I know I should like it, Nora, but I don't. He, on the other hand, wants to do "it" damn near every single night and can't understand why I'm not pregnant yet. It's been months, after all. God, even if I'm dog-tired, I absolutely dread going to bed every night because he just will not let me be. And, I *hate* it, Nora! What is wrong with me?" Ellie was so miserable, she was in tears and, Nora thought, almost on the verge of hysteria. And, Ellie almost never cried. Anymore.

Nora watched and listened to her sister lovingly, feeling helpless. Still holding hands. "I've got a confession to make, Ellie." Ellie tilted her head quizzically.

"You know how I always teased you when we were little about your big dreams being so silly? And showin' off? Well, truth is, I always loved to hear about those dreams and all the wonderful adventures you had planned. And, I didn't say it, but I always hoped you'd take me along." Ellie turned away as though the reminder of her true, original self was too painful to hear.

"Look at me," Nora urged. "I always thought that my big sister was the bravest and most exciting person in the world for wanting something so different and so much bigger than anyone else. And, I always wanted those dreams to come true for you. And maybe they still will, Ellie. Brady might surprise you!"

"You are such a dear sister. And, my very best friend in the world, you know. Thank you, Nora. Lord, maybe it *will* get better." Ellie took a sip of her lemonade and sighed. "What's wrong with me? We both know how many nasty heifers would have given *anything* to be close enough to get so much as a *sniff* of Brady, let alone *be* Mrs. Brady Renault. Why aren't I over the moon? And, why don't I just swoon when he comes at me with his thing?"

Nora's heart went out to her sister. *Could that bad thing that happened to Ellie so many years ago be having some kind of effect now?* She wondered. *No, 'cause Ellie doesn't remember anything about that terrible night,* Nora reasoned with herself. "Well, I am certainly not the right person to ask, Sister. But, you might consider approaching the subject with Marie. Did you know she is in the family way again?"

"Well, isn't that just the bee's knees? Wonder if Brady knows? Marie and Papa are multiplying like rabbits and we don't even have *one* bun in the oven. Jeez Louise."

"Recurring Nightmares"

"There's Mama's sweet baby. You just sit there like a good boy," Ellie cooed to the happy, healthy baby boy playing on a blanket on the ground next to her. Pregnant with her second child, Ellie was taking down clean, dry sheets flapping and snapping on a line in the wind. She breathed and savored their freshness, infused with nature's own special fragrant blend of sunshine, hydrangea-scented warm breezes, blue sky and puffy, traveling clouds.

"Hey there, Ellie. How's that fine little man doing today?" The Renault's neighbor, Lizzie Cass was also expecting, and gathering her laundry across the fence the two families shared.

"Hi Lizzie. Our little Master Evan is just perfect, thank you," Ellie smiled back at her son, happily clapping his fat little hands.

"You know, Ellie. I have wanted to compliment you on your maternity outfits. You wear the prettiest maternity clothes I have ever seen."

"Why, thank you, Lizzie," Ellie hollered back, continuing to harvest the laundry; but delighted that someone was admiring her handiwork. It had been so long.

"I know you make them yourself. How in the world do you find the time?"

"Oh, it's not so hard. Maternity clothes are really simple because they're mostly loose."

"Hmmm. Even so. I wish I had that skill. You're really lucky to be so clever with a needle and thread."

"Well, Lizzie, I'd be happy to make a few pieces for you, if you like." At the tail end of the neighborly banter, Brady pulled in from work. He parked his car, slamming the door shut.

Ellie quickly whipped her head around in his direction. "Hi Dear! How was your day?" Brady skulked into the house without saying a word.

A skilled multi-tasker, Ellie dropped the laundry basket on the table in the tiny, enclosed back porch; Evan perched on the other hip. She continued into the kitchen, slipped the baby into his high chair and gave him a bottle; checked the roast in the oven, then filled a cocktail glass with ice for whatever Brady wanted to drink.

"Would you like a refreshing gin and tonic on the rocks, Brady? You look like you've had a rough day." Ellie offered.

Brady's response was to knock the glass out of Ellie's hand, shattering ice, along with chunks and slivers of sunlight-prismed crystal all over the kitchen floor. He grabbed Ellie with one hand and a handkerchief out of his pocket with the other; then roughly wiped the red lipstick off her mouth.

"How many times have I told you I hate that red slut paint?" he demanded in a cold staccato voice. "You need to remember that you are a mother now, in addition to being a wife. *My* wife! And, I am not having any wife of mine leaving this house looking like a tramp. I don't care if it means just stepping foot in the backyard or the goddamn Eiffel Tower!"

"And, another thing," he reminded her, on a cruel, pissy-mood roll. "You can forget about making clothes for that fucking, nosey-ass heifer Lizzie, or *anyone* other than yourself, me or the baby!" Brady banged on the table to bring home the point that he'd *told* Ellie a hundred times that no wife of his was going to work; that he could take care of his family himself!

The screaming startled the baby, who began to cry. Ellie scooped him up, hissing back at Brady. "What the hell is the matter with you?!" Brady raised his hand to backhand slap her, but stopped himself in mid-air. Ellie clutched the baby tighter. She glared at Brady – not with fear, but with a look that *dared* him to touch her.

Ellie's and Brady's daughter, Dinah, was born four months later. Life was good for Brady Renault. He was blessed with the family he had always wanted . . . with the woman he had to have. He had been promoted to a shift manager at Ball Brothers Glass Company. Yet, he grew more dissatisfied with his life, more self-loathing and more resentful of Ellie every day. Brady started coming home later and later most evenings;

opting instead to spend his time after work at his old haunts. Dives that made the Low Down look like a four-star restaurant.

His favorite was the LooseLips. It was dingy, smoky and stuck in the backwoods off a side road leaving Okmulgee. That's where Jake Coursey observed his brother-in-law one late, rainy night. Jake had always had the bad-boy-bug up his ass and lived to drink too much, gamble, womanize and start as many fights as he could; but, he didn't have Brady's mean streak.

The music was blaring. Men and women were guzzling liquor like it was water, laughing loud and dancing – grinding and dry-humping right on the dance floor. All the hard drinking and carousing had taken a harsh toll on Brady's once-flawless face. He was even developing a paunch and looked at least a decade older than his 31 years. Jake, inebriated and hugged up with his own floozy, observed Brady at the bar, slobbering on a scantily-clad and heavily made-up woman who hung all over him; rubbing against him with her barely covered tits, which sat up on her chest like giant cantaloupes. Brady alternated between pulling on his cigarette, swigging his drink, stroking the woman's ample ass and laughing at whatever she was saying.

Jake's running around on his wife was one thing. His justification being that she knew he was a snake when she picked him up. Not to mention the 85 extra pounds Alice had gained since their marriage and three children. But, he'd be *damned* if he was going to sit back and tolerate his little sister being disrespected by her husband *right in front of his face*! He walked over to Brady and tapped him on the shoulder.

"Hey man, how're Ellie and the kids this fine night?"

"Swell, man. How's your little woman?" Brady chortled.

"I asked you first, brother," Jake retorted, not missing Brady's obvious slam against his rotund wife. "Excuse me, Miss, but brother-man here is *married*. To my little sister," Jake shared with the woman keeping Brady company.

Brady slurred, "Beat it," dismissing Jake. Cantaloupe-titty woman just shrugged and shamelessly eyeballed Jake up and down. She could have cared less about Brady's marital status. Lover-Boy here was nothing more to her than a few free drinks and the promise of a good time. *Who gave a shit about whether he was married or not?*

"Naw, I don't think so, Bro'. I think you're the one who's going to hit the road. My sister's waiting for you. And, frankly - " Jake waved his hand in front of his nose. "You reek! How the hell much hooch have you *had*, man? Damn!"

"Scram, man. You're killing my buzz."

"After you, brother. Or, we can stand right here and shoot the breeze into the wee hours. Whaddaya say?"

Brady wasn't up for a fight. He grabbed his companion, winked and tweaked her nipples with his fingers; then kissed her roughly on the mouth, smearing her lipstick all over her face. And his. "See ya around, baby." Jake, he ignored.

Back home, Ellie tucked 6 year-old Evan and 5 year-old Dinah into their twin beds in their pretty, shared bedroom. They had just finished their prayers when Brady slammed the front door downstairs. He bellowed for Ellie.

Ellie kissed the children goodnight, turned out their light, shut their door and headed downstairs.

Brady, visibly smashed, was in the kitchen opening and slamming shut the polished cabinet doors and yelling for his dinner.

"Brady, please," Ellie urged, hoping her calm would rub off on her husband. "Lower your voice. The children are trying to fall asleep." She took his plate out of the oven and put it on the table with a full place setting. "I tried to keep it warm for you without drying it out. The same ritual I perform almost every night lately."

"Well, you failed!" Brady spat. "This shit is both lukewarm and dry as dirt!" With that he hurled the plate and its contents to the floor.

Ellie refused to react. "It would still be hot if you were home where and when you were supposed to be, instead of whoring around! You can eat the damn food right off the floor for all I care!"

"Clean up this mess," he demanded.

"You're the one who made it. Clean it up your *damn* self!"

As Ellie walked away, Brady grabbed her by the hair, yanking her back to him. He slapped Ellie across the face so hard she stumbled backwards, grabbing the back of one of the chairs to keep from falling to the floor. He snatched her by the throat.

"You think you so high and mighty, don't ya? So much better than me with all of your stupid notions. All of those stupid, so-called pie-in-the-sky plans you went on and on about when I met your sorry ass. Well, *I* am the master of *this* castle, bitch!" Brady wasn't squeezing her throat, but Ellie was so stunned, at first she couldn't speak. Then Brady threw her to the floor and started to undo his pants.

Ellie jumped up, wildly kicking him and doing her best to beat the hell out of Brady with adrenalin-powered punches. "Have you lost your goddamn mind, you drunk, broke-down bastard? Don't you touch me! Don't you ever put your hands on me again!" Ellie's face registered some kind of memory. *Christ, had she had to fight like this before? Did she have a nightmare foreshadowing this real-life nightmare?"* She shook it off, concentrating on the present and bit Brady – hard – on his forearm, drawing blood.

When Brady yelped in pain, Ellie staggered away and reached for a butcher knife. She trembled with rage. Her breath coming in great heaves. There was a steely look of determination in her eyes as she spoke in an almost unrecognizable voice. "I promise you, Brady Renault. On my Mama's grave. If you *ever* raise a hand to me again, you sure as hell better kill me – because, if you don't, I *will kill you."* Her words and manner were so fierce, it gave Brady pause.

Brady managed to keep his temper under control for a few years. Until the "fear of God" Ellie put in him wore off. Just as before, it was another late night for Brady. The children were happy and surrounded by the love of their extended family, but they felt the tension between their parents. Both were well-mannered, good kids. Physically, they were good-looking, even blends of both Ellie and Brady. Evan was 10, Dinah, 9.

The children were fed and down for the night by the time their father stumbled into the house. First, he headed into the kitchen. It was clean. There was no trace of any dinner having been held for him. That was all the excuse he needed. Brady was just liquored-up enough to pick a fight.

He staggered up the stairs and into the bedroom he and Ellie shared now as simply roommates; yelling Ellie's name.

Ellie sat at her dressing table, resolute; brushing her hair. She could smell the whiskey on Brady's breath as soon as he entered the room. But, this time, she was ready for him as she stared into her stunning image with an emotionless, chilling *knowing*. Her free-hand curled around what she hoped she didn't have to use.

The same old arguments began – Brady accusing Ellie of thinking she was "so damn high and mighty" that she couldn't have dinner waiting for him; that he was "the *man* of the goddamn house, her goddamn husband." Brady began to unbuckle his belt. Ellie continued to brush.

Even angrier at getting no reaction, Brady grabbed Ellie's arm, snatched her out of the chair with one hand, hurling her to the floor, and raised his belt with the other. He struck her with it repeatedly, calling her a bitch and a piss-poor piece of ass to boot; then demanded that she look at him when he's talking to her.

Brady mistakenly thought that the slim silver-handled object in Ellie's right hand was a comb. With the fury of a madwoman, she grabbed the end of the belt at just the right moment, deftly pulled herself to her feet and lunged at Brady; jabbing him first in the arm holding the belt, then slashing him across the face when he released her in pain to grab the bleeding arm. He took a step back, staring at Ellie, stupefied!

Ellie held her ground, arms out, right hand clutching the knife so tightly the veins of her hand were popping out, ready to strike again; eyes blazing; voice almost growling. "You low-life, cowardly son-of-a-bitch. You are so weak and so fucking miserable, you are jealous of my every thought and action!

I told you before that if you ever laid your hands on me again, you had better kill me because I sure as hell am going to kill *you*! So, come on. Come on, you bastard. Come on and hit me again, please. *I dare you*! Please, give me a reason to cut you up into little pieces!" Brady was silent.

"No? Not so big and bad now, are you?" Knife poised, Ellie ordered Brady to sit his ass down on the bed, which he did. Reluctantly. Even though Brady was a foot taller and at least 90 pounds heavier than

Ellie, a dangerously dark fury in her eyes told him that she could – and *would* – kill him if further provoked.

Circling Brady on the bed like a predator with its captured prey, Ellie continued. "Ok, mothafucker. Here's how it's going to be from here on out. I have decided, out of the goodness of my heart, to let your pitiful, lying, poor-ass excuse of a man self, live. *This* time."

Ellie's eyes blazed and she never even blinked as she issued a not-so-veiled-threat. "Oh, and baby, if I were you, I wouldn't even *think* about closing my eyes to go to sleep tonight. Not with a high and mighty, and *really pissed-off,* crazy-ass bitch like *me* running around."

It was a miracle that Evan and Dinah didn't hear the commotion that night. Frightening them was Ellie's greatest fear. Certain that Brady got her message loud and clear, Ellie roused them up and put them in Brady's car, along with a laundry basket full of clothes and absolute necessities.

Ellie had never driven before. But, that night she negotiated the few blocks to Sam and Marie's home in the middle of the night. Sam opened the door, Marie at his side. They couldn't imagine who would be ringing the doorbell at this time of night. Her father lovingly ushered Ellie and her babies in, forcing himself to swallow the gasps that almost escaped his mouth at the sight of the swelling black and blue welts on Ellie's face, neck and arms.

Once Evan and Dinah were settled in with their same-age aunt and uncle, the adults – Ellie, Sam, Marie and Nora, who lived with her father and stepmother – sat in the living room where Ellie explained for the first time what had been going on in her marriage for years.

As he listened to Ellie's story, Sam's heart landed in his throat. He choked back emotion and held his daughter tightly, telling her over and over again how very sorry he was and begged her to please try and forgive him for failing her again; for not being there to protect her. Marie and Nora cried, but only Nora turned her face away, knowing why her father was *really* so grief-stricken.

Ellie didn't remember – *but Nora did. Nora was there, and her mind flashed back now to standing just inside the bedroom door, straining to listen while*

*her father and the doctor talked. It was right after Papa, Jake and Joe carried
Ellie home all bloody and dirty and raggedy and beat up. They had searched for
Ellie for an entire day and night after Mama's funeral. The doctor told her father
the terrible things that had been done to Ellie and Papa had cried then.*

"This is not your fault, Papa," Ellie tried to console her father.
"I am the one who decided to marry Brady. You didn't like or trust him
from the beginning, remember?"

"Oh, baby." Sam held Ellie and stroked her hair.

"I'm okay, Papa. It's alright, now. But, Papa?"

"Hmmm?"

"I'm confused about something. There is nothing to forgive you
for. You have always been here for me . . . for all of us. What did you mean
by 'failing me again?' You have never failed me."

"Well, not today. That's for damn sure!" Sam responded before
getting up and unlocking his shotgun from the gun cabinet.

"Sam Coursey, where are you going?" Marie asked with a
quivering voice.

"To send Brady Renault to hell."

It took all three of the women to hold Sam back. Ellie pleaded
with her father to please let Brady be – that Brady was not worth going to
jail for. She made Sam promise that he would not let Jake and Joe go off
half-cocked after Brady, either.

"I can handle Brady," Ellie assured her family. "In fact, I have a
plan. But, I need all of you to please love me enough to make it work."

"The Bitter"

The brilliant Oklahoma sun rose that next morning on a well-used coffee service, emptied coffee cups and half-eaten sandwiches in the Coursey sitting room.

"Ellie, please reconsider," Sam urged. "It is just not natural for mothers to leave their children!"

"I am not abandoning my children, for God's sake, Papa! I love them more than life itself. You *know* that! Nor am I leaving them alone. This is a plan for a better life for them and I am leaving them, temporarily, in the care of their grandfather and their aunt and the only grandmother they have ever known."

Ellie, like the others, was exhausted. But, she was passionate and determined, and spoke slowly and deliberately, obviously rehashing the same argument she had made all night long.

"Papa, I abandoned the life I wanted once. But, I clearly see now that I can still *have* that life. I also very clearly do not intend for my life or my children's to end up in the hellhole of Okmulgee, Oklahoma. I'm sorry, Papa and Marie. I know this is your home and you are happy here. And, believe me, I am happy for you! But, don't you see? It is not for me and never has been! I just settled for a life I never really wanted because I fell in love with and married Brady. Against my own better judgment, I might add."

"Ellie, Dear, you're not saying that Evan and Dinah were a part of your settling, are you?" Marie asked gingerly. Not trying to accuse, just understand.

"Oh, Lord, of course not! I love my babies more than life itself. They are the most wonderful thing that has ever happened to me. No, I never planned or wanted to be a mother. I admit that. But, I cannot imagine my life without them! They *complete* my life. Loving them and being their mother is the most glorious adventure I could ever know!"

Ellie closed her eyes and said a little prayer before continuing.

She *had* to make them all understand. "I do not think it is fair to my babies to traipse across the country to a big unknown. I want – I *need* – the opportunity to make a new life for them and for me. I all but gave up on my dreams before, and I got married because that is what everyone expected of me. Look how that has turned out!"

"Papa, please," Ellie pleaded. "If you have ever wanted to help me, please do it now. I am not abandoning my children. But, I cannot do this without you and Marie." The weariness was winning out, as tears seeped out, barely noticed. "If I am ever going to make any of my dreams come true, the time is now. There is no way in hell that I am ever going to so much as breathe the same air as Brady ever again. I would rather die."

With that, Sam's concern almost turned to anger. "Don't you ever say something like that again, Ellie Coursey Renault. Enough. I've heard enough."

"I'm sorry, Papa, I didn't mean it like that." Almost on the verge of hysteria, Ellie swore to her family that she *would* die, just a little piece at a time, if she stayed put.

"If I am forced to stay in Okmulgee, I will go mad and will forever hate myself for never trying. And, I am terrified that I might grow to hate you too, for not letting me try."

It only took a few days to make all of the necessary arrangements for both Ellie and the children.

Ellie had stayed in touch with former neighbors, Rose and Roland Turner. The Turners had also been members of Uganda Martyrs Church and got married around the same time as Ellie and Brady. Sam, Marie and Nora remembered them. Nice young couple.

A few years before, Rose and Roland joined relatives in Los Angeles, California; and from all accounts, really loved it. Rose was a maid for a rich white family that had something to do with the motion picture business. Her husband, Roland, worked as the gardener and the driver for the same family. The Turners even owned their own home in LA — with orange trees in the front yard! Other than Nora, Rose had been the only other person who knew how unhappy Ellie had been throughout her marriage. So, in a recent letter, Rose mentioned to Ellie that the people down the street from the folks she and Roland worked for were looking for a new housekeeper – one who could live in. Ellie wired Rose that she was coming to Los Angeles, so Rose told her boss, Mrs. Katie Gold, that she had a clean and dependable friend coming out from Oklahoma who would be looking for work – and a place to stay. According to Rose, this Mrs. Gold told Mrs. Helen Devane, and the arrangements were made. It was surprisingly simple, but apparently the women trusted Rose's judgment.

Ellie explained to her family that the plan was to save enough money to afford and find a home for them and be able to send for the children within a year.

At the Okmulgee Bus Station, Ellie felt as though her heart might actually stop beating; or break in half for real - from the pain of leaving Evan and Dinah; even though she knew she was doing the right thing for all of them. She was on her knees, her arms wrapped around the tearful little boy and girl.

"Don't you forget how much your Mama loves and adores you. You are both the center of my world."

"Then why are you leaving us, Mommy?" Dinah asked again, bottom lip quivering, giant brown eyes spilling slow rivulets of liquid sorrow.

"Oh baby. I told you. Mommy is going to make a better life for you, your brother and me. I promise. And, I promise that we will all be together again soon. Oh, I love you so much," Ellie squeezed them both to her tightly, choking back her own tears. *Dear God, please help me. Help me do what I know I must,* she prayed. Leaving hurt so bad Ellie could barely breathe.

The rest of her family stood close-by.

Also standing close by, lurking on the side of the bus terminal, was an intoxicated and irate Brady. As if bound and determined to get in his last licks, he let the insults commence. "Yeah, Miss High and Mighty, as old as yo' ass is, running after stupid pipe dreams. See you when you come crawling back with your tail between your legs! Don't 'spect me to take your ass back, neither. No suh! And, one thing's for sure," he slurred. "You sho' as hell can't keep my damn kids away from me!"

Sam had his arms wrapped around Ellie and her children. He straightened up. "I beg to differ with you, Brady. But, yes, actually, she *can* keep the children away from you. We all can and *will*. Come anywhere near these young'uns and you will answer to me."

Jake snatched Brady by the arm and "escorted" him to the back of the terminal. "Wave goodbye to everybody, Brady." Once they reached a remote spot, Jake thought for a moment about the promises he had made to Papa and to Ellie, then said aloud, "Oh, what the hell." He knocked Brady out cold with one good right hook.

It was time. Ellie boarded the bus, continuing to wave and throw kisses as it pulled off, beginning her journey to her future. Her children's future. Everyone she loved was getting smaller and smaller. Disappearing. Then, she couldn't see them anymore. *Oh, God, what was she doing?*

The doubts had been held at bay long enough and burst through the barely-there netting that had kept them out of Ellie's mind until now. Now they took up residence in Ellie's consciousness and unpacked their bags of self-flagellation and panic; making themselves right at home. *Was she doing the right thing? Was she crazy for leaving everything she knew and going to a big, fat - what? What the hell was she doing? What kind of mother ran off and left her babies, for God's sake? To do what?*

When her mind simply couldn't take the cacophony of uncertainty and second-guessing anymore, Ellie fell asleep. Blessed stillness took over. And calm. And subconscious prayer.

The bus spit and screeched to a stop several hours later, startling Ellie awake. Bus. A rest stop. Then, she remembered what she was doing. It was dark outside; but, inside Ellie's mind and heart, it felt as though someone had turned on a light. A crystal clear, brilliant light. *She, Ellie Coursey, was making her life happen.* She was on her way to Los Angeles, California with all of $7.00 in her pocketbook. It was all she had left after purchasing her one-way ticket, squirreled away over the years from the little bit of outside sewing she was able to sneak in without Brady's knowledge. A smile finally crept onto her lips. *Attagirl, Ellie*, she told herself.

ᴥ CHAPTER ᴥ
11
"Red Lipstick"

It was love at first sight. *Thank you, God!* It wasn't Paris or
New York City; but it was beautiful, vibrant and a million miles from
Okmulgee. Even though she missed her babies terribly, Ellie was
intoxicated with the most delicious sense of freedom she had ever known.

Rose and Roland Turner were right there to pick up Ellie from
the bus terminal and introduce her to the City of Angels. Ellie was so
excited she could hardly contain herself! In her eyes, everything here
was golden. The way it smelled. The palm trees - oh, she adored the palm
trees. The perfect warmth. The distinctly California houses which were
even better in person than in pictures – bungalows, Spanish Moorish,
ranch, Spanish haciendas, beach - big and small. The mountains rising
majestically and wondrously far in the distance on one side. The ocean
on the other. Sparkling. She just *knew* magic happened here! The Turners
were tickled by their friend's enthusiasm. They understood because they
had felt the same way.

The trio drove through the front gates of the Devane mansion,
which looked more like a museum to Ellie; one which she could not
quite classify architecturally, then proceeded around to the back, the
servants' entrance. Rose introduced Ellie to Helen Devane as the colored
friend from Oklahoma that she told Mrs. Gold about. Helen hesitated
momentarily, eying Ellie skeptically, before welcoming them inside. Ellie
caught Helen's not-so-subtle look and made a face of her own, as if to say,
Haven't you ever seen a colored woman before? It was behind Mrs. Devane's
back, of course. She didn't want to get fired before she'd even had a
chance to rest her hat.

After a few moments of initial introductory conversation, Helen
dismissed Rose, then directed Ellie to the maid's quarters behind the
kitchen. It was small, but more than adequate because she didn't have to
share it with anyone else *and* it had its own bathroom! Helen rattled off
Ellie's duties and what was expected of her as Ellie dropped off her purse

and small suitcase. She took off her hat, laid it on the bed; then followed Helen through the rest of the house.

During the tour of the luxurious Beverly Hills mansion, Ellie struggled to contain her amazement at the size and utter beauty of the house. She didn't want to appear like a complete backwoods Okie, of course. But, Ellie had never seen anything like it, except in her magazines.

The next morning when she donned her uniform shortly after sunrise, preparing to tackle her domestic chores, it suddenly occurred to Ellie that she was doing the exact same work as her mother. Even though she adored her Mama, Ellie had always felt cleaning the homes of white people was beneath a woman so talented and so beautiful as her mother. Even turned her nose up at it. Now, she understood that Callie was only doing what she had to do to make their lives work. Choices of employment were still very limited for an uneducated colored woman. Even an educated colored woman could not hope to be more than a teacher in a colored school – unless, of course, she was a famous writer like her idol, Zora Neale Hurston, or an actress like Fredi Washington and Hattie McDaniel, or owned her own business. And, how often did *that* happen? So, it was Ellie's turn to do what she had to do now.

Ellie scrubbed the Devanes' toilets and floors; polished furniture and silver; washed and ironed; cooked, made beds, and stood on a ladder admiring and cleaning the glistening crystals of elaborate chandeliers.

It helped Ellie feel connected to home to share her experiences, thoughts and feelings in regular letters addressed to *Dear Nora, My Dear Babies, and Dear Papa and Marie.*

> *Even though Mrs. Devane, insists, of course, that I wear a uniform, at least she appreciates the importance of well-manicured hands, and allows me to wear gloves. Actually, Helen Devane really isn't so bad, even though she is a white woman who, like the rest of them, considers herself superior to her help, and, of course, to all colored people. Mrs. Devane isn't much older than I am. Unfortunately, she and her husband, Daniel, are childless, after years of trying apparently. I think it's a shame to have such a big house with no babies or noise to fill it up. There's*

something about him, though, that just doesn't sit well with me. Please remember that this separation is just a means to an end so that you and I, my precious babies, can be together again soon. As for you Papa, and Nora and Marie, there is such a thing as visiting. I miss you with all of my heart and I close with my love to you all. Always, Ellie.

When Ellie served the Devanes' breakfast in the mornings, Ellie noticed that Daniel Devane rarely so much as looked at his wife, even when they exchanged empty, sparse conversation. He read the paper while eating his one soft-boiled egg in that ridiculously fragile-looking little eggcup, and sipping his coffee. Mr. Devane had an air of cruelty about him that made Ellie's blood run cold. She cringed when she had to address or be in the same room with him. And, her skin crawled at the way he looked at her when his wife was otherwise occupied. Ellie tried hard – and reluctantly – to keep her eyes cast down, but she was very much aware of his licentious glances. It was a lot simpler to just pretend not to notice; go about her business and try to stay out of his way.

Helen Devane didn't know it, but she was the best teacher Ellie ever had. Automatically assuming that Ellie was "slow" because she was an uneducated colored woman, Helen took her time pointing out, gesturing and explaining to Ellie in great detail which table and kitchen utensils to use for what; which wines to serve with what foods; the different qualities of china, crystal, silverware, linens, furnishings and art. She wanted Ellie to be able to service their home and their parties perfectly, so that she could impress her friends, her husband's business associates and most of all – her husband – as a flawless hostess. No matter Helen Devane's agenda, Ellie's eyes sparkled with excitement at every inadvertent "lesson." She soaked it all up with the intensity of a thirsty sponge.

Mrs. Devane doesn't know it, but she is providing me with the finest education I could ask for. She is supplying me with all the knowledge necessary to successfully run my very own elegant home. I never thought I would say this, but it is actually almost a pleasure to care for such a

beautiful home even though it isn't mine. So, I play a game with myself.
As I work, I pretend that I am the lady of the house, and that all this
finery does indeed belong to me and to my family.

On one of her first evenings off, Ellie – red lipstick and all – ran out the back of the house to get into the car with Rose and Roland.

"Well, hey, Miss Ellie. It's about time you got out of them white folks' house to see a little of *our* Los Angeles and have some fun," Rose teased when she climbed into the back seat. Ellie, of course, reminded both Rose and Roland that she was not here to have fun. She was in Los Angeles to make money so that she can build a better life for herself and her children.

"We understand, Girl." Rose added knowingly.

"Umm hmm." Roland nodded in agreement. "*Anything is* better than what Okmulgee has to offer." That last line merited hoots, hollars and belly laughs from all three Los Angeles transplants.

The unofficial Turner Tour took them through a radically different part of town – much smaller buildings and houses. But, they were pretty, neat and well cared-for. Rose welcomed her friend to Central Avenue, the heart of jumpin' South Central LA. She pointed out all the famous landmarks for Ellie – the fabulous Dunbar and Clark Hotels where all of the big colored stars stayed when they performed in town. Fine hotels for Negroes. Of course, she explained, big stars like Lena Horne, Duke Ellington, Billie Holiday, Louis Armstrong, The Mills Brothers, Cab Calloway and Billy Eckstine performed at rooms in the Beverly Hills Hotel or the Beverly Wilshire, but they can't spend the night there.

Ellie *swooned* at the mention of those famous entertainers. "Chile, I would *just die* if I would ever actually see one of them *in person.*"

"Well, we'd better go ahead and call the funeral parlor right now, then, 'cause I'm guessin' that you are gonna drop dead for sure right here. Right now!" Roland laughed. Ellie shrieked with delight when they pulled in front of Club Alabam. The club's name was in bright neon lights, as well as the name of the week's headliner – *Mr. Cab Calloway and his Cotton Club*

Orchestra! Ellie's eyes were as big as saucers as she watched finely dressed black people coming and going. And, it wasn't even a wedding or a funeral!

Inside the club, Ellie could hardly believe its elegance – beautifully and expensively decked out colored people sipping champagne cocktails and other fancy drinks out of beautifully cut crystal glasses at an exquisite bar and at intimate tables with crisp, clean white tablecloths and candlelight. Some were eating dinner. They were being served by very proper colored waiters, waitresses and bartenders, treating these patrons as well as they would treat white folks! The hostess seated them at a table right in front, and within moments, a tuxedo-clad waiter was at their service. After placing what seemed to Ellie like a luxuriously extravagant order of champagne cocktails and oysters on the half-shell, her attention quickly turned to the front of the room, where the curtains opened, revealing the orchestra and the man himself! The effervescent Mr. Cab Calloway!

Ellie had never felt so alive. Before she knew it, she was swept up by one of Roland's friends, a tall, ruggedly handsome, semi-sweet chocolate drink of water. Ellie didn't even catch his name during the cursory introductions; the music was pumping so loud! All she saw after he flashed a dazzling, genuine-looking smile was the dance floor. She and Mr. Friend-of-Roland had a ball jitterbugging and hi-de-ho-ing the night away. The exuberance and fun of Club Alabam was a joyful break from the reality of life for blacks in 1930's America. At least for those in LA fortunate enough to be able to take advantage of it.

All of the lights were out in the Devane house. A happy Ellie let herself in through the back door, quietly humming a catchy Cab Calloway tune to herself. She damn near jumped ten feet when she heard Daniel Devane's voice, coming from the dark in the kitchen.

"My, my, my. Looks and sounds as though *some*one had a high old time this evening," he commented dryly. "It becomes you. You look positively... *stimulated*."

As Ellie's eyes adjusted to the dark, she could see that he was leaning against one of the kitchen counters, drinking what appeared to be a glass of milk. Ellie blurted out a quick, "Yes sir. Goodnight sir," and hurried to her room, closing the door and locking it behind her.

Daniel Devane didn't flinch. He, however, did stare for some time in Ellie's direction, smirking like the proverbial cat that swallowed the canary; then drained his glass.

Helen Devane had been a twitter all day. She felt her reputation as a superb hostess depended on the success of tonight's cocktail party at their home. There was actually no need to worry. Ellie and the support staff Mrs. Devane had hired had everything under control. Ellie was an exceptionally quick learner with an innate sense of elegance and style, and could have thrown the entire soiree on her own. *Some day*, she fantasized.

It looked like a hit to Ellie. The Devanes' foyer, living room, sitting room, library and dining room were packed with laughing – cackling, really – drinking, smoking, bejeweled women and slick-haired men. Someone was playing the piano. Ellie moved gracefully through the crowd serving hors d'oeuvres and generally keeping an eye out for every detail. No empty glasses sitting around. Plenty of napkins. Plenty of constantly moving food and drink. No trash. Empty ashtrays. Enough toilet paper.

She was also very much aware that most of the men were ogling her. Their wives were aware of it, too, and whispered to each other whenever Ellie passed by. If looks could kill, Ellie would have dropped dead on the floor. But, Ellie reminded herself constantly that she had bigger fish to fry and couldn't concern herself with these silly women or their lecherous husbands. She resolved to not even allow herself to be thrown by Daniel Devane's almost constant lewd stares, damn near watching her every move. Daniel also watched the other men watching Ellie. Daniel himself wasn't sure whether the attention Ellie got from other men was making him jealous – or stoking his pitiful Johnson's embers. He enjoyed pondering the question, though.

Throughout the evening Ellie was busy furthering her education as she worked the party. Because of the additional staff Helen Devane had hired for the evening to accommodate the large number of guests, Ellie was inadvertently given the luxury of taking a bit of extra time as she served. She strained to listen to and absorb bits and pieces of conversations revolving around real estate, business acquisitions, sales, stocks, bonds, investments and the motion picture business.

The last guests left the party. Helen Devane, gracious hostess to the end, was finally ready to retire for the night. She beckoned hopefully for her husband's hand, inviting him to come upstairs with her. Daniel dispassionately kissed her on the cheek and brushed her off; informing her that he was going to enjoy another brandy in his study before coming up – just to unwind from yet another magnificent party his brilliant wife so brilliantly planned. Helen headed up the stairs wearily and a bit defeated. *No matter*, she told herself. When she comes down in the morning, everything will be as it should be. Ellie and the other staff will have made sure everything is cleaned up and put back in its proper place. Ellie almost felt sorry for her.

Ellie let the seven extra staff out the back door off the kitchen and locked up behind them, turning off the lights. Just as she turned to head to her room, an arm grabbed her from behind, with a hand wrapping across her mouth, as she tried to scream. His face was buried in her hair. Ellie's eyes were wild and terrified as he spoke, telling her he didn't mean to startle her. He just didn't want her to scream.

It was Daniel. He let her go and started laughing. A low, sinister laugh. "Why, I'm sorry, Ellie. From behind, I thought you were Helen," he lied. "It's dark, you know." He walked off. Cavalier. Entertained. Leaving Ellie, shaking and speechless.

The next morning, as Ellie served breakfast, it was business as usual. Daniel and Helen talked, for once, discussing the previous evening's success. Ellie was invisible to them as she efficiently took care of the morning's chores - the marketing, the laundry and the cooking. And, that was just the way she liked it.

Late another night, dressed for bed, Ellie went through her nightly routine. Double-checked the lock on her door. Turned on her radio, keeping the volume low. The day finally over, she sat down at the small table in her room to compose a letter to Nora. Talking out loud as she wrote, Ellie told her sister that it always surprises her how decent Mrs. Devane can sometimes be to her. She described how out of the blue, Helen Devane informed her one day that if she were able to complete her daily chores before starting dinner, Ellie could take those few hours for herself.

I don't know. Maybe it had something to do with the gorgeous gown I made for Helen (Her boss was only "Helen" in Ellie's letters.) *from my very own pattern design. I had made a stylish navy blue suit, trimmed with white collar and cuffs, by hand for myself. I reproduced it perfectly from a picture in one of Helen's Vogue magazines. Helen saw it when I was pressing it. When she found out I could sew, she bought me a sewing machine. It's the most beautiful thing I've ever seen – a shiny, black brand new Singer. Not even second-hand. Of course, I use it for household sewing and all of Mrs. Devane's tailoring as well. As I planned, I have saved almost every nickel I have earned so far. My only splurges have been on two pairs of well-made, smart-looking shoes with matching handbags. A decent pair of gloves. Two stylish, wear-with-everything hats to complete whatever look I might want to achieve. And, of course, a few pairs of sheer nylons in the same shade. That way, a run never has to be tolerated for any length of time. Then, everything works well with my carefully designed mix-and-match-to-look-like-more-wardrobe. One of the most important lessons I have learned is that you never get a second chance to make a first impression – especially in Los Angeles, it seems.*

Ellie had always been an efficiently quick – but thorough and accurate – worker, and, after preparing and serving the Devanes' breakfast, she handled her routine tasks of washing, dusting, sweeping, scrubbing and polishing in short order. Especially since Helen Devane had given her permission to take any extra hours during the workday for herself. Ellie changed quickly out of her uniform into something more appropriate for exploring Los Angeles. With one of her smart hats, gloves and bag, the ensemble was complete.

This particular afternoon, Ellie happened upon LA's garment district. It wasn't Paris, but Los Angeles; and this magical area of the city was definitely a step in the right direction. Ellie could *feel* it. It was something to behold, with block after block of wholesale houses, manufacturing plants, fabric stores, intimate designer shops. Ellie walked down Los Angeles Street, the heart of the district, marveling at the bustling, colorful atmosphere. Racks upon racks of beautiful clothes were wheeled up ramps, down ramps, into buildings, out of buildings and into waiting trucks.

Ellie stood in one spot, just taking it all in. Suddenly, she spun around, as if tapped on the shoulder. There was a sign in the window. "Seamstress wanted. Inquire within." Ellie's breath caught and she splayed the fingers of her free hand over her stomach, where butterflies had taken up residence. Not the nervous kind, but rather the kind that excitement and happy anticipation conjure. Ellie examined herself in the window's reflection. She smiled with approval at her crisply tailored navy blue suit, cleverly trimmed with white. The one that Helen Devane had so admired.

Once inside, the receptionist directed Ellie to a desk to fill out the employment application, appreciatively eyeing her smart outfit from head to toe. Ellie swallowed hard and took a few minutes to carefully read and complete the form, looking up once to flash a tentative smile at the receptionist, who watched her like a hawk.

Ellie hoped it wasn't obvious that this was the first real job application she had ever seen. Upon completion, she got up and handed the single sheet back to the receptionist who used the intercom to buzz Mr. Woodrow Harold. She explained to Ellie that Mr. Harold was the supervisor in charge of hiring, and that he would be with her in a moment.

When Mr. Harold opened his door and beckoned Ellie to come inside, she had to bite her bottom lip to keep from laughing out loud. Mr. Harold was the spitting image of Dagwood Bumstead in the *Blondie* comics serial.

Inside the office, Ellie took the seat indicated for her and explained to her interviewer that she made her suit herself when he complimented her on its fine quality. For the first time, Ellie realized that both Mr. Harold and the pinched-face receptionist thought she was white. He asked her a lot of questions about fabrics, lines, cut and quality, but never whether or not she was a Negro. The odd Mr. Harold was impressed, however, with Ellie's knowledge – as well as her good looks.

She was *in*. *Now she just had to make this work*. As he walked her to the sewing floor, Mr. Harold explained that the job paid by the bundle. So, since Ellie would only be able to work at the company a few hours a day, she may take work home with her. They would try the arrangement for a trial period of six weeks, to see whether or not the agreement would prove to be profitable for the company. Ellie was introduced to the floor supervisor, a stern-looking, no-nonsense woman named Miss Hecton. Everything was agreed upon. The entire process moved so quickly, Ellie felt as though she was caught up in a whirlwind. Quizzically watching Ellie leave the building, Mr. Harold couldn't help wonder why this particular young woman struck him as so much *more* than a seamstress.

"Grit & Old Ghosts"

My Dear Babies,

Guess what? I have a new job! Well, it's really a second job because I am still with the Devanes. But, this way I can make even more money and we can be together that much sooner. For that, I can hardly wait, my Dearest Loves and would dig ditches if I had to. But this is much better because I am a seamstress for a big company called Bass! And, want to hear something funny? The man who interviewed me looked exactly like Dagwood Bumstead.

Anyway, the job pays by the bundle. So, the faster a seamstress is, the more I produce, the more I get paid. Right now, I only work afternoons because I have to make sure that I keep up with my work at the Devanes'. The best part is that the company is allowing me to take work home with me, to see how that works. It's called a trial period. Like a test.

I get to Bass & Co. around noon, and leave a little before five. Your Mama can turn out more work in those five hours than the full-time girls do in eight. What do you think about that? I've got a routine. I get everything set up for the evening meal in the morning, after I finish my cleaning. Then, I change clothes and take the bus to Bass. When I get back to the Devanes', I change back into my uniform to serve dinner to Mr. and Mrs. Devane, clean up the kitchen and dining room, then head to my room and sew some more.

Whew, it wears me out just telling you about it! But, know what? Even though sometimes I am dog-tired, just thinking of the two of you and looking at the picture of you right next to my bed keeps me going because I know this is the means to the life I am working to make for us. And, I turn on the radio in my room to some energetic swing sounds and go to town.

I promise you both that I am going to pass this test with flying colors because – well, I've already said it, but it bears repeating. Making this extra money means that I will be able to send for you that much sooner! We will all be together again and will be so happy! I miss you, my Babies. Be good and please remember that your Mama loves you both more than the sun, the moon and all the stars in the sky.

Ellie's world at Bass & Company centered on an industrial sewing machine, an integral part of a symphony of whirring black Singers. She sat in the midst of the bustling sewing floor filled with white women playing the same quick-stitching instrument. For the first time in her life, Ellie was enjoying an enormous sense of accomplishment; as though she were doing something really important. The labels being sewn into the garments were *I Magnin, Saks Fifth Avenue, Bonwit Teller, Bullocks, Macy's.* Mannequins – most of them clothed in partially made garments, crowded the space. Racks of beautiful, completed garments were whisked back and forth.

Brown-skinned women – Mexicans – swept up around them, picking up fabric off the floor, fetching whatever was called for by one of the seamstresses. The Mexicans were never seamstresses.

Ellie tried to block the reality of her deception out of her mind, focusing only on her work; keeping to herself. Her co-workers didn't make it easy. She tried hard to block out the workplace conversation buzzing around her. She tried equally as hard not to show how much the conversations stung her.

There were concerns about "niggers" being hired on the cutting floor and jokes about keeping "them" away from sharp objects, "'cause you know how they like to cut each other." As most of the janitors and matrons were "wet-backs," they wondered what group was going to invade the company next – "gooks" and "japs?" Ellie sat quietly, seething on the inside, mentally screaming at the top of her lungs at the insults and ignorant cackling. *In her mind.* Outwardly, she dared say nothing. If she wanted to keep her job.

"By the way, Daniel, congratulations on your choice of domestic help." Ralph Edwards, one of Daniel's business colleagues garbled, puffing on his spitty cigar and gulping cognac. *Neanderthal*, Ellie thought. *Doesn't he know you're supposed to sip it?*

"So, what's the story, my good man? Is that little tart some lowlife poor white trash that you and your wife took in as charity? A poor relation, maybe?"

He's talking as though I am invisible. To him, I guess I am. Well, to hell with him, Ellie told herself. She was picking up after a small dinner party at the Devanes came to a conclusion. *This* yahoo stayed behind. He talked so loudly, the dead could probably hear him. *Cretin.*

"No, my friend. That fine specimen is a magnificent mulatto, a Negress, if you can believe it. Hot nigger blood running under all that gorgeous, creamy skin," Daniel gauchely responded. The men laughed at the prospect of how "hot" a nigger bitch could be. Ellie winced on the inside, but continued her cleaning with an exterior stoneface. She would never give them the satisfaction of thinking they upset her in any way. They could not touch her or interrupt her means to her end. She would not let them.

Ellie had just placed the last piece of silverware into the velvet-lined box, when she turned around to find Daniel lurking behind her.

He put his index finger to his mouth. "Shh-sh. Do not make a sound," he warned. "Helen just went upstairs with a headache, and we wouldn't want to disturb her, now would we? And you, my beauty, you wouldn't want to jeopardize all your hard work to be reunited with your *'chilluns'* would you now, *Mama?*" he mocked. Then he threatened, "Why, I can fix it so you *never* see your precious spawn again. If you open your goddamn mouth!"

Ellie froze. Daniel turned her around, deeply inhaling the fragrance of her hair, whispering demonically into her ear. His non-existent lips were so close she could smell the noxious, dead odor of his breath. Every instinct told her to kill him. Gouge out his eyes with her fingernails; then stab him to a bloody pulp. Instead, her body betrayed her; cementing her to the spot. It involuntarily stiffened like a stone at Daniel's unspeakably hateful threat. *He knew about her babies.*

"Ahhh," Daniel reacted to his reading of her body language. "I did not think so. And, yes, make no mistake. *I know everything.*"

His clumsy hands wandered, groping her breasts; working his way down to her thighs; rubbing himself against her firm, round behind. Ellie was terrified and didn't know what to do. She couldn't move. *Couldn't move!* Ellie could hear her own heart pounding so loud she feared it was going to burst through her chest and kill her. She closed her eyes, mentally willing herself somewhere else. *Anywhere* else. She bit her bottom lip so that she wouldn't cry. She would *not* give him that satisfaction.

Ellie heard Daniel unzip his pants, but he didn't raise her dress. He just continued to rub himself spastically against her, moaning. Then he emitted a final grunt. His masturbation against her uniform complete, Daniel released Ellie from his grip, zipped up his pants and simply walked out of the kitchen without uttering another word.

Ellie stumbled into her room, dazed and sick to her stomach. Her heart was still hammering and she couldn't breathe. She was gasping for air! After locking her door, Ellie ran to the bathroom and retched. Water soured by digestive acids with nothing to digest spurted out. She hadn't had time to eat that day. But, now, Ellie was so consumed with disgust and rage, her stomach would have shed and offered up its lining if it helped her to cleanse.

She dragged herself up from the floor in front of the toilet. Where *were* they? She spotted them in her room. As though in a trance, Ellie floated to the spot and grabbed the shears from her sewing table with a white-knuckled death-grip. With the furor of a madwoman, she then ripped off her uniform and sliced it to shreds. As much as she wanted to, killing Devane wasn't worth losing her children forever; so, she killed the dress.

Ellie then wandered back into her bathroom, pulled the curtain around the tub and turned on the shower. Once inside the almost-comforting womb of the porcelain shelter, Ellie stuffed as much of her washcloth into her mouth as it would hold; so she could scream without anyone hearing. After the silent howling, she broke down and sobbed uncontrollably. Furious sobs of anger and resentment over the violation she had just suffered. A violation that would never be avenged or even acknowledged because colored women were simply *there* for the white man's taking, beating or killing. No laws of man were broken when a colored woman was attacked by a white man. It would not even be *considered* an attack by any jury or judge in the country.

Ellie tore off her underwear while standing under the steaming stream of water; scrubbing furiously at her hair and her body with a bar of soap, damn near rubbing her skin raw. Finally, she collapsed in a heap. For a moment, the tub and its protective curtain felt like a temporary insulated cocoon, and almost reminded her of her root houses of so long ago.

God help me, the plan has to be expedited, Ellie silently prayed.

The next afternoon at Bass, inside one of the bathroom stalls in the employee ladies room, Ellie accidentally overheard an extraordinary conversation. One of the matrons was informing a co-worker that *she* heard that the young actress, Judy Garland, was looking for a wardrobe mistress. The matron's cousin apparently was a housekeeper in the same building where Miss Garland, her mother and sisters lived, and heard the family talking about it as they lay by the pool.

Ellie deliberated inside the stall. Part of her wanted so badly to throw open the door and tell the women she was colored, too – one of *them* – but she was afraid that blowing her cover would cause her to lose her job at Bass. The other part of her, though, had to make sure that *she* got that job with the actress before either of them – or anyone else – could. So instead, Ellie listened carefully, hardly breathing lest she missed a detail; and made a mental note of where the apartment building was located. She then coolly exited the stall, washed her hands, merely nodding in the direction of the matrons; and hurried to her work area for her hat, gloves and purse.

At first, Helen begged Ellie to stay on a while longer, but then became quite curt and dismissive when she realized no amount of pleading would shake Ellie's resolve over her decision. Ellie thanked Helen for "understanding" and apologized that she could only give one week's notice to the Devanes – days only, in fact - but Miss Garland was to begin shooting "Thoroughbreds Don't Cry" in less than two weeks.

Ellie jumped out of the car almost before Roland could put it in park. She squealed like a kid on Christmas morning just taking in the sight of the small but lovely, pink stucco bungalow. The very day she landed the job with Judy Garland and notified Helen Devane, Ellie moved in with the Turners, staying gratefully on their sofa. Her stay there was short-lived, thanks to Roland's connections and her scrupulous saving of nearly every penny over the last year. Though not high paying, the second job at Bass had been a financial godsend.

"Oh, my God! It *looks just like California*!" she exclaimed, running joyfully around the tiny, but pretty front yard, touching the flaming orange Birds of Paradise and each Bottle Brush tree. Ellie examined the hedge, which separated this house from the next. "Rose, are these what I think they are?"

"Well, I don't rightly know, Sweetie. What do you think they are?" Rose played her game with her, delighting in Ellie's exuberance.

"Ellie breathed in deeply. I think these are those deliciously fragrant Night-Blooming Jasmine bushes that I adore!" Rose, still smiling at her friend's contagious enthusiasm, nodded affirmatively. The home was on Neomi.

The trio's infectious excitement even rubbed off on the stilted colored realtor who met Ellie, Rose and Roland at the door with the keys, happy to point out some of the home's perks.

"Splendid thing about this location is that it is just two blocks away from Central Avenue. And, if we can step inside, I think you will be pleased that it is fully furnished with three bedrooms and two baths." Mr. Wallace Craig didn't have to offer a second invitation inside.

As they followed Mr. Craig through to the back of the house, he called their attention to the heavily-laden orange and grapefruit trees that shaded the backyard and the pretty little terra cotta tiled terrace.

"They are absolutely luscious-looking. This is all so heavenly; please pinch me to let me know that this is really happening!" Ellie whispered to Rose, restraining herself from jumping up and down with unbridled glee. She could work with the furnishings even though they weren't exactly her taste; but, most importantly, she could afford the rent! She'd take it!

The stars still twinkled on the stage of the midnight blue sky when Ellie caught the bus at the corner. Her new job began before daybreak. That was when she was scheduled to meet the young actress at the studio every morning. As wardrobe mistress, Ellie was charged with making sure that every stitch of clothing fit impeccably; was kept clean, pressed, and in proper repair; ready for whatever scene Miss Judy was working on, and getting her in and out of it. Over and again. That, and reassuring the insecure teenager daily that "No, Miss Judy, you are *not fat*." The job might have been a little tedious to others, but Ellie knew that there was much to be learned at MGM studios. And, even though the pay wasn't much, it was more than she made at either of her other two jobs.

Ellie had only imagined and dreamed that it was possible to feel so fulfilled; happy even – although work consumed her days and most of her nights. But, it was *happening*! Here she was living in a *real* city and living on her own for the first time in her life. She had gone after opportunities to make money doing what she loved (albeit on a bottom-rung-of-the-ladder level) – and it was more exhilarating than her most vivid imaginings! She *knew* she was well on her way to the kind of life she had always wanted for herself and her children.

Ellie tried to put her "passion" into words for the people at the table. "It's not that I'm in love with dressing, undressing, and taking care of the movie wardrobe and whims of a spoiled rotten little white girl who gets paid good money for playing pretend; or even that I get to see famous movie stars walking the back lots of MGM every day," she tried to explain one night while sipping champagne cocktails at Club Alabam with the Turners and a group of their friends.

The lively party hooted and "amened" to Ellie's narration. "Wowee. Sounds pretty exciting to me, girl! Movie stars? Well, if that ain't it, what *is* it?" asked Maybeline, another new friend sitting around the elegant, linen and crystal-dressed table.

"Yes, Miss Coursey. I'd like to know as well. What is it?" The question came from the rich baritone of the "tall, ruggedly-handsome, semi-sweet chocolate drink of water Friend-of-Roland" whom she had danced with the first time she had visited the club with the Turners. He was standing right behind her.

"Hey man. Take a load off. Join the party!" Roland invited. Rose nudged Roland and the group all moved over one chair to make room. Friend-of-Roland took the seat now vacated at the table, right next to Ellie.

"Everybody," Roland went on. "Y'all know my Ace, Mr. Sonny Duran, don't ya?" Sonny nodded all around.

"And, Sonny, I know you remember our friend, Ellie Coursey. Another transplanted Okie," Roland continued, winking at Ellie, who had completely clammed up. "So, what's your poison, man?"

"Whiskey. Neat. Another champagne cocktail for you, Miss Coursey?" Sonny turned his attention to Ellie, flashing that dazzling genuine smile that Ellie couldn't help notice the first time.

She offered a half-smile and nodded "yes." Ellie didn't mind dancing again with Sonny Duran, but she sure as hell didn't like the idea of the group somehow unanimously deciding to make room for him right next to her. If they were trying to set her up, all of them were barking up the wrong tree. *However, nothing wrong with having another friend,* she reasoned.

"So, go on, Miss Coursey, please. I'm sorry. I interrupted you. You were telling everyone about your job. What you love about it. Please go on. It sounds fascinating." There was that smile again.

"Well," Ellie began, and then fixated – mesmerized - on the miniscule bubbles dancing in her fizzy concoction. For a fraction of a second that seemed like forever, she identified with their busy, joyful effervescence. In spite of all the insults, abuses and hardships she had had to endure, her life now seemed to be bubbling with new possibilities. She took a sip of the cocktail and continued. "I make clothes. And, I take care of clothes."

Sonny's head craned forward, his eyes widening with an expression that clearly yet wordlessly said, *where's the rest of it?* "And?" he asked. "You sounded so excited before. Don't let me be the wet blanket. Please."

"Well," Ellie went on tentatively. "I love making clothes. Always have. Creating something out of nothing. Working with beautiful fabrics. And, both of my jobs combined give me the opportunity to do that. Well, to a degree. But, it's a start!"

"Girl, tell him about the movie star part!" Rose spurted with a "go on" wave of her hand.

"Yes, I work at MGM," Ellie offered reluctantly. "But, you all *know* I don't care anything about all those movie actors," Ellie playfully shot back, intentionally including the entire party in the sweep of her eyes so as not to give Mr. Duran the satisfaction of being singled out by her attentions. "Although I *do* love movies," she added demurely.

Her animation returning, Ellie explained that she had always enjoyed sewing and dressing up; but it just recently dawned on her that the rough patterns she had drawn and cut from paper bags all her life were actually the art of designing!

"At Bass, I make clothes that ultimately make it to all the most exclusive stores and at MGM – well, I don't plan to be a wardrobe mistress for*ever*. That was just getting my foot in the door!"

Sonny simply smiled, enjoying Ellie's enticing enthusiasm. He listened with genuine interest to every word; noticed every gesture. Ellie stopped in her tracks, realizing that she was doing all the talking.

"Yikes. I'm so sorry. You must think I'm a motor-mouth. Going on and on like that." She took another sip of her champagne cocktail, embarrassed.

"That's perfectly alright," Sonny laughed. "I enjoy listening to you, Miss Ellie Coursey. And, I find your zeal for your work quite charming. And, a powerful weapon, I'm sure. It will get you far in this world."

"Well, I guess we'll see, won't we? Thank you for your kind words, Mr. Duran. But, I know I can get carried away. Please, tell me a little about yourself. I know you're a friend of Roland and Rose; but, that's *all* I know."

"Well, my story is pretty straight-forward. Nothing particularly exciting. I'm a first generation Angelino."

"That's it? Well, excuse me, Mr. Duran, if I think there is more to your story than that," Ellie responded coyly, oblivious to the alluring effect she was having on Sonny. At thirty years old, she had never had occasion to practice or test her feminine charms before. Not even with Brady in the early days.

There was that low, sexy laugh again. "Well, don't say I didn't warn you. But, I'll try to give you a thumbnail sketch so I don't bore you to death." Even though a big part of her would never admit it, Ellie wouldn't have been bored no matter *what* came out of Sonny Duran's mouth. In spite of herself, she was rapt by the light dancing in his sagacious, molten nut-brown eyes, framed by the most lush, blackest eyelashes she had ever seen – on a man or a woman. Lord! She heard the words, but was captivated by the vessel which released them. The friendly, wide, full lips parted to reveal the whitest, most perfect teeth she had ever seen; and the mouth was kind. No curl or twist of cruelty anywhere. Kind, like the eyes.

By now, the rest of the party was involved in any number of lively separate conversations, paying no attention whatsoever to Sonny or Ellie.

"I'm a business graduate of Howard University," Ellie heard, snapping out of her reverie with Sonny's countenance. "I came back to Los Angeles after graduation to help run my family's funeral home business. But, I'd like to ultimately branch out into other entrepreneurial opportunities." Now *Ellie* was staring.

"Hello, Miss Ellie? You still there," Sonny chuckled, waving his hand in front of Ellie's face.

"Oh, yes. Sorry. I was listening. It's just that I never actually met a Negro who has graduated from college before. Or, even *attended* college."

A quizzical look crossed Sonny's face. Ellie continued, answering his expression. "My brothers and my younger sister all graduated from high school, and that was really an accomplishment where I come from. As for me, I never made it past the fifth grade. We moved to Oklahoma from a tiny little parish – um, town – in Louisiana. My mother was uneducated. It wasn't important, I guess, for me to have a formal education either back then. Especially being a girl. Of course, those kinds of old fashioned notions are ridiculous nowadays."

Sonny grabbed her hands in his in a friendly, non-threatening manner. "Well, you know what, Miss Ellie Coursey? Yours must have been one helluva grammar school because I've never met a smarter, brighter or more interesting lady. And, I wasn't humoring you before. I really am interested in what you do. Now we have established, I believe, that you enjoy making clothes; which is quite a talent. I don't even know how to sew on a button or darn a sock. But, what is the rest of it? The thing that has you so – what's the word I want – passionate?"

"Well," Ellie began. Everyone at the table was looking her way now. "Well, working for Miss Judy Garland at MGM studios has given me the opportunity to meet Alberto!" The group all glanced at each other, clueless.

Who the hell was Alberto?

"Cinema Queen"

Alberto was the fabulously talented and somewhat flamboyant head costume designer at MGM. He was born Albert Adolph Greenburg in Connecticut. After graduation from the prestigious Connecticut School of Fine Arts, he designed for musical revues and Broadway shows! That's when the name Albert evolved into *AlBEARto*. Hollywood took notice of his elaborate yet clean designs and *had* to *have* him; so, he began designing for DeMille Studios in 1926. MGM made him an even bigger offer – one that he couldn't refuse - in 1928. By industry accounts, he single-handedly defined the look of an entire generation of major stars – like Greta Garbo, Jean Harlow, Norma Shearer and Joan Crawford. Alberto's avant-garde and almost universally-flattering style was so popular, retail versions of his fabulous creations were mass-produced and sold in high-end boutiques and department stores throughout the world.

On any given day, as soon as Ellie finished dressing Miss Judy for a scene and catering to whatever needs the young star may have had – like making sure the water in her dressing room was consistently at the same room temperature with plenty of lemon in it – she hurried to Alberto's design area. There she shadowed and assisted the slightly built, boyishly good-looking artist in any way she could, eagerly hanging on to his every word.

In return, Alberto took quite a liking to the young Miss Garland's new wardrobe mistress. He immediately recognized and appreciated the quick study Ellie proved to be; along with her obvious talent, boundless imagination and her wonderful eye for color and line. Ordinarily an unyielding taskmaster who could not be less interested in the ideas or suggestions of those in his employ, Alberto sought Ellie's opinion and comments. He found himself genuinely pleased by her refreshing hunger to learn, and was impressed by her spunk and effortless flair. The keen curiosity of the king of women's costume design was also piqued by this mysterious beauty.

Between pinning and draping one hectic afternoon, sandwiched between discussions about whether they should add a couple of extra inches of fabric because Madame Cinema Queen with whom they were working seemed to be "somewhat expanding in girth," Alberto decided to pop the question. "Speaking of cinema queens, Ellie Darling, surely a girl as beautiful as you have a most delicious story. Why aren't you being adored on screen by thousands? Millions, even? You are certainly as lovely and charming as any movie siren I've ever seen or worked with; if you will forgive my being so forward."

Ellie laughed. "That's quite alright, Alberto. You're not very good at being subtle or sneaky, you know." She paused for a thoughtful moment, placing the draping of the gown they were piecing together just right. "But, in answer to your question, I have never had any interest in being in the spotlight. And, from what I've heard, I certainly have no interest in participating in any of the uh – athletic competitions I've heard of that are played on the so-called casting couches at the studios."

Leaving the MGM lot late one evening, Alberto happened upon a ruckus out on the parking lot; just far enough away from the guard shack not to be immediately noticed. At first he dismissed the escalating quarrel as probably just a lovers' spat between some spoiled rotten starlet and her indulgent-to-a-limit, married paramour and/or benefactor. But then, his curiosity getting the best of him, Alberto peered a bit more closely. It was that ridiculously pompous Daniel Devane, one of those boring Harvard Business School types who thought they knew everything about the motion picture business. And – was that Ellie? Devane had her cornered. What the hell was he saying? Alberto strained closer to hear what was going on.

Was Devane *threatening* Ellie? What the hell would a studio adding machine care about a wardrobe mistress in the first place? Their paths would *never* cross!

"I'm warning you, you little bitch. You need to think long and hard about what you're saying 'no' to," Daniel was growling.

Ellie stared Daniel squarely in the eyes. "I said no and I mean no. You can say whatever you want to whomever you want. I'll just find another job. I don't care."

"Why, you little mongrel piece of trash. To whom do you think you are speaking?" Daniel spat, raising his hand to strike.

Alberto emerged smoothly from the shadows. "Darling Ellie, I do so apologize for my tardiness and beg your forgiveness." He kissed her on both cheeks and gestured to his car, which was "right over here." Alberto acknowledged Daniel's presence as an afterthought, waving him off with a dismissive and superior "Oh, hello, Devane. I see you've met my brilliant apprentice. There is simply no way I could crank out all of those award-winning designs for the studio without her. Come along, Dear, or we'll be late."

Ellie gladly took Alberto's proffered arm. Deflated, though his burning eyes squinted with anger and suspicion, Daniel stiffly nodded in Alberto's direction, and watched the two walk away. Unfortunately for Daniel, he knew Alberto was golden to the studio and therefore untouchable; but he also knew full well that women weren't Alberto's cup of tea.

"So, my Sweet, where shall I whisk you off to?" Alberto turned to Ellie as soon as he had driven them outside the gates of MGM. "I and my chariot are at your beck and call."

Ellie looked at Alberto with grateful eyes. "Have you ever heard of Club Alabam?"

"And the Sweet"

It was a magnificent golden Saturday morning in the City of Angels. For Ellie, it was her birthday, Christmas morning, New Year's Eve and the 4th of July all rolled into one. She was so excited, she thought she very well might jump out of her skin before the bus pulled in! There it was. All the way from Okmulgee! Evan, almost 12 and little boy-turning-into-young-man handsome and looking a foot taller to his mother and skinny as a rail, stepped off the bus first; followed by his sister, 10-year-old Dinah, a maple-honeyed doll baby version of Ellie; and then her beloved Nora.

"Oh my God!" Ellie rushed to her babies, barely letting their feet hit the ground. With one arm wrapped tightly around Evan and Dinah, she clutched Nora to her with the other, hugging and kissing all three as though she could have eaten them alive!

"Mama, I can't breathe," Dinah's tiny voice made it through the loving din, but was muffled because her face was smashed against her mother's chest.

"Wha - ?" Caught up in the joyful satiation of delicious hugs and kisses after a year of starvation, Ellie didn't realize she was nearly smothering her children. She quickly released the too-happy-to—be-weary travelers; and they all burst into laughter. Unadulterated hilarity blended with the kind of tears that flow because such joy was simply too much for the heart to hold.

"Oh Nora, thank you," Ellie hugged her sister separately this time and whispered in her ear.

"No, Darling Ellie. Thank *you*. You did it! Just like you promised," Nora whispered back, her heart as proud as Ellie's was grateful. "You did it."

The sisters pulled apart, still grasping each other's hands; smiles of happy incredulity fixed on their lovely faces as they stared at the still mirror-images of their grown-up selves; wispy snatches of long-ago root house whisperings and dreams playing in each of their heads.

Ellie quickly snapped out of the sweet reverie and blissfully focused her attention back to the sweeter reality of her children. "Just look at the two of you! Ooh, I need me some more of that good sugar!" Ellie cooed playfully, grabbing Evan and Dinah again as they giggled, wriggled and joyfully showered their Mama back with all the hugs and kisses they had stored up. Just for her.

Everyone grabbed bags and followed Ellie to the Turner's big, casket-gray 4-door Chevrolet sedan. Roland had polished it to gleaming perfection especially for this occasion, insisting that Ellie take it to scoop up Los Angeles' three newest residents.

Evan's and Dinah's eyes widened as round as saucers when Ellie slid deftly behind the wheel of the automobile. "Mama, do you know how to drive?" Dinah breathily asked, sounding both astonished and concerned. Their mother had never driven back in Oklahoma, except for that one night when she herky jerkied their way to Grandpa's house in Papa's car.

"When did you learn how to drive, Mama? Will you teach me?" Evan chimed in excitedly.

"Ah now, my Dears," Ellie winked at Nora, nestled in the passenger seat next to her. "Your Mama has discovered many magical powers I didn't even know I possessed. Driving a car is just one of them. So, which do we want to do first? Go straight to our new house or do a bit of sight-seeing of the City of Angels?"

"Sight-seeing!" the children sang out in unison, gleefully bouncing up and down in the sedan's sprawling backseat.

"I was hoping you'd say that," Ellie laughed, reaching into her handbag. She then turned around to hand Evan and Dinah each a pair of something absolutely wonderful that had not yet been widely seen on the streets of Okmulgee - sunglasses. "Here you go. Put these on." The children hurriedly obliged. Mama *was* magical!

"Ah, yes," Ellie and Nora nodded approvingly. "Now, you look like real Angelinos. And, here you go, Aunt Nora." Ellie pulled out another pair and turned to her sister. Like the children, Nora squealed with delight as she accepted and quickly tried on her gift. "We can't very well leave you out of the fun, now can we? Perfect," Ellie adjusted the shades on her sister's face, flipping down the visor so Nora could take a look. Then, she dug into her bag one more time. "Now, I'll put on a pair and no one will ever know we aren't movie stars," she laughingly teased.

An awestruck Evan and Dinah were practically hanging out the car's windows – exaggerating the act of inhaling but inhaling, nonetheless - the faintly perfumed, blossom-infused air as their mother squired them all through many of the best-known and lesser-known neighborhoods of Los Angeles. Like Ellie, Evan and Dinah immediately fell in love with the gracefully exotic palm trees and the magnificent vastness and smell of the ocean.

They were enthralled by the clear view of mountains to the north, by the immensity of the movie stars' homes and the larger-than-life, rolling "Hollywood" sign. Nora was equally enchanted, but tried her best to maintain some semblance of what she thought should be adult decorum. Her involuntary "oohs" and "ahs," however, still managed to slip through.

On the way home, Ellie took the most pleasure in sharing with her family some of the Los Angeles that she loved best – Black Los Angeles, the Central Avenue corridor.

"This," Ellie announced affectionately, "is the heart and soul of the colored community in LA." She explained that, by day, "The Avenue" was the bustling economic center of the community.

The proud corridor extended from Alameda on the east to San Pedro on the west, and from First Street on the north more than forty blocks southward to what was known as the Furlong Tract. The lively area that some even called "Little Harlem" because there was always "somethin' going on," boasted all manner of businesses, both large and small. You could find doctors, lawyers, dentists, churches, libraries, banks, theaters, museums, restaurants, shops, hotels and nearly all of the most powerful black organizations in LA; including the NAACP, the Urban League, the Liberty Building & Loan Association, the Masons, the Elks, the Federated Women's Clubs, all of the black Greek fraternities and more.

"Mama, this is like that part of Tulsa a long time ago that got burned down," Evan interjected thoughtfully.

"Yes, baby. That's right. Did you learn about Greenwood in school?"

"No, Ma'am," Dinah chimed in. "Grandpa, Uncle Jake and Uncle Joe told us. Our Monteigh cousins lived there, they said. But Cousin Eddie and Cousin Ollie don't like to talk about it."

"That's right, baby. They don't," Nora cut in. "But, what I want to know, Miss Ellie, is what happens on Central Avenue at night; as you've only been telling us about what happens in the light of day?" she asked, one eyebrow cocked in mock disapproval, wanting to keep the children focused on the happy new memories they were making right now. No sad history today.

"Well, to be quite honest – not that I can speak from experience, mind you," Ellie winked at Nora. "Central Avenue transforms into a whole different place after the sun goes down. It's like it comes alive or something! There are fancy nightclubs, bars and some very famous hotels – like the Dunbar. That's where all the big colored entertainers stay when they're in town. And, right over there, that's Club Alabam. I've been there with Roland and Rose. We even saw Mr. Cab Calloway and his Cotton Club Orchestra there one time! Oh, and look here," Ellie pointed to the impressive edifice they were passing. "That's the Golden State National Life Insurance building. Colored folks own that, too – and started it!"

"Is that a castle, Mama?" Evan pointed to the fawn colored ashlar stone building on the corner.

"No, baby. It's actually a mortuary – or funeral home. In fact, a friend of mine owns it. Well, his family owns it. They call this kind of structure a mock castle." A neighborhood-sized replica of an authentic Gothic European castle, Duran Funeral Home *was* something special to behold with its distinct rounded corners, miniature towers, turrets, arches, balustrades, merlons and elaborate cornices.

Between their last encounter at Club Alabam and picking up her family at the bus station on that splendid Saturday, Ellie and Sonny Duran had spent nearly every weekend and several evenings a week together – in spite of her two, almost three, jobs. And, in spite of her protests.

Although she hadn't told him where she lived (Roland, she surmised, took that upon himself), Sonny dropped by early one evening with dinner in hand. Ellie, of course, had been stunned to see him; but Sonny's timing was impeccable. She was dog-tired, still had several pieces for Bass to complete and hadn't felt like cooking anything that night. So, even though she hadn't been particularly up for company, she waved him in the door. They ate, laughed and talked easily. About everything. On that evening and many more. Without realizing it, Sonny Duran was becoming her closest friend.

Ellie found out that Sonny's family had relocated to Los Angeles from Raleigh, North Carolina in the first wave of the so-called "Black Invasion of Los Angeles" in the early 1900's. Sonny, Sr. and his wife, Penelope were both born second generation free blacks. Just before they were born, Raleigh seemed like a promising place for colored families after slaves were freed and Reconstruction took the place of the Civil War. For a brief time, black political leaders even rose to power; but that utopia of equality was short-lived as white southerners refused to stand for what they termed "Negro Rule." The Ku Klux Klan and their less obvious devotees terrorized with their usual unspeakably monstrous violence – murder, mayhem and torture; and moved their kind into public office. Those lawmakers quickly passed Jim Crow laws that sanctioned every kind of discrimination against blacks imaginable. Disfranchisement, segregation in housing, jobs, economics, education, services, a non-existent legal system. Sharecropping opportunities had dried up and the positions available in the growing textile industry were for whites only.

Sonny, Sr.'s parents had established a small funeral parlor in the city which provided a dignified and appreciated service. He took over the reigns when his father, Jeremiah Duran, passed. The funeral parlor consistently turned a modest profit before the Klan swept in and destroyed it, as was their modus operandi. Desperately seeking to escape the shackles of Jim Crow, legions of black families migrated up the East Coast, largely to New York. Others headed to Chicago. Sonny, Sr. and Penelope wanted to get as far away from the South as possible and chose California.

Because they were childless upon their arrival in Los Angeles, the Durans spent their first few months cramped in one room in a colored boarding house. Though not formally educated, Sonny Duran, Sr. was a shrewd businessman and a patient man. At the time, housing covenants were popular in Los Angeles. These were contracts entered into by white folks which put restrictions on the titles to their property. The restrictions stated that the property could not be sold or leased to a person of color for a specific number of years. Like many other ingenious black residents, Sonny Duran, Sr. made it his business to regularly search titles for those properties whose deeds had run out. With his initial purchase, the first Duran Funeral Home was officially established in his adopted city. He and Penelope made their home on the top floor of the modest three-story structure. Sonny, Jr. was born there in 1905. His sister, Josephine, followed in 1908. In 1912, the Durans opened their second funeral home; and bought a separate residence for their family in the Adams Street District, a once white neighborhood that quickly integrated after the first Negro families moved in.

LA's official Black elite hadn't yet fully come into its own when Sonny, Jr. and Josie were coming up during the teens and early 1920's. Nonetheless, the intimate number of black professionals and entrepreneurs who lived in LA at that time still managed to live in the same community clusters, move in the same close social circles and worship at the same handful of churches. Because of their family's success and because Sonny, Sr. and Penelope saw the possibility of a life for their children that they never could have imagined, Sonny, Jr. and Josephine were nurtured in a relatively sheltered life of a beautiful home run by firm yet doting parents. Their cloistered, privileged Negro upbringing abounded with educational opportunities, tennis, etiquette, dance and music lessons, organized ice cream socials, art showings, fancy teas, book clubs, strictly chaperoned dances and meticulously executed cotillions.

Sonny, Jr. wanted to experience life outside of his protected environment and chose to attend Howard University in Washington, D.C. for college. Howard was considered the Mecca of excellent colored education in the United States, and the District of Columbia was relatively safe – more "up south" than south. However, Jim Crow was still a resident there, albeit perhaps a part-time rather than a full-fledged citizen. Josie chose to stay closer to home and attended UCLA, which was integrated.

These past few weeks, Sonny had gently (He didn't want to overwhelm her or scare her off) introduced Ellie to a world she had only read about or imagined. They listened to lectures and attended readings by literary and

philosophical greats (and her idols) like W.E.B. Du Bois, E. Franklin Frazier,
Alain Locke and Zora Neale Hurston. Sonny wined and dined her at elegant,
candlelit dinners. They walked down Central Avenue on lazy yet invigorating
Saturday afternoons languorously licking ice cream cones – and occasionally their
sticky fingers - and window shopping. Ellie experienced her first ladies' tea with
Sonny's sister, Josie. (Being a guest instead of a server was such a pleasure.) And,
she attended her first Black Greek fraternal dance. The sweetheart ball of the
Los Angeles graduate chapter of Sonny's fraternity which he had pledged at
Howard, Alpha Phi Alpha. To Ellie, the event, which was held in the Grand
Ballroom of the Dunbar hotel, was a black and gold wonderland!

Even though bringing colored people together socially was one of the
major roles of the fraternity, especially in college apparently; Sonny shared
solemnly that the men of Alpha Phi Alpha were his brothers for life. Like all the
black Greek organizations, the primary focus of the Alphas was to "uplift the cause
of the Negro race." Wanting Ellie to know everything he knew, Sonny schooled her
on the other Greek organizations, as well. Black men could also join Kappa Alpha
Psi or Omega Psi Pi. Women had their own Greek organizations – sororities. There
was Alpha Kappa Alpha and Delta Sigma Theta. Ellie loved learning that
colored people had so many magnificent choices in the world. How life had
changed from LeBeau, Louisiana and Okmulgee, Oklahoma. She loved Sonny's
stories and his lessons. And, even though formal education was not a reality for
her; she knew she wanted it all for her children. Sonny Duran was her dear friend,
companion and mentor.

"Ellie? Ellie, are you alright?" Nora was gently squeezing
her forearm.

"Yes. What? I'm sorry. You were saying?"

Nora looked at her sister with a different interest. "No, my dear.
You were saying. You were talking about the people who own that
castle we just passed back there. Then, for an instant, your mind seems
to have wandered."

Ellie smiled at Nora, then at her precious cargo in the back.
"That's right. But who wants to talk about a dreadful ole' funeral parlor.
Know what?"

"What?" Evan and Dinah answered in unison.

"I think you are both going to absolutely love your new school. You know what is so wonderful about Los Angeles and much of California?" There was hush in anticipation of their mother's answer. "Well, like everywhere else, the workplaces and the restaurants, hotels and places like that are segregated, but - everyone attends the same schools. Blacks, Asians, Mexicans and even some whites. My babies are going to have a wonderful education," Ellie enthused. Ellie had thought she heard incorrectly when she learned that children of all races attended the same school. The mixing of all kinds of people is exactly what she had dreamed of for her children. "You're going to experience all kinds of people and have a wonderful introduction to the rest of your lives. The school is right here in our neighborhood. And," she paused. "We are here. Welcome home." With perfect timing, Ellie parked the sedan right in front of their new house.

Evan and Dinah shot through the house like happy whirling dervishes, making it in record time to the terrace and backyard with its pregnant fruit trees.

"And, Nora," Ellie motioned towards the third bedroom. "This is your room. For as long as you want it."

Tears of uncorked emotion welled up once again. Ellie and Nora looked into each other's eyes – and burst into wild peals of laughter.

"Ooh, Lord, Ellie!" Nora joyfully collapsed back onto her new bed with its coral and rose patterned spread. "Chile, you did it! Look at you with your own pretty house all your own. Ain't nothing a colored woman cain't do. You have proved it to me, Sister."

Ellie plopped down, belly first, on the bed right next to her, just like they did when they were children. She had laughed so hard, she could hardly catch her breath. "Well, thank you, Sister. *We* did it. As a team. 'Cause, if you and Papa and Marie hadn't taken care of my babies for the last year, wouldn't have been no house. No Los Angeles. No new life. Nothing. So, I thank *you*, my Nora. We are some powerful colored women, aren't we? Can't tell us *nothing!*" Ellie playing tossed a throw pillow at her sister.

Rose and Roland arrived later that evening to pick up their car and join in the reunion celebration. They hadn't seen Evan or Dinah since they were toddlers. And Nora had been barely out of her teens. Ellie had invited Sonny to the little party, but he thought it was best if the children had some time with their mother all to themselves before she introduced him.

The next morning, Sunday, the family enjoyed the luxury of eating breakfast outside on their house's little terrace. Ellie had baked biscuits, which she served with strawberry jam, thick slices of ham, fried eggs and grits with lots of butter; just the way Evan and Dinah liked them. The children's hands were sticky with the juice of the grapefruits they ate; plucked from the trees in their own backyard. The fresh-squeezed orange juice Ellie served also came from their very own home-grown fruit.

Ellie just loved watching her children eat. Such a simple, ordinary act. But, it had been so long. "Alright, now. I certainly want the two of you to enjoy your breakfast, but remember, we're going to be leaving for Mass shortly. So, let's try not to dawdle too much." There was a smile in Ellie's voice as she gently nudged Evan and Dinah along.

Their perfect petit dejeuner was abruptly interrupted by a loud knocking at the front door. Ellie dabbed at her mouth with her napkin and excused herself from the table. "Finish up, now. I'll get it. It's probably Rose," she continued talking to all of them and no one in particular as she walked through the house to the front. "Although I don't know why she didn't just walk around back. I told her we'd be having breakfast on the terrace. Don't you love the way that sounds? Breakfast on the terrace." Ellie chuckled to herself, carefree and content; and unlocked the door. "Good morning, Rose, how are -," Ellie started as she swung open the door. Her heart dropped and her stomach lurched.

It was Brady – with a suitcase in one hand and flowers in the other.

As though nothing had happened and no time had passed, Brady, paunchy and faded, wasted no time dropping the suitcase and pulling Ellie close to kiss her.

"Aw, Baby, I've missed you so much!" Ellie immediately jerked back and shoved Brady away. Her mind was racing. *What? How?* She was horrified. Confused. And angry.

"What the hell are *you* doing here?" she demanded.

"Now, is that how you greet your husband? After how long? But, to answer your question, it's easy, baby. I want my family back. So, I followed Nora and the children all the way out here so I could plead my case. Whadaya say, Doll?" He handed her the bouquet. Ellie pitched it right back at him.

"Have you lost your goddamn mind? Showing up on my doorstep like nothing has happened? When I left your sorry ass more than a year ago? And, take your flowers! This is California. There are flowers everywhere, you fool! I can pick my own damn flowers right out of my yard anytime I want. So, just turn right back around and march yourself back to Okmulgee. Or, better yet, go jump in the Pacific Ocean for all I care. There's no place for you here, Brady Renault."

"Aw, Baby. Don't be like that," Brady purred, failing miserably at recapturing his old charm. "I know what a fool I was not to appreciate and cherish you as the greatest gift God could ever give to me. I'm sorry for being such a horse's ass and I want you back, Ellie. And, I want us to work. You, me and our kids."

Ellie's body instinctively stiffened. On guard; ready to fight. She was in shock. *Could this be happening?*

"Alright, Brady. I don't know what you think you are doing here or what kind of game you may *think* you are playing. But, it's not with me. Or, maybe you really *have* lost your goddamn mind once and for all. Either way, get this straight! I. Do. Not - want anything to do with you. Now or ever! So take your raggedy-ass suitcase and get the hell out of my house and out of my life."

Just as Ellie ended her tirade against Brady, Nora entered the living room with Evan and Dinah. Spotting Brady, all three stopped in their tracks. Nora was speechless. And, neither Evan nor Dinah knew how to react. They had only seen Brady a handful of times in Okmulgee. Grandpa Sam wouldn't allow it. Even though no one actually told them, Evan and Dinah figured that it had something to do with all of the screaming between their parents; and the bruises that sometimes appeared on Mama's face, neck or arms. They loved their father, but they knew he did something bad to their mother and they did not want to upset her now. Evan and Dinah had been permitted to kiss Papa goodbye just a few days ago. And, now here he was in California, too, bending down and opening his arms to them.

Ellie saw the confusion on her children's faces; so, she backed up and backed off a bit, and gave the children a slight "okay" nod. Evan and Dinah then tentatively walked to Brady and allowed him to hug them.

Not wanting to upset her children, Ellie simply and calmly stated that Papa was there for a visit, but would not be staying with them. "He will, however," Ellie softened slightly; only because Brady *was* their father, "be staying on the sofa in the living room for a day or two until he is able to make other arrangements."

"'Morning, everyone. Sorry I'm late," Rose called out cheerfully and a little breathless, running up the front stairs right behind Brady. Still standing just inside the doorway, he turned around to surprise Rose. "Oh. Brady! Uh, hello. I haven't seen you in years! How *are* you?" she rambled, then threw a "*what the hell?*" look at Ellie, knowing their history - chapter and verse.

"Rose." Brady nodded in her direction.

"Rose, would you mind taking Evan and Dinah on to church with you? Brady just got here and we need to talk about a few things," Ellie interjected.

"My pleasure. And, if it's okay with your Mama, maybe we could get ice cream afterwards."

"Can we Mama?" Evan asked.

"Of course. Nora, would you mind staying behind with me? I'd like to share a few more details about the house with you while the children are out."

"Absolutely," her sister responded, thinking, *Uh oh. Ellie's going to blow a gasket.*

"Kiss Mama bye, now," Ellie offered and accepted fresh hugs and kisses, which she still couldn't get enough of.

"And Papa, too?" Dinah almost whispered.

Ellie swallowed. "And, Papa, too."

After Rose, Evan and Dinah headed out for Mass at Holy Trinity, Ellie spun around to face Brady, who was still standing. Nora was sitting in one of the chintz-covered armchairs; bracing herself for the storm she knew was brewing.

By the next afternoon, Brady had contacted and was able to move in with his cousin, Carlos, and his family. Carlos, who had reminded Ellie of a grisly, mottled-brown Santa when he visited once in Okmulgee, had enthusiastically assured Brady that because Los Angeles was steadily growing; Brady would have no problem finding work as a day laborer in the construction industry.

Ellie was highly skeptical that Brady had changed either his ways or his temperament, but she didn't want to deprive her children of a father – in the event there was a modicum of truth to his mea culpa and self-proclaimed transformation. She promised Brady that he could see the children whenever he wanted to. However, she made it crystal clear that their marriage was over and had been for years. Ellie had dropped her married name, Renault, since the day she left Okmulgee; although Evan and Dinah still carried their father's name. She had also recently filed for divorce.

ᴥ CHAPTER ᴥ
17
"... And Eating It, Too."

The children flourished and thrived in their new, sunny
environment. As their mother predicted, Evan and Dinah loved Fairling
Middle School and made friends easily. They were able to see Brady nearly
every weekend, when they weren't attending a birthday party, church
social, young NAACP activity or one of the many lessons Ellie
had involved them in.

Ellie was busier than ever with her two jobs; but was also happier
than she ever thought possible. Her babies and Nora were safe and happy
with her; and, now with their own home, she had a telephone and was able
to speak to Papa, Marie and even Beth – every Sunday. Life was better
than good. It was wonderful.

At her primary job, the bustle of activity in the design, cutting
and sewing rooms at MGM had become Ellie's classrooms. And, in
addition to being her mentor, Alberto was her number one fan – even
more so after their evening at Club Alabam.

After he "saved" her from Daniel Devane's obnoxious advances
and threats, Ellie felt safe – and relieved – to bare her soul to Alberto
and spill her whole story. God, it felt so good to get it out to someone.
To be able to trust someone she worked with everyday. Alberto couldn't
have been more delighted. Ellie, his very own little protégé, was a lovely
Negress trying to make her way in a world that despised her! How
deliciously exotic, so "Imitation of Life" he gushed dramatically, after she
shared her reality with him.

"The Daniel Devanes of the world," Alberto confided to Ellie,
"hate your kind even more than they loathe Jews and homosexuals.
It would be my great pleasure, my dear Ellie, to guide you through
Hollywood's treacherous waters to the success you are so hungry for."
That's what they toasted to at the club, where Alberto was welcomed
with open arms by the friends she had made there, including Sonny. The
hospitality was not missed by Alberto, who loved the club and was moved

to making an impassioned declaration Alberto-style to his new friends. "Those pasty-assed crackers could learn a thing or two from you, my brown brothers and sisters, about playing nicely together – and with such exquisite taste!"

Thanks to Ellie's intervention, Nora had found her professional niche as well. Ellie maintained her relationship with Bass & Company for two more years while she worked at MGM. Her supervisors at Bass appreciated her skill and she appreciated the extra income. Because the only Negroes employed at Bass & Co. were, along with Mexicans, custodial workers, Ellie introduced the stunning Nora to Mr. Harold as her Indian friend straight off the reservation in Oklahoma. Being Indian apparently was an acceptable minority. Nora was hired as an inspector, checking for irregularities in the garments.

During those late nights at home, when the children were asleep, white folks supplied the comic relief. Recounting the events of their day, sometimes Nora and Ellie would fold over in laughter, giggling until tears streamed down their faces over how incredibly *stupid* white people could be. "Fooled 'em again!" was their evening mantra. Clinking their glasses of lemonade, the sisters would toast to their very own "sweet revenge" for all the prejudice any colored person had ever had to suffer. Ellie the "white woman" and Nora the "Indian" were making more money than they ever had in their lives!

Sonny had become something of a fixture in the Coursey-Renault home. He would have dinner with the family most nights, rather than taking Ellie out because she had already missed too many moments with Evan and Dinah and wanted to be there with them. To help with homework. To listen to the latest news from school. To huddle around the radio to shudder together to the mystery of "The Shadow," laugh to the "Charlie McCarthy Show," or even swing dance around the living room to the latest jazz or big band sounds. On the weekends, Sonny worked around the kids' schedules to take the entire group to enjoy the many wonders that Central Avenue LA had to offer.

On the occasional evening, one of the older teenaged girls or neighbor ladies would stay with Dinah and Evan while Ellie and Nora enjoyed grown-up fun. It was on one of those outings – a social at Sonny's church, Second Baptist Church, that Nora met and was smitten with a dashing young tavern owner, Mel Johnson. The feeling was mutual. Nora and Mel were nearly inseparable from their first chat at the punch bowl in the Church hall.

And then there were two.

Sonny knew Ellie was terrified. He loved her and he knew she had feelings for him too – even though she might never admit it. He had enjoyed every moment with Ellie. Seeing everything new and fresh through her eyes was a joy he had never experienced with anyone else. Knowing how she had changed her life gave him greater appreciation for her courage and resolve. Watching her with her children showed him how deeply she loved; and made him love her even more. Looking into her eyes and seeing the depths of the hurt that was there – though masked by stunning beauty and an insurmountable spirit – made him want to eradicate any shred of pain she had ever felt and to protect her from any future threat of pain.

But, tonight, he fixed her dinner. They would be alone. For the first time in weeks. They had enjoyed going to see the all-colored cast film *The Green Pastures* at the Florence Fields Theater last week without the rest of the family and enjoyed a quiet dinner afterwards; but that hadn't felt like alone to Sonny. Too many other people around. But tonight, he would have Ellie all to himself. True, she had never been to his home before. But, they had been alone before – before the kids and Nora arrived – so why was it so unnerving now?

Because he was cooking, Ellie had insisted on getting to his place on her own. The doorbell rang. "Coming!" Sonny called out as he lit the candles on the dining room table.

"Good evening." Ellie's smile lit up the room and Sonny's world.

"Good evening. Please come in."

"Oh, so this is how a bachelor lives?" Ellie commented, admiring Sonny's spacious and beautifully appointed foyer, living room and dining room.

"Well, yes. This is it. Uh, have a seat. Dinner will be ready in just a few moments. How 'bout I get you a drink?"

"I'd love one, thank you. But, can I help with something in the kitchen?" Ellie was as nervous as Sonny. She hadn't ever been in a man's home alone before. Even though it *was* Sonny. And, it was a lot bigger than she thought it was.

Ellie and Sonny breezed through the comfortable and delicious meal of pot roast, potatoes and carrots and homemade rolls. Fresh strawberries and cream for dessert. The sherry added warmth and calmed the nerves.

A lover of dreams and business talk, Ellie reveled in Sonny's blow-by-blow description of his latest business investments – two rental properties – an office building and a multi-unit apartment building. Both within the confines of the Central Avenue corridor. Even though housing covenants weren't as severely enforced as in years past, they still existed. If whites didn't want to sell to blacks, they had the law behind them. If no covenant existed for a piece of property, a white seller could always find some devious way to challenge and prevent the purchase.

On the couch in the sitting room after dinner, Sonny slowly began kissing Ellie the way he had long wanted to. They had kissed plenty of times before, but it was always quick. Tentative. One or both of them always pulled away. Tonight, Sonny's mouth lingered on hers. Sweet. Slow. And, Ellie didn't push him away. He was undoubtedly the most wonderful man she had ever met – a perfect blend of everything she could ever want in a man - smart, successful and ambitious; yet also kind, gentle, genuine and interesting.

But, she couldn't.

"I love you, Ellie."

"What?"

"I said I love you. I love you so very much." Only then did Sonny pull back, searching Ellie's eyes. She said nothing. "Ellie? Ellie, you don't have to say anything. I'll do all the talking. I love you, Ellie Coursey, and even if you say nothing, I know you have feelings for me, too."

Ellie nodded "yes," terrified of what she knew in her gut was coming next.

"I'm 32 years old, Ellie. I should have been married with a family long before now. But, I couldn't. There have been women, but none of them were right. Until now. Until you. You are everything I ever could have dreamed of in a woman. Please do me the honor of marrying me, my sweet Ellie. Let me love you. And, Dinah and Evan, too." Sonny then pulled a tiny, black velvet box out of his backpocket. In it was an exquisite round-cut emerald surrounded by a double halo of sparkling diamond baguettes.

Ellie gasped, then spoke; her eyes filled with tears. "I do love you, Sonny. With all my heart. I thought men like you only existed in songs and movies and stories. I love you, but I can't marry you."

ᴄᴀ CHAPTER ᴀᴄ
18
"Emerald City"

Even though it had been just short of three years, Ellie was promoted to the highly coveted position of assistant costume designer at MGM. Hearing the news through the company's internal grapevine, Daniel Devane did his best to have her fired. She's colored, uneducated and a fraud, he charged. However, the studio heads chose to turn a deaf ear on Devane's rants. They didn't see a colored woman; and *where was the proof?* Just Devane's word. And, Ellie's work spoke for itself. Most importantly, Alberto believed in her talent so much, he threatened to resign if she were let go. MGM's new big-budget fantasy film, the biggest role yet for the studio's golden girl, Judy Garland, had just started production. It was called "The Wizard of Oz." Ellie was in the middle of working with Alberto on the elaborate, top-secret costumes for the movie. No, the top brass decided that letting Ellie Coursey go at this time would not have been a smart move if they wanted to keep the costumes for the project top secret.

Because of the demands of her work on the new film, Ellie was forced to resign her position at Bass. Nora stayed on as an inspector; happy that her new husband, Mel, didn't mind his wife making her own money.

Ellie and Sonny remained close, though not betrothed. Sonny, though, continued to half-playfully hint at marriage every now and then. The night Sonny proposed to Ellie two years before, they sat for hours as she poured out her heart. The dam of her emotions broke, spilling her long-held feelings and fears about marriage; and how all those fears had been realized - and then some - with Brady. She begged Sonny to please let them stay the way they were without ruining it with marriage. Ellie had been so distraught, so terrified, Sonny didn't have the heart to push her. He loved her too much.

Ellie was thrilled that the two men in her life – Alberto and Sonny – got along so well. One evening, after dinner on her little terrace and after the children had gone to bed, Ellie confided that she finally felt as though she might actually dare to believe that her dreams and goals were coming true. For the first time in her life, she actually had a fairly significant amount of money in the bank.

Ellie's keen business sense and all of her self-teaching, told her that she now needed some investments. The first step, she reasoned, was to move out of her rental house and become a homeowner. So, she wanted to talk real estate.

"Well, since we've ruled out buying a home with me and being my wife, why don't you and the kids just move to one of my properties where you can live rent free? Then, you can pump your resources into other investments," Sonny offered.

Alberto took a swig of his scotch and rolled his eyes at Ellie. "Ellie, Darling, you know I worship the very ground you walk on. But, you, Precious, are out of your ever-lovin' mind. You'd be wise to take this man up on his offer before he pulls it off the table one of these days."

Ellie leaned over to lightly kiss Sonny and blew one to Alberto, trying to lighten the mood with her usual, "Sonny knows I adore him. I'm just not the marrying kind of gal."

With most of her savings and $600 borrowed from the Golden State Insurance Company, Ellie was able to purchase her own home – with a small swimming pool for the kids – on Van Ness, a little further west. It was close enough to their old house, that her children were able to attend the same high school as the rest of their friends; all of whom had also finished Fairling.

Dinah, like her mother, was a whiz at numbers and was developing into quite a beauty. She was also a spitfire like her Mama. Ellie knew early on that two such females under one roof presented the possibility of some challenging moments, maybe even fireworks, as Dinah grew up. Evan, very serious, though sweet and gentle – so unlike his father - had assumed the role of the man of the house. Once he became a teenager, he asked his mother to please stop calling him her "little man." That was for babies, after all. Although both children were excellent students, Evan was more in love with learning than his sister. Because of that love, he had evolved into the family bookworm. He was particularly fascinated by science; especially anything having to do with airplanes or aviation.

A business idea had been percolating in Ellie's head, but she knew she needed the absolute support of both Alberto and Sonny to pull it off successfully. This particular evening, the trio enjoyed cocktails in the living room of Ellie's new home.

"I want to design. On my own," Ellie announced.

"Bravo!" Alberto enthused. "Brilliant idea. It's about damn time that my little chickadee left the roost."

Sonny was a bit more reticent. "You know I have the utmost faith in you, your talents and your instincts, Ellie. And, I certainly support your entrepreneurial goals. I just don't know that much about the fashion design industry. So, I'm not sure I can advise you one way or the other. You seem to love your job so much. Is it worth it to leave a major studio?"

Alberto took it upon himself to do the convincing. He feigned an apology to Ellie as he playfully pushed Sonny down on the couch. "Listen up for the bottom line, tall, dark and handsome. Our fabulously multi-talented Ellie has gone as far as she can in the studio design system. I myself certainly have no plans of leaving MGM as head designer any time soon, so *my* job is off-limits. Edith Head is the untouchable Grand Dame of design at Paramount. Warner Brothers has Orry-Kelly, Walter Plunkett is Mr. RKO. Jean Louis is lead designer at Columbia Pictures and so on."

Sonny listened thoughtfully. "So, there is literally no where else for her to go."

"Exactly. And, what do all of these name studio designers have in common, including yours truly?" Alberto asked rhetorically. "Impeccable professional pedigrees – fashion illustrators, art directors and designers in other mediums, and educated at art institutes throughout the country and around the world. And, all are lily white which, God knows, is certainly nothing to brag about; but is simply fact."

Ellie knew her friend meant well; but, couldn't help wondering, half-amused, where Alberto was going with this soliloquy.

"Please don't misunderstand. None of this is to put down darling

Ellie. However – as gorgeous and brilliant as she is, alas, our Ellie is a Negress with a fifth grade education. That despicable, snot-nose Daniel Devane has already tried to have her fired, to no avail, thank God. But, my loves – chances are this is *it* for our girl. She cannot go any further in the system, so our job is to support her in her endeavors for independence and greatness! If Dorothy could find the Emerald City with that rag-tag crew she traveled with, then so can our Ellie!"

Within days, Ellie's goal to design on her own mushroomed into a joint venture called ESA, which incorporated the initials of the first names of each partner in the enterprise. And, within just a few more days, Alberto had already identified the perfect location for ESA, Limited. The trio stood in front of a lonely-looking vacant warehouse on Sunset, which just happened to be right down the street from Ciros, an exorbitantly priced nightclub for the beautiful people.

"The rich," Alberto exclaimed, "can spend their money here first on the beautiful clothes they'll wear to dance and dine in later that evening at their snotty little club." Made sense to Ellie and Sonny.

To acquire the space would require playing Ellie's favorite game – "Fooled 'em again!" Even though this space wasn't protected by a housing covenant, all three were savvy enough to know that the owners of the property would never have sold such a prime piece of property to them if they knew a black man – or woman - was involved. So, Ellie and Alberto acted as the "front" partners with Ellie again passing as a white woman to get what she wanted. It was so easy to use white people's ignorance to their total advantage. Sonny had no trouble being the "invisible" partner in public.

During the closing, Ellie and Alberto couldn't even look at each other, lest one or both of them burst out laughing. Ellie practically drew blood, digging her nails into her palms in order to contain her glee at "getting over." She and Alberto finally exploded into joyous screams and squeals when the sellers left the building after the papers were signed. Sonny soon joined his partners, a bottle of chilled champagne and three glasses in hand. He joined in the laughter, shook Alberto's hand, and then hugged Ellie right off her feet; triumphantly twirling with her in his arms.

Ellie believed in spreading the wealth. She was thrilled to hire Nora away from Bass and Rose away from the Golds.

"OK, Gang. Welcome to the team. Our job now is to turn this empty cavern into a stylish shop, showroom and design space and then make it run like clockwork." Ellie sounded like a drill sergeant. All three women stared out into the vacuous space wondering where in the world to begin.

"Yikes," Nora involuntarily squeaked.

Ellie ignored her, pulling on her brave front. "And, it has to be nothing short of fabulous because I poured in every dime I had and took a second mortgage on my house for this rather ambitious undertaking. If it's any help," she continued. "All we have to do is the initial clean-up for now. The carpenters and painters will be in tomorrow to put a real face on it. OK? Are you with me? Nora? Rose? Are you with me?"

"You bet!" Nora giggled in exaggerated military-speak.

"Me too!" Rose chimed in.

Dressed in overalls and headscarves, and armed with rubber gloves, rags, brooms, dustpans, and trashcans, all three women went on the attack against the mess in front of them.

Initially, Ellie and her own small army of seamstresses worked in her home diligently on the first batch of women's clothing for ESA. A massive design, cutting and sewing floor was part of the warehouse's re-design with a smaller shipping room right next to it. Next to the shipping room was a spacious business office with three desks. The front of the building housed the showroom and dressing rooms. Should ESA prove successful, the partners would invest in a more comprehensive manufacturing operation.

It didn't take long for the workmen and Ellie's own personal team to transform the warehouse's vast nothingness into a beautiful, plush shop and showroom. The tasteful sign outside the stylishly renovated building read ESA, Limited. On this day, the grand opening, a head-to-toe glamorous Ellie greeted patrons, directed traffic and adjusted clothing. There were racks of intricately beaded gowns, garments of flowing silk, metallic lame, crepe-de-chines and fine wool crepes. Some of the outfits were hanging; others were being showcased by models of every hue. Ellie's store; Ellie's rules. And, no one raised a stink. Rose, Nora and other ESA representatives (known as sales staff in other shops) answered any and all questions on the clothes, escorted patrons to dressing rooms, passed out champagne and wrote up sales – lots of them.

Well-heeled and or well-kept women walked out smiling, armed with bulging shopping and garment bags. Alberto made an appearance, taking the hands of the many women who were thrilled just to meet him. Sonny sipped champagne and kept tally of the sales and all other business issues in the office. When no one was watching them, Alberto and Ellie exchanged "Oh my God, we *did* it!" grins. ESA was indeed a hit! As Alberto reminded Ellie, "With your flair for creating fluid, uncluttered silhouettes and my fame and worldwide reputation; and Sonny's crack-the whip business management acumen – well, Dahling, how could we miss?"

In addition to the wives of doctors, lawyers and business titans, Ellie's first spectacular spring fashion show was packed with movie stars in the front row – Joan Crawford, Bette Davis, Rita Hayworth and even her former employer, Judy Garland. Helen Devane was there, too, along with her friend and Rose's former employer, Katie Gold. Helen threw sidelong stares at Ellie every chance she got during the event. Finally, she leaned into Katie and whispered with nervous entitlement, "Katie, tell me it couldn't be. The "E" in ESA couldn't possibly be my former maid, Ellie, could it?"

"Oh my God! Well, I can't imagine *how*, Helen. But, I do know that's Rose over there. I just waved to her," Katie whispered back, having a lovely time washing down her caviar topped toast points with champagne; her eyes fixated on the dazzling evening gown collection the models were currently showing.

Ellie had spotted Helen in the crowd early on. After the show, dressed to the nines and basking in all of the congratulations and praise, Ellie made a point of gliding to Helen's side. Smiling sweetly, she took Helen's hand in both of hers. "Helen, how lovely to see you again. Welcome to my salon. Hello Katie. It *is* Katie, right?" Ellie turned her smile to Katie, who was not quite as shaken as Helen that a colored woman, a former maid, was addressing them by their first names. Although you couldn't really tell by her face, which was – like Helen's - deepening with the most unattractive, red rash-like color.

As difficult as it was to contain herself at this curious yet satisfying moment, Ellie maintained her composure. "Tell you what. I'm going to give each of you – just the two of you - a special discount on any of my designs that tickle your fancy. For old time's sake. Hmm?"

Losing any semblance of graciousness, neither Helen nor Katie seemed to be able to shut their gaping mouths.

"Bountiful"

Sam and Marie were visiting California for the first time – without their children. As thrilled as both Nora and Ellie were to have Papa there, Ellie, being the big sister mother hen, was concerned that Nora was not taking the best care of herself. Nora was expecting her and Mel's first baby and had been looking like she would bust if you stuck a pin to her belly! Ellie had practically had to threaten her sister with bodily harm if Nora came back to work at ESA before the baby was born. But, being part of a long line of stubborn Coursey women, Nora insisted on making dinner at her own home at least one night during Papa's visit! Dinner for the entire family, which included Sonny. With no help from Ellie, who had arrived late, anyway. Nora's husband, Mel Johnson, still owned a popular neighborhood tavern not far from his and Nora's home, in addition to a large four-family flat that they owned together and rented out.

"That's the beauty of investment property, man. You buy some undervalued piece of property or something that just needs a little fixing up. And, once you give it that old spit and polish to either rent or sell at a tidy profit; it's like making money in your sleep," Sonny was sharing with his captivated party. Even Marie and Sam had already fallen under Sonny's spell. Like Nora and Ellie's children, they loved him.

"You are so right, Darlin'," Ellie added, in between bites. "I've learned so much from Sonny, Papa. He is a genius in business. And, he's such a good teacher, I'm thinking about buying a piece of investment property of my own. In fact, there's this apartment building over on La Brea that I've had my eye on."

Before anyone could respond or react to Ellie's announcement, Nora abruptly dropped her fork, attempted to grab at her belly and moaned. Mel snapped to attention immediately, panic commanding instant custody of his heart, eyes and voice. "What *is* it, baby?"

The other adults stopped eating and stared. For just a second.

They *knew*. Evan and Dinah were 15 and 14, and weren't too well versed on babies actually being born. They just knew Aunt Nora sure looked like she was about to pop. And, it seemed as though it was going to be right then and there!

"My water just broke," Nora answered in a tiny voice, as she felt her insides twist and lurch with the first contraction.

"Well, I think it's time to get the midwife," Sam interjected, trying unsuccessfully to remain calm. He rushed to Nora's side and kissed his youngest daughter on the forehead. Everyone except Nora had jumped up from the table by then, scurrying into action.

"Mel, Sugar, why don't you get Nora's little suitcase from your bedroom?" Ellie ordered in her most calm, soothing voice. "Where are your keys? Sonny, would you help Papa get her to the car?"

"What?" Sam looked bewildered.

Ellie chuckled while she hunted on the phone table for the phone number of Nora's physician. "This is 1939, Papa. Modern women have their babies at hospitals today. I'll call your Doctor, Nora, and tell him you're on your way."

"Well, we still have babies at home back in Okmulgee. But, I think I like the way modern women here in Los Angeles have them a lot better," Marie chimed in, beginning to clear the table. With the others fussing over Nora, she needed to feel useful, too. "Why don't I stay here with the children?" she offered. "Sam, dear, I know you and Ellie want to be at the hospital waiting room with Mel. Sonny?"

Mel rushed back to the front of the house with Nora's bag and the car keys. Sonny and Sam were nearly carrying Nora out the front door, as she writhed in pain. Ellie followed behind.

"We want to go, too!" Evan and Dinah protested.

"Tell you what," Sonny called back over his shoulder with the solution. "Why don't you guys and your Grandma Marie finish cleaning up the dinner dishes? I know your Aunt Nora and Uncle Mel would appreciate that. Then, I'll come back and take you all back home. We'll wait there together for your Mama's call about your new cousin's arrival."

It was a girl.

Early the next morning, Nora happily cradled her perfect, beautiful, new daughter. The new mother was propped up and nestled in crisp white hospital bedding. The baby slept contentedly in her arms; and Mel's arms lovingly wrapped around both of them. Nora and her little girl were surrounded by pink floral arrangements, baskets of fruit and a zoo's worth of stuffed pink animals. And, of course, their family. "I'm going to name her Callie," Nora announced to the beaming audience.

"Callie." Sam repeated in a soft voice.

"Mama." Ellie murmured reverently.

The eyes of Sam and his girls were wet with memories, both happy and heartbreaking.

Mel, Marie, Evan and Dinah nodded from some fundamental place of understanding.

Nora and Little Callie were back home within a week. She, Sam and Ellie thought that adding the "Little" in front of the baby's name as a nickname, would help to distinguish her from her grandmother; while still honoring their beloved lost Callie with the moniker.

Sam and Marie extended their visit an additional couple of weeks, so they could help Nora – and Mel – become acclimated to their new life. And, of course, to spoil their new granddaughter a bit; while further enjoying their getting-way-too-grown-too-fast teenaged grandchildren.

Ellie gushed over her new niece as well, in between cranking out new designs for ESA, as well as helping Sonny run the business. Determined to give her children the best of herself as well as the best life possible, Ellie spent most evenings with Evan and Dinah; and a good portion of most weekends shuttling them to lessons or social events designed specifically for privileged colored teenagers. Then, there was the task of directing the crew that gutted and rebuilt the apartment building she ultimately purchased on La Brea. She also bought the empty lot right next to it. The building's upgrade was so impressive; Ellie already had prospective buyers nipping at her heels.

"You know you're wearing yourself out, don't you?" Nora observed on one of Ellie's rare free Saturday afternoons. Brady had actually volunteered to squire Evan and Dinah to the day's scheduled activities. So now, Ellie enjoyed coffee, peach cobbler and visiting with Nora and Little Callie in their cozy kitchen.

"Oh, please," Ellie shoed her sister off. "I love everything I'm doing. So, how could it possibly wear me out?"

"Because even *you* are but a mere mortal like the rest of us, Miss Ellie!" Nora had just finished feeding the baby. She handed the happy, wiggly little girl to her Auntie to burp.
"Here, take Little Callie while I finish kneading the dough for the rolls. Mel's favorite."

Little Callie obliged with a deceptively loud burp almost as soon as Ellie took her. So now, Aunt Ellie was free to admire the youngest Coursey woman while holding the precious bundle on her lap. Babies are always kissable, especially when their naturally sweet, intoxicating "baby smell" is infused with baby powder and lotion. Ellie couldn't resist inhaling that sweetness and stealing some sugar from the delicious plump cheeks. "You know, Nora, I believe this little princess favors Mama more and more every day. These gorgeous giant eyes are the same color as this pretty chocolate skin. Just like Mama. Remember?"

"Ah-hem! Of course I remember. But, speaking of pretty chocolate skin, Jeez Louise, Ellie! When are you going to let Sonny make an honest woman out of you?"

Ellie was smiling and making funny faces at her gurgling niece who rewarded her aunt with a radiant, gummy smile. Aunt Ellie continued their game by answering her sister in an "I'm playing with the baby" voice. "Why, Mommy, you of all people know why that can't happen! You know perfectly well how Aunt Ellie feels about marriage."

Nora turned to face Ellie. Her tone far more serious. "Oh, honey. I know how much Brady hurt and disappointed you. But, please. Don't let your rotten experience with Brady ruin the possibility, no – the promise – of happiness with a man who truly treasures you. Sonny loves you so much."

"I know that. And, I love him, too. I do. But why does anything have to change? I absolutely love my life exactly the way it is! I have my children. You're here. And, Los Angeles has agreed with you. Right, Little

Callie?" Ellie steals another yummy kiss from the baby. "My children and I live in a beautiful home. They have friends and are thriving. I run a successful business. My designs are sold at stores all over the country. *Mine*, Nora. Isn't that amazing? We're making more money than even *I* ever dreamed of. And, Sonny is right there participating and sharing in all of it. So, why fix what isn't broken?"

Nora looked at her sister sadly. "Yes, it's all wonderful, sweetie. And, you know I am so very proud of you. I love you and I've always only wanted the best for you. For your dreams to come true. I'm just afraid that if you're not careful, you may become a very rich, but very lonely woman."

"A Dollar Above Starvation"

Ellie held on to her beautifully renovated art deco style apartment building. All of the units were rented immediately at a pretty penny. Apparently the parking lot was heavily coveted by the church across the street for an annex or school. So, a tidy profit was made with that sale. Ellie's ESA office was doubling as her real estate office.

"You know, I love designing clothes. And, I really love selling them! But, I had no idea that buying and selling real estate could be so much more – exhilarating!" Ellie rhetorically announced out of the blue one afternoon in the office she shared with Sonny.

She sauntered over to Sonny's desk and perched seductively on the edge. "Hey, big boy."

"Yes?" Sonny looked up from his paperwork, intrigued by Ellie's tone.

"I've got a proposition for you."

"I'm all ears," Sonny answered, his interest piqued.

"Good. Because I want to buy The Southway Hotel. With you. It's small and very successful. And, the owners are elderly with no offspring and are ready to sell. You and I are such a fabulous team. So, what do you say? Partner."

Sonny's face fell. Ellie was so caught up in the excitement of a prospective new deal, she misinterpreted his disappointed expression.

"Oh, you don't think it's a good idea?"

Sonny paused for what seemed like a long time to Ellie. "No, Ellie. My brilliant, beautiful Ellie. I think it's a great idea and I am 100 percent certain that you would be able to turn it into something even more successful than it already is."

"Me? I'm talking about *us*, baby. You and I buying it together."

"Yes, I know. And, I'm going to have to decline."

"Decline? Why? The Southway is a cash cow, just waiting to be properly milked."

"And, I'm sure you're right, Ellie. But your idea of 'us' and mine just aren't jiving anymore." Sonny smiled a doleful smile and shook his head. "You know I adore you and your spirit and the fact that your amazing mind can both create clothes that are almost works of art, and cut business deals as well as any business schooled mogul. But, I can't be your silent partner any more. No matter how successful we have been. It's just not enough for me. I want a real 'us.' Can you do that now? Are you ready? Do you love me enough to be my wife, my partner for the rest of our lives; not just in business?"

Ellie's throat was constricting with the tears she choked back. "I love and adore you, too, Sonny Duran. You know I do. I just cannot marry you."

Sonny nodded and leaned back in his chair. "I didn't think so. Well then, there's something I need to share with you."

"What?"

"I've decided to branch out into importing. I'm flying to New York in a couple of weeks to sail to Europe. All of the major cities – London, Paris, Rome, Barcelona, Amsterdam – as well as smaller, more rural areas. I might even continue through parts of Asia. I know how much you've always wanted to travel abroad, especially to Paris. For some crazy reason, I convinced myself that this time you would say 'yes' and the trip would be our honeymoon. And, then some."

"Oh, Sonny, I'm so very sorry. I – "

Sonny cut her off, placing one finger over her lips. "Shhh. No. No more sorrys. It's alright." He rose from his seat, pulled Ellie off the desk and wrapped his arms around her. They held each other that way for a piece of forever.

Ellie purchased the Southway on her own. She wanted to give her guests a sense of celebration and luxury, so she had the entire hotel – inside and out - overhauled in the modern, streamlined art deco style that she so favored. Ellie renamed the club inside the hotel's lobby The Coursey Room – which, with its pink upholstery, black lacquer and glass décor, was even more elegant and glorious than Club Alabam. The new Southway was opulent and filled with monied black patrons when it opened its doors. The club's opening night was packed. Nora and Mel, Alberto, Rose, Roland and all of her friends were there to support Ellie and toast her latest achievement. Everyone except Sonny.

Brady had heard all about the new Southway Hotel and the hoity-toity Coursey Room. He would have gone, he told his aces, but "hanging around a whole roomful of uppity niggas all night long" wasn't exactly his idea of a good time. Sitting in the East LA speakeasy throwing back endless shots of his old friend, Jack Daniels, it seemed the old Brady was back. "I'm sick and damn tired of playing by my wife's rules. Ex-wife. Who the hell does she think she is, anyway? Miss High and Mighty with her fine house, fancy clothes and big car. Even got folks working for her."

"Hey, Brady. Maybe you've had enough, buddy," the otherwise nonchalant bartender interjected. It was his job, after all, and it sounded like Brady was getting himself good and worked up. He wasn't in the mood to have to break up a drunken brawl.

Brady ignored the bartender, demanded another drink and continued to slur his building resentment against Ellie, steadily spilling his twisted guts. "Hell, I was married to her when she was nobody, after all. *And*, I'm them kids' Papa. Don't that entitle me to *half* her money and shit – or at least a *cut*? Why should I stay put, living in not much more than a lean-to, slavin' away every day while *she* is living in the lap of damn luxury? Why? Because she *say* so?" The bartender just nodded.

Brady made his move one evening under the guise of waiting for the kids to get home. He knew they had tennis lessons after school that day, but feigned forgetfulness. Ellie was on the phone when he arrived. She was closing another business deal and told Brady to make himself a drink and have a seat while he waited for Evan and Dinah.

"Or," Ellie added, covering the phone's mouthpiece with her hand, "you could just leave, and learn to call first like a civilized person the next time you want to see the children. They *do* have schedules, you know."

The festering sore of resentment burst. Brady's face contorted with it before he opened his mouth. He leaped up from the chair, snatched the receiver out of Ellie's hand and slammed it in the cradle.

"Bitch! Who the hell do you think you talking to? I am so sick of all your shit!" Brady screamed. "But now – now you think you're something just because you're out of Oklahoma and making a dollar above starvation. Yeah! You still think you better than me. I'll show you better!" Brady grabbed a stunned Ellie by the arm and slung her across the room. And, just like the old days, Ellie got up and lunged at Brady, her anger making her a madwoman. She had gone through too much, had come too far – to take this, ever again!

Brady pinned Ellie down on the floor, loosening his belt and trousers to "give it to you just the way I know you like it." In freeing his left hand, he freed her right. In the blink of an eye, Ellie reached under her skirt to her garter belt, and pulled out a tiny, pearl-handled pistol. Being in the club business taught her to be prepared for anything at any time. With all her might, she whacked Brady across the face with the gun.

Brady staggered to his feet, grimacing with pain and shock, grabbing at the bloody gash on his cheek. Ellie scrambled up more gracefully, gripped the gun steadily with both hands and promised to blow Brady's brains out if he ever even *thinks* about raising his hand *or* his voice to her ever again. "And, just for the record, you *will* play by my goddamn rules. Yes, *my* rules, you crazy bastard. I have *earned* the right to make them *and* enforce them!"

Brady reluctantly got the message and skulked out of Ellie's house with his tail between his legs. But, Ellie needed insurance. She put down the gun, picked up the phone and dialed, hands shaking.

"Hello Ronnie? It's Ellie. Listen, my ex-husband was just here. He needs to learn to keep his damn hands off of me! . . . No, I'm fine. Thanks. . . . What? No, don't kill him. Just scare the hell out of him." Yes. Being in the club business definitely had its advantages.

↝ CHAPTER ↜
21
"All Grown Up"

On another flawless blue and gold Southern California afternoon, the entire proud family gathered to watch Evan Coursey Renault graduate from high school. The class of 1941. Grandpa Sam, Grandma Marie and their now pretty-much-grown children were there. As were Uncle Jake and Uncle Joe with their families. Ellie's older sister, Beth and her husband Beau had even made it from Texas. Ellie was thrilled to be able to fly in all of her loved ones to share in the joy. And, of course, Nora and Mel sat with a very active Little Callie in tow. Dinah sat with her family and a few giggly girlfriends, all of whom had secret crushes to varying degrees on Evan. Brady was in attendance, too, but sat a few rows behind the rest of Evan's family.

Tall, handsome and brimming with all the glorious possibilities life had to offer, Evan beamed as he majestically strode across the outdoor stage in his cap and gown. So did his Mama, who was full to overflowing with love, pride and the sweetest memories. Her baby boy. How was it possible the time had flown by so quickly?

That evening, the Coursey Room was closed for a private function. A fabulous graduation party in Evan's honor - and his entire class! All 72 of them and their families. Because fabulous and bigger-than-life were Ellie's favorite ways to celebrate. Balloons, "Congratulations Class of '41" banners and streamers in Manual Arts High School colors of maroon and white filled every previously vacant spot on the club's ceiling and walls. The Coursey Room had gained such celebrity in Negro entertainment circles; Ellie had no problem convincing the Ink Spots to provide the music for her son's soiree. They were in full swing and the party was in full blast. The female vocalist accompanying the Ink Spots for the evening belted the hell out of Billie Holiday's *What a Little Moonlight Can Do* and *God Bless the Child*. The revelers went crazy.

"Thank you, Mama. Thank you so much!" Evan gratefully hugged and kissed his mother regardless of any ribbing he might consequently endure from his buddies.

Ellie held Evan's beautiful chiseled face in both her hands. "You are so very welcome, my wonderful, amazing son. My precious baby boy. Just look at you! All grown up. High school graduate. Headed for college!"

"Aw, Mama. I guess even when I'm old and gray I'll still be your baby boy."

"Um-hmm," Ellie nodded in absolute agreement.

"Did you see the fancy gift Sonny sent?"

"Yes, baby, I did. Very handsome. Sonny loves you and Dinah. You knew he wouldn't forget you on your special day. Why don't you get on back to your friends, hmm?" Sonny's import/export business was doing so well, he spent much of his time these days in Europe. As Evan was on his way to being a "Morehouse man," Sonny had a hand-made attaché case of the most buttery-soft espresso leather sent from Milan. And, of course, Evan's initials gleamed in golden letters.

Sam was so proud of Ellie he could hardly contain himself. She had told Papa she had a surprise for him. Until that day, Sam had no idea that Ellie had given the club their family name.

"My wild, wonderful little girl. All grown up into one hell of a woman." Sam held Ellie close. Ellie sighed deeply, feeling safe in the shelter of her father's arms.

"Your old Papa couldn't be more proud of you, you know. I want to thank you for sending for all of us to be here. And, my Ellie, I want to thank you for not listening to your old man. Thank you for not listening to me when I tried to keep you in Okmulgee."

"Oh, Papa, I know you were just telling me what you thought was best. You were afraid for me. To tell you the truth, a little part of me was afraid for me, too."

"No, baby. That was good. A little fear is normal. Even for my brave, brilliant daughter. I now know I was being very selfish and narrow-minded. I just wasn't blessed with your vision or your ability to dream, my sweet girl. Most of us probably aren't. We're just common folk."

Ellie stepped out of her father's arms and turned to face him. "I love you, Papa. And, I want to thank you for loving me enough to let me go and for taking such good care of Evan and Dinah until I could send for them."

"That was the least I could do, daughter. But, I have to say – there is one area where I'm afraid you aren't being very smart. Sonny. He's a wonderful man, Ellie. It pains me that you have put up a wall to your own happiness. That man loves the ground you walk on. And, he's a real man; the kind I have always wanted for you and your sisters. He's nothing like Brady."

"But - " Ellie tried to interrupt her father.

"No, daughter. I have one more thing to say. And, I want you to listen to me good! Don't throw your happiness away. You have all the 'things' and trappings and success you've always wanted. But, love, child. Don't forget about love. These children are grown and leaving you. Next year will be Dinah's turn. Nora's married with her own family. If you know where Sonny is, well, I think you should go to him and see if you can set things right."

The threat of tears were stinging Ellie's eyes; but she'd be damned if she let them fall. She knew her father was right, though. Everyone was right. But, it was too late now. Sonny had spent most of his time in Europe for nearly the past two years. *Yes, it's too late*, her mind told her. That realization, however, didn't stop her heart from aching with his loss; or with the love it held for Sonny, kept so tightly bottled up by Ellie's fear. She lightly kissed her father on the cheek.

"Thank you, Papa. I listened to every word. But, right now, I think I'd better continue to mingle. Why don't we go and find Marie?" Just then, Dinah was pushing through the lively crowd, trying to reach her mother. Ellie heard her daughter's excited voice over the din before she even saw her.

"Mama, Mama! Look who I found loitering in the lobby!" Dinah was calling out.

"Darling, I was on my way in when this lovely young vision spotted me. Swear to God, Ellie, she's you! But – surely you knew I wasn't going to miss your Evan's big soiree. He deserves this. And, so do you, my love. You have been the most remarkable mother! Honestly, between the children, ESA, this place and your other properties, I don't know when you sleep." Alberto was trailing just behind Dinah. He kissed Ellie on both cheeks.

"Oh, Alberto. Thank you. Thank you for everything and thank you so much for coming. Have you seen Evan yet?" Even though Ellie was thrilled to see her friend and – nearly invisible these days – partner, her heart had leapt; and, now dropped.

"I wouldn't be anywhere else, dear Ellie. But, sweetie, you seem a bit disappointed. Expecting someone else, perhaps?" Alberto queried, nimbly lifting a glass of champagne from a passing tray.

"Disappointed? Of course not," Ellie protested. "I am so very delighted to see you, my dear friend. I've missed you. So, don't stay away again for so long, alright? Papa. Papa," she called to her father. Ellie turned her attention back to Alberto. "You know, Alberto, I don't think you've met my father and stepmother. And, Evan will be delighted that you're here. Come with me." Ellie took Alberto's free hand to navigate him through the dancing, eating, talking and laughing multitude.

"Congratulations, Ellie. You must be very proud."

Alberto smiled knowingly. Ellie froze in her tracks. It couldn't be. She slowly turned around, hearing no other sounds in the room – not the music, not the party noise. Just *his* voice.

"Sonny?"

The familiar dazzling smile lit up the room.

"Sonny!"

For Ellie at that unbelievable moment, there was no one else in the club. Any sense of decorum or caution or fear or embarrassment was miraculously nonexistent for her. Not sure how Ellie would react to seeing him after such a long time, Sonny just opened his arms for a hoped-for hug. When Ellie unabashedly leaped into them, and wrapped her arms around his neck, there was no one else in the room for him either. They pulled back for only a fraction of an instant to look at each other, then melted into a kiss filled with all the passion and longing each of them had tried to bury. Neither Ellie nor Sonny cared or heard that all of the guests in the club had broken into applause, cheers and whistles – led by Ellie's family. And Alberto.

As corny as he knew it was, Evan ran up to the bandstand to whisper in the ear of the closest musician. The Ink Spots broke into *I Only Have Eyes For You*. The party guests loved it. Evan had graduated from high school. But, he and the rest of the family knew their Ellie had graduated from herself.

❧ CHAPTER ❧
22
"Game Changers"

Having the entire family in town for Evan's high school graduation made it the perfect time to host an intimate ceremony right in Ellie's meticulously manicured backyard. The reception would immediately follow by the pool. Marie, Nora, Beth and Dinah couldn't put the wedding together fast enough, which was a good thing, since they only had days. Luckily, Alberto was more than happy to step in as the wedding coordinator. Sonny's mother and sister were happy to pitch in as well. "It's about damn time," was all anyone could say when told the news of the engagement – with big, happy smiles.

Peach colored roses and orchids smothered the white trellis. White wooden upholstered chairs sat on a bleached-white hardwood floor constructed on the grass for the guests. After the ceremony, it would double as a dance floor. Open white tents, draped with graceful peach and white swags were set up around the pool. The tents covered elegantly dressed round tables. They were set with the finest white and peach linens, sparkling Baccarat crystal stemware, and translucent peach R. Lalique plates nestled in gold chargers; bordered by gold flatware. Each table held its own precious R. Lalique bowl of fragrant roses and orchids. The surface of the water in the pool itself was filled with happily floating miniature bouquets of roses and orchids, commingling with the dozens of lit votive candles resting peacefully on lily pads.

Sam was delighted to give his daughter away. This time. Ellie was breathtaking in her own design – an off-the-shoulder pale peach, tea-length creation. The bodice and hips were fitted, flowing out into a gentle fish-tail hem. She carried roses and orchids, with one perfect orchid tucked behind her ear. Because the ceremony was simple, only Dinah served as a bridesmaid for her mother. She wore a more modest version of her mother's gown that was far more appropriate for a sixteen year old. Because Sonny had no brothers, Roland stood up for him – as it was Roland who introduced them at Club Alabam. Little Callie served as the adorable flower girl in her tiny, frothy, ballerina princess-worthy dress; not at all afraid to be part of the center of attention.

The curtain of the heavens provided a glorious backdrop for Ellie's and Sonny's sunset nuptials. It radiated gradated corals, magentas, golds and deepest lapis – all beautifully coordinating with Ellie's colors.

So, on that perfect evening of June 9, 1941, Eleanor Marie Coursey willingly, joyfully and fearlessly gave herself in holy matrimony to Sonny Jeremiah Duran, Jr.

Ellie and Sonny decided that Sonny would move into her home *temporarily* and sell his; then they would buy something else together. Since money was not an issue, that selection didn't take long. Just a week prior, Sonny began looking into their newest joint real estate venture while the women – and Alberto - planned the wedding.

After Sonny and Ellie came up for air during Evan's graduation party, Ellie shamelessly asked Sonny to "please ask me again." At first, Sonny wasn't sure what she meant; but, it didn't take long for him to catch on. So, Sonny said "yes." Then, Ellie gave her "yes" quicker than greased lightning when Sonny asked her - this time around - to share his life as his wife and equal partner. She was not going to lose him again!

The magnificent new home of Mr. and Mrs. Sonny Duran sat in one of Los Angeles' gated luxury communities. It was everything that Ellie had ever dreamed of. Once owned by some long-dead, eccentric film star, the house boasted lustrous Italian marble floors, a majestic winding staircase; five marble-framed fire places; open, airy, spacious rooms and opulent appointments.

"Oh Baby, I just *know* this is the last house we will ever buy – to live in, that is. I love it! We will grow old together and die in this house, I swear to God!"

"I had a feeling you might like it, Sweetheart. My only question is – what are we going to do with all this room?" Sonny asked playfully, knowing full well that Ellie would love the enormous size.

"I'll tell you what we're going to do with it," Ellie responded, dreamily strolling through the empty rooms. "We're going to pack this house with grandchildren one of these days. Besides our grandchildren, we have to make sure that our nieces and nephews have plenty of room to run and play when they visit. And, of course, parties. Lots of parties! With white people as servers. Wouldn't that be a hoot? White servers." Ellie laughed and reached up to slide her arms around her new husband's neck, covering his face in kisses. "Besides," she added. "If we don't buy it – where will we put all of that gorgeous furniture and artwork we're going to purchase on our honeymoon in Europe?"

"Excellent point," Sonny nodded.

"Sonny?" Ellie almost reverently whispered his name.

"Yes, my love?"

"Thank you."

"For what, Baby?"

"For absolutely everything. For truly making all of my dreams come true. Including those dreams I didn't know I had."

The blended Coursey-Renault-Duran family enjoyed a wonderfully sweet summer. After their three-week honeymoon throughout Britain, France, Spain and Italy, Ellie and Sonny moved their family into their new home. Evan and Dinah seemed to host cookouts and splash parties for their friends every other day! Ellie loved the constant activity because it kept them happy and at home. And, to her, a home was supposed to be filled with children and friends and laughter. Even if the "children" were nearly adults. Evan would be leaving at the end of the summer for college; so, having him at home for these few weeks was precious to her. Sonny loved Evan and Dinah, too. Their happiness and the happiness of their mother meant the world to him.

"Mama, can I talk to you?" Evan sat on the end of the chaise where his mother relaxed while sketching pieces for her new line.

"Of course, Baby. You know you can talk to me anytime." Both Evan and Dinah had always been so open with her. So, Evan's asking set a gnawing in motion at the pit of Ellie's stomach. And, Evan was fidgeting, nervous.

"What is it, honey? Are you getting nervous about going so far away to school? Is that it?" Ellie reached.

"Well, see, that's the thing. School. I mean, I look forward to attending Morehouse. I really do. Just not right now."

"What?" Ellie sat up, startled. "What did you say?"

"Mama, I've enlisted in the army."

"You *what*!?" Ellie nearly shouted, certain she had heard her son wrong.

"I said I've enlisted in the army."

Try and stay calm, Ellie told herself. "What do you *mean* you've enlisted in the army?"

"I've thought this through, Mama. You know that working on planes – building them and flying them – is what I have always wanted to do. It's *all* I've ever wanted to do. Well, there's a war going on in Europe. In the army, I can be trained to fly fighter planes. After the war is over, I can come back and take my place at Morehouse. I don't plan to miss college; don't worry."

"Oh, Dear God in Heaven." Ellie got up, lit a cigarette and began pacing.

She took a long drag and slowly exhaled a chimney's worth of smoke. "Let me get this straight. You are just days away from leaving for college to prepare for a fabulous life. Just as we planned and talked about and looked forward to all these years. You threw college away to enlist in the goddamn army, the white man's army? What the hell were you *thinking*?" No matter how hard she tried, Ellie was on the verge of hysteria.

"I was thinking that - " Evan began. His mother cut him off.

"And you're only 17! A baby!" Ellie exploded.

"I'm a high school graduate, Mama. And, well, I told them I am 18. Which wasn't even really a lie because I will be 18 next month, after all. A man; not a baby."

"The point is, Evan, *they* don't care! The white man's army doesn't care about you and they sure as hell don't *want* your black ass in their army!" Ellie was frustrated and terrified by her son's naiveté. "Baby, the army isn't going to let a colored boy, colored man or colored anything else fly a goddamn fighter plane! If anything, they'll make you some kind of fry cook or janitor. They won't appreciate your intellect or your gifts or your goodness. They will beat you down. Make you feel less than who you are. No! I will not let you go! I won't let you! We will *fix* this somehow!"

Ellie dissolved into tears and tried to take another drag off the cigarette. Before she could get it to her mouth, Evan snatched it out of her hand, threw it to the ground, and stomped it out. Then, he took his mother's hands in both of his.

"I love you so much. You know that, don't you, Mama? And, both Dinah and I appreciate everything you've always done for us our whole lives. Please believe that I'm not doing this to hurt you. Or, to defy you. I joined the army because it's something I really feel very strongly about. I promise you that I have no intention of abandoning my education. I'm just postponing it a little."

Ellie listened, but was too upset to speak. Evan looked deeply into his mother's eyes, and continued.

"Mama, you of all people should understand how important it is to follow our dreams. How impossible it is *not* to. Isn't that how you've always lived? What you've always done? Isn't that why we're here in Los Angeles living this wonderful life you fought so hard for by following your dreams? For us? Please try and understand."

Ellie sighed and kissed her boy. God help them, he was right. And, she had no right to try and stop him. For better or for worse, Evan was even more like her than she realized.

❧ CHAPTER ❧
23
"Taken"

On September 1, 1941, Evan boarded the bus for boot camp in San Diego. Dinah, Ellie, Sonny, Nora, Mel – and Brady – were all at the depot to send him off. Amidst tearful goodbyes, Evan promised to write at least twice a week. On the outside, Ellie put on the brave, supportive mother face. Inside, her heart was broken. And, this time, there was absolutely nothing she could do about it.

Dinah, Ellie and Sonny were determined to make their first Christmas in their sprawling new home on Wellington Road as merry as humanly possible. By December 1st, their halls were decked with glittering Christmas trees in nearly every room, fragrant bowed evergreen garlands hung on every fireplace and wound down the staircase; golden and crystal cherubs, miniature Santas and cinnamon infused candles shared spaces on tables and shelves with Baccarat bowls of silvery ornaments and Christmas cheer. Ellie and Dinah knew Evan would love it if he were home. Christmas was his favorite holiday.

"I hope these fruitcakes and cookies get to Evan in one piece," Dinah laughed, elbow deep in cookie dough. Dinah, Ellie and Nora were having a wonderful time baking Christmas goodies. Even Little Callie was helping. She was in charge of shaking the sugar sprinkles on the sugar cookies in any color she chose. By the look of things, red was her favorite.

"Dinah, baby, read Evan's letter to us again."

"OK, Mama. Let me just wipe my hands off first."

"Ellie, sweetie, we've already heard it three times," Nora interrupted, trying to help Callie get more sprinkles on the cookies than on the table and floor. "Are you sure it's making you feel better?"

"Of course," Ellie insisted. "It makes me feel that much closer to him. Go on, Dinah."

> *Dear Mama, Dinah and Sonny,*
>   *Hawaii is truly a tropical paradise. It kind of reminds me of*

LA with all of the palm trees, but it is lush and exotic and more beautiful than I ever could have imagined. Mama, you would love it. And, even though I am not in Atlanta at Morehouse – yet - at least I am seeing the world. Even though the colored army is separate from the white army, it's not so bad; and I've almost gotten used to it. But here's the best part! Have any of you heard about the Tuskegee Airmen? I just found out about it. It is an all-colored flying combat unit that the Army Air Corps has just set up down in Tuskegee, Alabama. My superior officer has made several inquiries and I am being transferred to the Tuskegee Army Air Field right after Christmas for aviation cadet training for the 99th Fighter Squadron. What do you think about that? Isn't it swell? I am going to fly airplanes, Mama, just like I wanted. Right now, I am working as a mechanic's apprentice, which I really like because even though I knew how planes fly in theory; now I am learning all about how planes fly first-hand. Enough about me. Little sister, do me a favor and try not to break the hearts of too many boys at school this holiday season at all the dances and balls. Mama, try not to work too hard. That goes for you, too, Sonny. Thanks again for finally making an honest woman of our mother. That's a joke, Ma. Would you give a big hug to Aunt Nora and Uncle Mel for me? And, to Little Callie from her big cousin, Evan. I hope you all receive the Christmas presents I sent before the holiday. And, of course, I hope you like them. Thanks again for all of the wonderful care packages, but I've got to confess that my greatest wish for Christmas is that I could be there to celebrate it with all of you. I've got a nifty idea – maybe all of you will be able to visit me soon in Tuskegee! Will you? That would be the best present I could ever receive. Please remember how much I love and miss you all. Evan.

When the news of the surprise attack at Pearl Harbor broke just days later, Ellie, Sonny and Dinah, along with their friends, were glued to the radio in the Wellington home den for updates. Ellie was sick with worry that Evan might have been somewhere near that naval base on Oahu. Nora and Sonny tried to reassure her that Evan was in the army, and was probably no where near the naval base – and, wasn't he stationed on a different island? From that Sunday morning, December 7, 1941 through Monday evening, Dinah, Sonny, Nora, Mel, Rose, Roland and Alberto all took turns staying awake to listen to the news reports. Except for Ellie. She didn't want a turn. She simply refused to sleep. *Couldn't* sleep. Until she heard from her son. Between listening to the news reports, Ellie paced, staring at the phone, drinking endless cups of coffee and smoking one cigarette after another. She was determined to will the damn phone to ring with Evan on the other end telling her he was okay.

The extended-family group, exhausted and horrified, listened to the terrible statistics over and again: The U.S. fleet all but destroyed by Japanese torpedo planes, bombers and fighters; thousands of U.S. military casualties. The mood in the house remained somber as they all listened to President Franklin Roosevelt declare that terrible Sunday "a day which will live in infamy;" and listened to the report on Monday, December 8, that Congress had declared war on Japan.

By Wednesday, everyone was gone, save for their housekeeper, Juanita, who was going about her daily chores. Juanita was praying the rosary for Señora Ellie, Señor Evan and the rest of the family under her breath as she changed the bedding. Dinah was at school. Sonny was needed to put out a fire at ESA, even though it pretty much ran like clockwork these days. So, except for Juanita, Ellie was alone in her fabulous, exquisitely decked-out-for-the-holidays showplace of a home. Still chain smoking; still listening to the radio and looking like hell. She hadn't bathed or even brushed her hair. *Please God, someone has to tell me something, she begged. Please. Please tell me that my son is safe.* The phone rang and jarred Ellie out of her stupor of worry.

"No, Papa. We haven't heard anything. I don't mean to be rude, Papa. I love you for checking, but I want to keep the line clear, just in case Evan tries to get through."

When Dinah got home from school that afternoon, she found her mother sitting in the dark in the library; all the drapes drawn.

"I tried to get her to eat something, Señorita Dinah, but she refuse. Señor Sonny call. He be home shortly."

The doorbell rang.

"Excuse me. I'll get it." Juanita was startled by the man dressed in a military uniform. Inherently, she knew it was bad. When she stepped away, Ellie appeared with Dinah at her side.

Ellie's eyes immediately zeroed in on the telegram in the man's hand. Before he even opened it, Ellie shrieked like a wounded animal. "Noooooooooo!" Dinah, herself in shock, caught her mother as she collapsed. Ellie's weight was too much, and they both ended up huddled in the doorway. Juanita tried to wrap her arms around both of them, empathetic tears streaming down her face. She had three children of her own, including two little boys. Juanita believed her own heart would just stop beating if anything happened to one of her babies. Poor Señora Ellie!

The young man at the door was himself devastated at delivering such pain, dutifully reciting what he had been trained to repeat. "I'm sorry, Ma'am. You have your country's sincere condolences and gratitude." He handed the telegram to Juanita and turned to make his way back down the winding walkway.

Sonny pulled up just as the soldier was walking to a waiting car. He leaped out of his car before barely putting it in park and tore up the driveway to the front door. "Oh, no. Oh, no," he murmured softly, as he took Juanita's place holding both Ellie and Dinah. Their woeful sobbing and moaning drowned out all of the other normal late afternoon sounds – children laughing and dogs barking in the distance. The vroom-vroom of automobiles, with the occasional honk. The birds still chirping away in the trees. Life somehow went on even as theirs seemed over.

Sonny lifted Ellie in his arms to take her upstairs to their room. "I know, baby. I know. Let it out, Sweetheart; it's okay," he lovingly whispered in her ear; his own eyes wet, his face stricken with grief. Dinah followed them up. Juanita shut the massive front door.

"Shall I call Señora Nora, Señor Sonny? And, perhaps the doctor?" Juanita called up to Sonny, anxious to help. She loved this family. Even though she came in every weekday to take care of them and their home, they treated her more like a family member than an employee. She had only been with the Durans for three months when young Evan left for the army; but, she saw what a good boy he was. So smart and so kind. So full of life and laughter and promise. The kind of son any mother would be proud of. The kind of man the entire world would benefit from. The kind she prayed her boys would grow up to be.

"Yes, thank you, Juanita. Thank you," Sonny called back, barely audible.

As soon as Sonny put her down, Ellie stumbled into her bathroom and threw up. *Oh, God. Why? Why?* She crumpled onto the floor heaving and screaming. Sonny and Dinah rushed in to help her. Tears and snot running because of her own sense of unbearable loss at the news of her brother's death, Dinah nonetheless lovingly wiped her mother's face and mouth with a cool washcloth.

She stroked her hair while helping Sonny get Ellie into bed. "It's going to be alright, Mama. It's going to be alright," Dinah managed to whisper in between painful cries that stuck in her now raw throat.

Ellie stared into space. "Why does everyone always say that? It's *not* going to be alright. It's *never* going to be alright! Oh God! Evan! *Evan!*" Hysteria had finally taken over. Certain that she was losing her mind, Ellie thrashed and hollered and fought Sonny with the adrenalin of unspeakable sorrow. Even though her husband was twice her size, Sonny struggled to hold her still. Dinah stood helpless, watching in horror with her hands clasped over her mouth.

Nora rushed into the bedroom and crawled right into the bed with Ellie, talking in the most calming voice she could muster; her own tears silent. She gently took her sister from Sonny as though she were handling a small child. "There, there, Darlin'. I know. I know, baby. We are all hurting with you, Ellie. We all loved Evan so much. He was such a wonderful young man. Wonderful. And, you know why? Because you are a wonderful mother, that's why. And, Evan is right here in this room with us, hating that his Mama's heart is broken. He loves you so much, Ellie. And, he *is* here. I promise you. Evan left this world chasing after *his dream*. That made him happy, Ellie. He was working to achieve *his* dream. Just like his Mama always has. He was *happy*, Ellie. Happy because you loved him so much you let him go. And, he knew how much his Mama loved him." Nora rocked her sister back and forth, praying to God that she was saying the right things. Trying to ignore her own pain at losing her beloved nephew because her own pain didn't count right now. Ellie had lost a *child*. The worst tragedy any parent could suffer.

Juanita escorted Dr. Jones upstairs to the master bedroom. The doctor expressed his condolences to Sonny, Nora and Dinah; then took a hypodermic needle out of his bag and filled it with a sedative.

"This is something to help her relax. She'll probably go to sleep, which is the best thing for her right now," Dr. Jones addressed Sonny as he pushed the needle into the soft flesh of Ellie's arm. She didn't flinch; but rather stared now into space, seeing nothing. Sonny, Dinah and Nora all held each other, more concerned with Ellie than they were with their own unbearable sorrow.

Now, just six months after Evan's joyful graduation from high school, his entire family gathered once again on a clear, beautiful Southern California day. This time to say goodbye much too soon. A mournful rendition of "Taps" filled the air. This time, there was only the absolute absence of joy. Utter sadness dwelled on all the faces and in all the hearts as the body of this precious boy child was lowered into the ground.

Ellie's eyes were bloodshot and swollen from crying, blueblack circles rimming them. She stared straight ahead as though in a trance. Her daughter helped her get dressed that morning. Wearing a simple, unadorned black suit, Ellie refused the application of any make-up, but did permit Dinah to brush her hair back into a chignon.

Dinah sat on one side of her mother, leaning her head on Ellie's shoulder and holding her hands. Sonny sat on Ellie's other side, his arm protectively in place around her shoulders; determined to stay strong for his new family. Sonny's lips and jaw quivered with his own pain. He had loved Evan as though he were his own flesh and blood. Nora, Sam and Marie sat on the other side of Dinah. Mel was walking back and forth with Little Callie, who wouldn't stop whimpering, although at two years old, she couldn't have had any notion of what was going on. An unshaven, red-eyed Brady sat behind Ellie with his own family members who had come in for the service. Even though neither he nor they were very involved or demonstrative with the children, they did love them; and were devastated by Evan's death. Rose, Roland, Alberto and an intimate collection of friends and acquaintances pulled up the rear.

After the service, the officers folded the American flag that had draped Evan's coffin and handed it to Ellie. She took it, but stared at them as though they were from another planet.

At the crowded repast back at Ellie's and Sonny's home, Nora and Sonny gently guided Ellie upstairs to their bedroom. Ellie was zombie-like, so they lay her down, slipped off her shoes and clothes and pulled up the covers.

"Do you think we should let her be further sedated?" Sonny asked Nora as they padded softly downstairs to the guests.

"Yes, I think it's best for her. She can't take it," Nora replied thoughtfully.

"No, I'm afraid she can't. I'll get Dr. Jones."

Nora and Sonny both knew that sleep was a blessed escape for Ellie now. Dr. Jones left a prescription bottle with Sonny, giving Ellie two more of the tablets after Sonny brought him back up to the bedroom. When the doctor left, Sonny climbed onto the bed next to Ellie, fully clothed in his dark suit and polished shoes; and curled his body around hers. He enveloped Ellie with her head resting in the safe place where his shoulder and chest met. Sonny, in turn, rested his cheek against the top of Ellie's head. He kissed it over and again and gently caressed her hair. It was as though he was physically trying to protect his precious Ellie from the hurt. Trying to absorb it into himself. If only he could.

Later that night, when all of the company had gone and Dinah had cried herself to sleep – again - in her own bedroom, Nora and Sam sat down to talk with Sonny. Juanita had cleaned up everything and left fresh coffee for them before saying goodnight and heading home. Marie had gone back to Nora's to take care of Callie. Mel had to leave to cover the tavern that night.

"Sonny," Nora started tentatively. "There's another reason why I thought sedation was a good idea for Ellie." Slowly and sadly, Nora and Sam recounted the terrible story from so long ago in LeBeau, after Callie died. Sonny buried his face in his hands. His heart was breaking again for his Ellie. He now understood so much more.

The holidays were long over. Ellie immersed herself in work to save herself. To shield herself from feeling anymore. Even her look had changed. Ellie Coursey Duran was still glamorous – but hard. Severe. The softness, warmth and fun were gone.

At one of their real estate meetings with possible new, outside partners, Ellie was arguing vehemently for a questionable new venture. "Gentlemen, I am not the one who has decided that the West Coast is vulnerable to Japanese attack. Our very own U.S. government has. And, it makes sense.

Los Angeles is, after all, the hub of American aircraft production, and is a prime target for invasion. I, for one, agree with the government that ethnic Japanese in California would automatically aid and abet such an assault on our shores."

Sonny couldn't believe what was coming out of Ellie's mouth! Surely, she didn't actually believe what she was spouting? "C'mon, Ellie! The government is being paranoid and just plain *wrong* by displacing Japanese American residents by the thousands. They are forcing people to leave their homes to be herded to interment camps with no evidence whatsoever of their disloyalty to the United States. The government is calling them relocation camps. But, we all know that's bullshit!"

"Oh, don't be such a boy scout," Ellie chided her husband. "The government is simply being smart. Striking first this time. You and the others, my darling, are not seeing the bigger picture here, which is the opportunity to make millions of dollars! Those hasty upheavals mean that hundreds, maybe thousands of homes and properties are essentially going to be abandoned. They will either be foreclosed upon or sold at a fraction of the value. I want to be the one to buy them! Or, at least as many as I can afford. And, if we don't act right this minute, we lose!"

Sonny tried to make Ellie see that that any kind of profit made on these properties would be blood money. Money made by taking advantage of the misery of other people. People who were almost as hated as they were. "It would be unfair and blatant discrimination, Ellie! Something that you, me and a whole hell of a lot of us know a little something about. Did you know that entire families were corralled out of their homes like fucking cattle? People had clothes on the line, food still on the stove and tricycles in the yard. We *know* what it's like to be thought of and treated like less than human. So, how in God's name could we, as colored people, Negroes – or whatever we call ourselves - turn around and discriminate against anyone else?"

Ellie's reply was cold. Unfeeling. "Easy. Ask me if I give a damn about discrimination against the Japanese. Did the Japanese care when they killed my baby? *Did* they? No! So, *fuck* them! *Somebody* is going to profit from this – so why shouldn't it be me and my partners? But, if none of you gentlemen are with me – then, so be it. I don't need you. I don't need anyone!"

Ellie purchased acres of Japanese-American owned property on her own; only to shrewdly turn right around and sell specific parcels of the highly desirable real estate back to the city of Los Angeles for a small fortune. It was a coup for both parties. The city didn't want the houses. It needed the land the houses sat on to expand its airport.

Sonny understood Ellie's motivation, but he made it clear that it was wrong. And, had she been herself, she never would have taken that avenue. "You're different, Ellie. You know I would never do or say anything to hurt you – but, you have changed since Evan died. I love you very much, but I can't honestly say that I like you right now."

They stood in their well-stocked and cozy library that evening. Ellie poured herself a scotch to go along with her cigarette. "Is that it?" she asked without blinking an eye.

"No, as a matter of fact. It's not. This isn't you, baby. You've changed. I know you've been to hell and back, but this cold and unfeeling person you seem to have become isn't you!"

"Says who? Maybe this was me all along and I was pretending before. Hmm?"

"Stop it, Ellie. I'm your husband. I love you. And, you still have a daughter; a lovely little girl getting ready to graduate from high school who needs her mother to be involved in her life. Her *mother* - not the money-making machine you've become."

"You know what, Sonny? I don't give a damn what you think of me. I love Dinah. She knows that. As for you, if you don't like what you think I've become, then leave! Can't stand the heat? Then, you know what they say - get out of the damn kitchen. Get the hell out! No one has a gun to your head to stay with me! *Least* of all me!"

Ellie slammed down her glass and turned to stomp out of the room. Sonny grabbed her by the arm.

"No, Ma'am. I am *not* leaving my own damn house. If you want to go, then you're welcome to camp out at any of your other properties. If not, there is enough room in this big-ass museum we call a house for ten families. But, I'll tell you what. I am more than happy to move my shit to another bedroom in *our* house until my wife decides to come back! Because I can't stand being around *this* version of you another goddamn minute!"

This time it was Sonny who slammed down his glass and stomped out of the room, sweeping right past Ellie.

Ellie took Dinah and stayed in the Bridal suite – the finest suite at the Southway – for a week. Dinah was able to invite her best pals for elaborate slumber parties in the suite on both the Friday and Saturday nights they stayed in the hotel. Music, boy talk, painting nails, styling hair and all the ice cream sundaes they could eat. To Dinah, living in the hotel was a special treat just for "the girls" – she and Mama. Even though she knew her mother was different after Evan's death; initially, she had no clue there was any kind of wedge between Mama and Sonny. She was just thrilled to have her mother's full attention.

Dinah's high school graduation was something less of a celebration than Evan's the year before. Even though she fully understood that the entire family – including herself – were still in mourning, that didn't make the teenager feel any better. This was her big event, so couldn't there be a little hoopla?

Instead of a full-blown soiree, Ellie hosted an intimate, elegant family dinner for Dinah in The Coursey Room. She sent for Sam, Marie, her brothers and sister and their families, as before. Like Evan's party, there were balloons and streamers and a band; but on a much smaller scale. And, despite best efforts by everyone, the atmosphere was devoid of joy. Ellie tried to explain to her daughter that things were simply different now.

"None of us asked for this, baby. I understand how you feel, Dinah. I do. But, I need for you to understand that even though we are all so very proud of you – and we *are* – the fact of the matter is that no one is in the mood for a big, noisy party. We haven't yet gotten over Evan being gone." Ellie reminded Dinah sadly.

"I know, Mama. And, I do understand. Remember, I lost Evan, too. He was my brother and I loved him. Losing him was like losing part of me! We did almost everything together. The year you were gone, we prayed together every single night. Grandpa let us stay in the same room because that way we could talk about you when one or both of us woke up during the night with bad dreams or missing you. And, that happened a lot, Mama. Mostly with me. I cried the most and Evan always made me feel better by talking about you and all the things we would do when you sent for us. Sometimes he would re-read your letters to me. I don't know how I would have made it without my brother. So, you see, Mama, I miss Evan just as much as you do. But, Mama – " Ellie stopped.

"Yes, baby. What is it?" Ellie was searching her daughter's eyes. Perhaps searching for herself in their mirror.

"Well, sometimes it seems like you have forgotten that I'm still here, Mama. And, I *am* still here." Dinah's beautiful face bespoke of pain and loss as the tears spilled and rolled down her cheeks. She finally uncorked feelings that she kept bottled up since she lost her brother.

"You weren't the only one who lost him, Mama. Evan was my best friend as well as my brother. When he died, it almost killed *me*, Mama. But, then, when you became different – it was almost like I'd lost you, too. Like both my brother and my mother had died."

Dinah's profound and honest outburst somehow seemed to release her mother from the semi-alive state she had been living in since

Evan's death. Ellie looked at Dinah, really *looked* at her as though she were *seeing* her daughter for the first time in a long time.

"Oh my God, my beautiful baby girl. I am so sorry. So very sorry. Can you please forgive me? I have been so selfish. My darling Dinah, I love you so very much. You know that, don't you?" With the fog finally lifted, Ellie tearfully opened her arms to Dinah. She rocked her daughter for a long time, kissing her and stroking her hair and telling Dinah over and over again how much she loved and cherished her. The others at the table - the rest of the family and Sonny – all looked on, smiling relieved smiles. They knew that they – and Ellie – were going to be okay.

To celebrate their one-year (plus two months) anniversary and to give Dinah the fabulous blow-out bash she deserved before she left for college, an extravagant joint celebration was planned. Ellie and Sonny decided to renew their vows. All three of them decided to host the vow-renewal-bon-voyage-to-college party in their own backyard. Unlike Ellie's old backyard – which was lovely – the yard in the back of home on Wellington Road home was more like a park. There wasn't a more gorgeous setting in all of Los Angeles. This time the tents were dressed up in swags and elaborate flower garlands of Dinah's favorite new color, Carolina blue. White twinkle lights were discreetly intertwined in the garlands. Ellie had ordered every luscious blue bloom she could find - Irises, Calla Lilies, Hydrangeas and Tulips. To complement all that color, hundreds of white roses were clustered with the blue flowers. The arrangements lavishly adorned the bandstand and every table in the yard. And, of course, brilliant blossoms blanketed the shimmering surface of the pool. Carolina blue and white were the proud colors of the college Dinah would be attending, Spelman. Dinah had been accepted by every college she applied to, but chose Spelman College, a prestigious historically black college for women in Atlanta. As Evan would never have the chance to make it to Atlanta for school, Dinah reasoned that she was going "for both of us."

ᴀ CHAPTER ᴀ
25
"Blessed Changes"

With lucrative real estate investments throughout Southern California, Ellie and Sonny and their descendants were set for life. The management company Sonny and Ellie formed, S&E Holdings, oversaw the day-to-day operations of all of their properties. Sonny was the CEO of S&E. Ellie served as President.

Because of the blessing of her financial successes, Ellie made sure that all of her little half-brothers and sisters were able to attend college and have spending money in their pockets to boot! None of her family wanted for anything. She also funded the education of her nieces and nephews. The children of Joe, Jake and Beth all opted to attend Lincoln University, the colored college in Jefferson City, Missouri. Nora's daughter, Little Callie, was now a senior in high school and had her heart set on college back East, preferably in New York.

ESA had evolved into a mass manufacturing company of upscale women's clothing, designed primarily now by a creative team handpicked by Ellie. Sans the salon. For a while, Ellie had continued to sketch the skeleton of every design; and, her team provided the meat on the bones. But now, the creative team all but ran the show. Ellie's personal creations were almost non-existent. She was more businesswoman than artist these days. When time permitted, she did sometimes allow herself to think back wistfully to the ESA heyday of exclusive salon shows; but times were rapidly and radically changing. Everything was faster, bigger and mass-produced, it seemed. Private, more personalized, self-contained shops weren't as popular as they once were.

Ellie especially missed Alberto, who had unexpectedly retired from MGM and amazed everyone by marrying and running off to the South of France with a very eccentric and very wealthy film star of yesteryear to live happily ever after in her castle. Developing cabin fever behind ancient castle walls, however, would not be a problem for the unusual but fabulously happy couple; as they spent a good part of each year cruising along the French Riviera on Geneviève Benoit's fully-staffed and fully-loaded yacht.

Among Alberto's and Geneviève's most frequent and welcome guests, Ellie and Sonny had enjoyed several weeks over the last few years sharing in Alberto's new glorious, decadent lifestyle. Shameless hedonistic luxury was the order of the day – and nights – as they would cruise up and down the Côte d'Azur; hitting the seaside resorts of Cannes, Antibes and Saint-Tropez. Occasionally, they would stay over in Monaco to party, gamble and mingle with the "beautiful people" from all over the world. The best part for Ellie and Sonny was that they were never turned away or treated differently from anyone else when they were in Europe.

It was during one of the foursome's fabulous evenings at Monaco's Le Grand Casino de Monte Carlo that Ellie came face to face with one of her lifelong heroes, Josephine Baker, who had successfully established herself as a world-famous entertainer. Now an official citizen of France after being stung one too many times by the venom of American racism and forced segregation, Josephine and her then-husband Jo Bouillon were on holiday, too.

The Bouillons and the Durans became fast friends. Ellie and Sonny often added trips to Castelnaud-Fayrac, France to their European Itinerary to stay with Josephine, Jo and their twelve adopted children at Les Milandes, their sprawling chateau. The children were happy, healthy and of many ethnicities and relations. Ellie loved Josie's nickname for her lively brood. Her Rainbow Tribe.

Life was good. Better than Ellie the Dreamer had ever imagined; except for the loss of her Evan, which stayed with her everyday – but no longer poisoned her spirit. Since Dinah's graduation from high school so many years before, Ellie only carried in her heart the love and beautiful memories her son had given to all of them; and the abiding love she had for him.

Dinah graduated from Spelman one week; then turned around and got married the very next week to a handsome and promising last-year medical student at Meharry Medical College. The back-to-back life changing events had provided something of a challenge for Dinah's party-planning-perfectionist mother; but Ellie, with her usual panache, pulled off both an extraordinarily festive graduation party, and the fairytale wedding of the season for her daughter. The couple had met when Dinah was a freshman and Jonathan was a senior at Morehouse. From that first exceptionally well-chaperoned mixer at Spelman, Dinah and Jonathan were practically inseparable. Their young romance managed to stay strong and mature as Jonathan went on to Meharry in Nashville. Dinah did not share her mother's legendary reluctance to settling down.

Now, Dr. Hamilton, a gifted cardiologist at Mt. Sinai Hospital in Beverly Hills, his wife Dinah and their 9 year-old daughter, Faith, lived just blocks from Dinah's parents. Ellie couldn't have been more delighted. And Faith – her bright, funny, effervescent, gorgeous granddaughter Faith - was the delicious icing on Ellie's cake. She and Sonny both doted on the little girl from the moment she made her appearance into the world.

Four years after Little Callie was born, Nora gave birth to twin boys, David and Donovan. They were now 13 year-old high school freshmen and loved ripping and running throughout Aunt Ellie's and Uncle Sonny's "museum." That's what the house on Wellington Road was now fondly referred to by everyone. The name stuck the night Sonny "put Ellie out," as they jokingly recalled whenever the story was retold.

Little Callie's young life was a whirlwind of activity between school, French club and drama club, preparing for college, and her busy social life thanks to Nora's membership in Jack and Jill of America. Jack and Jill was one of the relatively new national organizations created to cultivate and nurture children of the so-called Negro elite.

As Sonny and Ellie loved their "museum," and saw no reason to move, they opted to simply revamp the entire house. Some of the work was necessary maintenance after years of living – like new plumbing, electrical wiring, new paint and wallpaper throughout, driveway and roof replacement and pool re-surfacing. Then there were all the "fun" touches. The gourmet kitchen was brought up-to-date with the latest in modern 1950's appliances and cabinetry and imported glazed black granite for all the countertops. The tile was pulled up and replaced with hardwood cherry floors. The bathrooms were fitted with Swiss showers and bathtubs deep enough to swim in. Furnishings, carpets and artwork throughout their museum were hand-picked by both Ellie and Sonny from their travels around the world. Every piece was lovingly selected from showrooms, galleries, antique stores, charming hidden-away shops and garrets filled with treasures, and even from street vendors.

And, even though masterpieces by artistic geniuses from Romare Bearden to Jacob Lawrence to Pablo Picasso and Henri Matisse adorned the walls, the Duran home was always a place where children could run and play; and adults could comfortably relax. Part of that was because Ellie had created an atmosphere of warmth; despite the house's intimidating dimensions, expensive furnishings and accouterments. She had strategically hung her collection of priceless paintings in between equally priceless and elaborately-framed crayoned and finger-painted works of art by her children, her niece and nephews, and her granddaughter.

"I have eclectic taste," was her simple answer when asked about the unique exhibits.

Yes, the entire world was changing and Ellie was so happy to be alive and part of it. The most important change for her, for all of them, was the way Negroes were fighting for their rights. En masse. Across the country slowly but surely. Praise God. *It was about damn time*. Just two years before, the United States Supreme Court declared that racial separation in the country's public schools was unconstitutional. *Blessed change*. In theory, anyway. Then, that courageous woman down in Montgomery, Alabama refused to give her seat up for a white man on a crowded bus last December. Ellie had been scared to death for Mrs. Parks, but her heart leapt with joy and pride at her act of brave, common-sense defiance. That one act seemed to have inspired an entire movement! Folks down in Montgomery boycotted that bus company for a year and now Negroes all over the country were doing the same thing; sitting at lunch counters, picketing their banks, office buildings, department stores and employers. It was terrifying and dangerous; but wonderful.

The introduction of television a few years back had been a colossal change, too. What a miraculous invention. Who would have thought that one day people would be able to actually *watch* their programs in their own homes, in addition to listening to them? *Would wonders never cease?* Ellie had pondered to herself. She and Sonny purchased for their library a large television encased in a handsome console; and put smaller televisions in every bedroom and in the kitchen. Ellie was in love with "I Love Lucy!" On the other hand, even though she adored seeing Negroes on TV, she was less enchanted with "Amos and Andy."

And, as if planes zipping across the country and around the world weren't enough, man was even exploring the idea of poking around in outer space. Amazing. Her Evan would have loved it all, and would have been right in the thick of all of these wondrous advancements and developments. *If only Evan had lived,* Ellie would often sigh.

She mused to herself that Evan would have also been tickled that his mother was tooling around in a car he would have gone gaga over – a fire engine red Ford Thunderbird convertible sports coupe. Sonny liked a little more automobile around him and drove a big, white Cadillac convertible. Tangible symbols of the American dream realized in 1950's California. At least on the surface.

Through their joint business interests, their travel, Ellie's association with fashion and MGM, and her participation in civic and social organizations throughout Los Angeles, Ellie and Sonny had cultivated an eclectic coterie of friends.

Still a fun-loving and stunningly handsome couple at 49 and 51, the Durans both enjoyed cozy gatherings of friends. They never needed a special occasion for a good time. Even though the parties took place in an elegant, expensive setting; theirs were usually good ole' low-down house parties with plenty of conversation, music, dancing, food, laughter and libations.

On any given evening – like this particular late spring night - the guests might include Nat King and Maria Cole, Sidney and Juanita Poitier, Lena Horne and her husband, composer Lenny Hayton, Harry and Marguerite Belafonte, and James Baldwin; along with Nora, Mel, Rose, Roland, Dinah and her husband, and whomever else might drop by.

This night, the jazz on the stereo console turntable was hot; and so was the conversation. Miles Davis' trumpet achingly blared in the background, a soulful milieu for the tinkling of ice cubes in highball glasses, blended with serious group tête-à-tête.

And, because it was de rigueur, the air was thick with cigarette smoke.

Everyone was particularly interested in James Baldwin's perspective on the budding Civil Rights movement, as he was largely watching from the sidelines as an expatriate in Paris most of the time. "Well, I think living abroad truly gives one a clearer perspective on one's homeland. Even though the United States is quite possibly the most bigoted, segregationist, and elitist country in the world; it is simply a matter of time before America realizes that the American Negro really is an integral part of this country. And, when that happens – and mark my words, it *will* – then and only then will these United States truly become a nation; possibly a great one."

"Man, you talk just like a writer," Sonny joked good-naturedly. Everyone laughed, but Sonny was right. James spoke as eloquently as he wrote. And – what he said was true.

"Seriously, though," Harry Belafonte continued James' train of thought. "Nothing is going to happen until we get a president in the White House who will, at the very least, have the balls to enforce the Supreme Court's decision in Brown versus the Board of Education in Topeka. Hell, the Supreme Court ruled and white folks still don't want us in their schools! No offense, Lenny."

"None taken, man. You're right on point." Lenny responded, raising his glass in agreement to Harry.

Lena Horne agreed with Harry, too. "Yes you are, Harry. But, I'm keeping my eye on that young minister in Alabama, Martin King. I like his nonviolent resistance approach and I honestly believe it's going to catch on across the country. I really feel like that young man is going to make a difference for the Negro in America. He knows how to stir things up."

"You're right about that, Lena," Harry continued. "I've met him and there is truly something special about this fellow. Martin Luther

King, Jr. is his full name. I do believe he's the one we've been waiting for."

The wheels of Ellie's mind were turning as she listened thoughtfully to everyone during the discussion. "Well, I haven't yet met this young Rev. King, but I certainly look forward to it. I swear to God I can *feel* the change coming. All of us just have to make sure we do *our* part to help end racial discrimination and to actually promote economic power and self-sufficiency among Negroes."

Knowing his wife, Sonny turned to Ellie. "I recognize that tone, baby. You've got something in mind. Spill."

Just then, a pink pajama-clad Faith bounded down the stairs. Since her parents were spending the evening at Nana's and Grandpa Sonny's house, Faith came too, and was put to bed in her own pretty pink and white bedroom in the museum, decorated to her own specifications.

"Young lady, what are you doing out of bed?" her father gently scolded, already up from his seat to take her back upstairs and tuck her in. Again. But, Faith had already spotted him.

"Uncle Sidney!" she called excitedly, and ran into his arms. Sidney swooped her up off the floor.

"Gotcha," he laughed and kissed her on the cheek. "Hi, Sweetheart. Look at how tall you're getting! Would you do your Uncle Sidney a favor and stop growing so fast, please?"

Faith giggled. "Nope. Sorry, can't do that. I'm gonna be just like Mommy and Nana."

"Yes, indeed you are baby. God help us," Jonathan joked as he took her from Sidney. "Now, say goodnight to everyone and I'll take you back to bed, princess."

"Aw, Daddy. But, I can't go to sleep. I can *hear* all of you down here. Can't I stay? Just for a little while? Please?"

"It's Friday night, Jonathan. Come on. I'll take full responsibility if she's cranky in the morning," Ellie offered, winking at Faith conspiratorially. Jonathan and Dinah exchanged feigned looks of surrender.

"Ok. But, just a little while, young lady. Got it?" Dinah added.

"Yea!!! Thank you, Mommy. Thank you, Daddy!" Faith squealed, jumping up and down. She loved grown-up parties and she loved having her Nana on her side!

Ellie playfully crept to Faith's side and leaned down to whisper in her ear. "And, tomorrow, we'll pick up David and Donovan and see what we can get into. Whaddaya say?" Faith nodded enthusiastically, grinning from ear to ear.

"I heard that," Nora chimed in, but she couldn't help chuckling. Save for nearly 40 years having passed, Ellie was pretty much the same Ellie she had so adored when they were little girls back in Louisiana. Her confidante and wonderful partner in crime. *No, make that the leader*, she corrected herself.

❧ CHAPTER ❧
26
"Slow Grind"

The centuries old "There but for the Grace of God go I" was one of Ellie's and Sonny's favorite proverbial mantras to remind them of their blessings.

Even though the wheels of change for Negroes in America were slowly grinding; Sonny and Ellie knew that they and their friends were the exception, not the rule. They were living in the lap of luxury. Such was not the case for the vast majority of Negroes and other minorities in 1950's Los Angeles. Racism in LA might not have been as blatant as it was elsewhere in the country, but Los Angeles was nonetheless one of the most segregated cities in the United States.

Some of the resulting scars left behind from the disease of institutionalized racism were evident at the place where Sonny, Ellie, Dinah and Faith were now standing. Six years before, Ellie had sold her beloved Southway Hotel because the once-thriving jewel that was the Central Avenue corridor had lost its luster. Working and middle class Negroes converged on Los Angeles looking for jobs during World War II. And, the city-imposed racist housing covenants achieved exactly what they were designed to do: restrict Negroes to primarily owning and renting property only within that designated, boxed-in South Central Los Angeles area of Main-Slauson-Alameda-Washington and Watts. People were living on top of each other and employment opportunities were in short supply. Whites who previously lived in the corridor were either moving out and taking their businesses with them; or they terrorized black families with fire bombings, gunfire and even burning crosses on lawns. Negroes retaliated with so-called black mutual protection clubs. Sadly, those protection clubs eventually morphed into territorial, weapon-wielding gangs in some neighborhoods. Maintaining the previous integrity of the corridor and South Central Los Angeles was an uphill battle.

Sonny and Ellie were used to such battles. That's why Sonny

backed Ellie's plan 100% and was proud as punch of her for coming up with it.

He, Ellie, Dinah and Faith tread gingerly through a dense carpet of debris strewn all over the floor of a cavernous, boarded-up, long-vacant, three-story building in the heart of South Central. At Ellie's sensible urging, they had all dressed in overalls and work boots.

"Careful now," Sonny warned.

Ellie was in her element and was energized. "Can't you just see it now? Look around you. Just visualize it! ESA, Limited - reborn!" She had missed the fashion business so much since she all but abandoned it to run S&E Holdings with Sonny. But, now that her accomplished and talented daughter had agreed to take over the running of Ellie's part of that business for her, Ellie could concentrate on opening a new, fabulous store right here. She was determined to put her money where her mouth was and truly do something about "promoting economic power and self-sufficiency among Negroes." Ellie didn't have two nickels to rub together until she was 30 years old, so she understood the importance of economic power and self-sufficiency better than most.

The new ESA would be part of that effort.

Dinah put on her CPA and MBA hat. Those graduate degrees were earned at UCLA after she and Jonathan moved back to LA from Nashville. "Mama, no one could ever question your incredible business instincts. But, you brought me here because *you* trust my business knowledge and training. It is therefore my responsibility to tell you that in my professional estimation, an elegant women's clothing store might not do so well in this part of town. And, I urge you to think of the resources it's going to take to get this place fixed up; let alone getting the business up and running."

"Ah, but you're not seeing the whole picture, my darling," Ellie responded firmly but lovingly.

"Dinah, baby, you know you might as well save your breath. Your mother has made up her mind. And, I'm on board with it as well. Ellie and ESA South have the full backing and cooperation of S&E Holdings."

Ellie reached up and pecked Sonny on the cheek. "Thank you,

baby. You know, I just so wish that Alberto were here to join in the fun of starting something new and shaking things up a bit. I miss him so much. His energy, his flair. You know?"

"I know, sweetie." Sonny gave Ellie an understanding squeeze. Ellie was on a mission, so she bounced right back to the project at hand.

"Well, with or without Alberto, it's about damn time I get back to what I absolutely love! I want to be excited again about my work."

Dinah was genuinely puzzled. "You've made millions in real estate, Mama. You love the art of the deal. Wasn't all of that exciting for you? You travel the world and do everything you want to do! Isn't that fun? I mean, what more could anyone want?"

"Well, of course, honey. In spite of everything, I've had lots of fun. And, closing deals and making money *was* exciting – especially when you start out with nothing like I did. On a bus cross country to a strange place with $7.00 in my purse. Lord, have mercy!" Ellie had to laugh at herself at the memory. "I must have been out of my mind. Well, come to think of it, I guess I was!" They all chuckled with her on that one.

Ellie regained her composure and focused on both Dinah and Faith. "But, both of my baby girls, I believe that being able to do something that you really love that also happens to benefit other people in the process, is a gift! Always remember that. It's what I think keeps us alive. And, believe you me, I certainly have no intention of just counting my money and turning into some little old lady waiting to wither up and die."

"Don't worry, Mama. I hardly think you're in danger of ever turning into some little old lady. Withered up or otherwise," Dinah laughed.

"No, not my Nana," Faith agreed, totally in love with her grandmother.

"Probably not. But, think about this, my sweet Dinah. We've had this talk before. You've enjoyed a beautiful life. And, your brother did, too. Until he, well – until he was taken from us way too soon. Both of you deserved the best that life has to offer. It's what I wanted for you – and for me. That's why I sacrificed and lived an entire year without my babies and why I worked so hard. Do you know how incredibly lucky that makes us?"

"I know, Nana!" Faith rang out.

"I know you do, baby. So does your Mommy," Ellie smiled. She could hardly wait to bring her plan to fruition. "That's why we are going to give the women in South Central lovely, exclusive designs that will also be affordable. These garments will still be high quality, but will not carry outrageous price tags like the merchandise in the old Sunset store."

Dinah, Sonny and Faith had settled themselves on top of a couple of sturdy crates. Ellie walked around as she spoke, envisioning all the activity she described. "And, we can hire people from the area to work on the construction crew as well as in the shop. Wow," she paused, her mind turning and creative juices flowing. "When you think about it, we're talking about a considerable number of jobs because this store is also going to be the self-contained manufacturing center for all of the pieces we sell."

"Can I help, too, Nana?" Faith asked, getting caught up in her Grandmother's enthusiasm.

Ellie gave her a big hug and kiss. "You bet, my little love. You can be right by Nana's side every day after school and in the summers – *if* it's alright with your Mommy and Daddy, of course."

Dinah could only smile and shake her head. How could she possibly stop either of them? They were just alike! Dinah actually wished *she* were more like Ellie. Even though they might not always see eye to eye, she loved her mother's passion, drive and never-ending ability to dream for others, as well as herself.

Mama is right. This is a wonderful venture. Besides, Dinah reasoned, *maybe this would keep both of them out of trouble!*

"Evolution... Revolution"

For several years, ESA Limited South flourished in the
Watts section of South Central Los Angeles. Fortunately, Dinah had
underestimated the appreciation the women of South Central – as well
as women throughout other parts of the city as the word spread – would
have for fashionable clothes that were well-made, luxurious and expensive
looking, yet easily affordable. Affordable because Ellie didn't need or want
a huge mark-up on the garments; and her overhead was a lot less in Watts
than it was on Sunset Boulevard.

In addition to the satisfaction ESA South brought to its clientele,
Ellie created a plethora of jobs. After the massive construction job
was complete, there were sales clerks in the front of the shop and the
stockroom handlers in the back. Additionally, Ellie tapped local South
Central talent to actually make the clothes.

Instead of shipping the work out to a less costly sweatshop, ESA
South's entire second and third floors were transformed into design,
cutting and manufacturing areas. She had scouted all of the high schools
in the area to find the best and brightest seamstresses in home economic
classes. Ellie knew that many, if not most of those young people, were
not headed to college. The high school dropout rate in South Central was
disproportionately steep. Ellie hoped to provide for high school students
a skill and a way to make a decent living. For those who did plan to attend
college, ESA South was a great way to make money for school. She hoped
that the promise of a salary and flexible hours to accommodate class
schedules would be an incentive to both graduate from high school and
give college a shot.

High school art students who were seriously interested in fashion
design were encouraged by their teachers and counselors to submit their
creations to ESA. Ellie also contributed money to the schools to help
keep their art programs alive. And, she found a new joy - mentoring many
budding, young designers in the years she ran ESA South. All of them had

the satisfaction of seeing their creations come to life with the ESA label and were able to build their portfolios at the same time. As a welcome bonus, the fledgling designers were paid well for their talent. Some of the young artisans furthered their design education. Some were able to land positions at larger fashion houses in New York, Chicago and Miami after working for ESA. It was a win-win all the way around for both the community and Ellie.

True to her word, on most afternoons after school and on Saturdays, Faith happily assisted her grandmother and anyone else who needed an extra hand in the shop. From fifth grade all the way through high school, where she was now a junior. Faith loved the work and she loved the people she worked with. Their stories and gumption touched, fascinated and inspired her. So much so that Faith had a pretty good idea of what her career path was going to look like.

She and Nana became joyfully and totally ensconced in the fabric of the neighborhood where ESA South lived. They joined the Watts Business Owners Association. At Faith's insightful suggestion, Ellie purchased a boarded up eyesore at the end of the block and the weed-choked vacant lot next to it. She hired a professional demolition crew to raze the building. Then, over a couple of sweaty weekends, Faith, Ellie, Sonny and a small army of their new friends and colleagues cleared the now two vacant lots and planted a neighborhood victory garden that doubled as a park.

Creating and planting the garden was a sweaty labor of love and potluck fun. Everyone brought something different. Ellie and Sonny provided the grassy sod, orange and grapefruit saplings, lacy wrought iron park benches and planting tools. The volunteer partners brought seeds for collard and mustard greens, tomatoes, cabbage, carrots, radishes, turnips and onions. Music. A couple of grills. Hotdogs, hamburgers, chips and all the fixings. Coolers full of ice-cold beverages. Surrounding neighbors and business proprietors saw what was going on and joined in the good time. The labor of love evolved into an impromptu block party. Both weekends. And the end result was glorious, green and abundant. Faith took pictures and wrote all about it for the Neighborhood Business Association newsletter.

She now understood exactly what her grandmother meant when she said that *being able to do something that you really love that also happens to benefit other people in the process, is a gift*! Faith felt as though she was opening a wondrous new present every day.

Both Ellie and Sonny were also involved with the Los Angeles chapter of the NAACP. They provided financial support to countless NAACP legal efforts around the country and led phone and letter-writing campaigns. Faith accompanied her grandparents to most meetings. During the summer of 1961, she vigorously lobbied her parents and grandparents to join the "freedom riders," groups of student volunteers who spent the summer taking bus rides through the South testing new anti-segregation laws at bus and railroad stations. The students – both black and white - were frequently attacked by angry white mobs.

The answers of both her parents and grandparents were "no" and "hell no."

Now, two years later, the NAACP, along with the Student Christian Leadership Conference (SCLC), the Congress of Racial Equality (CORE) and the Student Nonviolent Coordinating Committee(SNCC), organized buses and trains full of people from all over the country to converge on Washington, DC for the March On Washington.

On August 28, 1963, black and white alike marched for Jobs and Freedom, led by the Rev. Dr. Martin Luther King, Jr. Faith was thrilled to join her grandparents for that monumental event; along with her parents, Aunt Nora and her family. Nora's boys, Donovan and David, had chosen Uncle Sonny's alma mater Howard University and had already arrived in Washington a few days earlier to start their junior year. Now 24 year-old Callie (she begged her family to drop the "Little" after high school) had graduated Cum Laude from Columbia University in New York, with a degree in English literature. She fell in love with the city and decided to stay, working happily as an elementary school teacher in Harlem. But, today, they were all together – physically, spiritually and emotionally – with legions of others.

With more than 250,000 participants – both black and white, it was the most magnificent display of humanity at its best that any of the people present had ever witnessed. Ellie and Sonny were moved that their friend Josephine – so passionate about integration and the belief that all men were truly brothers that she created it in her own family – had flown in from Paris and also spoke to the masses that day; the only woman to do so.

As Ellie's family stood captivated by the chill bumps-in-the-sweltering-heat power of Dr. King's "I Have A Dream" speech, they – along with every man, woman and child present that day - knew that life would never again be the same for any of them.

❧ CHAPTER ❧
28
"Faith"

Unlike her cousins, Faith decided to stay close to home for college. She already knew what she wanted to do with her life, so she didn't feel the tug that many young people experienced to explore their options as far *away* from home as they could get. Faith loved home and she loved the work she had been doing for the last nine years at ESA South and the Watts community. ESA South was her home away from home. The people who worked there were her extended family.

Most of the news stories coming out of the Watts area in the papers, on radio and TV were typical of white coverage of black communities – stabbings, shootings, miserably poor test scores, staggeringly high drop out rates, increasing poverty. The majority media never came into the area to witness the volunteers who mentored, tutored and encouraged – or the youngsters who excelled. There were never stories on the beauty of spirit that gave rise to the success stories that were all around. Hell, other than the faithful *Los Angeles Sentinel*, the black weekly newspaper, there had never been a story on their miraculous victory garden and park which was lovingly tended by an entire community to yield fresh fruit and vegetables every season; and which provided a lovely, safe place to just *be* and enjoy.

Faith wanted to tell those stories and so much more. So, she applied to and enrolled at Pepperdine University, where she would be a sophomore Journalism major in the Fall. She had it all planned out. Even though black reporters were fairly few and far between, the pressure was on, thanks to Dr. King and the momentum of the movement. She would intern at the *Los Angeles Times* and do such a fabulous job they would *have* to hire her. At least, that's the way she planned for it to work.

Then, there was Chris.

They had met at a civil rights rally on campus during the first semester of her freshman year. Chris Desjardins was a second-year law student, an *older man*. Faith was intrigued the minute she heard his impassioned call for more student involvement in the movement, no matter how dangerous it might be.

He urged his fellow students to give serious thought to getting up off their "cushy asses" to work on the side of what was right. To volunteer during their school breaks to help southern blacks register to vote. To work to overcome the "tyranny of racism and elitist entitlement that was embedded in the arrogant establishment in this country."

Faith was smitten.

She wasn't alone. As Chris stood on the riser, microphone in hand, he picked her right out of the crowd. Faith inherited the gift of height from her father, towering over her mother and grandmother since she was 15. A runner, she was lean and athletically built. Even though Faith was proud of being so much like her grandmother, and being around design and glamour most of her life gave her a keen appreciation of fashion; she preferred simple. No fuss. The fresh faced young beauty also eschewed make-up. Thankfully, she was also blessed with flawless deep amber skin and didn't need it. Faith usually just settled for a smear of berry lip-gloss, the best thing to come out of America's current infatuation with all things British as far as she was concerned. Except for Paul McCartney, maybe. Her tawny, curly hair was pulled back into a long, loose ponytail; with wispy ringlet escapees framing her face. Her big golden brown eyes rimmed with dense ebony lashes sparkled with light and life.

At the rally's completion, Chris gravitated through the mass of students, right to Faith.

"Hi, I'm Chris."

"I know. I was listening to you. I'm Faith."

"Faith," Chris repeated. "Wow. Beautiful. Strong. Faith. Would you think I was just handing you a lame pick-up line if I said that your name suits you?"

"Maybe," Faith smiled back at him.

"Wanna go for coffee?"

"Sure. Why not?"

Faith and Chris spent the next several hours talking and laughing at a coffeehouse not too far from campus. She found out that Chris planned to work as a member of the NAACP Legal Defense team after he graduated the next year. As a member of the Student Non-Violent Coordinating Committee, Chris had been a part of Freedom Summer. He and hundreds of other mostly white students from the North and West traveled to Mississippi that summer and helped form the Mississippi Freedom Democratic Party.

They risked their lives helping to register tens of thousands of black voters and taught civic classes to uneducated Mississippians.

"As you might have heard – although the news establishments are pretty selective in what they choose to report - we lost a lot of good people last summer. Southern whites didn't take too kindly to our presence. Probably half of us were arrested at some point when we weren't being beaten, shot at or stabbed."

"Oh my God. Were you?" Faith was both impressed and horrified.

"Which?"

"Any of them!"

He smiled. "I know what you meant. I was just trying to lighten things up a little. Yeah. I did spend a couple of days in some backwoods jail. And, I was shot in the shoulder while running for cover with a kid I swooped up who was right in the line of fire. Cowardly bastards. I think they would have shot him if I hadn't been able to get him out of the way. He was just a little kid. But, those Klan dickheads don't care. All they saw was that he wasn't white."

"You were shot, but you're fine?" Faith's voice was involuntarily growing higher with alarm.

"Sure. I'm tough. I got patched up and wore a sling for about six weeks. That was more than two months ago. I'm cool."

Yes, you are, Faith thought to herself, as she took another sip of her second cup of coffee. She admired this guy's moxie; his integrity and principles. Plus, he got bonus points for being really cute. Shaggy, almost-black hair; crystal blue eyes that were even more stunning because they were framed by the kind of long, black lashes that somehow seemed only to be given to boys. Long, lean body. *Thank God his nose is crooked or he might be perfect,* Faith quietly chuckled to herself.

"What's so funny?" Chris asked, watching the beautiful girl's face just as intently as he slowly sipped his java. It was getting cold, but Chris didn't care. He could have sworn that Faith's intelligence and very *soul* shined through her hypnotic, dancing brown eyes. *But, what color brown were they?* Hazel? Golden? He could stare into them all day and night. And that sexy mouth and perfect skin. He couldn't help wondering what she tasted like. But, her gorgeous eyes kept drawing him back. He wished he knew what she was thinking; what kind of heart she really had. He wished he were a *part* of her thoughts. He wondered if he could ever be a part of her heart. *Whew, shake it off man. You're getting way ahead of things,* he chided himself.

"Oh, nothing. Sorry. Got another question for you."

"Shoot. Oops. Now *I'm* sorry. Poor choice of words," Chris laughed this time.

"Why does a rich white boy like you care so much?"

"Whoa. You've got me pegged wrong, I'm afraid."

"What? You mean you're not white?" Faith smirked teasingly.

"No. You've got me there. But, I'm far from rich. The exact opposite, actually. My mother struggled to save money to send me here. And, I worked two jobs during the school years and summers to supplement. I've got some financial aid and loans, too. So, I'm going to be paying for my education for a long time."

"Oh. Ok. But, you could do anything. Instead of working as a civil rights lawyer, you could make a gazillion dollars probably working in some big white law firm. Right?"

"Yeah, I guess I could. But, working for some big firm doesn't appeal to me. I believe in what I'm doing. I believe that everyone should have the same rights. And, it makes me sick that human beings are hated, abused, oppressed and even killed because they just want to be treated like everyone else and enjoy the most basic of rights. Just because we don't all look the same. I mean, how stupid is that?"

"I admire your work, what you do, Chris. I do. But, you could be killed helping people register to vote in the South." Faith felt a lump in her throat as she was swept with a feeling of intense sorrow. "Like those three civil rights workers on the news. They were in Mississippi last summer the same time you were."

Chris nodded. "Yes, James Chaney, Andrew Goodman and Michael Schwerner. We met them. Great guys. Had the keystone cops down there handed us over to the Klan instead of just letting us go - well, yeah. Sure. But, there but for the Grace of God go I."

"What did you say?"

"There but for the Grace of God go I. It means - "

Faith playfully rolled her eyes. "I *know* what it means, for heaven's sake! It's just that my grandmother always says that. My Nana. She says it's her favorite saying because it reminds her that that everything good in our lives is because of the Grace of God. Especially when we escape something terrible that happens to someone else. It could always be us."

"And your grandmother is right. Look, I've done almost all the talking here. Going on and on about myself. I want to know all about you, Faith - . Wait. I don't even know your last name. "

"Hamilton."

"Faith Hamilton. So, are you from California?"

"Yes, as a matter of fact, I am. First generation Angelino."

"Cool. Where are your folks from?"

Ever the colorful storyteller, Faith shared her parents' background, which eventually went back to her Nana's difficult but providential journey on the bus from Oklahoma to California with all of $7.00 in her purse.

"Wow. Way to go, Grandma. Sounds like my kind of girl."

Faith smiled both on the outside and the inside. Somewhere in Faith's heart, a little voice was telling her that she was quickly developing feelings for this boy. Feelings that could grow into something *really big*. Chris got her back to her dorm before curfew that night. From that point on, they studied together in the library, frequented poetry readings, listened to jazz at smoky little holes in the wall in Venice Beach, and took long walks on the beaches there in Malibu. They also attended political rallies on other campuses.

On more Saturdays than Chris liked, Faith drove back to Watts to work at ESA and tend to the victory garden. Chris wanted to go along, and Faith wanted to include him. But, as hot as things seemed to be those days, it didn't seem like the smartest idea to bring her white boyfriend into the ghetto.

"So when are we going to meet this boy?" Dinah asked cheerfully one Sunday around the dinner table.

"Yeah baby," Ellie chimed in. "He sounds fabulous from everything you've told us. I like where the boy's head is at. We just want to see if he's as good as he sounds. See if he's really good enough for our Faith, that's all. Just don't be like your Mama and get joined at the hip before you've had a chance to check out the other fish in the sea."

"Mama!' Dinah protested. Faith just chuckled.

"Sweetheart," Sonny cocked an eyebrow. We're not going to have *that* discussion ever again, are we?"

Jonathan agreed with his mother-in-law. "Mom, I, for one know what you mean. God knows I'm not ready to even think about my baby girl getting hitched to none of these knuckleheads out here. And, Dinah baby," Jonathan turned to his wife, planting a wet one on her, "I would do it all again the exact same way for you. But, that was good for *us*, sugar. Back in the 40's. This is the 60's. And, I like what your Mama said." Jonathan broke into a really bad falsetto version of the Marvelettes' current hit. "Too many fish in the sea-ee. Too many fish in the sea."

"Oh Daddy, please!" Faith laughed. "You're hurting our ears."

"Don't like that one huh? Well how about this?" Her father proceeded to break out into James Brown's "Papa's Got A Brand New Bag" and pulled a muscle while failing miserably at mimicking Brown's famous spin and split moves.

Faith had wanted to introduce Chris to her family. She knew they would love him. *Great-Grandpa Sam was white, after all; so they would be okay with Chris,* she told herself. She dragged her feet because she was embarrassed. Her family had money. Her father was a successful cardiologist; her mother a high-powered CPA and her grandparents were rich. Faith had never had to struggle. *What would Chris think of her when he found out where she came from?*

She shared her trepidation with her mother and grandmother.

"Honey, Chris would be proud that you come from such strong stock," Ellie told her. "Remember, my mother – your great-Grandmother Callie - cleaned houses in New Orleans to help Papa make enough money to move us all to Oklahoma. When I first moved here I worked as a maid and worked in what was nothing more than a sewing sweatshop. Then I waited hand and foot on a spoiled rotten little white actress until I got my break in designing. That's not exactly being born with a silver spoon in my mouth. Both of your parents work. Ain't nobody around here sitting on their asses. We've worked for everything we have, so bring that boy on over here if you want him to meet your family. Because we certainly want to meet him."

They settled on a barbeque in the backyard of the "museum" instead of her parents' slightly more modest home. *Might as well get the worst over with*, Faith told herself. Besides, Nana had a knack for making people feel right at home.

"You didn't tell me your grandmother was white," Chris whispered after all the introductions were made.

"She's not," Faith whispered back. "Her father is, and she took after him."

"And, you didn't tell me your family was so rich."

"We're not. Only Nana and Grandpa are. And, I told you how she got here. Nana had balls. Still does, as a matter of fact." They both burst out laughing.

Jonathan and Sonny did the grilling themselves. Chris stood close by as the sous chef handed them utensils, seasonings, platters and whatever else they called for. Mel whipped up exotic drinks behind the elaborate new tiki bar. The women prepared all of the side dishes. It felt odd that there were no children left to play in the pool. At least, not until Faith and her cousins decided to reproduce. For now, all of the cousins, except Faith, lived on the East coast. Callie still taught school in Harlem and was engaged to a promising songwriter. Donovan and David had graduated from Howard undergrad the previous year, but were now pursuing graduate degrees there – David in the School of Law and Donovan in the School of Dentistry. When they got together, all the "kids" joked that any reproducing to be done was on Callie's shoulders. Callie always rolled her eyes and fussed at everyone to "stop rushing" her.

Well, at least Faith, the baby of the family, was still a teenager. That was almost like still having a youngun' around.

Everyone sat around the picnic table enjoying the feast. Chris fit right in to the conversation. Faith's family was as fascinated by Chris' experiences in Mississippi and throughout the South as Faith had been.

"Do I detect a bit of a Southern accent?" Nora asked.

"Heck. And here I thought I had completely lost it," Chris replied.

"Chris is from Louisiana," Faith interjected for him, tickled that everyone was having such a good time.

"Really, where in Louisiana? That's where Nora and I are from," Ellie's interest piqued.

"I thought you were from Oklahoma," Chris responded after swallowing a mouthful of potato salad.

"Well, we are. By way of Louisiana. After our Mama died back in 1919, Papa moved us all to Okmulgee, Oklahoma. Everyone except our older sister, Beth, who got married and moved to Texas," Ellie explained.

"1919? Damn, we're old, Ellie!" Nora blurted jokingly.

"Speak for yourself, Sister," Ellie shot back. She stood up to strike a mock glamour pose, then took a long sip from her champagne flute. Everyone cracked up.

After the group had regained its composure from their hollering belly laughs, Dinah managed to ask Chris a follow-up question. "So, where in Louisiana are you from, baby?"

Chris explained that he grew up in a miserable backwoods piece of swampland called Dupree, filled with miserable people. It sat between New Orleans and another tiny black and Creole parish called LeBeau. He shared that he mostly grew up ashamed of his name and his family. Not just because they were poor white trash. "And, we were. No point in sugar coating it," Chris stated flatly. Worse, his card-carrying Ku Klux Klan member paternal grandfather had done something despicably inhuman when he was a young man. He and one of his no-count fellow Klansmen. The grandfather boasted about the heinous act for years and passed it down to Chris' own father as an act to replicate. Chris' father was a second generation hatemonger, who tried to infuse Chris with the legacy of hatred as well.

Just before Chris was old enough to attend high school, he and his mother crept away in the middle of the night for points north and west. They ended up in St. Louis, staying in a rundown boarding house until they'd saved enough money to move to a small apartment near a decent school. To the best of his knowledge, his father never tried to contact them.

"Probably because I was such a disappointment to his Klan heritage. Thank God," Chris closed his story.

"Thank God is right. Chris, what exactly did your grandfather and his friend do?" Dinah wanted to know.

"It's too terrible to repeat," Chris hung his head.

"What did he do, Chris?" A knot was growing in the pit of Nora's stomach.

Chris retold the horrific tale as it was told to him of the night his grandfather, Crowbow Desjardins and his crony, Lizard stole a little Creole girl from a hidden place in a Cypress tree. A place that she thought she was safe.

"Oh, that poor little girl." A small sad wail escaped from Ellie as they listened to the vicious tale. Dinah, Jonathan, Mel and Faith could only shake their heads in disbelief, silent involuntary tears welling up and spilling over. Nora and Sonny exchanged pained glances. It was worse than they ever could have imagined. And, only the two of them knew the rest.

ᴪ CHAPTER ᴪ
29
"Up In Smoke"

August 11, 1965

The Fall semester would start in just a few weeks. This summer, Faith and Ellie had embarked upon a neighborhood redevelopment project in the area surrounding ESA South. There was still much to do before she went back to school, so Faith was spending as much time as possible at the Community Center she and her grandmother planned to open on the block, with the able assistance of their volunteer partners. The same people who lovingly tended the victory garden and kept the park pristine. The Center housed an after-school program, two classrooms for adult education, a small but well-stocked library, a community room where parties or meetings could be held and a well-stocked kitchen to provide nourishing, hot meals to whoever needed one. They built it in response to the steady decline of resources and hope in the area. The infestation of inner-city squalor had set in with full-force, complete with bad schools, high joblessness, poor housing and stubborn injustice.

The Center might have been viewed by some to be a small thing, but it was a step in the right direction and would open to much brouhaha on Friday. Faith had even wrangled a commitment from a reporter at KTLA to cover the event. *Where was Nana anyway?*

Chris had spent his summer with Dr. King, accompanying and assisting him at marches, speeches, meetings and lobbying in Washington for Congressional passage of the Voting Rights Act of 1965. He and Faith had been able to speak on the phone once a week since he'd left right after the last semester ended. Chris couldn't wait to see her face when he surprised her by showing up at the Grand Opening on Friday. Then, they'd have more than two weeks to spend together before classes resumed the day after Labor Day.

"Baby, wait and let me go on over there with you," Sonny had caught Ellie on the phone before she left for ESA. He and Dinah were wrapping up over at S&E Holdings. "It's getting late. You're going to run into traffic. So, just wait. I'll go with you. Afterwards, we can grab Faith and go someplace for a nice dinner."

"Thank you, Sweetie, but I'm already late. I had a ton of paperwork to handle here first. That's why I'm leaving so late. So, I've got to scoot. Faith and I have so much to finish before we open that Community Center on Friday. I'm so excited."

Sonny had to chuckle. He loved his wife's enthusiasm, even if she was eternally hardheaded. "Ok, Ellie. I know how you are when your mind is made up. You and Faith just get out of there before it gets dark, though. Will you at least do that for me?
I know you love it, but that damn neighborhood is getting worse and worse. They don't like white folks over there you know. Especially all our new "power to the people" brethren who aren't crazy about Dr. King's whole non-violent approach. And you, my love, still look like a white woman, even though you hate to admit it. A fine-ass white woman, I might add."

"Mmm-hmmm. Thank you, baby. But, you worry too much. Everyone over there knows me and knows *us*. We're part of the community. Gotta go. I love you. See you back at home in a few hours."

At 6:45 p.m. that evening, Carol Bailey, the manager of ESA South, locked the doors to the shop. Business was closed for the day. She headed two doors down to assist Ellie and Faith in putting some final touches on the Community Center. Carol admired how Ellie refused to settle for less than perfect. Tonight, they were painting cheerful and motivational murals on the walls of the after-school program rooms. She hoped the fans were working. It was still hot as hell out.

Not too far away, at the corner of 116th and Avalon, an erratic driver was pulled over by a traffic cop. Marquette Frye was wasted. Even though such an arrest by a white officer was a routine sight, a crowd started to form to watch this one. Marquette failed the sobriety tests, including walking a straight line and touching his nose. He was arrested, which really pissed off his mother, who was a passenger in the car; along with Marquette's brother, Ronald. Mrs. Frye began screaming. The group of onlookers rapidly grew from dozens to hundreds. Ronald got out of the car spewing his two cents worth and a full-blown argument ensued. The officer arrested all three family members. Someone in the crowd threw a rock at the officer. Then another, yelling about police treatment. It didn't take long for the building volcano of anger, frustration and racial tension to blow. All hell broke loose.

"Looking good, ladies." Ellie stepped back to admire their work.

"Yeah, the kids are going to love it," Faith joined her.
Carol jumped down from her perch to grab a look.

"Um-hum. We're geniuses. Wait. Shh. Listen." Carol squinted, cocking her head towards the front of the building.

"What's that racket? Sounds like glass breaking. Oh, shit! We've been lucky all these years. Hope no one has decided to rob us now." Ellie ran over to the window to peek out the drawn shades and investigate the noise.

"Oh, my God!" Ellie couldn't believe her eyes.

"*What*, Nana?" Faith and Carol flew to the window to take a look.

Throngs of people – angry people - had filled the street. Bedlam ensued. *Was everyone fucking possessed?* Ellie's mind screamed. All the storefront windows on the block were being smashed by flying bricks, chairs, baseball bats; anything people could get their hands on. There was a fire blazing at the end of the block. It was the victory garden. *Someone had set the trees on fire*! People were running with couches, lamps, televisions, radios, anything they could loot and carry.

"Call the police!" Ellie barked.

"Nana, *no*! You can't go out there!"

"I'll be damned if those bastards will destroy my store!" Ellie was out the door.

Dinah was home preparing a late dinner. Jonathan was on his way home from the hospital. She turned on the TV to keep her company.

The news anchor's account was booming and sensational. "Racial tension in the South Central Los Angeles neighborhood of Watts this evening exploded in an outburst of killing and destruction. The rioting is allegedly being perpetuated by angry, out-of-control Negro residents of the area." As if someone had just doused her with ice water, Dinah's head jerked up, panic taking control of her entire body. She picked up the phone with shaking hands and struggled to dial Sonny, barely able to get the words out about the news of the rioting.

"Sonny, oh my God! Those damn fools are rioting in Watts. Turn on the TV! For God's sake, Faith and Mama are over there working on that damn Community Center! We've got to call the police! We have to *go*, Sonny! Jonathan is on his way home and I won't be able to reach him. Oh, my God!" She was hysterical.

"I'm on my way. You make the call to the police, Dinah. Now! I'll be there in two minutes."

Ellie arrived just as rabid looters hurled the Molotov cocktail through the storefront window of her shop. It was too late. Brown plastic faces and appendages blown to pieces like bodies in a war zone, swirled through the air in a hellish blizzard of glass, metal and wood. The arms and legs landed at awkward angles, their fashionable mini-dresses and bell-bottomed hip huggers that Ellie had been so proud of, now just smoldering shards of fabric. A single head bounced off the charred broken glass of the display window, before landing on concrete, and rolling to just inches from Ellie's feet; its frozen painted smile still in place.

"What the hell are you *doing*?" she screamed frantically, lunging at the perpetrators. *Had everyone lost their damn minds?*

"Get that old white bitch!" one of the looters barked.

"Stop! Leave her alone!" Faith screamed, catching up to her grandmother. "Nana!" As Faith reached for Ellie, she was violently flung against a wall.

Hands grabbed Ellie, throwing her to the ground, where she was kicked, punched, beaten and spat on repeatedly by the manic mob of angry young black men.

"Nana! Get off her! She's my grandmother! Get off her, dammit!" Faith, mustering strength she didn't even know she had, was up and fiercely elbowing her way through the frenzy. She shoved the riotous attackers out of the way.

"Get the hell away from her! Nana!" Faith sobbed, kneeling on the ground next to Ellie. She gently lifted her grandmother's bleeding head into her lap. "I'm here, Nana. I'm here. Stay with me, please. Please, Nana. Oh, God!"

Ellie's assailants froze momentarily, puzzled looks colliding with the senseless rage on their faces; stupefied by the brown girl, this Negro girl, taking up for the old white woman.

Carol witnessed it all, horrified. She joined Faith and Ellie on the sidewalk. "I've called for an ambulance, Faith. And, the police are already here. Oh, Ellie. Ellie." Carol's stricken face was streaked with tears. As was Faith's, who jerked her face upwards, glaring at the perpetrators with piercing eyes that forced a smidgeon of reluctant shame.

Her words dripped with utter abhorrence. "She's *black*, you cowardly sons-of-bitches. She's as black as *you* are, you *fucking ungrateful, dumb-ass low-lifes!*"

Ellie's beautiful face was now grotesque – bruised, cut and distorted. She opened her eyes, wild and blazing; calling out in a little girl's voice for her "Papa" to please help her.

That's how Sonny and Dinah found them. They had abandoned the car blocks away. Sonny held Dinah's hand and used his size and strength to powerfully sprint through the melee.

"Oh, dear God in Heaven, Mama!" Dinah fell to her knees. Sonny knelt beside her and touched Ellie's face.

"We're here, Sweetheart. And, help is on the way. Help is on the way, my love." He couldn't stop the free-flow of tears, knowing how much pain Ellie must be in from the vicious, cruel beating she had suffered. Sonny looked around, almost blinded by his tears and seething anger. He was going to kill whoever did this to Ellie. At that moment he *didn't give a damn how down-trodden or beat-down these mothafuckers were. Ellie had devoted the last nine years of her life trying to make shit better for them. And, this is how they repaid her? Ignorant bastards.*

"Papa?" Ellie called again, appearing to look straight at Sonny. "Papa, please help me."

Sonny glanced over at Faith. She just shook her head sadly.

Dinah was holding on to both Faith and her mother, staring only at her mother's face.

There were shouts of "Burn baby, burn" in the air, which was now choking with smoke. The aggressors tried to scatter, but other neighbors and business owners caught the thugs and pinned their asses to the ground, getting their own licks in on Ellie's behalf. Police officers rushed the crowd, wielding clubs all around them and attempting to make arrests.

At last, EMTs were lifting Ellie onto a gurney. Sonny, Dinah and Faith all climbed into the back of the ambulance to ride to the hospital with her and escape the madness around them. Ellie, totally disoriented, continued to whimper for Papa before blacking out.

"Awakening"

"I don't *care* if he's been camped out in the waiting room for a day and a half. I don't want to see his ass. Now or *ever*!"

Faith was not backing down. She refused to leave her Nana's bedside. And, after what she'd learned, she refused to see Chris. Ever again.

When he heard the news of the Watts riots, as the news media was now calling the three days of death and destruction, Chris immediately flew from Washington to Los Angeles.

Ellie had pulled through the surgery that repaired her broken ribs, shattered arm and punctured spleen. A plastic surgeon had been called in to stitch the gashes in her face so that there would be minimal scarring. Told of Ellie's delirious rantings before she lost consciousness, the neurologist was concerned with possible brain damage, due to the blows to her head.

The family kept vigil around the clock. Even though Sam was now well into his eighties, he had flown out to LA as soon as Nora called him. Joe, Jake and Beth were there as well. The others took turns, but Faith would not leave the room. Nor would Sonny. Jonathan was now the head of cardiology at Mount Sinai, so he was able to secure the vacant bed in the room adjacent to Ellie's for Dinah. Sonny folded himself to nap on the not-quite-long-enough couch in Ellie's suite. Faith slept in the chair by Ellie's bed.

When Ellie had finally opened her eyes in her room some 36 hours after the surgery, she had murmured a barely audible, "I remember." The neurologist was called in immediately to examine her. Against the "two people in a room at one time" rules, Faith, Sonny, Nora and Dinah had all piled in the suite and stayed there.

Dr. Gupta shined a light in each of Ellie's eyes. "What do you remember, Ellie? Do you know where you are? Do you remember what happened to you?"

"I remember what those bastards did to me."

"Do you remember anything else?"

"I remember how they stole me from the secret place and tied me up and beat me. They tore my clothes and the new bloomers my Mama made for me. And they, and they - "

"She's still delirious," Dr. Gupta turned to Sonny. "She's talking out of her head."

"No, I'm afraid she's not," Sonny responded sadly.

"Dear God, after all these years, why does she have to remember now?" Nora intoned. "Hasn't my sister suffered enough?" she asked rhetorically.

"What? What is she remembering?" Dinah and Faith cried, themselves becoming hysterical as Ellie became more agitated. Restrained by her bandages, Ellie began to scream, flapping about in the bed as vivid memories of that terrible night slapped her in wave after wave, forcing her to re-live that terror of nearly 50 years before.

"Help her, dammit!" Sonny demanded, trying to hold Ellie still so she wouldn't hurt herself.

"It's alright, Mrs. Duran. You're going to be just fine," Dr. Gupta soothed as he took a hypodermic needle and medication from the nurse who had rushed into the room. He emptied the tranquilizer into Ellie's IV. "Yes, here we are. This will help you to relax."

Within moments, Ellie's breathing came easier and she was able to close her eyes in the artificially induced peace. Ever her sister's protector, Nora took charge and ushered both the doctor and the family out of the room. In the waiting area, she told them all . . . everything.

Later that night, Nora climbed in next to her sister on the cramped hospital bed. Faith was asleep in her designated chair. Sonny was folded up – exhausted - on the couch. Nora stroked Ellie's hair. Ellie, only half-asleep by then, opened her eyes and turned her head towards Nora. Her eyes were full of questions.

"Did I dream it?"

Nora shook her head, no.

"So, then, it's true?" she murmured.

"Yes," Nora whispered.

"How much do you know? How much *could* you know? You were just 10 years old – a baby - and you weren't there when they found me. I think I remember that. And, Papa crying. Carrying me." Ellie turned her head away from Nora as if staring blankly. But, her gaze was staring at the horrific movie playing in her head; her usually sparkling eyes dulled by sadness.

"I was at home when Papa, Uncle Paul and the boys came in with you. It was so scary, Ellie. You were just a baby, too. Just 12 years old." Nora choked back tears.

"Tell me."

"Oh, Ellie."

"Tell me, please. I remember what those sons of bitches did to me. And, I remember Papa's face, but the rest is so fuzzy."

Nora closed her eyes, unable to hold the deluge back any longer. She swallowed hard and continued.

"Well, Aunt Lucille and Aunt Agnes were there with me. I was so afraid we were going to lose you, Ellie. I-I thought you were dead. You were limp and black and blue all over. And covered with blood and - just filth and - ." Nora sobbed quietly, hoping not to wake Faith or Sonny. Then she sat up so she could see Ellie face-to-face.

Ellie's heart broke for her sister as well as herself. The women clutched each other's hands tightly.

"Oh, Ellie. They raped you and beat you so badly. I'm so sorry. So sorry that happened to you," Nora continued, the words tumbling out of her mouth more and more quickly. "Your beautiful face was almost unrecognizable. Joe and Jake ran to get the doctor. Then, Papa laid you in the bed so Aunt Lucille and Aunt Agnes could wash you. So gently. So carefully. I remember bowls and bowls of water on the night table beside the bed. I helped empty and refill them as the water blackened with dirt and blood. Lots of fresh white towels that became all bloody and filthy. We threw them away. Then, they changed the bedding again. By then, Dr. Kennard – I think was his name – Dr. Kennard was there and examined and bandaged you up.

When he was done, I got into the bed right next to you. It was my way, I guess, of soothing you or protecting you – I don't know, Ellie. I just know that I loved you so much and you were hurt and I could hardly stand the thought of it. Papa and Dr. Kennard closed the door behind them and talked in the hallway. I don't know why, but I crept out of the bed to listen at the door."

Ellie watched her sister lovingly as she spoke. Her precious Nora; her best friend. Always. As close as any sisters could be. Ellie hated to put her through this pain, but she had to know. "Do you remember what the doctor told Papa?" she asked softly.

Nora repeated what she'd heard through the keyhole, because the two men were speaking in hushed tones. Suddenly, her whole expression brightened. "Ellie, you produced miracles."

Ellie tilted her head on the pillow, a puzzled look on her face.

"One thing I remember Dr. Kennard saying is that there was a lot of bleeding, Ellie, from where those bastards raped and sodomized you. He told Papa that because of the internal trauma, he didn't know if you would ever be able to have children. But, you did, Ellie! You did! Dinah and Evan are miracles!"

"Yes, they are, aren't they? My babies. Oh, God, my Evan!"

"Shh-shhh. Don't cry, Sweetheart. Don't cry. It's alright. It's alright now. Evan is fine now. And, you know he is right here with you! You *know* that. He loved you so much. You were a wonderful mother to him and to Dinah. You still are. Look at the beautiful life you built for both of them. Hell, for all of us. It was all you, Ellie. No one could keep you down. Not those monsters back in LeBeau. Not your crazy, lowlife of an ex-husband. Not all the racist white folks in the world. Not those ignorant boys back in Watts. No one. You have created miracles all around you, sister. And, I love you so much. All of us do."

By Saturday morning, Ellie was able to sit up in bed without assistance. After she drifted back off to sleep, Nora went to stay in the room next to Ellie's with Dinah. Faith, who had spent the night sleeping in the chair next to Ellie's bed, woke up when her grandmother stirred.

"Nana?"

"Hi baby," Ellie responded weakly.

"Grandpa, Nana's awake," Faith called to Sonny, who had to take a moment to unfurl in order to get on his feet.

"Morning, Sweetheart. How are you feeling? Did you sleep well? Unh," Sonny groaned, arching his back for a quick stretch. "Sorry, baby. Just a little crook in my back. Slept wrong, I guess." He leaned over to kiss Ellie on the forehead.

"Thank you, my Darling. I'm pretty sure I slept a helluva lot better than you did. I love and adore you, Sonny Duran; and you, too, my Faith. I am so grateful to you both for staying in here with me. Thank you. But, I think I'm in the clear now, so I want both of you to sleep in your own beds tonight. Okay? And, no offense to either of you. But, both of ya'll sure do stink to high heaven."

"Honey, you're going to have to face Chris at some point," Ellie told Faith. Ellie was following the doctor's orders to rest. She was grateful their museum had enough bedrooms to comfortably accommodate all her company. It was wonderful to be so loved by her family. . . and to have been able to provide a happy ending for all of them. Thank God. But, she was worried about this one. Despondent, Faith lay on the bed next to Ellie to talk and watch their favorite soap opera, "The Guiding Light."

"But, Nana, I hate him for what his grandfather did to you."

"Did you hear yourself? Did you hear what you just said, Sweetheart? You said 'I hate him for what his *grandfather* did.' His insane, sub-human, racist monster *grandfather*, Faith. That horrible, terrible nightmare had nothing to do with Chris."

"I don't care. I still hate him."

"Faith, baby. You know who you sound like?" Faith shook her head, no.

"You sound like my Faith of maybe 12 or 15 years ago. My *little* baby, Faith. As much as it pains me to admit it, you're a young woman now, Darling. So, listen to me with that strong young woman's heart and brilliant mind. I should hate the monsters – note that I don't call them *men* because they *aren't* – I should hate them for what they did to me. Hell, I should hate Crowbow Desjardins for what he tried to do to that lovely young grandson of his. But, I don't think I do."

"Why not? And, how can you not?" Faith wanted to know.

"Well, I know I *would* have just a few years back. And, come to think of it, I believe I did hate their guts when the memories first came back to me last week. Last week. Nearly 50 years of oblivion until just last week." Ellie paused thoughtfully. She wanted to be honest with her granddaughter, but she wanted to make sure she chose exactly the right words.

"I don't know, baby. Maybe it's true that ignorance is bliss. Now that I know the truth, I am sick when I think about what they did to me. I feel so badly for that poor little girl. But, that was lifetimes ago and, somehow, I've got this peculiar feeling of detachment. Almost as though it happened to someone else. I certainly hate what happened - but, now, I think I'm stronger because of *everything* that has happened to me. I mean, I'm still here. It's as though everything, good and bad, has made me the woman that I am. And, you know what? I like her. A lot." Ellie patted Faith's hand lovingly. "Oh, don't look so puzzled, my Faith. It's really very simple. It's just like you young people talk and sing about these days. Love, all you need is love. As corny as that sounds, I do believe it is true. Hmmm?" Ellie took a long pause, adjusted the bedding around her; then sat up in the bed a little taller. "This must be what they mean when they talk about being older and wiser. You know I hate the 'older' part. Think I do appreciate it, though."

"But, what about those bastards who hurt you last week? And, destroyed our store, our garden and the community center? I'm pissed and I hate them, Nana. Don't you?"

"Language, sweetie," Ellie teased, smiling at her granddaughter. Then, she sucked in a deep breath and shook her head.

"Oh, honey. Those poor, sad, angry young men. As difficult as this might be for you to understand, my heart breaks for them. None of them ever had even a sliver of the love and advantages you've had. And, look where hatred got them. Jail sentences and a burned-out neighborhood. They killed it. True, it might have been on its way; but they finished the job. Now, there is nothing for them to go back to except worse conditions, more frustration and more ruined lives than before."

"But, what does any of this have to do with Chris?" Faith asked.

"Exactly. What *does* any of this have to do with Chris? Why are we talking about hate and Chris in the same breath? That boy didn't do anything wrong. In fact, partially because of his evil-ass grandpa, it seems that Chris has dedicated his life to doing the exact opposite. Doing *good*. My sweet, brilliant and beautiful granddaughter, if you're punishing him on my account, don't. Please. There has been enough punishment to go around, and God knows, he doesn't deserve any of it."

"But, Nana. You've *hated* white people. I know you have! Except for Great-Grandpa Sam, of course. Their sense of entitlement and superiority, the racism, the Jim Crow laws, the Klan, the decades of lynchings and destruction, segregation, the hatred just because they're white!"

Ellie looked at Faith with nothing but love. "Well, for one thing, Sweetheart, your Great-Grandfather isn't really white. At least, not in his soul. And, a person's soul and heart are all that ever count, my Faith. I was wrong before. I hated what white people did and *do* to me, my family, to all black people. But, I just got an ass-whipping from my own last week, now didn't I? So, what am I going to do? Have it in for the whole human race? Life is too short and too precious to be wasted on hate, Sweetheart. Growing up, my Mama – your Great-Grandmother Callie – used to always tell us 'two wrongs don't make a right.' Just because someone does us wrong doesn't mean we do them wrong back. Hate shouldn't beget hate. That's a lesson your Nana had to learn. Because we all know that I did more than my share of begetting. But, the wonderful thing about life is that we get to learn from our mistakes. We get to heal. And, we get to make different choices – if that is what we want. We get to choose. Hurt or healing. Love or hate. Misery or joy. Always our choice."

Ellie's combo smile of mischief and contemplative thought suddenly appeared; the smile which Faith loved best.

"*What*, Grandma? What are you cooking up?"

"Nothing, baby. I was just wondering why the good Lord didn't just make us all gray and be done with it."

Finally, a giggle from Faith. "Ewww. Gray. Well, that would be kinda boring, wouldn't it? Everyone all the same?"

"Mmm, maybe. Maybe not. Well, it didn't happen that way, now did it? Even if it had, folks would probably just get even more riled up over everything else that wasn't the same as them. Besides, I don't think a gray complexion would be a good look for you and me, Sweetie." Ellie and Faith shared a laugh and a hug.

There was a knock at the door. Sam and Nora poked their heads in. "Can we come in?"

"Sure. Join the party," Ellie invited.

"Faith, baby. You have a guest downstairs." Nora announced, well aware of Faith's refusal to speak to Chris. She threw her hands up in playful mock defense. "Don't kill the messenger. I'm just giving you the information to do with what you will."

Faith got up off the bed; kissed Nana, Aunt Nora and Great-Grandpa Sam, then checked herself in the mirror.

"Hey Sweetie," Ellie called out.

"Yes, Nana?"

"When you go downstairs, send Grandpa Sonny, your Mama, Daddy, uncles and aunties up here, too. Would you please?"

Faith grinned. "Sure, Nana."

"Oh, and Baby – first ask your Daddy if I'm allowed to partake of any grown-up libations yet?"

That was her Nana. "Got it, Nana!" Faith chuckled and bounced out the door.

"What was that about, daughter?" Sam asked, kissing Ellie before sitting on the side of the California king-sized bed.

"Oh, nothing, Papa," Ellie winked at Nora. "Just a little something between us women. New day, you know. Being the sixties and all. By the way. Have I told you recently how much I love you?" She took a deep cleansing breath as the rest of her family filed into the vast, beautifully appointed peaches and cream master bedroom. Ellie patted the bed for everyone to take a seat.

"Come on, people," she laughed at her family. "You're moving like you're old or something. I have an idea. Since I'm not that mobile yet, let's have a party right in here. Right now. We have a lot to celebrate. I've been rode hard, but not put away wet – so whadaya say?"

The End

Acknowledgments

You know how it takes a village to raise a child? Well, completing, "raising" this book took an *army* of loving and supportive family and friends scattered throughout many cities in many states. Throughout the good, the bad, the ups and the downs, they have unfailingly encouraged me, lifted me up and *put up with me*; even when I *know* I was no day at the beach. I am so very blessed to have such unconditional love. My cup truly runneth over. *Thank you.*

Thank you to my beautiful, brilliant and wonderful grown-up baby girl, Morgan Laura Banks-McKenzie, for always being your Mommy's number one cheerleader; even when you were a teenager 5 minutes ago. (*I'm not sure, but I'm thinking that might have been a violation of the official Teenager Handbook.*) You are my dream come true. Thank you to my beloved legal eagle brothers, Richard Banks and Vincent Banks for being my best guys throughout our entire lives (even when we were fighting). The two of you have lovingly kept me from drowning on more occasions than I can count, and have been in my corner no matter how crazy you thought your sister was. We lost our Daddy, VA Banks, many years before we lost our Mama. This is for you, too, Daddy, for being the best father that you could be. I love you. To my other precious "babies," my nieces and nephew – Austin Celeste Banks, Jessica Ruth Banks and Richard (RJ) Banks, Jr. – thank you for your constant joy, love and inspiration. And, thank you to our stepfather, "Ninja" – Bill Gillispie – for being part of the family and for giving my manuscript an early read.

My dear Aunt Oneida Johnson, this book is alive because of all of the fascinating stories you shared with me. Thank you for that amazing steel trip mind and memory of an elephant, even until you left us at age 93. To the elegant and learned Dr. Maceo Dailey and Sondra Banfield Dailey, the wondrous Sweet Earth Flying Press team, thank you for your brilliance, insight, guidance, friendship and for taking a chance on me. My dear writing mentor Brian Bird, you have been with me on this journey the longest. How can I thank you enough for your incredible generosity of talent, time and spirit over all these years since *Touched By An Angel?*

You are an angel. Thanks to you and my always sage college friend, Allison Davis, for nudging me into turning my movie dream of Bittersweet into a book first, along with my other longtime B.U. BFFs Flo McAfee and Alfre Woodard. My dear lifelong friend Chuck Hamilton has also been an unwavering angel on my shoulder from the beginning. Thank you so very much for lifting me up, supporting and encouraging me, along with every creative idea I have ever had – without question.

Thank you to my Aunts Agnes Cosey, Tekie (Bessie Marie, quiet as it's kept) Turner and Ann Delaney for filling in the blanks, and to all my other aunties and uncles (some by blood; all by heart) for always being there: Georgianna Broadus, (Uncle Big) Dave Cunningham, Rose and Ed Tripp and Grace and Charles Gamble. I could not possibly have provided as much of the historical accuracy without the help of my lovely Oklahoma cousins, Helen and Donald L. Hopings, Florice Thompson and James Cazenave, Jr. Thank you, cousins. To my "other mother" Etta McAfee, your beautiful, positive, joyful outlook on life has meant so much to me. Thank you for your ever-present love and encouragement during this journey... and always.

I cannot imagine where I would be on this exhilarating roller coaster ride without the fiercely constant love and support of my darling SisterCousins: Mercedes Lee Akounou, Linda DeYampert, Linda Fuller, Miriam Ha, Carol Johnson, Carol Broadus Moore, Nikki Moss, Eve Riley, Robin Stratton Rivera and Cheryl Broadus Staples.

To my precious SisterFriends whom I love and cherish so much, thank you for your unconditional love, friendship, inspiration and nurturing and for *always* being there to "lift a sista up," which has involved laughter, tears, listening, preaching, praying, fussing, adventures, misadventures, heartbreaks, triumphs, copious champagne consumption and every combination thereof. All with so much love. Please know that all of you helped birth this baby, no matter at which point you joined me on the journey: Marva Allen, Betty Banks, Sheron Chin Barnes, Patricia Boyd, Debbie Bragg, Lorita Brown, Marie Canada, Ruth Clark, Jennifer Coke, Bonda Lee Cunningham, Dellena Cunningham, Debbie Johnson Daniel, Sandy Epps, Gaynelle Evans, Thommie (*are you writing?*) Fillmore,

Barb Goldenhersh, Kimalica Guynes, Karen Hardwick, Pat Hercules, Rosalind Hodges, Camille Howard, Kia Jefferson, Susanne Kersey, Rita Kirkland, Lyah Beth LeFlore, Robin Lewis, Beverly Lewis-Rachal, Tammy (Hope) Lindsay, Linda Lockhart, Renee Kirkland Magazi, Del Mattioli, Charlene Mitchell, Edna Lee Moffitt, Denise Molini, Carylon Morris, Elaine Natale, Ayanna Najuma, Yolanda Parks, Geraldine Pearson, Denise Quarles, Tina Rahman, Rosemary Reed, Stacie Royster, Delores Silvera, Cathy Smentkowski, Larissa Steele, Diva Sister Rochelle Tilghman, Deborah Tang (in Heaven, but still with us), Alleather Touré, Monica "Wisdom" Tyson, Virlynn Atkinson White, Brenda Atkinson Willoughby, Kim Wilson and Grace Virtue.

How blessed am I to also have had such wonderful men in my life. I am sending buckets of love and gratitude to my "BrotherCousins," Stephan Broadus and (His Honor) David S. Cunningham, III. As with my girlfriends, my "brothers from another mother" have also listened, supported, prayed, loved, counseled (and occasionally provided free manual labor). Thank you dear Joseph Barnes, Warren Boyd, Clay Chavers, Dr. Julius K. Hunter, Duane (Smokey) Jackson, John D. Lindsay, Jr., Ed Maddox, Don McCann, Father Maurice Nutt and Anthony Rachal. I love you guys.

Thank you to my extended family: Mary, Michael, Monica and Susan McKenzie, for your help with our girl. As she has always been my number one priority – you have, in turn, helped me, too. Special thanks to my story's "first responders –" Herman Jimerson and Linda Leon. Thank you to D. A. Thigpen and Gayle Thigpen-Allen for their season. Thank you to the amazing Zane Strebor for giving me the *so* appreciated boost I needed when you said you loved my story. Lastly, but most importantly, Thank You to our Heavenly Father for... Everything. Love, Sheila

10670492

THE LORD OF THE LAST DAYS

ALSO BY HOMERO ARIDJIS

Novels:

**1492: The Life and Times of Juan Cabezón of
Castile**

Persephone

Poetry:

Blue Spaces

Exaltation of Light

THE LORD OF

THE LAST DAYS

Visions of the Year 1000

HOMERO ARIDJIS

TRANSLATED FROM THE SPANISH
BY BETTY FERBER

WILLIAM MORROW AND COMPANY, INC.
NEW YORK

PQ
7297
.A8365
S5813
1995

Copyright © 1994 by Homero Aridjis

English translation copyright © 1995 by Betty Ferber

Originally published in Spain by Edhasa and in Mexico by Alfaguara as *El señor de los últimos días, visiones del año mil*.

All rights reserved. No part of this book may be reproduced or utilized in any form or by any means, electronic or mechanical, including photocopying, recording, or by any information storage or retrieval sytem, without permission in writing from the Publisher. Inquiries should be addressed to Permissions Department, William Morrow and Company, Inc., 1350 Avenue of the Americas, New York, N.Y. 10019.

It is the policy of William Morrow and Company, Inc., and its imprints and affiliates, recognizing the importance of preserving what has been written, to print the books we publish on acid-free paper, and we exert our best efforts to that end.

Library of Congress Cataloging-in-Publication Data

Aridjis, Homero.
    [El señor de los últimos días. English]
    The Lord of the last days: visions of the year 1000 / Homero
Aridjis; translated from the Spanish by Betty Ferber.
    p. cm.
    Includes bibliographical references.
    ISBN 0-688-14342-3 (alk. paper)
    I. Ferber, Betty. II. Title.
PQ7297.A8365S5813 1995
863—dc20   95-1140
                                      CIP

Printed in the United States of America

First U.S. Edition

1 2 3 4 5 6 7 8 9 10

BOOK DESIGN BY BRIAN MULLIGAN

32012664

To Betty, Chloe and Eva Sophia

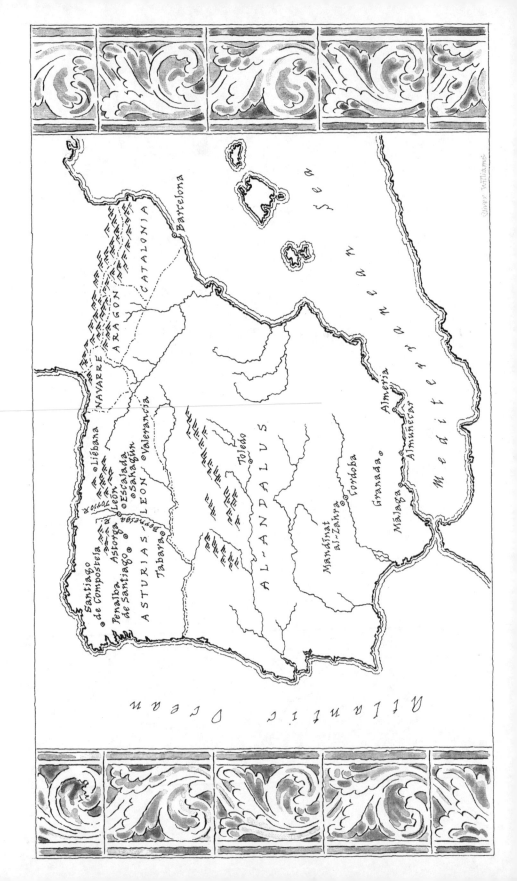

Mediterranean Sea

Atlantic Ocean

Mediterranean Sea

Barcelona

CATALONIA

ARAGON

NAVARRE

Liébana

Tower

Escalada

León

Astorga

Sahagún

Peñalba

Santiago de Santiago

Tábara

Santiago de Compostela

ASTURIAS LEON

Valerancia

AL-ANDALUS

Toledo

Madīnat al-Zahrā

Córdoba

Granada

Málaga

Almería

Almuñécar

Oliver Williams

And he laid hold on the dragon the old serpent, which is the devil and Satan, and bound him for a thousand years.

The Apocalypse, or Revelation of Saint John
the Theologian 20:2

His traces on earth will tell you his story as though you were witnessing it with your own eyes.

Ibn Idari, *Bayan* 11. Kamil on al-Mansur ibn Abi Amir

Facanos Deus Omnipotens tal serbitio fere ke denante ela sua face gaudioso segamus. Amen.

Glosses of St. Millán, tenth century, said to
be the first sentence in the Spanish language

I am the psalm lips utter, I am the tongue created by the Word to utter the psalms, I am the silence that follows the psalms.

Alfonso de León, *Visions of the Year 1000*

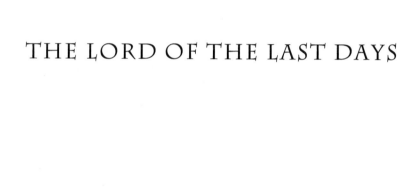

THE LORD OF THE LAST DAYS

VISION I

The year 1000 of the Incarnation of the Lord was dawning when my brothers set out on the roads of this world. The nocturnal shadows had not yet withdrawn from the ground, and they were already descending the promontory where the monastery was situated. With their mules laden with crucifixes, statues of enthroned Virgins, loaves of bread, cheeses, honey and water for the journey, they forded the swollen stream and took the first path they came upon on their left, eager to publish the signs of the Last Judgment throughout the villages of the kingdom.

Some of their number, fleeing before the terrors of the millennium, fell prey to unknown terrors in the lands of the Saracens and in the Murky Sea. No one knows what they found in that sea—darkness, monsters, storms or peopled islands. Propelled onward by the waves, they disappeared into the unbeheld.

Seven infants, who had been offered by their progenitors to the mon-

1

astery of San Juan el Teólogo in ritual oblation to God during the Offertory of the Mass, went with the monks, those ephemeral men who had passed through the so-called ages of Saint Isidore: *infantia, pueritia* and *adolescentia,* repudiating their temporal life.

The seven oblates who, years and months earlier, clutching an offering of bread and water in their hands, had been led to the altar by their parents to be presented as living sacrifices to Abbot Andrés, knew no other world than that of the monastery, being forever bound to the monastic community.

Martín Meñique, the hairy, pinched and pallid brother who would keep the four- and five-year-old oblates in his custody during the journey, was responsible for shielding their innocence. He himself had been an oblate. His father, Recafredo, and his mother, Liliosa, had donated him to the previous abbot when he had not yet turned seven. In the monastery he was the one in charge of examining the children whom the peasants wanted to give to Father Andrés, not for the love of God, but to be rid of them, for they were often blind, leprous or deformed.

At night, by the faint light of a candle, Martín Meñique patrolled the dormitory where the oblates were sleeping, and made sure that each lay in his own bed; he strictly forbade them to sleep together or to visit the latrines alone until they reached the age of discretion and could defend themselves against the Enemy. Every day, he allowed them to partake of four modest repasts, to play outdoors for one hour and to nap between Matins and Lauds. Scrawny, shy Faustino, who at the age of five already gave evidence of an old man's wisdom, was his inseparable companion.

The formidable Brother Anselmo disciplined the older boys, ordering them about as if they were his servants, beating them unmercifully and assigning them the harshest penances. The mere sight of him drove any thought of sin from the minds of the nearly fifteen-year-olds, and made them shrink from overly intimate physical contacts.

On that cold and rainy morning, the children set out on the roads silently and in crocodile file as they were wont to enter the refectory for meals. I, Alfonso de León, scribe and illuminator of the Apocalypse, remained behind, sprawled on the floor. Amid the bundle of sticks which monks call a bed, I found the thorns put there by Abbot Andrés to mortify my flesh.

Opening my eyes, I espied Jimena, who from the arched aperture in the tower was watching the clerics below scurrying in the rain. Ignorant of the plans of my colleagues in benediction, she wondered what she was seeing, but time made clear to her the reason for their departure.

My brothers went into the towns and countryside to preach the end of time, which, they affirmed with certainty, would occur in the year 1000, which was beginning. In obedience to Abbot Andrés's instructions, they made their own the words of Lord Christ, which Saint Eulogius reiterated in the *Memoriale Sanctorum:* "Go forth and teach all the nations: That which I say to you in the darkness, you must say in the light. That which I say into your ear, you must preach in the houses. I send you like lambs into the midst of wolves, but fear not those who would slay the body, for they cannot slay the soul."

"The wretched folk who congregate in the squares and marketplaces of the Spains must ready their souls for the Judgment of the Last Days," Don Froilán, bishop of León, astride his white horse and about to go to his estate adjoining the Bernesga River, declared to them on the second day following the Nativity of the Lord. "The coming of the Messiah is nigh. Let no one lead you into error, for first will come the Apostasy, and the man of iniquity, the son of perdition, will rebel and seat himself even in the temple of God, pretending to be God Himself."

"Contrary to the course of nature, women will love amongst themselves. Men, inflamed by love for each other, will surrender themselves to the turpitude of male to male, and the wages of their sin will be visited on their persons," Abbot Andrés said. "When this universal fornication comes to pass, boys and girls will be shocked in their souls and abused in their bodies."

"In the year lately come to a close, Otto III, crowned king of Germania at the age of three and Emperor of the World at sixteen, has aspired, as head of the Holy Roman Empire, to revive the glory of the ancient Romans by governing the world from Rome," Don Froilán stated.

"Gerbert of Aurillac, the son of most humble parents, was elected pope under the name of Sylvester II in the year 999, the year of triple nines, which add up to the number twenty-seven, which when again added makes nine," Sampiro, the royal notary, declared. "The pope of the year 1000 will bow to the Emperor of the World in matters religious as well as secular.''

"Henceforth you must prepare yourselves to receive your corporeal death. An angel has revealed to me in a vision that this will take place on a Sunday,'' Don Froilán announced before riding off toward a hill over which the bloody sun was setting.

"Do you see the skeleton beneath the skin?'' Abbot Andrés asked Sampiro.

"I certainly do, and I would rather be in heaven than in the clay,'' the royal notary replied.

"My sleep is already troubled by this procession of martyrs dressed in the purple of my monastery,'' said our spiritual father.

The morning my brothers set out to journey this earth thick with mountains and cravings, hatreds and rivers, I was immersed in a second sleep, in which all that happened was true, or so patently false that it did not seem fraudulent.

And then such a feverish and foreign confusion pervaded me that I came to believe the creatures bustling inside me were alive and walking about the cloister.

I dreamed that while I was drawing a *P* with a human shape, whose head and chest were the bowl of the letter, in the Apocalypse, or the Revelation of Saint John the Theologian, the Virgin's lips parted to say something to me about the date of the Day of Wrath, but the *P* turned into a *G* and then an *S,* and the secret names became blurry.

I can remember my soul's vague desire: "If I should die while I am laboring over the sacred miniature, let my remains be buried in the church, together with the volume I am illuminating.''

In my dream I drew letters with eyes, words that stared back at the person who was reading them, portents of fate that unveiled themselves to the man who was drawing them.

Abbot Andrés came to find me. He usually visited the dormitory at the hour of the morning twilight when dawn dampens the earth, when the monks have finished saying Matins and their bodies are resting before Lauds. To prevent acts of sodomy, he would walk through the dormitories and satisfy himself that each of us was in his own bed, eyes closed, and not leering sideways at his neighbor.

Neither he nor Martín Meñique appeared to see me. Either my body was lying stiff and dead on the cot, or it was gone. However it was, I saw them pass through the doorway, utter my name and depart, leaving me there behind. It all happened in the wink of an eye, and I felt no wish to wake up or to detain them. I remained mute, and I remained distant.

One by one, the monks filed by, peering into the dormitory. One by one, they crossed the threshold that separated the monastery from the century, flipping their hoods over their heads against the rain. All wore short broadswords beneath their habits, fearing to encounter al-Mansur's Saracen hordes, who were devastating the countryside, raiding monasteries, razing walls and temples, capturing clerics and oblates, ladies and abbesses.

I watched them moving off, hugging the poplars lining the bank of the Bernesga River, until they became black dots on the horizon. It was winter, the sky was cloudy, the sun hidden from sight; the earth was puddled and muddied from the rains.

Far away I could barely make out the adobe huts of the peasants of Santa María who, with their voluntary labor, fill the granaries of León's churches each year.

Not a trace of the monks remained in the distance. The sarcophagi outside the dormitory were brimming with water. They were narrow sarcophagi, hollowed out into the shape of a body with an indentation for the head and tapering toward the feet.

Then I went to the scriptorium, where the Apocalypse, the manuscript on which I have been working for a long time, is kept. I had in front of me the Commentary of Beatus of Liébana. The book, illuminated by Maius, was lent to our monastery by the monastery of San Miguel de Escalada.

Overwhelmed by the words of Saint John and the images of the painter, I went outside. From the portico, between the columns surmounted by horseshoe arches, I surveyed the valley and the river. Rain was falling on the pebbles, on the roof, on the poplars. Through the window to my right, I could see the rocks with their mossy hair, the patches of mud, the river running faster than it seemed to be at first glance. I felt the cold water pelting my hands, my face, my hair and my clothes.

Leery of the lightning bolts, which were splitting the sky, although there were no thunderclaps, I returned to the dormitory and lay down on Abbot Andrés's bed, a framework supported by joined planks resting on four flimsy legs. I slept, I know not if for seven hours or seven days.

My soul awoke confused and trembling. Fear of darkness had over-shadowed my childhood. And fear of being eaten by one of the women in the harem, who seemed to devour everything with their eyes and with their mouths, and fear of being castrated in the dark, like one of those eunuchs from remote lands brought by the Saracens to al-Andalus. The night was so dense that even when I held my hand before my eyes, my body remained invisible.

I hastily lit the bronze sconce, which was chained to the wall, to see myself, to find myself. One after another the candles, thrust by threes into the clay arms like trinities of light, cast a triple shadow—mine—on the wall and the floor.

So goaded was I by hunger, so thirsty that I hurried to the kitchen, Doña Miguel's territory, in search of food. There I ate my fill of some cheeses she had left at the mercy of mice and worms. And, lest a gust of wind plunge me again into darkness, I stopped the chinks in the door with bits of twigs and rags.

At Matins I climbed the stone tower to observe in the upper reaches of the air the *stella crinita,* that comet which, according to the ancients, had coalesced into a round mass from the warm effluvia of the earth and the breath of the planets and the sun. They had dubbed this raveled matter "hair," but it more closely resembled a smoking star whose long tail shed light on the gloomy regions of the world. Sometimes the tail took on the shape of a curved scimitar; other times, a woman's thick tresses. The luminous globe, glowing in the mysterious sidereal darkness, remained visible for a while.

The timorous claimed it heralded the following calamities: the death by poisoned arrow of the child king Alfonso V; the birth in Córdoba of a caliph even more cruel than his predecessors, who would slaughter Christians; the renewed devastation of León and Santiago at the hands of the

Saracens; a terrible earthquake, itself a sign of the Second Coming of Lord Christ.

The early hours of the morning were cold, though not so cold as the walls of the crypt where Abbot Andrés was wont to lie on freezing nights until sunup, or as the sarcophagi outside the dormitory, where I hoped never to lie.

With my eyes fastened on the stars, which the ancient sages say are stationary, I endeavored to discern their size, height and girth, their composition, ordering and movement, and to understand the wanderings of the days and nights and ascertain the hours and times, but I discerned little, and gave up.

A few days before departing, Abbot Andrés had confided to me that in the year 955, prior to the dethroning of Don Sancho the Fat, who was unable to reach his head with his hand, or to put on his crown himself, or to wield his sword unaided, the igneous features of a fiery face had been seen. And so, in expectation of new revelations, I awaited the appearance of the hairy star. The cawing of invisible crows surrounded me in my vigil.

Standing in the arch-shaped opening in the tower, alone with the firmament and my own grandeur, I recalled that on the last day of the year a living botch of nature, with two heads, four legs, and both a woman's and a man's parts between each pair of legs, had been abandoned at the monastery gates. Abbot Sabarico had hurried to show the prodigy to Doña Elvira, Alfonso V's mother, but the monster vanished with a squeal before the widowed queen's very eyes.

I thought back: On the fifteenth day of December in the year just concluded, a creature of some fourteen years, a native of Toledo, whose face and chest were as furry as the most heavily bearded man's, was brought to León by her parents. She went by the name of Dominga, and her progenitors claimed that she was born hairy and with a horn on her palate, through which she spoke in unknown tongues.

"We have bid all clerics to abstain from braggery and drunkenness and to shun the company of minstrels and forbear from entering taverns, unless there be need or urgency, to keep them from hatching children of this sort into the world," Bishop Froilán declared to the little man from Toledo, who was the creature's father.

There came a hush. The comet appeared, blazing in the depths of the bluish sky. Enthralled, I gazed intently at its long, long tail, similar to a dragon's. Suddenly a hateful face congealed in that ball of ice and frozen dust, a face with flaming eyes, donkey ears, the body of a reptile and iron teeth in its belly.

It was the ancient Adversary. I fell to my knees in a murky puddle, perhaps of water, perhaps of ashes, for I spattered black drops in the chill air. My eyes shut tight, my arms open wide, I stammered a prayer, hoping that the face would be gone when I finished. But when I opened my eyes, the comet streaked across space like a raging beast.

"This must be the Red Dragon, the Ancient Serpent, the incarnation of evil," I said to myself. "Antichrist has already been born, in Córdoba. His mother is a fornicating nun, his father, a Moor drunk on Christian blood. At the instant of conception, of the abominable coupling, the devil slithered into the whore's belly to ensure the offspring would be the personification of the Evil One. The apostle warned us that he who was born in Corozaim would be raised in Bethsaida and would rule in Capharnaum, that all three cities would pride themselves in his person, and that after their elevation to heaven, they would descend together into hell."

My head filled with the buzzing of wasps and the hissing of snakes: "Zacharias, Zebedee, Zamzummims, Zenagas. Zas. Zas."

I spoke, addressing the world:

"I, a man of the last days, have the mission of finding the devil's son and striking him dead before he can grow up, take arms and propagate his errors throughout the earth. For under the rule of the Iniquitous One, the saints and the righteous will be persecuted, the animals will be exterminated, the trees cut down in the forests, the mountains disfigured, the lakes and rivers awash with poisons, the cities fouled, and nature will begin to die. Six hundred and sixty-six legions of demons, each attended by six thousand six hundred and sixty-six servants and commanded by sixty-six princes of evil, will endeavor to annihilate the earthly paradise. Only the Immaculate Virgin Mother, who is the fountain of grace, can save us from the final death."

At the summit of the tower, my shadow detached itself from the uniform darkness. The long hair that covered my monkish tonsure seemed to fan out over the ground. Huge eyes gleamed above the roof of the church, owls hooted in the poplars.

"Not far from here, a blessed woman will conceive the seed of the Lord of the Last Days and give birth to the anointed one, who will confront Antichrist and defeat him," I exclaimed. "Once the Messiah has slain the son of perdition, the millenary kingdom, which lasts for one of God's days, will be established, and filled with the word of life, the righteous will shine in the firmament. Thus saith the apostle."

I looked at the lurid comet. The owls flew by unseen. The wind blew. I continued:

"Somewhere there is a worshiper of Satan who has remarked this secret sign, and henceforth he will not relent in his search for the woman who shall conceive the Child of God, to kill it."

Then, for some reason, I suddenly thought about Córdoba, the capital of the caliphate, and what happens there in the month of January, *Yanayr* for the Muslims. I pictured the Guadalquivir with the mist rising from its lukewarm waters, the hawks building their nests, the cows calving, the men driving in stakes to prop up the olive and pomegranate trees. I pictured the early narcissi blooming.

Once it became light, I went down to sing psalms of praise for the Circumcision of Jesus. At the foot of the stairway I stumbled over a soft body, and my hands brushed a bristly snout, an animal profile.

It was the guard dog, which Abbot Andrés kept to discourage beggars and lepers from approaching him for alms, especially those unfortunates whose gums were eaten away, who disgusted him most. The bitch was a few weeks away from whelping. Someone had stabbed her with a knife.

Darkness turned blue, the celestial vault brightened over the fields. Within and without the ancient walls of León, silhouettes loomed up: the monasteries of San Lucas, San Marcelo, San Adrián, El Salvador and Santiago, the church of Santa María de Regla and the Square Tower. The millenary morning was much like any other, except for the bloody rays furrowing the sky from west to east.

Today the year 1000 began.

VISION II

"Eye, hand, foot, house, horse." A man was teaching his son words in the new Spanish, as both sat beside the beggar's gate on the ground outside the monastery. "Knife, dove, chest."

As the boy, about four years old, remained silent, the man added,

Heare are beastes in this howse,
Heare cattes make yt crousse,
Heare a rotten, heare a mousse,
That standeth nighe togeither.

The air was still. When the rain stopped, the afternoon had briefly turned golden. After Vespers, a treacherous and chilly blue mantled the harsh Leonese landscape. It was the month of February, the feast of the Purification of Holy Mary, and the sisters Casta and Larga had donated an

10

estate in Valdesabugo, between the Torio and Porma rivers, to the monastery of Santiago after Abbot Andrés's efforts to persuade them to donate it to us had failed.

"The vixen barked, the snake hissed, the pig grunted, the crow cawed, but no one answered," said the man, whose red tunic hung to his knees. He wore neither cloak nor hose.

A stone's throw from them, a horse whinnied as it galloped by unseen. Fearful lest a Saracen be lurking nearby, I began to cast my eyes over the cemetery. There were no Moors. I did see a man of my own size and stamp striding swiftly across the sodden fields. As I studied him I had the feeling that he was I, or if not myself, someone very similar. But what was I doing out there, with no idea of where I was going or coming from or what my name was? The creature slipped among the poplars.

Along came a plump woman, not over thirty, somewhat on the homely side but quite sprightly, fancifully dressed in rusty, threadbare garments. In her hands she held a clump of twigs and grasses, which she had gathered among the graves. The shirt-clad boy sought her arms. She did not offer them; he was too big to be carried.

I was standing behind one of the cloister walls, spying on them through a chink in the stones. In my hiding place a spider was spinning its web to catch a fly. No sooner was the trap laid than the fly fell in. But a gust from my mouth blew away web, spider and fly.

"There are all manner of flies," the man was explaining to the boy as one of these insects lit on his hand. "Some shit on meat, others worm into cheese, others sting your tongue, others fidget in your hair, others buzz in your ears."

"And what do you feed on?" the woman asked him.

"The fat fish of dreams," he replied.

"I invite you to my inn, and you'll dine on cheese," she said.

"Remember those rich men who were eating and throwing bread crumbs to those who were standing around the table, looking on," he murmured.

"To us." She nodded.

"Oro María," the man said to her, "come to breakfast, all my imagination is yours." He held out an imaginary plate.

"Meals of air are tasty," she agreed.

"A minstrel is always wretched and wanting, always infamous, always famishing," he declared, raising his tunic to his waist, where a dagger hung, to amuse the boy.

"The minstrel, who is neither cheat nor cripple, cleric nor vagabond, though lacking and luckless, gladdens the humble folk in the towns and countryside," she said, tickled that her son was mimicking all her movements.

"Gómez plays the drum and dances; he'll be a minstrel like his father," the man affirmed. "He won't be a sharper or a sot or a braggart."

"Could he but talk, he'd be a jester and singer of songs in the new tongue that is aborning; he'd go from castle to castle, to markets and public squares, rejoicing the plain people," said she who was called Oro María.

"The crow is careful not to caw, for with his warbling Sancho Saborejo gives more joy than any other minstrel," the man cried in celebration of himself.

"Oro María, the strolling woman, earns her keep with her daily wage. Even when asleep, her feet are always twitching; she dreams she's dancing and drumming in the marketplace," the woman added.

"Dancing at the minstrel's side, she sways her shoulders and hips," Sancho Saborejo observed.

"Come Wednesday, fourth weekday, we're off to the market in León to peddle song and dance for cheese and meat," she announced.

" 'Hapless whore, vile jade, fit to be whipped in the square by the hangman,' you heard how Don Gimeno, bishop of Astorga, railed at you," Sancho exclaimed.

"He, who is so bountiful he gave a greyhound, a hawk and a costly spaniel to King Vermudo, and to his wife, Doña Elvira, Islamic carpets and brocades and a horned diadem to adorn her brow, was base to me," she recalled.

"A tedious minstrel is reviled in the person of his wife," he acknowledged.

"I'll tell you a tale that's going around." Oro María jumped up.

Sancho Saborejo took Gómez by the arm. "Once the crow stole a son from a dove. And the dove went to the crow's nest and begged him for

her son back. And the crow said, 'I will give you your son if you can sing.'
And the dove began to sing.''

The minstrel imitated the dove. Oro María enjoyed it more than the
boy, who was unable to laugh.

The bells clanged. Doña Miguel rang the small bronze hemispheres by
hand, and the faithful, who could hear them at some distance, were thus
notified of the death of a monk, or summoned to the divine offices and
the prayers appropriate to day or night. Decades earlier, Count Fernán
González had presented the bells to the monastery of San Juan el Teólogo,
knowing that the Saracens detested their sound.

I left my hiding place near the horseshoe-shaped door, which was usually
guarded by Brother Anselmo. Through that door, which no oblate or monk
was allowed to cross without the abbot's permission, came the things
needed to provision the monastery.

I confronted the intruders, who had camped outside the church since
the night before. They had pitched a tent, planting its poles in the mud.
Beside them lay their belongings: an empty wicker basket and a pouch
holding pointed utensils.

"Is this the road to Santiago?'' the man called Sancho asked.

"Yes.''

"We are looking for an inn, to spend the night,'' she murmured.

"In León you will find the bishop's inn.''

"Our horses died on us in the mountains from exhaustion, and in a
wood, thieves who murder travelers for their purses robbed us. We are
hungry and in need of shelter,'' Sancho said frankly.

"Why are you going to Santiago?'' I asked.

"To see the relics of our lord the apostle.''

"Why were you teaching an infant who cannot speak words in the new
vernacular?''

"So he may know the names of things which are inside and outside
him.''

"What are you doing in the monastery, you pair of devils playing at
minstrels?'' I demanded.

"Master, upon my life, we have come from the limits of Sahagún, and
here we lost our way. We have not stopped walking since the feast of the

Conversion of Saint Paul. We go from castle to castle, from place to place, singing of ancient deeds in the newborn tongue. We give delight to the downtrodden, mirth to the motherless and solace to wronged widows.''

"You seem a bad minstrel, shrill and shouting, one of those who visit virgins and widows in the house of bawds.''

"*Domine,* pastor, in Córdoba my enemies the Muslims seized me; they put me in prison though I was blameless. In Oviedo, for mocking the heavens, I was marked with this contortion in my face. My star paled in Toledo when the city was taken. I am an historical man, I have suffered centuries.''

"What do you have in your pouch?''

"Live rocks: the rock that sucks blood, the rock that hinders sleep, the rock that shuns milk and the rock found in the swallow's stomach. Would you like to see them?''

"What I've heard is enough.''

"A monk should have recourse to a minstrel on occasion, to comfort him in his sorrows and cares,'' he countered. "Charity begins at the gate. Where is your porter? When does the foot-washing begin?''

"I don't wash feet, I wash out sinners' mouths.''

"The body makes us sin in five ways. I sin in all of them, although more by seeing and hearing than by touching, smelling and tasting.'' Sancho Saborejo skipped to and fro.

"Here you will make such penance as the law ordains. Doña Miguel, who is churchwarden of the parish, will give you what you require,'' I said.

"We are poverty-stricken minstrels; we have naught to pay you the price of hospitality. As the Hebrew says: We are the century's guests and pilgrims; give us aught to eat so we do not die of hunger.''

"The proverb goes: A whore and a minstrel have a hapless dotage, their season is past and they are cast off. I would think the mishap must strike them on a lean night.''

"Master, don't preach overmuch to us needy folk, for the raven of hunger is eating at our vitals. Down by the stream we saw a cleric pushing along an enormous appetite, far too big to carry, in a two-wheeled barrow;

we offered to help him with his victuals, but he defended them with a lance."

"This belly makes me look like a crumpled wall, and I'm not even pregnant from the Holy Ghost," said Oro María.

"The belly, in man as in brute beasts: amen," and I made the sign of the cross in jest.

"Almanzor and his Muslims have laid waste to the fields of the poor, they have stolen wine and kine. Winter has come, and in mountains and meadows there are no grains or grazing," Sancho Saborejo complained.

"When dogs find a dead beast they feed on it, while ravens and crows circle above, waiting for the dogs to be gone. Once the dogs are sated, the birds pick the bones. And thus do kings and cardinals raven on the flesh of vassals and peasants, as if they were dumb beasts. And when they are sated, chaplains and squires come to gnaw on the bones. This example is going round," said Oro María.

"You, Sancho Saborejo, and you, Oro María, his wife, will remain here. For the labors you will perform on my estate, I will lend you twelve solidi to hire a yoke of oxen for one year, so that you can till the fields properly. Husband and wife must inhabit the house and the land with their bodies and remain there as faithful and obedient vassals," I explained to them. "It is your obligation to furnish me with kids, pigs and fowl, spun linen and hemp; to sweep the threshing floor, to mind the oxen, to dig and delve, to prune and mow in accordance with the custom of the kingdom."

"Anything else, *domine?*" Sancho asked.

"It is ordained that no one may chop or cut so much as a single branch from the mountain that belongs to the monastery, else he will be clapped in jail."

"*Domine, ego,* Sancho Saborejo, and Doña Oro María will thatch the roof; we will layer sticks and stones on the walls to keep the rain from soaking in; and we will sow the earth," the minstrel promised.

"Leave the gleaning to lesser women, for I am a lady minstrel, not a peasant, and my son is of tender years. We are not made to earn day wages in the sodden fields," Oro María protested.

"No need to be wayward and aloof," I replied. "If she does not want the wage, the lady minstrel may depart whenever she pleases.''

"Doña Velasquita *regina,* may God keep her, is my protectress,'' Oro María declared. ''I met her when she and Don Vermudo granted certain properties to the monastery of San Andrés de Pardomino.''

"Doña Velasquita went to live in Oviedo with her daughter Cristina after she was repudiated by Don Vermudo ibn Ordoño.'' I quickly silenced her. ''Then he married Doña Elvira García, the granddaughter of Fernán González.''

"They were first cousins, or nephew and aunt, and their love waned,'' Sancho Saborejo remarked. ''Because of that incestuous union, Almanzor wasted our lands and took the Christians captive.''

"Was not Velasquita the woman Don Vermudo the Gouty delivered to Almanzor to pacify his lust for Christian lands?'' Oro María asked.

"It was his own daughter, and not a repudiated wife, whom Don Vermudo offered to the *hajib* of Córdoba. Her name was Teresa, and she was his concubine. While they were escorting her to Córdoba, the Leonese nobles begged her to intervene with al-Mansur on their behalf, for better treatment. 'A kingdom defends its honor with the lances of its warriors and not with the buttocks of its women,' she answered them,'' I recounted.

"Why, I have come from a distant land to find that very Don Vermudo you're talking about!'' Sancho exclaimed.

"*Veremudus serenissimus et pius princeps* has paid the debt of his earthly life; he is dead. He left a legacy of one king and several bastard children,'' I went on.

"Ramiro III and Vermudo II, who are each other's cousins, asked al-Mansur to help them accede to the throne. Ramiro swore to be his vassal, Vermudo, his soldier, and the kingdom of León became a tributary province,'' Sancho Saborejo said. ''Ramiro perished from disease and from pride, meager talent, paltry prudence and great greed.''

"Did the infamy end there?'' Oro María asked.

"Vermudo became impatient with al-Mansur's haughtiness and disdain when receiving his complaints, and he drove out the Moors. Al-Mansur attacked León to punish him. Vermudo, who was suffering from gout, sallied forth with all the weakness of his realm to confront him,'' Sancho continued. ''Borne in the forefront on a litter on villeins' shoulders, Vermudo fled on all sides, even from his own shadow.''

"Vermudo sued for peace and returned to his kingdom so bereft of authority that even the dogs pissed on him," Oro María broke in. "The nobles took away his lands, his cattle and his servants; petty hidalgos, to whom he had previously entrusted castles, rose against him in rebellion, made jests about his person, and by dint of jesting killed him.''

"He really died last year," I said.

"We encountered him on the old bridge. In his hands he held an astrolabe, to find out his fate and which road he should take to reach Santiago. Always looking to the stars, he never suspected that his downfall was right in front of him," Sancho said.

"The bishops and abbots of León counseled him, and he did penance, gave alms and performed acts of charity. But all these were of no avail; he gave up the ghost in El Bierzo and was buried in Villabuena. A few months ago, at the age of five, Don Alfonso V succeeded his father to the throne," I added.

"Count Meneando González and his wife, Doña Mayor, raised that infant in Galicia," Sancho declared.

"The count's name is Menando, not Meneando," I corrected him.

"Master of mine, I ask you if the widow Doña Elvira has married for the second time," Oro María broke in.

"In the Council of Toledo they ordained that it is an execrable evil and all too frequent iniquity to aspire to the royal bed of his surviving wife when the king is dead," I responded.

"On second thought, we will not need the twelve solidi for the yoke of oxen, for we have no intention of laboring in the mud of San Juan," Sancho Saborejo conceded.

"We want only to sleep in the monastery for a few days, until the feast of Saint Eulalia Virgin Martyr, before we resume the road to Santiago," Oro María stammered.

"We haven't come from Sahagún, we've come from Toledo, the town where the table of Solomon, son of David, was found, along with other treasures," Sancho confessed. "We have been walking for nine days."

"We are very tired; we have crossed cold mountains and long solitudes. Here the Leonese have become puffed with pride," said Oro María.

"We made a vow to visit one of the great sanctuaries of Christianity, to see if the holy bones of the apostle, which are preserved in the most distant reaches of Hispania, facing the *mare Britannicum,* can perform the miracle of making Gómez speak again."

"When and in what manner did he lose his voice?" I inquired.

"One day at dawn two years ago he saw the devil," Sancho said. "Since then, he is always afraid."

"We set out on this penitential pilgrimage to expiate our sins and seek pardon from Lord Christ," the woman explained. "When we leave here, we will continue our pilgrimage barefoot."

"Ut per te, beatissime Iacobe apostole, remissionem peccatorum meorum ante dominum Ihesum Christum," I invoked the saint.

"Like the first pilgrim, Don Gotescalc, bishop of Le Puy, and Simeon of Armenia, who crossed all France, my wife and I are journeying to Santiago with increasing devotion, for throughout the land we have heard the faithful proclaiming miracles," Sancho declared.

"We still don't know if it's Santi Yague Major, the son of Zebedee, or Santi Yague Minor, the brother of Lord Christ, that we're looking for," said Oro María.

"We only know that the body of one of the two was translated by the hand of God from Jerusalem to Galicia in six days," said Sancho.

"They call this saint Yago, Yague, Sanctiago, Santiago, Jacob, Jacobo, James and Iago, but they're all the same one," I explained.

"I have heard tell that he came by himself over the waves, sitting on a stone by way of a boat, and disembarked in Iria Flavia," Sancho said. "That night, burning lights and angels appeared in a nearby hamlet—"

"I heard that the angels transported his body through the air with no help from any living creature, and that Bishop Teodomiro discovered his grave and transferred his remains to the *campus stellae,* now Compostela, to be honored," I interrupted. "The basilica Alfonso III built for him was razed by al-Mansur, who carried off the gates of the city and the bells from the church. He used the latter as lamps in the mosque of Córdoba."

"We ask charity of you, for the poor pilgrims of Santi Yague carry no money," Oro María pleaded, pointing to a cockleshell fastened to her clothing. "We went from Burgos to Fromista, from Fromista to Sahagún,

from Sahagún we came to Léon, and from here we will depart for Astorga.''

"To travel with a lady and a struck-dumb child over roads infested with
thieves and Saracens is very dangerous, even though we poor have nothing,'' Sancho Saborejo explained, nodding toward his wife and child.

"The bodies you see before you are our sole wealth, and we do not
want robbers or ravishers to murder or defile them,'' Oro María said,
looking at me narrowly.

"You are minstrels and pilgrims, so I owe you hospitality: Be welcome
to this monastery. Doña Miguel will give you a place to lie and take
repose,'' I offered when I noticed their skin showing through their worn
garments. "All I ask is that you wash your bodies and your clothes, which
stink to high heaven, without delay.''

"A minstrel's wage is for drink and stew and a glass of good wine,'' I
heard Sancho Saborejo say as I turned toward the monastery.

"Master, sir, what may your name be?'' Oro María asked.

"They call me Alfonso de León,'' I replied. "Keep your ears open, for
soon you will hear me much mentioned.''

"You are the one I am seeking,'' she cried, feigning knowledge of me.
"You are the saint of these parts.''

"I am no saint,'' I replied, and I pretended to leave, so as to spy on
them.

Both minstrels entered the church, which was dark at this hour. Their
attention was drawn to a reliquary near the altar that contained the leathery,
fleshless hand of an unknown saint. The fingers made the sign of the cross,
the little finger doubled over. It was a small hand, though not a child's,
belonging to a thin, slight man.

Gómez remained outside, studying his bare feet, whose toes twitched.
Then he went to the cemetery to look for I know not what among the
tombs. He was visibly attracted to the graves of children, which were apart
from the other dead. They had been buried to the sound of psalms and
antiphons, and their bodies sprinkled with holy water in keeping with their
purity and virginity.

Sancho and Oro María stood open-mouthed before a reliquary that displayed a set of jaws with two molars on either side. Saint Genadio had

found it in a cave and decided that it belonged to Saint John the Baptist.

Gómez suddenly began searching intently among the tombstones, as if seeking one in particular. Perhaps it was the tablet of a peasant's son who shared his name and had died a short while ago. It was then that a disembodied voice spoke to him from behind a leafless tree. The boy looked up at the branches, trying to discover who was talking to him. White crows blanketed the tree and filled the air with cawings, which only I could hear. The warbling of a fabulous bird echoed in the distance, as if it would go on for a thousand years. It lasted but a moment.

Now the church was enveloped in a sticky silence, which oozed up the stone terrace that was the tower's foundation and arrested the ringing of the bells. Through the wall, through the trees, over the graves in the cemetery, a procession of transparent floating creatures in black garments and hats appeared. With slow and solemn step they advanced, bearing a coffin aloft. In keeping with the world's order, a limping priest came first, followed by a warrior, a tonsured layman, and a shirted bumpkin whose feet were wrapped in rags.

Seated on the box was a woman of high rank, dressed in opulent black clothes, whose shaggy, snarled hair rose like a rampant snake. Her bluish face and fiery eyes gleamed through black veils. Her head was so transparent that it seemed made of the damp green of the hills and the riverside poplars I could see beyond it. Her hands disappeared at the edge of her sleeves. Her silvery slippers sparkled in the light of the setting sun.

Perhaps the cortege came from Córdoba. White crows followed it in the air. At the forefront, astride a vicious horse, rode a foul and forbidding female dwarf dressed in yellow. The man who resembled me, the man I had seen crossing the fields a short while before, trailed behind. He was my size, he had my eyes, and if I was not mistaken, the expression on my face. The only differences between him and me were that he was dressed in Saracen fashion, his cheeks were noticeably wrinkled, and his long hair, hoary. Otherwise he looked like me. When the person on the coffin spotted me in my hiding place behind the side wall of the church, her eyes, filled with loathing, were riveted on my chest. The leafless tree's branches blazed, but there were no flames or smoke.

The procession passed by. The face of the person on the coffin became blacker and blacker. Ahead, an acolyte carrying a brass bucket sprinkled the air with holy water. He was followed by a subdeacon with a cross, bracketed by two more acolytes holding unlit candles. The deacon came next, a black book pressed to his chest, then the celebrant in a black cope.

Ghastly, greenish beings beckoned Gómez to come nearer; they held serpentine wands in their hands. From the sounds they made I thought they were weeping or chanting responses. Here and there voices murmured, *Sed libera nos a malo; Libera me Domine de morte; Qui Lazarum resuscitasti; Qui venturus es judicare vivos et mortuos; Et clamor meus. Oremus.*

Gómez did not understand the summons of the black-clad figures. One detached itself from the rest, gliding toward him with outstretched hands. Just then Sancho Saborejo emerged from the church and walked straight through the dark figure, neither seeing nor touching it. He spoke to the child.

Silent, unseen, like spectral travelers, the procession of creatures passed through the trees, through the church, and down the dreary road until it disappeared from sight.

Gómez waggled his hands at the minstrels. Oro María could barely understand her son's mute mouthings. She explained to her husband that the boy had just looked upon the face of a beautiful woman, who was being borne on a litter toward Santiago by people in white garments. The face was radiant, bright as day. She had said something to him, but he had not known how to read her words.

The boy was dumb. It was odd that the minstrel would bother to teach him words in the new Spanish.

In the funeral, Gómez saw a virgin, I, a fiend.

VISION III

I, Alfonso de León, am tall and slender of build, with a fine and pleasing countenance. My hair is black and juts over my ears like eyebrows. I have well-proportioned shoulders and delicate hands. I am a man of good sense and agreeable conversation, circumspect and straightforward, discreet and cheerful, prudent yet bold, moderate in eating and drinking, albeit somewhat mournful and fussy. I am cleanly in my dress and in my person, I have a great love of books, and I give myself easily to women. Perhaps more easily than befits a monk. As a child, I was duped by the Saracens into becoming an Islamite, but I recognized my error and broke with them, leaving Córdoba not only to defend my life but to save my soul as well. My lineage is an ancient one: On my father's side there are caliphs or Jews (only God knows which), on my mother's, kings. I have a twin brother who is a Moor.

I am writing down my story on parchment, using the words of the new language that is taking its first steps. In these incipient idioms, I fix the visions that are taking shape within me. Little by little, like an infant or a barbarian, I am learning to express my own discourse and the deeds of the year 1000 in words that are born in my mouth.

How strange that a tongue should be born when the world is dying, because when a tongue is born, earthly man is born, dreaming is born, poetry is born. With a tongue, a man can name the creatures who come and go around him; he can talk about his affections, passions and imaginings; and he can recall the expressions of his own face.

This verbal east is dawning in the west, and the livelier and richer it grows, the more it seems threatened with ruination, as if a thousand years of life could come to an end in a few days, or a thousand years of hell commence. Be that as it may, a thousand years are but a breath, the wink of an eye, a nothing compared with the Word Incarnate and the word in the making every day.

Although I know my name, and I know the body I will die in, in this final hour I do not know if I am Alfonso de León or if I am Abd Allah, if I personify Lord Christ or Antichrist. Perhaps I am none of them, perhaps I am only the letter A, which figures in the firmament of verbal signs in an infinite possibility of combinations.

At the moment of death, each man has his Apocalypse, each man comes to know his own end of time. For each man the seven sacred seals are loosed. But only for his soul, because at that hour of grace and misfortune, the light silently fades from his eye.

With her habitual shrewishness, Doña Miguel, the bearded woman Abbot Andrés received as part of a donation of estates and villas, and who belongs to the monastery, says I have a squat, stubby body and an ugly face, that my neck is short, my nose long and my eyes unpleasant, my beard over-grown, my shoulders misshapen and hunched, my head, chest and arms overlarge. But say what he/she will, my face does not resemble that of any other man. God made it thinking of me alone.

Nevertheless, this woman who first appeared in this place on Friday, the twenty-ninth of May of the year 980 (I can see her still, entering the monastery, barefoot, disheveled and stinking), insults me by saying I am slovenly and dirty in my person and dissolute with women, that I would not spare my own mother if I found her naked in my bed. She tells everyone that my wit is woeful and that I am so miserly I wouldn't help my parents even if I saw them at death's door.

This virago has taken my measure and found me ambitious to command and govern, vengeful, melancholy and superstitious. She has noised about León that when my father died, murdered by the Saracens of al-Andalus, my inheritance was so paltry my mother was forced to earn her bread by reminiscing in public about her life in the harem of Córdoba. Sheer slander.

What is absurd is that Doña Miguel takes care of me in the monastery. She, or he, does work proper to both male and female and dresses as one or the other, as befits the day and the occasion. I am certain that she will discover her real gender only at the moment of her death, and she will be the first hermaphrodite to be commemorated in the *sanctorale,* listed among the saints. The clerics of León call her "the she-man."

He helped lay the foundation stone of the monastery of San Lucas and raise the adobe walls of a house of mine in San Juan de Esla; he introduced cattle into pastures belonging to our monastery, upward of thirty sheep and goats. Never lazy or late, he has kept the neighbors from cutting and selling grasses and trees from our mountains; he has gone out to hunt hares and gather wood on those mountains, to sow and plow the earth in our estates; he has slaughtered two-toothed rams for us to eat and brought pitchers of wine. During this month of March alone, from the day of Saint Nicephorus until the feast of the Conception of the Virgin Mary, she pruned the vines, worked at the distaff and hauled water from the well; she scoured the latrines, went to the mill and the market, swept the floors of the church and the monastery every Saturday, cooked for me and laundered the clothes. He has strong arms and hands, matted hair, and is taller and more burly than I. She is pale and pink-cheeked, has a snub nose, coarse features, broad shoulders and hips; in shape and swagger, he's more man than woman. Occasionally, to the monks' surprise, he dons Islamic raiment and dances like the Moorish women in the harem. She is ugly to look at.

Doña Miguel has a headstrong gait, is quick to anger and rash in her speech; with the peasants' children, she is charitable, and no one goes away from the gate without being given bread. Fearful lest the infirmities of others adhere to her body and soul, she shuns the sick as though they were the plague incarnate, convinced that merely seeing and being seen by them is sufficient to infect her.

She takes pleasure in the company of prudent men, especially that of Abbot Andrés. She likes hearing Sancho Saborejo's rhyming couplets and his tales of hoodwinked Vices, although when she first set eyes on him, she scolded me in a virile voice. "What is that inventor of lies doing here? Didn't we have enough with our own sins without bringing in other, unfamiliar ones?"

"The Author of all creatures never ceases to astonish those innocents who practice charity, because the eagle does not always climb to the heights on outspread wings. At times it plummets to the ground, its wings wet with water," I answered, and I reminded her of the day he had arrived at the monastery.

" 'I thoys pore end unpepylled placys, my faderen techyd me the scole of lif, nought the *trivium*.' " I reminded her of how she had spoken in his faltering Spanish. " 'Weth the yarde of justise my faderen wippen me . . . saven me the chirche.' "

I reminded her of it, because Doña Miguel's father was a wrathful man, and she grew up mistreated and miserably poor. Not minding the ill-usage or his avarice, she suffered him patiently, until a Saracen, who had taken him captive, stabbed him to death in Chozas de Abajo.

Ever since she was brought to the monastery, Doña Miguel had concealed her real nature, or natures, from the monks. Only Abbot Andrés has seen her naked, and that was to his delight or to his horror, or to determine on what part of her he could inflict the greatest suffering. At that time he set her the penance of putting her head and arms in three iron rings until her skin turned black and blue.

Sabarico, the abbot of the monastery of San Lucas, confided to me one day that Doña Miguel was Abbot Andrés's concubine, and that I should look for his features in the face of the creature that was found one morning abandoned at the gates of the monastery of San Juan el Teólogo, whose birth was the work of the Holy Ghost. The creature answered to the name of Jimena. The Holy Ghost was called Andrés.

According to Sabarico, our fortunate abbot had left the cloister every night of the year 985 and made his way to the hermitage of La Anunciación in the orchard, there to pass long hours in prayer on the irresistible bulk of Doña Miguel.

"For as long as we dwell in this vale of tears, clothed in mortal flesh, let us enjoy the power of our prayers, let us not despise the worldly goods with which God regales us in rich abundance, provided that we always remember that we are dust and ashes," he affirmed, psalter in hand.

Jimena, who by now had turned fifteen, called the abbot priest or *pater* when she encountered him. For his part, when he played with her, he called her daughter—of the flock of Lord Christ. And he expressed his hope of one day seeing her wearing the crown of martyrdom, her breasts amputated, her body quartered and roasted on a gridiron.

"You, who are both father and husband to this virgin, are also her son," I said to the abbot one afternoon.

"Woman gives us death with her belly, resurrection with her mouth," he replied.

"The spirit is male, the soul, female," I said, citing the words of a saint.

"Jimena should be flagellated like the martyr Eulalia, then quartered, burned and hanged from a cross. Only thus can she expunge the ugliness from her face," he insisted.

Jimena had, however, a comely visage, ruddy cheeks somewhat spotted, a small mouth, rosy lips, large dark eyes, black hair hanging down to her waist, a tall stature, broad hips, and an ample breast. The clerics of León, wed to chastity with the Virgin Mary or Saint Leocadia, tried not to look at her when she went by; she was too tempting.

According to them, the Enemy, the Envious One, the accursed Beast, the devil, was lurking in the monastery of San Juan el Teólogo. Nightly he troubled the friars' sleep, emblazoning women's buttocks and he-goat pizzles on the dormitory wall, or depositing Jimena's voluptuous body in my bed. More than once I had to hurl the Tempter against the wall, ignoring his resemblance to a Toledan prelate, a Santiagan pilgrim or a Slavic eunuch. They knew that, in the quiet of the cloister, the Evil One had threatened me because I had made him so ugly in the manuscript. Me, a humble scribe, barely able to rough out the letters that praise the Glorious Blessed Virgin Mother of God and to paint her name in gold, blue and pink. I, Alfonso de León, who doesn't believe in myself, much less in what people declare and say about me.

Now that the monastery is depopulated, it is all mine. Brought to ruin by the ravages of men, San Juan el Teólogo survived, thanks to the holy life of its servants, in particular its founder, Abbot Alfonso, whose cell was a cramped prison.

Cordoban Christians, who fled with Father Alfonso from the persecution of the Saracens, labored tirelessly on the monastery's construction during the first years of this century, as the tablet above the main gate attests. Together, the abbot and the faithful searched for a site suited to silence, remote from the turmoils and flesh of the world, and here they found it, near the stream that swells with the rains beneath the cloudy sky of León.

Stones from Roman and Visigothic monuments and temples served the *must'arib,* or Mozarabs, as building material for the church and the cenoby, the latter with two patios, one of them the cloister. Many a time the devil came to sit on the stones so that they could not lift them, and he toppled walls, crushing several monks. The church was consecrated by Bishop Genadio, who came from Astorga in the year 913. During the ceremony he wrote the alphabet on the floor, from left to right, from the spot farthest east to the spot farthest west, and with his pastoral crozier he sketched letters, which quite possibly contained all the prayers, toward the four cardinal points.

Seven monks first dwelt in the cenoby, and seven oblates were offered to Abbot Alfonso. Seven was the number that always prevailed in the monastery of San Juan el Teólogo, in homage to Saint John and to the Seven Gifts of the Holy Ghost. In the church were seven enthroned virgins, seven lamps and seven candles burning day and night. Not only were stories from the lives of Lord Christ and his glorious Mother Mary carved on the capitals crowning the columns, the fiend and his followers were depicted as well, to remind the Christian flock to beware of falling into his clutches, and that he and his disciples were at the root of all the century's upheavals.

Although no day in San Juan went by without a soul's being freed from the power of evil spirits, thanks to the offices celebrated in the church, the monks still had the task of delivering from purgatory the millions of souls of all the deceased who had ever existed in the world, a number that swelled daily with the newly dead. To alleviate this endless toil, the abbot established the feast of All Souls, when it was possible to rescue thousands at a time. He also established the custom of inscribing each departed monk's name in a memorial, and when a brother was at death's door, he ordered the others to rush to his bedside to chant a Credo, to fortify him in his final battle with the Enemy. According to the abbot, the faithful were not lying dead in their graves, they were merely resting until the Last Judgment.

When Abbot Alfonso died, the monks of San Juan el Teólogo fought with the monks of San Lucas over his relics. "The abbot is our property, and he should repose in our cemetery. While alive, he worked miracles here, and he will continue working them here until the Day of the Resurrection of the decease faithful," my colleagues in benediction argued. But the quarrel went on for months and years, and one morning it was discovered that his body had disappeared, purloined with coffin, shroud, fingers, hair and nails by a cleric named Lupicino. "He was no saint after all," the new abbot declared of Alfonso, "because he let himself be stolen."

Ever since then, although they live apart from the world, the devil has pursued our monks and nuns with lust, the daughter of perdition. The Seducer and Slanderer attacked Abbess Onnega and Brother Odoino, who wandered like lunatics, wanton and insatiable, over the peaks and ravines of this land. The Great Betrayer deceived Gundisalvo, the hermit who prayed perched on a rock in the River Torio; he peopled his solitude with temptations, and Gundisalvo, unable to defend himself from himself, embraced his hallucinations as though they were real.

With the Rule of Saint Benedict, Abbot Andrés brought other rules to the monastery: *Regula Communis, Codex Regularum, Liber Ordinum, Poenitentiale Vigilanum, Regula Monachorum,* and other books, such as the *Etymologiae* of Isidore of Seville, the *Ecclesiastical History* of Eusebius, the *Code* of Alaric, Saint Ambrose's *De Paradiso,* the *Lex romana visigothorum,* Beatus of Liébana's *Commentarius in Apocalypsin* and the *Biblia Latina,* which begins with the prophets and includes the New Testament. This Bible, made for Abbot Maurus and copied and painted by Juan the deacon, with help from the presbyter Vimara, swarms with creatures and monsters. These ecclesiastical treasures were kept in the crypt, for fear of the Saracens' campaigns, and of thieves.

Among our number, Brother Martín Meñique showed the greatest passion for relics, having become devoted since his monastic infancy and childhood to the bodies of Saints Cecilia, Columba and Marina, which were enshrined in the crypt. All night long, he would abandon himself to the contemplation of the uncorrupted remains. With superstitious reverence, as if they were still alive, or were members of his family, he caressed with his eyes, but never with his hands, those fingers, those bones, those garments, those tresses.

It fell to him to provision the monastery with spiritual protectors from the kingdom of León, from al-Andalus and from Rome. Above all, his mission was to discover the places where the relics were to be found, to translate them to the church, and to see that suitable tombs were built where the faithful could come to venerate them. Often, after exceedingly arduous journeys, he returned with the bones of unidentified dead, and Abbot Andrés was obliged to invent their names and lives.

Martín Meñique justified his purchases by arguing that, although he had tried to acquire relics of famous saints, the bones he brought back were the only ones available, because the monasteries refused to sell him their most miraculous bishops and abbots.

"When a saint dies, his body becomes public property, and the faithful pounce on his hairs, teeth and clothing in search of relics," he told me one afternoon. "The faithful want to know everything about his life, the details of his final throes, his last words. The saints in their tombs are more alive to them than are the living, and if properly invoked, they can act through their remains."

A portico with eight horseshoe arches and marble columns, crowned by capitals carved with plant and animal motifs, led to the small church, which was divided into three naves, each with its own apse. Two rows of arches and columns separated the naves and held up the roofing. Halfway down, four columns with their respective arches kept the worshipers apart from the officiant. Above, on both sides, six off-center rectangular windows allowed light in; several had marble latticework, others were crossed by bars, which served as grilles or to hold glass. There was a window at the head of the central nave, and before the altar stood two stones, both consecrated, on which graven letters revealed that within were bestowed the relics of Saints Acisclus, Christopher, Bartholomew, Stephen and Genadio, adding to the considerable quantity of these righteous men's mortal remains known to be in the monasteries and churches of León and other lands.

There was a doorway on one side of the portico, so low and narrow that the officiant had to hunch over to go through it and down the steps. The parishioners entered by another door toward the middle, next to the holy-water font. On the outside, curvilinear chapels disguised the roundness of the church.

When it was my turn to celebrate the divine service, standing between the columns, my back to the altar, I contemplated the flesh and faces of the human sheep, in particular, the female sheep. Or, while the cold rose from the slate floor to my feet, I watched the slender shadows of the columns creeping across the floor and climbing the red-painted walls. Or I listened to the partridges and goldfinches.

Adjoining the church was a cemetery walled like a cloister, where burials, almost always of children who had not yet reached the age of ten, took place. These infants were orphans or newborns wrapped in bloody rags, abandoned at the hour of Matins at the monastery gates. In this cemetery we denied church burial to pagans and Jews, infidels, heretics and apostates of the faith, to schismatics and public excommunicates.

On a stone set into a wall were inscribed the names of dead kings and queens, counts and knights, bishops and monks, abbesses and nuns, converts and laymen. Such were the ghostly inhabitants of our holy ground, all silently imploring our brothers and sisters to pray for pardon of their sins. The women had died immaculate, the men chaste. The necrological stones were writ with colored inks in various handwritings:

✝ On the eighth day of the Epiphany, feast of Saint Hilary, died Legundia, *puella,* a virgin.

✝ Today, feast of Saint Engracia, died Menendo Menéndez, presbyter of this monastery. He died old and shriveled at the age of forty.

✝ Today died Trastemiro Trastemiriz, who left the monastery ten solidi in his will.

✟ Today Rutilia died, consecrated bride of Christ in the monastery of Santiago. Her remains were transferred to this cemetery so they might lie next to her sister Adosinda's until the Day of the Resurrection of the Dead.

✟ Today died Sarracino, who served as sacristan in this monastery.

✟ Alpha and Omega. Here beneath the weight of this stone lies the soldier Miguel of worthy memory. Let us pray to Dominum for the remission of his sins. Amen.

Flush against one wall, as if guarding the monastery's back, was a hillock with a cave containing seven open graves. These the monks had dug for themselves, sized to their bodies, expecting life to be brief. A niche in the rock had been turned into an ossuary.

Beyond the stone cross, which marked the boundary of the monastery, the tonsure no longer afforded protection. Even the dead had to remain within the demarcated space. The souls that dwelt here were not supposed to leave these confines; to do so, they needed permission from a living person. The peasants of the district had been born under the protection of the parish and, like their parents and their children, had been baptized and wed here, and here they had celebrated the feast days. They were confident that, once in the other world, their spirits would be in our care.

Notwithstanding his bodily absence, Abbot Andrés still haunted me. No one knew better than he how to mortify the flesh with flagellation and fasting, how to punish gluttony with a diet of hunger, how to keep us humble by dressing us in shabby clothes. Scourge in hand, our spiritual father practiced on his sons the precept that the body is meant for death and the best way to atone for its existence is by making it suffer.

Anselmo, the forbidding friar who was posted at the monastery entrance and responded to those who called at the gate with a *"Deo gratias"* or a "God bless you," maintained that Andrés was the illegitimate offspring of the elderly Count Orosio, and that he had a sister named Gaudiosa, equally bastard and devoted to religion; that one day, each on his own, they had both sought the Lord in the hermits' caves near Peñalba de Santiago, nourishing themselves with grasses and water. Afterward, Andrés had taken to the road, to preach to children who did not yet enjoy the knowledge of God.

"Vices acquired early in life can never be shed," the abbot explained to the oblates, whom he did not want anyone to see naked.

"Few men in the world reach the age of discretion, even though they achieve old age," Martín Meñique remarked, looking pointedly at Brother Anselmo.

"There is always a desire embedded like a thorn in the depths of the soul which betrays faith and chastity. This desire manifests itself while we are sleeping," Abbot Andrés stated, glaring at me. "Some brothers are visited in their dreams by voluptuous ladies, and upon awakening notice that they have wet their beds."

"Litanies and the psalms of David, toiling in the orchard, drawing water from the well and baking bread, taking singing lessons, studying grammar, arithmetic, Latin and liturgy are all useful against nocturnal emissions. In wintertime it is prudent to read a book from start to finish, without skipping pages. And at all times, I recommend that you devote yourselves wholly to the service of God," Martín Meñique cautioned us.

"To thwart the snares of the Instigator, it is advisable that neither bodies nor beds of monks come in contact with each other during day or night, nor should they visit the latrines in pairs or without a mentor, nor frequent lonely places in the company of a child. Above all, I exhort you to be as innocent and tender as one of those oblates," the abbot entreated us.

But Andrés was strict, even with the infants offered to the monastery. He forbade them to ask for bread between meals or to talk during religious offices, and he required perfect obedience of them under all circumstances. Twiddling the rod of punishment between his fingers, he spent days explaining to them by any means available the horror of having genitals, the meaning of penance, communion and excommunication, and the importance of controlling their appetites, their sorrows, their tempers, their secular laughter. He had developed a language of signs and gestures for the oblates and for us, which never broke the silence of the refectory.

After night fell, he would burst abruptly into the dormitory, his intention to enforce respect for virtue rather than to keep us company, to ensure that our bodies were tightly wrapped in the wool and sheepskin coverlets and far from the oblates', rather than to see whether we were cold. He also made certain that the candle burned all night long and that each brother had lain down with his clothing on.

He arose before Matins and went to pray in the church, or he could be found standing in the cloister, contemplating the stars in the firmament. When we saw him there, indifferent to the world and the freezing cold, the rest of us, still drowsy, with darkness still clinging to our eyelids, hastened to go to chant the nocturnal prayers.

With grave face and hooded eyes, he watched as we entered the church and examined us. Standing before the altar, holding the heavy psalter in his hands as we took our places in the nave, he made us feel there was no distinction of rank among us, either by virtue of birth or by intelligence. Nevertheless, life was miserable for anyone who could not endure the raw mornings, who was perpetually famished, whose appetite was not satisfied by the monotonous rations of bread, cheese and egg. Companionship meant "sharing bread," but in the monastery it meant sharing hunger.

On days of abstinence, he made those of us monks who had arduously attained the age of discretion sleep near the urns in the crypt, or on vine twigs on the church pavement, or on the grave of a recently deceased child. Or he compelled us to spend three days and nights shut up in a dank, dark chamber. All this was meant to induce spiritual anguish and corporeal exhaustion, so that no one could fall asleep or think bad thoughts.

The abbot believed in the mysteries of the holy faith, but he believed even more in the practice of flagellation, both the kind the individual inflicts on himself and the kind administered by others, and on the eve of every feast he gave us not three, not five, but one hundred and fifty lashes, honestly applied, to mortify the body.

He delivered the blows with his eyes closed, careful not to give one more or less, for he was fair. I clenched the psalter between my teeth and hands, enduring the pain of being a believer. And since I had to chant aloud each one of the one hundred and fifty psalms, I called these sessions the hour of song. To make us God-fearing, at nightfall, dawn and mealtime, as if by chance, he left the scourge in full sight, its branches smeared with blood and bits of skin, skin he had torn with fervor from our virginal flesh.

Abominating the creatures of night, he anathematized those who accepted vampires and witches as real beings; those who drank the blood and urine of animals and men, who conjured up storms and worshiped heavenly bodies and idols; those who lacerated their faces and limbs upon the death of a relation, clamoring in the darkness, filled with grief and anger.

The guardian of the gate, Brother Anselmo, hypocritically humble, spoke in Latin to the wretched faithful who could neither read nor write, or he insulted them with words from the new Romance tongue, which they did not yet understand. Or, self-righteous and implacable, upon learning our sins he threatened us with hell.

Never far from the abbot, always vigilant and pitiless, thanks to Anselmo's zeal, some of my brothers preferred the privations of the century and the inclemencies of the open road to his Christian piety, more terrified of the penances he imposed on them than of the horrors of the year 1000.

VISION IV

That Good Friday, al-Mansur ibn Abi Amir appeared on his armored horse. A golden coif sheathed his forehead, mouth, half his nose, and his neck. His white coat of mail glittered in the sun. His sword with the grooved blade was known as The Terrible One. It was said that the sword's gleam bewitched its victims, for a mortal fire flickered along its edges.

By the light of the setting sun, the one whom the Christians called Almanzor rode at the head of his hosts, coming to a halt before the church doors and near the cemetery. Among the cattle and booty taken during the expeditions—embroidered silks, garments of merino wool, brocade tapestries, weasel skins, crosses, chalices, and jewels of gold and silver—were the captives and the slaves, and the carts adorned with the wives and daughters of kings, counts and knights. Men castrated in their childhood guarded the females.

Al-Mansur governed al-Andalus. The reigning Caliph, Hisham al-Muayyad billah, prayed, made love and grew weak in the court harem, immersed in the flesh and the Koran. A virtual prisoner of his *hajib,* or prime minister, the son of al-Hakam II lived surrounded by guards and spies who observed his every movement. He was a stranger to his people, who had glimpsed him only once, in the streets of Córdoba, and that was in a gilded cage, in the midst of his retinue, scepter in hand, wearing a tall turban swathed in a burnoose, like one of the women accompanying him.

After al-Hakam II expired in the arms of his eunuchs Faiq and Chawdar, al-Mansur, being a great hater of literature and the arts, accused anyone who read books about philosophy, astronomy and other sciences forbidden by religion of heresy, and with his own hands threw the library onto a bonfire and buried it in one of the Alcázar's wells.

Among his pious and secular works were the enlargement of the principal mosque of Córdoba, which he accomplished with the riches looted during his campaigns in the Christian North, and the expansion of the city, as much to increase its splendor as to afford shelter and services to the foreigners come from the Muslim world and from the Berber tribes of Ifrikiya. These tribesmen, who had arrived in Córdoba in rags, riding broken-down jades, had, thanks to his favors, rapidly acquired mansions, finery and mettlesome horses.

Ambitious and ostentatious, al-Mansur erected a palace for his lover, Subh, al-Hakam II's favorite concubine and the mother of Crown Prince Hisham. He moved from the al-Rusafa quarter to be closer to Madinat al-Zahra, and called his new residence al-Amiriyya. Finally, he built and installed himself in a palace city he named Madina al-Zahira, took control of al-Andalus and announced to the world that the Caliph Hisham would devote himself entirely to spiritual exercises. On the seventh of July in the year 981, he took a surname reserved for the Caliphs, al-Mansur billah, "the victorious one of Allah," and he compelled the populace to address him as *malik karim,* or noble king. He insisted upon being paid royal honors, and even princes of the blood and viziers had to kiss his hand. Murderer of generals, governors and eunuchs, he always carried a Koran, copied out in his own hand, to draw God's blessings toward himself during his travels.

Respectful of others' faith, he made Christian and Muslim soldiers alike keep Sunday. A worshipful devotee of Allah's, he saved the dust that clung to his face during his campaigns against the infidel. Each time he stopped to rest, his servants put the dust in a bag, which he carried wrapped in the shroud his daughters had embroidered for him. In case he died, his followers were to bury the bag with him.

Sustained by the armed Prophet and with his Berber, Slav and Christian cavalry, in the year 987 al-Mansur so thoroughly devastated Coimbra that the city could not be inhabited again for seven years. The following year, he attacked the kingdom of León, razing towns, castles, villages, monasteries and churches, and killing or capturing everyone who crossed his path. The city resisted, thanks to its Roman walls, its stalwart towers, and its marble gates, but he succeeded in forcing the South Gate, sacked the town, and massacred its populace. The governor, Count Gonzalvo González, who was ailing, was stabbed to death on his litter. King Vermudo the Gouty, who had provoked the war by expelling the Muslims, fled just in time. In his destructive rage, al-Mansur left one tower standing near the northern gate, so that men of the future would know how mighty had been the city he had ruined.

That same year, al-Mansur entered Galicia by way of Portugal. Abetted by the Christian counts of the region, he crossed the fields, rivers, canals and mountains of the country and marched against Santiago. On Wednesday, *Xaban* 2, or August tenth, he pitched camp before the city, which had been abandoned by its inhabitants, and profaned the church, setting it on fire, which the relics of the apostle were unable to prevent. Two secretary-poets were at his side during the expedition, Ibn Darray and Abd al-Malik ibn Idris, who would later celebrate the annihilation of *Shant Yaqub* in a poem.

Before departing, al-Mansur took the smaller bells from the church to use as lamps in the mosque of Córdoba, where he would place the gates of the city in the ceiling of that house of prayer. When he entered Santiago, all he found was an elderly monk seated beside the saint's tomb. He ordered that the sepulcher be spared.

"Why are you sitting there?" he asked the monk.

"To do honor to Sant Yago," the old man replied. "You will pay for what you have done with your life, and with the life of your son and successor, for one day not far distant your palace will be burned down, and the only man to remain faithful to you, a Christian count, will lose his head. You, Victorious One, will be defeated. You, Immortal One, will die, and you will be buried in hell.''

''Leave him alone,'' al-Mansur commanded when the Berbers moved to behead him. ''Twenty thousand soldiers do my bidding, but none is more miserable than I.''

The prime minister shrank from the monk in superstitious terror. For two days he devoted himself to demolishing the walls, the palaces and the church. Then he left the city. Leading his cavalry, he reached the peninsula of San Mankas and came to a halt before the ocean until, laden with spoils, he commenced the return to Córdoba. Asking the Christian counts who had collaborated with him in his campaign against Santiago to file past him, he gave them garments and skins from the plunder. One man, Rodrigo Dávila, took away a cross of gold and precious stones.

According to legend, on his way back, al-Mansur came upon a house whose walls and roof were covered with ivy, and was curious to know what person might live there. His men dragged into the sunlight a rheumy-eyed hermit with a white beard and frightened face.

''Have you seen al-Mansur?'' al-Mansur asked him.

The monk gazed at him mutely.

''We are searching for him to kill him, for he is a prodigious murderer of hermits and has beheaded many of them in their caves and hermitages. If you happen upon him, come and tell me, and I will hurry here to cut off his head,'' said the *hajib* and rode off at the head of his armies.

Such was the man to whom the Castilians were obliged to give one hundred handsome, marriageable maidens in tribute, the man who had abducted the abbess and sisters from the convent of Santa Cristina, and nuns from other monasteries in León, and who kept two of Doña Flora's aunts in chains—if they had not already died. He was the supreme general who led the Saracen armada on expeditions. With him rode Berbers and black slaves annexed by al-Hakam II to the royal forces; squadrons from the Banu Birzal; *al-Khurs,* or mutes, so called because they could not speak the Arab language; bought or captured Slovenes; Andalusians, who didn't know how to ride with stirrups and could barely speak any language, but were cunning in battle. Foreigners also followed him: Leonese, Galicians, Franks, Castilians and Navarrese, all poor Christians impelled by greed to serve him in his campaigns against other Christians.

At that moment, in their separate columns, the volunteers for the holy war, who had joined the troops on their way to fight against the infidels, were engaged in military or religious exercises. Some of them had given information about the state of the Christian kingdoms. As a child, I had seen the cavalry and the infantry mustering for days beneath the walls of Córdoba, the location of their next campaign a secret. I remember watching them depart in the summer for the Christian lands, after a ceremony in the Great Mosque during which they tied banners to their lances. And I remember seeing them return in the fall, laden with riches and captives.

That afternoon al-Mansur seemed omnipotent on his mount, which was worth more than one hundred sheep, thirty oxen and fifty asses. I faintly heard that he was going to, or coming from, Toledo and Medinaceli. Near him, Wanzammar ibn Abi Bakr, the Berber who spat Arabic when he spoke, was glaring at the Christians. "Lord," he had once said to al-Mansur, "please give me a bedchamber so I don't have to sleep outdoors." "Didn't I already give you a big house?" the *hajib* asked. "Yes, Lord, but I filled all the rooms with grain, and there's no room for me," Wanzammar replied. The poet Mutanabbi wrote these lines about him and other Berber horsemen: "You would think the horses were born under them,/or they were born on their backs."

The Berbers, men of the Banu Birzal clan, carried their trophies of war, heads impaled on pikes and lances. It was they who shepherded the long procession of captive Christians, men and boys plucked from villages, roads and fields to do the hardest, dirtiest work, or for sodomy.

The women, ladies of the court and abbesses or peasants and servants, would swell the harems of powerful Saracens or be sold in the slave markets of Córdoba and Almería, where females from the North fetched the best prices. The slave merchants crowded around them, draping lengths of silk cloth over their bodies to see if they could pass for Christian princesses at sale time. In Zamora, in Simancas, in Barcelona, al-Mansur had taken captives.

Behind the women prisoners a man on foot, goaded by a Berber's lance, pulled two mules. The Arabs jeered at him, calling him King Rodrigo. The bizarre figure wore a crown of parchment, rabbit-skin gloves, and counterfeit regalia similar to that the Goth king had used.

Farther back, eight captives with shackled feet carried their chains in their hands so that they could walk. Barefoot and barechested, bearded and hairy, they wore brightly colored short skirts tied at the waist with a rag. Puny of build, they seemed small and slight by nature and by misfortune. Four more were squatting in the mud like so many starving dogs. Already poor, these wretches were now also slaves. A heavily armed, malevolent mute stood guard over them.

The Saracens let their horses and cattle graze among the graves, as though the cemetery were a stable.

Because it was Good Friday, we were forbidden to bury and say mass for the deceased, unless decay made it necessary to inter a corpse quickly. That morning I had chanted a responsory for the soul of a peasant boy brought to me earlier by his parents. The earth was still fresh, and the animals, scenting decomposition, were nosing in the ground.

Several Moors thrust their swords and lances, festooned with blouses and sashes, rings and kerchiefs, at nuns and peasant women.

"Her torso is a branch swaying above her hips. The branch is bedecked with two golden moons," I heard a man they addressed as Marwan say in his own tongue.

"Women, my lord, being born into a state of servitude, are fit only to bear and suckle children," said a certain Banu Sabarico, who may have been Marwan's servant.

"After he had reigned for almost fifty years, the caliph Abd Rahman III al-Nasir could remember fourteen happy days, fourteen days without clouds. I have counted fourteen women who have given me fourteen nights of pleasure, on such and such a moon, month and year," Marwan remarked.

When al-Mansur met the captive women, he removed his mail coif, perhaps to get a better look at them, or for some fresh air, or to give orders. He scrutinized them one by one, as if deciphering in their bodies and faces the delights they could offer him. They, in turn, looked with fear and fascination at the bearded visage of the *hajib,* about whom they had heard so much.

He was accompanied by a man dressed in a tunic of black cloth, a turban of the same color and a black leather cloak strewn with flowers, animals and birds, so expertly embroidered in gold that they seemed to be walking or flying over the garment. His hose were black, as were his mare, saddle and weapons. The mare's tail, mane and forelock had been curled and tied with the same golden thread. Black Dawn, for so she was called, snorted as if an inner bellows were urging her to run even when she stood still.

The man himself looked sinister. His black hair spilled over his shoulders and back, and a black beard brushed his bulky chest. He wore no coat of mail, no helmet on his head; in one hand he held a desiccated snake, and in the other a black sword, so broad and long that it was hard to imagine anyone resisting its strokes. The man displayed it almost angrily, ready to use it at the slightest provocation. Horse and rider kept listening to the air around them for invisible enemies who might attack them at any moment.

"Where is the man who gives orders in this monastery? Let him prostrate himself before me," the Black Rider said insolently as al-Mansur searched for the most beautiful damsel among the women assembled before him.

No one answered, and the Black Rider's gaze flitted over the captives, spurning them one by one.

"Do any of you know a *muladi,* one of those renegades who ran away from al-Andalus, who goes by the name of Alfuns?" he asked. "I know he lives hereabouts. Should you meet him, tell him that Abd Allah of Córdoba is looking for him."

An insignificant cleric called Rodríguez, from the monastery of San Lucas, opened his mouth, but the words stuck in his throat when he saw a brawny eunuch glaring at him.

Gómez, the minstrels' son, stepped to the monk's side as if about to speak, but his face merely screwed into a grimace.

The Black Rider bristled when he caught sight of the monastery's stone wall, knowing perhaps that I was behind it. Then his hands gripped the saddle, and his fingernails gleamed redly beneath the setting sun. There, where his eyes had lit, he stared hard.

"Does anyone here speak *aljamia,* the barbarous jargon of the Castilians? I think these Christians lost their own language and couldn't learn *arabia,*" he taunted them.

"A few years from now, the gibberish of the Spaniards, spoken in the mountains by a handful of Christian freedmen, will have vanished forever, there will be no recollection of it, our lord al-Mansur says," said a man who relayed to everyone whatever the *hajib* wished said to them.

The Christians made no reply, struck dumb by their dread of al-Mansur, the warrior who had razed León and Santiago. Appalled by the Black Rider, they wondered in silence what his presence among the Moors could mean. The most some dared was to move nearer to examine the captive women, afraid they might recognize a relative among them. The rest stood quietly in place.

"Lord, don't waste words on those oxen. They can't understand what you say," Wanzammar ibn Abi Bakr told al-Mansur.

"*Muley,* tell me your name," Sancho Saborejo said to the Black Rider.

"Don't answer that cur, I'll take this dogmeat to be a slave," said a Sevillan captain, who answered to the name of Banu Angelino and whose gaunt hands, bony face and rusty skin resembled a corpse's. It was evident from his tangled hair and shabby clothes that he seldom dismounted.

"The Prophet has said, 'Go and cut out his tongue, and thus will you shut his mouth,' " exclaimed a grim dwarf, very like the one I had seen in the ghostly procession on the feast of the Purification of Holy Mary.

"Everything that Christian dog has said will be annulled by the sword, the sharp-edged sword, which hungers and thirsts for men, the polished sword, which sheds blood and skewers necks. Its caresses turn coats of mail into shrouds," Banu Angelino declared.

"Even a bad blade, which cannot cut or behead, a dull, nicked and rusted blade, whose blows bounce off flesh and bones?" Wanzammar ibn Abi Bakr bantered. "I refer to the pruning sword the Christians employ, with which, in battle, they wound the legs and ears of the horses under them, or hack their own feet."

"Fall ruthlessly upon the puppy they are rearing to oppose you, before they can send it against you full grown and more furious," the cadaverous captain advised. "Punish impiety with death."

"Goad the file of slaves onward," Wanzammar commanded one of the mutes, who had a cruel, violent face, and the latter immediately poked his lance into the flanks of old Count Orosio, being led with a rope around his neck.

"Al-Mansur says a fine animal carries your weapons on the road to Destiny," the man beside the *hajib* remarked. "If your dream comes true, this creature will engender a lineage of excellent horses."

"I protect her from death with my body, and she shields me from spears with hers," the Black Rider replied. "Here I am, fleeing Destiny on all sides and meeting it in myself day and night."

" 'Death does not daunt me. I never escaped it by running away from myself,' my lord the *hajib* answers," exclaimed the man beside him.

"I hear her whinny in my dreams, the hoarse breathing of her gallop, her voice when she asks for food, and I feel as though I were already in battle, my shout rousing her to a homicidal frenzy," the Black Rider continued.

" 'The lance fell from your arm of iron; it would seem that the lance is no longer a lance,' al-Mansur will say when he sees you have neglected your weapon," the man said.

"The Prophet had four lances, four vertical nooses of death, serpents which pierced throats and bore into entrails," the Black Rider declared. "The warrior who holds them in his right hand is great, and grows greater."

A touch irreverently, Sancho Saborejo studied the supreme general of the Saracens. Then he examined Count Orosio, who gazed back more plaintively than the most downtrodden peasant on earth.

"Orosio, your reputation for courage has traveled throughout the known world, for which I challenge you to fight to the death with the weapons of your choosing," the Black Rider said to him.

"Milord knight, if what you want is to slay me in a duel, you will be disappointed," Count Osorio answered. "My keenest wish is to join Almanzor's hosts, and for him to be my king, he, the Victorious One."

" 'Praised be Allah,' says al-Mansur, who doesn't deign to glance at you, 'praised be the man who puts you to death,' " declared the man at the *hajib*'s side.

The Saracens fell silent, awaiting the signal from al-Mansur to continue on their way or remain where they were. The Black Rider circled the count on his black mare and, steely-eyed, observed the faces of the Christian men and women. His black brows arched, his black beard trembled with rage. Standing in his stirrups, he brandished an ax in his left hand and jeered, "What? Are these the warriors of León whose fame has reached Córdoba?"

"The valiant Christians are no better than rabbits," Wanzammar ibn Abi Bakr scoffed.

"They are not rabbits, they are swordless riders. They bear no arms, like women," exclaimed Banu Angelino.

"Let the count come forward, al-Mansur commands it," shouted the man next to the *hajib*.

The count knelt on one knee in the dust. "Your magnificence obliges me to humble myself before you," he murmured.

"Give him weapons, let him face me," the Black Rider said, twisting around on his saddle.

"It's not claws that make the lion, but teeth," said the female dwarf with a laugh.

The famished, flea-bitten captives began to walk, bent over beneath their burdens. A few of them carried al-Mansur's traveling bed on their backs. They were whipped on amid the horses and stolen cattle, muttering a plea for the celestial intervention of the apostle James, who was of no help to them.

"Look at that wretched hag," the Black Rider pointed at Doña Miguel. "Time spares no human being from ignominy."

The virago was standing with Jimena behind the minstrel.

"What are you doing here?" Sancho Saborejo asked her. "Do you want al-Mansur's hosts to rape and ravish your daughter? There's always a great demand for Christian women in the slave market of Córdoba."

"The *hajib* does not acknowledge you and says to be quiet," the female dwarf chided him.

Doña Miguel frowned at Sancho for having made public her folly and imprudence. Soon afterward, scowling and crestfallen, she headed back to the monastery with Jimena in tow.

" 'Do you fancy the milk of the young she-camel?' al-Mansur asks the Black Rider," the man alongside the *hajib* said to the horseman.

"I've had my fill of Christian udders," the Black Rider replied, leaning forward in the saddle.

"What is her infidel name?" the female dwarf asked Sancho, referring to Jimena.

"Buraiha," lied the minstrel, aware that this was the name of the *hajib*'s mother and daughter.

" 'Whoever touches her will die a dog's death,' says al-Mansur," warned the man beside him.

"Bring me that creature, he'll do for a eunuch," said the courtesan, dispatching two soldiers to arrest Rodríguez the cleric. "We can castrate him in Córdoba."

One of the Berber captains, mounted on a horse with creamy hooves, gave a whistle, touching the tip of his tongue to his palate.

"With Allah's blessing and aid, one day we shall conquer all of Christendom," Wanzammar ibn Abi Bakr spat out in his own language.

"Oh Commander of the Faithful, only the sea can set borders for the Muslims," the Black Rider said to al-Mansur.

" 'I am merely a soldier of the Prophet, may Allah bless him and give him peace,' says al-Mansur," declared the man beside the *hajib*.

"It is said by Omar, son of Mohammed, son of Abdelaziz, son of Said, son of Abdelmelic, may the Lord have mercy on him, that the day is not far off when the Victorious One of Allah will be caliph of Córboda," the female dwarf prophesied.

" 'I need not be caliph to reign in al-Andalus,' replies al-Mansur. His eyes are trained on the mountains of Asturias, already searching among the peaks for the Castilian count Sancho García and his ally García Gómez, who have formed an alliance against the Moors," said the man at his side.

When al-Mansur advanced, an escort of dozens of noble youths of high estate, with burly bodies and bearded faces, armed with silvery spears and gilded blades, clustered around him. He was followed by knights in armor and men with crossbows and lances, and by the Saracen and Christian common folk on foot. Litters with hidden women, guarded by armed eunuchs, were borne forward. The noise of drums and trumpets deafened the ears as al-Mansur set out in search of his enemies.

Gómez ran among six horses wearing saddles and bridles of the caliphate that several grooms were leading so that al-Mansur could change mounts during his journey north to the land of the Asturians. The Black Rider made as if to slice him in two, but Sancho reached the boy in time and began to scold him with words and gestures.

"Who was the man in black clothing next to Almanzor?" asked Oro María, suddenly beside me when I left my hiding place.

"Abd Allah of Córdoba, my brother," I answered.

"He's looking for one Alfonso de León, whom I happen to know," said Sancho Saborejo.

"May God keep you!" Oro María exclaimed.

"What does he want with you?" the minstrel asked.

"He wants to kill me," I replied, turning toward the west where, like the day, al-Mansur and his army were gradually fading away.

VISION V

April was not yet over when Isidoro, the Messiah of the Poor, appeared at the monastery gates.

Doña Miguel came to the scriptorium, where I was illuminating the Book of Revelation, to inform me that a strange creature, dressed in animal skins, accompanied by a tatterdemalion troop, was demanding to see me immediately. I hurried out to keep this miracle worker—who owed his fame to his power to cure the mute and the blind and to his broadcasting of the terrors of the end of the millennium—from entering the monastery buildings.

Isidoro was in the cemetery, amid the tombstones, surrounded by disciples and a swarm of flies. They were clever flies who seemed to understand what was afoot, for at times they hovered in the air, and at times they clustered on a patch of wall to peer toward the church.

"I order you to put before me all the wealth of the monastery, to wit, chalices and crucifixes, vessels of gold and silver, monstrances and caskets filled with relics of saints, and ornaments of diverse sorts, that I may choose among them and take what seems best to me," the foul-smelling man commanded as he came toward me.

I made no answer. He continued. "I want Saint Mary Magdalene's thumb and a splinter of the cross of Our Lord; in their stead I will leave dog bones and teeth."

I remained silent. He added, "I will make a blessing over the candles, I will say a prayer over the dead, I will bring the bones to life and, garbed in cope and crozier, I will lead a procession."

The Messiah of the Poor had matted hair and a shaggy beard. His body was frail and his face so sallow that it looked as if dirt and grass had dried on his cheeks. His name and birthplace were unknown. He was always on the move, more to escape from his enemies and persecutors than out of humility and love of anonymity. He worshiped being worshiped, and a forked staff served as his cane.

"Famines, plagues, wars, earthquakes and the appearance of false prophets will be signs of the end of time. Those 'Christs' will work miracles to lead the chosen into error. Thus saith the apostle," he declared before his faithful.

Isidoro's flock was composed of hungry paupers, premature dotards, blind starvelings, hunchbacked beggars, orphaned imbeciles, foolish prostitutes, crippled widows, casualties of war, and sufferers from eye ailments, Saint Vitus's dance and the diseases named after Saint Lawrence, Saint Lazarus and Saint Blaise. Some were so ragged that their clothing revealed their privates, and so flea-ridden and lousy that they scratched incessantly at their heads and bodies and scraped pellets of insects from behind their ears. The most fetid of all beamed a snaggle-toothed grin at me.

Former prisoners, down-and-outers, debtors and exiles, married and single servants, bumpkins, peasants, fugitive slaves, hermits, and vagabonds were also among his retinue. A separate group was made up of monks who had renounced both Islam and Christianity; spurious priests; rogues and traitors; criminals; grovelers; heinous sinners; shammers; and charlatans posing as the incarnation of the Holy Ghost, of the Spirit of Truth, heralding the imminence of the Third Testament; ecstatics praying for the Second

Coming of Lord Christ and the Kingdom of the Righteous and the Holy Saints.

In his sermon of the previous afternoon, delivered at the gates of the monastery of San Lucas, Isidoro denounced the envoys of the Evil One and the canting messiahs and the lunatics who roam the earth deluding other lunatics, declaring himself to be the sole anointed one of God.

"Should someone say to you: Behold, here or there is the Savior, do not believe him, for false prophets will arise and enumerate great signs and portents to seduce you," he warned his audience.

"The Son of Man will summon the beasts from the fields and the fowls from the heavens and exhort them, saying to them: 'Assemble and come forth, for I am preparing a great sacrifice for you: Eat the flesh of the mighty and drink the blood of the great,' " his disciple Nauj exclaimed, appropriating the words of Ezekiel.

Standing on the wall, his arms spread in a cross, Isidoro proclaimed himself the Messiah of the Poor and, as was his custom, withdrew from beneath his clothes a celestial letter, signed by the Lord Jesus, which attested to his divine condition and authenticated him as the true Son of God.

According to Sancho Saborejo, who stood nearby to hear him better, at the end of his preaching Isidoro recited parables backward and distributed among the poor garments, animals and crockery given to him by other poor. The people crowded round him, trying to snatch relics from his person: a hair from his donkey, a scrap of his rags or a hair from his head, amulets purportedly of use for curing the sick, protecting against enemies and exorcising the possessed.

"Saint Genadio is not a great saint, because he has worked only one miracle," a peasant said to Isidoro, whipping the ground contemptuously with a bit of cloth, which had belonged to the bishop, to humiliate him.

"In his dreams a place in the cenoby of San Lucas has been revealed to my lord where lies the incorruptible body of a saint more powerful than Genadio. We have only to disinter his bones and transfer them to any church we choose," Nauj asserted.

"The saint who will be uncovered is the prophet of the Messiah of the Poor," Sacul added.

"Let us pray, let us invoke the names of the fallen angels: Adin, Tubuel, Sabaok, Simiel," Socram urged them all.

From that moment on, it was noised abroad in León and the surrounding countryside that Isidoro could interpret the present, foresee the future and work miracles merely by squeezing his eyes shut or whispering a prayer. They said he was born chaste, that he had never tasted flesh or wine, nor had his hands ever caressed women or gold. As for his spirit, rumor had it that when he visited Jerusalem, Lord Christ had appeared before him and asked him to preach the end of the world and the coming of the kingdom of God.

His followers were now in the cemetery, foraging among the graves for holy relics, and, far worse, were preparing to spend months on end there. Death was edifying to Isidoro, and the crosses on the graves served him as reminders of eternal life. To me, he and his sheep were no more than handfuls of dust with eyes, mouths, hands and an astonishing capacity for sinning.

It was said he could hear voices berating him from afar, that he collected bony remains in cemeteries and packaged them in little caskets to sell as relics of martyrs and saints, whom he baptized with outlandish names, concocting such lives for them as came to mind and seemed appropriate.

Sancho Saborejo told me that yesterday afternoon, outside of San Lucas, when various unbelievers questioned Isidoro about Saints Adrián and Natalia and wondered aloud how he had been able to find so many relics, he gave implausible answers, such as, the martyrs had appeared to him in spirit, and still did, to inform him of the exact spot where their remains were buried. They directed him to break them into tiny pieces to enable more Christians to benefit from the miraculous power emanating from their garments and their hallowed bodies. An angel had guided him to their sepulchers and had revealed to him everything he wanted to know. This had occurred twenty-three times, and he had brought with him twenty-three male and female saints, from different kingdoms and counties, who had suffered a variety of martyrdoms.

In front of the monastery of San Juan el Teólogo, Socram, the greediest of the disciples, swore that he had for sale the body of Saint Sebastian, which he had acquired in Rome, along with the arrows that brought about his death. Nauj offered the ears of a hermit, endowed with the power to make the deaf hear. Two women displayed hairs, fingers and fingernails of Saint Stephen and other saints, which they, too, had brought from Rome.

When a matron asked Isidoro if the influence of the bodies and the garments impregnated with divine grace would not dwindle if they were parceled out, he replied that the mystery inherent in them remained untouchable and unreachable because both bodies and clothes were endowed with an unfading supernatural potency. It sufficed to touch or to invoke them to be cured.

"Monks and nuns, princes and kings want to buy my relics for the altars of their churches and the chapels of their palaces, but I will not sell to them," Socram crowed. "My lord has promised to distribute the relics among the needy of this world on the day of his triumph."

"The people hereabouts are so poor that they have need of marvels merely to stay alive. The bones and belongings of the saints are these marvels," said Isidoro, raising his voice before demanding from me, in the name of Saint James the Apostle, food and lodging for himself, his disciples and his beggarly flock.

I refused him, not only because we lacked provisions and sleeping space for so many, but for fear that they might stay here forever, especially should they learn that the monks of San Juan el Teólogo had gone off to preach the end of time, and that only Oro María, Sancho, Gómez, Doña Miguel, Jimena and I remained in the monastery.

I told him they could not spend the night in our domain because we had several monks dying from the plague, which was then scourging the countryside, and because demons haunted the monastery after dark.

"I am gifted with supernatural powers, and I can cure the sick with my touch," Isidoro replied. "I also drive out demons."

"Even the strongest succumb to these evils," I warned him.

"People now in health, tomorrow will be ailing," he said, looking me up and down meaningfully. "I predict that soon disasters and calamities never before seen will befall the kingdom of León, due to a dearth of loving acts among its inhabitants."

"I speak to you with just cause—" I started to say.

"Tell no lies. The ignoble reasons are plain on your face," Isidoro interrupted.

"A very few days ago, the monks in the monastery of Sahagún denied us charity, and during the night we saw black dwarfs crawl out of their bodies, demons of avarice that they had nourished inside themselves," Socram exclaimed.

"I know my demons, and I am not harboring misers. I cannot receive you," I said firmly, turning my back on Isidoro.

"You will be ashamed of this," he shouted, waving a cross at the sky.

I had heard that, when he was on the road, Isidoro habitually brandished crosses and exhorted people to pray to him in the Communion of Saints; that in Toledo he had married a woman named María, whom he had rebaptized Airam, because she was his wife and not his mother; and that one Sunday morning, before the assembled throng, he had pronounced the sacrilegious words that joined him in matrimony with that vile simulacrum of our Glorious Mother.

"Here you see," he brayed, "that I have taken to wife the virgin Airam. Bring on the wedding gifts. Maidens, put yours in this chest; youths, put yours in this other one."

He brazenly claimed he had been full of the grace of God since his mother's womb and was his Father's chosen one since birth. Days before her confinement, his mother had dreamed that a lamb burst out of her right flank—Lord Christ was born from the Virgin's right side. And, like Jesus, at a tender age he had distributed among the needy in Muslim and Christian lands alike whatever gold, silver and garments he owned. Socram bore witness to this in his gospel.

Isidoro made the maidens who devoutly followed him lie down by his side, that they might receive from him the mark that would grant them Eternal life. And once lying by his side, so that they might procreate the redeemer, he made holy their bellies with his seed. The redeemer, who would reign in the era of the 1000 Years of Isidoro, would come after the Day of Judgment. To the apostles, whom he had baptized with the names of Noel, Saduj, Ordep, Socram, Nauj, Sacul, and Soetam, making anagrams of the holy names, he confessed that he enjoyed the personal services of the angel Tubuas, a member of the highest celestial hierarchy. Although he was protected by the angel, Isidoro had armed his followers with cudgels and knives, lances and swords, and charged them with defending him from his earthly enemies, for the bishops of Astorga and León had spread the word that he worked his miracles with the help of the devil.

Since a week ago, Bishop Froilán II had savagely turned against him. Two messengers sent by Isidoro had appeared at his house; one was naked, with fleshless gums; the other, in rags and emaciated from hunger. Both had announced the messianic mission of their lord, the anointed one, who was coming to save the world, León and Froilán himself.

That Sunday, Isidoro prudently waited near the Count's Gate for the return of his envoys. When they came back empty-handed, he immediately dispatched others more foolish still. When Isidoro entered León the following day, instead of welcoming him with hosannas and drums, Bishop Froilán attacked him with sermons and rumors, published his heresies among the faithful, and warned that he only resembled an angel of light, like his master, the devil.

Isidoro made his reply that Monday, at the gates of the monastery of San Lucas, accusing the clerics of León and its surroundings of cohabiting with nuns, calling the dormitories bawdy houses, and maintaining that the sacraments were not valid if administered by the hands of copulators. Standing on a pulpit of stones, he declared that the cloisters were no better than the harems of the Moors, and that the harlots in the brothels were more sincere than the sisters, because they were practicing Christian charity by coupling with men they did not love. Finally, he enjoined the common folk and peasants not to pay tithes to the ministers of churches on earth.

"Each of you must fashion your own god. Make him from clay or wood or stone or ivory or crystal or iron or gold or silver, depending on your means. Carve the image with love, paint it in bright colors and give it human eyes. Once it is finished, put your own head in it and worship it," he preached.

That same day a procession arrived, droves of scruffy men and women carrying lighted candles and singing, bands of hapless widows and children, flocks of the blind and the lame, freed peasants with no possessions whatsoever, peasants who had abandoned fields that no longer sustained them, peasants free to die of hunger or to eat animals rotting on the dung heaps, creatures who, if they did not die by the sword of the Saracens, would die of cold and injustice, and others who, to obtain bread and money, assaulted wayfarers, robbed noblemen and stole from churches and monasteries.

Isidoro boasted of bringing shreds of Saint Luke the Evangelist's clothes, hair and nails of Saint Leocadia, bones of Saint Ubaldo and Saint Odilia. He claimed to own an ark containing the hand of Alfonso Pérez, a hermit who had lived in penitence and perpetual abstinence from the flesh, and to possess the bones of Saint Genadio and Abbot Vicente, whose body, kept in our chapel, smelled so sweetly that the believers called him "saint."

Noel bragged of having a casket with the three hairs of Mahomet which his companion Abu Zama'a al-Balawi had plucked from the Prophet's beard. In a small reliquary box, Socram kept the finger of an infant, whose name nobody knew, which worked miracles.

Two blind men arrived in search of Isidoro, holding on to a stick carried by a ragged boy.

"You who have dwelt in the caves in the Valley of Silence, give me back my sight," bawled the first, stretching out his hands.

The second said nothing, merely tilting his face in the direction where he supposed the false prophet to be. Socram emerged from the crowd to sprinkle Isidoro's head and chest with holy water.

"When your beautiful eyes crack open, we must extract two mice from the black holes," Isidoro murmured, touching the frayed, dirty bandages and bony sockets of the sightless men with his long fingers.

The blind men went off howling that they could see.

The Messiah of the Poor was reputed to have lived in the caves near the monastery of Santiago de Peñalba, where Bishop Genadio had retreated from the world to devote himself to penance and prayer, divination and magic. But this was a lie. Isidoro had built a small church on the riverbank dedicated to the worship of himself.

Because of his knowledge of the Rule of Saint Benedict and the lives of the saints, he was thought to have been a cleric before he discovered that he was a redeemer of souls. Moreover, he had commenced his preaching dressed as a monk. His eloquence was considerable, and the crowds hearkened to him as if he were the Son of God. It was said that his presence in León had been foretold at the beginning of the year by the appearance of a comet.

"When the day comes, those men who remain in power through tyranny and the sword will be obliterated from the face of the earth," he railed outside the monastery of San Lucas. "The barbarians who have come out of the desert thrive on the desolation they cause. Being corrupt, they draw others into corruption; being loathsome, they breed hatred."

"Isidoro walks barefoot over mountains and plains, from city to city, from village to village, from castle to castle, from monastery to monastery. In squares, hospitals and marketplaces he preaches the end of time, the judgment of the living and the dead and the punishment of sinners by fire," Sancho Saborejo whispered to me. "In rain and cold, by night and by day, hungry and weary, on foot or riding a donkey, like Jesus, Isidoro condemns greed, silken clothes, attachment to earthly goods and human wickedness."

"Our lord Isidoro says that the date of his birth is more important than the day of his departure from the century," Noel exclaimed.

"Our lord Isidoro says that today he clearly remembered the afternoon when, as a ragamuffin, he was pursued by the dogs of a miserly cleric, because it was on that fearful afternoon, sitting in a tree, that he glimpsed for the first time the divine light that shone on his person," Socram said.

"Our lord Isidoro says that after being incarnated as a rich man he became poor, like Lord Christ, and by becoming impoverished, he enriched us with his poverty," Sacul proclaimed.

"Should someone come to you saying, 'I have naught to feed myself, I am naked,' what will you answer? Will you sell the adornments of the church and its liturgical paraphernalia so the man can eat and clothe himself?" Isidoro asked me with fierce delight. "The monastic life and acts of charity are one and the same."

"Have you seated the hungry at your table, and have you broken bread with them?" he asked me next. "Have you gone out to do battle with kings and bishops in defense of orphans and widows? Have you relinquished your pillow so that the poor man has a place to lay his head? Have you shared with good humor and generosity the austerities of the destitute? Until the end of time, the clamorings of the wretched will not cease to be heard."

I made no reply. He challenged me.

"Will you join me tomorrow in laying the first stone to build the City of the Second Millennium? Will you be the gatekeeper with me of that City of Charity, Love and Justice? Will you fulfill with me our obligation to the poor man, will you wash his feet? Will you worship Lord Christ in his person?" His malevolent eyes sized me up. "Do you believe that the Son of Man will find faith among the sons of Ishmael, as I have found it?"

I calmly answered, "The apostle said, 'All those who are from Israel are not Israel.' Similarly: All those who call themselves Christians, like yourself, are not Christians."

His voice became louder. "In these times of apostasy, all are infidels, and even kings and bishops, envious and cowardly, bow to the power of the Saracens, serving their gods and not ours."

"In the era of Ishmael, there will be no more offices or sacrifices in the churches. The sons and daughters of the Christians will be slaves of the caliphate," Sacul interjected.

"The sons and daughters of the Christians are and will be sold by their parents to the Saracens to obtain material advantages in exchange for the captivity of their own blood. Their servitude will be as bitter as it is cruel," Isidoro added.

"When the time allotted by God for the Saracens' dominion over this land comes to an end, they will undergo eras of misfortune, hunger, epidemics and slavery, and their kings will prostrate themselves in the mud and dust. No one will pay them tribute. And upon arising, their viziers will find only emptiness and silence in their hands," I said.

"It will take centuries for that to happen," Isidoro grumbled.

"The slave maidens and youths will return to their nations and their parents, to Greece and Africa, to Galicia and Toledo, and they will multiply and bear children who are free. Peace will reign over the earth," I continued.

"The sons of Ishmael, masters of Persia and Sicily, al-Andalus and Toledo, will say, 'No one and nothing can ever release the Christians from our grasp,' " he asserted.

Just then Gómez appeared, as if from nowhere. He cowered before Isidoro and held out to him a gift, wrapped in a soiled, shabby cloth.

Isidoro undid the wrapping in the sight of all, exposing an arm bone. It came from Saint Genadio, our church's most precious relic. Gómez was still standing beside Isidoro, who spoke to him. The boy made a face.

"Don't you know how to talk?" Isidoro asked.

Gómez grunted.

"Are you dumb?"

The boy nodded.

"If you believe in me, the next time I come to León I will restore your speech. You shall bear witness throughout the land to my power to cure the tongueless."

It began to rain. The sky teemed with swift, cold drops. When Isidoro saw that I was returning to the monastery, he shouted at my back: "Man, repent!"

"We will soon be back, and you will fling open the church doors to us, you will ride with us in the name of the living devil!" the man called Socram screamed at me.

"You will gather in the sheep at the wrong time under the wrong sign, because this monastery will be destroyed before the waning of the millennium," Noel prophesied.

"You will cry out in vain when you see ghosts dancing on the rooftops, for you will be alone amid the desolation," Sacul warned me.

"The peasants have a saying: 'I'm not asking you to go, but I'll make sure you leave,' " I replied as he vanished, whether from my sight alone or among other people I could not tell.

Nauj proffered a cross made from two sticks to Isidoro, who took it in his left hand and began to walk, leaving black footprints in the mud. Holding a candle in one hand and a small box containing a splinter of the true cross in the other, Socram took his place at the head of the throng of faithful, who were singing hymns. From his legs dangled tiny bells whose jingling was meant to ward off evil spirits. At the rear of the crowd, Noel flailed the withered arm of Saint Genadio like a weapon. The congregation followed Isidoro to the river, threaded its way among the poplars and turned into the road leading to Astorga.

The guileless folk believed that this despicable man was the Messiah of the Poor. They were mistaken. The real Messiah, the Lord of the Year 1000, is I. The time for my revelation has not yet come.

VISION VI

I was born near Córdoba, that patrician city of old now aptly called the jewel of the world. I first saw the light far from the debauched, unruly masses, the day that al-Hakam II al-Mustansir billah, son of Abd al-Rahman III, acceded to the throne. That crafty and ambitious ruler had declared himself Caliph, successor to Mahomet and Commander of the Faithful, in the year 929, lengthening his name with the honorary title of "He Who Defends the Religion of Allah," may God have mercy on him.

Abd al-Rahman, the eighth Umayyad emir, died in the seventieth year of his life and the forty-ninth of his reign. Those who knew him, or glimpsed him during his lifetime, reported that he had blue eyes and short legs and was so wealthy and powerful that his coffers contained twenty million gold coins and his harem more than 3,600 women of diverse ages and origins. They also said that no fewer than 3,750 slaves of both sexes dwelt in his palace at Madinat al-Zahra, and that, being a monarch of

implacable justice, he had witnessed the beheading of, or had perhaps beheaded with his own hand, his son Abd Allah al-Zahid, accused of con-
spiring against his father and brother in order to usurp the caliphate.
Invincible in military matters, his navy and his armies dominated the seas
and the Christian kingdoms. At the height of his glory, tribal chiefs from
the north of Ifriqiya flocked to his Andalusian courts, as did ambassadors
from the Emperor of the East, Constantine VII Porphyrogenitus, from the
Emperor of the West, Otto the Great, from the Frankish kings, and from
the popes of Rome.

I was born one Thursday in October of the year 961 in a house in
Madinat al-Zahra, "the city of surpassing brilliance." My first whimper was
drowned out by the coronation feast and the bustling of the new Caliph's
concubines who, being confined to the harem, were spying on the ceremony through the marble window screens.

Al-Hakam II al-Mustansir billah, "he who seeks the victorious help of
Allah," took the oath in a hall of the palace. Supposedly my half brother,
he never knew it. He was forty-six years old, with blond hair, black eyes,
aquiline nose, jutting jaw, short forearms, short legs and delicate health.
The chief eunuchs were lined up in order of rank to his right and left as
far as the gallery. They wore their swords girded against their white tunics,
in mourning for Abd al-Rahman III. The slave eunuchs, wearing long mail
shirts and jeweled swords, were ranged in two orderly files. There were
more eunuchs in the arcades, white-clad Slavs holding swords. Behind them
stood the servants, covered from head to toe with armor. Then came the
archers, the infantry troops from the Dar al-jund, and the black slaves.
Sentries and soldiers guarded the al-Sudda Gate. On the other side were
mounted horsemen as far as the portico.

In the *Book of Times*, the day following my birthday was recorded thus:
"According to the *Sindhind*, the Sun passed from the sign of Libra into
Scorpio; on the twentieth day the inhabitants of Córdoba began to sow
onions, the harvest of olives was counted, and the cold became so intense
that men and women changed their white garments for others of raw silk
and wool; the cranes and starlings arrived, and people boiled syrups of
quince and sour apple."

The palace city of Madinat al-Zahra was Abd al-Rahman III's masterpiece. Begun, according to some, in 936, according to others, in 940, its construction took twenty-five years. The site occupied a surface of 990,000 cubits, and every day 1,000 men, 1,400 mules and 400 camels labored on it. Each day thousands of blocks of carved stone and irregular stone were used, and five hundred loads of lime and plaster. Altogether, four thousand columns of white, green, pink and mottled marble, brought from Ifriqiya, Byzantium, Carthage, Rome, the land of the Franks, and al-Andalus, were employed. Five hundred doors, some of carved wood, others with iron plaques or burnished bronze leaves, were hung in the halls, bedrooms, streets and corridors. The streets and passageways beginning at the gates linked houses and buildings and had set-in stone benches where the officials could sit while the guards remained standing. The southern gate, the Gate of the Statue, connected the city to the rest of the world.

Once it was finished, ministers, generals, officials, water bearers, grammarians, servants, horses and mules, eunuchs, women, and slaves belonging to the Caliph came to reside in its buildings. There were marvels of East and West for its embellishment, objects of gold and silver, ivory, precious stones, carpets, furnishings and fine textiles. The wall, flanked by square towers, enclosed palaces, houses, mosques, gardens, pools, baths, barracks, storerooms, workshops, jails, stables, markets and fountains. The architect's name was Maslana ibn Abd Allah.

The Caliph's residence was built on the highest level of the Alcázar. From his dwellings the Caliph could behold Córdoba and its countryside. Indeed, the entire construction had been conceived to exalt the magnificence of his person, the areas destined for prayer as much as those assigned to pleasure, as much for the movements of his body as for those of his eyes.

The garden was the image of paradise, with water at its heart. Trees grew in this earthly Eden: cypress, ash, bay, juniper, white mulberry, poplar, holm oak, willow and palm; others bore fruit: lemons, walnuts, figs, apples, pears, apricots, plums and pomegranates; and there were eggplants, broad beans, lettuces, cucumbers, asparagus, artichokes, radishes, onions, chick-peas and watermelon. Vines and honeysuckle climbed the walls, the lawns were planted with mint, chamomile, anise, sesame, mustard, fennel, rosemary and oregano, myrtle, oleander, strawberry trees, spikenard, wall-flowers, violets and lilies.

These gardens, made of foliage and shade, of fruits and fragrances, of flesh-and-blood houris and castrated youths, were the Eden promised by the Prophet to his followers. The pleasures he had offered to the chosen of Allah in the next life were also enjoyed by the Caliph on earth.

My mother, Adosinda de la Vega, gave birth to twins in one of the bedrooms on the lower level, but not many people knew of it, because the sound of her panting was muffled by the noises of the palace city. That very night, far from her and her toils, the eight brothers of the new Saracen monarch were installed in their lodgings, legitimate brothers who, during the ceremony, took their seats in the East and West Halls and were the first to swear fealty to the enthroned sovereign.

I was born first. Squalling, my brother followed, after tussling with me in the womb. He wanted to be born before me, with all his soul he yearned to be the firstborn, and he wouldn't let me out . . . until they wrenched me from his grasp. Much later my mother told me that at the moment of birth he grabbed my feet and pressed his hand against my face, trying to smother me, but I pushed him aside and foiled his attack.

No sooner did I emerge than my body was carried to a room in the seraglio, and everyone marveled at my face and shining eyes, unmistakable portents of my luminous destiny on earth.

"Purple with rage, your brother Abd Allah came out after you did, his face bloody, his eyes unseeing, his fists clenched; with long nails and sharp teeth he tried to bite your flesh and claw my breasts. His cry was more a howl than a wail," Adosinda confided to me. "When I first saw him and he opened his eyes, I knew I had begotten a creature not of this world."

After that she always kept me apart from him and held me in her arms, lest he do me harm. If she was careless for an instant, my skin was soon covered with the marks of scratches and blows.

Adosinda was born and brought up in the harem. She was the daughter of Froila, a Leonese nun captured by Abd al-Rahman III at the onset of his reign. The Caliph regarded my grandmother as his property and changed her name to Ualada. One day Adosinda became her father's lover, and we, sons and grandsons of both women's seducer.

In that world of stallions, my grandmother and mother had names and bodies only when they were taken to one of the seventy-two bedrooms for pleasuring the Commander of the Faithful. Otherwise, they disappeared from his sight and with difficulty survived the competition of maidens recently brought from the Christian North.

Unusually, my mother was sent to school as a child. There she met Aixa ben Ahmed, daughter of the poet Abulhosain. But the day she began menstruating, they veiled her face, and her life of seclusion began. She was shut away in the area reserved for women of the harem, where she learned to play the lute, recite poetry and spy on the world through the marble window screens.

"The veil should cover a woman's face, clothing should conceal her body, and the house should encompass her entire existence," the eunuch Luna said to her one morning.

"A woman should not speak, because the timbre of her voice lays bare her person, and a woman's life must pass in the strictest anonymity," the eunuch Crepúsculo told her.

"It is no more the sun's fault that you are feminine than it is a man's fault when his concubine conceives a female," the eunuch Luna added.

"Being female rather than male has been an unfortunate blessing for your mother," the eunuch Crepúsculo remarked to me years later.

The concubines who accompanied my mother in the eunuchs' custody were Galicians, Navarrese, Catalans, Andalusians, Slavs and Africans; some had been purchased in the slave markets of Córdoba, Seville, Mérida, Almería and Toledo. Whether they were captured during Saracen forays into Christian kingdoms, or taken prisoner from defeated tribes, they soon became accustomed to life in the harem, although they were suspicious and jealous of one another, seeking the Caliph's preference.

To entertain themselves during their long days of seclusion, the women exchanged wondrous stories in which the characters were snakes as big as palm trees, monkeys spitting fatal poison, rhinoceroses with horns on their backs, salamanders who lived amid the flames and died at the touch of water, and nasnas with only half a body, one leg and one hand, who spoke the language of Babylonia, although they couldn't understand it, and were hunted down with dogs and eaten. Zuleykha and Zafira talked mostly about a dead lake in Galicia where all life perishes, about a city of bronze built by King Solomon in al-Andalus, about Saint Torquatus's olive tree, which flowers only one day a year, fruits, and then turns black. Aysha revealed the secrets of the Prince of Believers of Baghdad, a descendant of the prophet Mahomet, who had imprisoned and shackled his family because he was afraid they would conspire against him and kill him.

"That Caliph, who shows his vassals only the brightness of his visage once a year, has a palace where he confines people who become crazy from the heat," she told them.

On her night of glory, Adosinda was deflowered by her father, Abd al-Rahman III who, in his paradise of buttocks and breasts, had no recollection of having begotten her nor of having seen her before. In exchange for her virginity, he gave her an ivory casket and a gold necklace, and told her that no one on earth was her superior in beauty; that her body was made of the stuff of clouds swept toward his celestial bed by the hurricane of desire; and that he was like a dissolute beast grazing on the flowers of her garden as if they were grass.

"Do not ask my age when you see the gray in my hair and the wrinkles on my face, for I have lived only for one moment, the moment in which I met you," he confessed to her one day at dawn.

"Don't be sad, sadness turns souls rusty, like iron," he said to her one afternoon. "Allah knows that I walk the earth clad in a tunic of defiled chastity," he declared on another occasion. Finally, in a burst of passionate fervor he vowed that he no longer wished to have children with any woman but her, if she would consent to it.

She assented, and he began reciting to her verses by poets of his court in which he was hard, stony ground covered by the tender vegetation of his love for her. Andalusian singing women came to her bedroom to enliven her with dances and lute playing. Pouches filled with gold coins appeared nightly hanging on the wall across from her room, so that when she opened the door to take possession of them, he entered paradise.

Before his arrival Adosinda would perfume her bedroom with incense or scented golden candles, which burned all night long; she imbued her clothes with fragrances and obtained aromatic potions from the pharmacy to cure herself of colds and sore throats, and cosmetics to treat her hair and skin.

"Ambergris, musk and camphor are good for maladies of the heart and brain; the first is extracted from whales, and the other two come from India and China. They are very dear, and they make more desirable gifts than a horse, a slave or a gold box," she told me years later, showing me an ivory receptacle in the shape of a statue, which the Caliph had given her years before.

Suddenly a sprightly Byzantine slave on the brink of puberty was brought to the harem. Her breasts were like honeyed moons and her loins like a celestial mare's. The Caliph called her Estrella and likened her walk to a cluster of narcissi rippling in a glade. He admitted falling into the flames of her body like a moth into fire and declared that when he gazed upon her his eyes knew not where to stop, as her beauty had no limits. From the eunuchs and other women in the harem, Adosinda learned that he preferred to mount her at dawn. "There is no other paradise but your crupper," he had confessed to her.

The Andalusian women no longer came to Adosinda's chamber to play music; the pouches brimming with gold coins were hung on other walls. Once she had lost the Caliph's love, she had to live day and night in the same room with her rivals and share him in rotation. She was allowed occasional visits from female friends. Bedecked in jewels and served by slaves, she still had me (and Abd Allah), for, by conceiving, she had ensured herself against transferral to another harem or sale to a brothel in Almería. Virtually repudiated, she devoted herself with patience and wisdom to spinning and weaving the future of her son.

"Oh Commander of the Faithful, you who cast away the rose after plucking her, give her to me for my pleasure," one of the Berber captains said to Abd al-Rahman when he saw how he disdained her. "Show me your affection and generosity by this live present."

"I cannot do that, because she has conceived my seed," the Caliph replied, so enamored of the young slave that he asked the chief eunuch to drown her in the Guadalquivir River to free himself from the passion he felt for her. Luckily, the eunuch disobeyed him, for the very next day the

Caliph ordered him to bring the houri to his bedroom.

Adosinda told me that under those circumstances, she gave milk only to me. She nursed me until I was four years old, and I sucked blissfully, my face slobbery between her fleshy moons. I can remember that when I returned from play, she would let me satisfy my hunger at her aching breasts.

My brother was suckled by several wet nurses who took turns because of the pain his teeth inflicted on their nipples. But there were times when Adosinda took Abd Allah in her arms by mistake, believing he was I.

Banished from the beatific presence of the woman who gave life to us both, Abd Allah grew up green with hatred in another house on the palace grounds. I spent my infancy under the patient tutelage of my mother and early on learned words in the new Romance tongue and in Arabic, speaking my own and others' thoughts.

The birth of Prince Hisham, future Commander of the Faithful, in the year 965 afforded much joy to the reigning Caliph, a man already advanced in years, but caused the attention paid by the courtesans and eunuchs to us twins to diminish.

Meanwhile, whenever my brother became angry with me, he would ram his head against a tree until blood flowed from the wounds. Or he would try to injure himself by flinging himself to the ground on stones. Whenever he did this, my own body ached. On other occasions, maddened by jealousy, he would glare at himself in the mirror and insult his reflection. In this way he could offend me. We had both discovered that our likeness was spiritual as well as bodily. We understood each other by movements of the hands, by grimaces and furtive glances, and by signs that went unnoticed by everyone else.

The language we used, a mixture of Arabic and *aljamia,* sounded to ignorant ears like a foreign tongue because we spoke it rapidly with an altered pronunciation. Abd Allah liked to say words backward. Our voices often resembled the cawing of ungainly birds.

Abd Allah tagged after me for years and months; he was my living shadow. Neither he nor I had friends. And we did not want anyone to approach us or speak to us. We were both easily embarrassed, and we blushed if we so much as found ourselves in the presence of the women of the harem or the eunuch guardians of the beds.

There was one maiden, and only one, whom we allowed near us. She was a pious girl by the name of María Sabarico, the daughter of a Mussulman and a Christian woman. She lived in Córdoba and was companion to us both. And we were both in love with her.

"Are you always together?" she asked us one morning.

"Yes," I answered.

"Who are you?" she continued. "Whom do you tell your dreams to when you dream? In whom do you confide your most private desires?"

We both remained silent, each afraid of revealing the other's secrets.

"Whom do you love above all else?" María persisted.

"God," I replied.

"Nobody," muttered Abd Allah, although no voice issued from him, and his lips did not part.

People sometimes thought that Abd Allah was possessed by me, or I by him. Everyone wanted to know which of us was the stronger, the dominant one. But he and I merely stared at each other in the face of so much questioning. We were so indistinguishable that we confounded our taunters.

We lived in the palace city all year round, and we continued to live there even after the Caliph stopped residing in the Alcázar during the spring and autumn months. Al-Hakam II was to die in the year 976, and al-Mansur would found another city to the east of Córdoba, called Madina al-Zahira, where he would take up residence and transfer the court and its administrators. In that city he built a fountain of black amber in the shape of a lion, which may have stood for his own person. But I do not wish to get ahead of events.

We dressed alike. Others looked us brazenly in the face, comparing us, attempting to determine our differences. Finding none, they laughed at the identical creatures. It was to avoid these jeers that I gave up the heavy, somber clothes of winter and the light, white ones of summer; in April I started wearing long, colored silk *jubbas,* and in October and November I donned dyed, quilted garments. I cropped my hair and left my ears and neck bare; I sprinkled myself with the perfumes introduced into Córdoba by the freedman Ziryab.

My mother and I contemplated the outside world from a stone bench near the North Gate: Above were hackberry, poplar, olive, cypress and ash trees, and down below, the wooded valley of the Guadalquivir, where Córdoba lay. The sun hurt our eyes, burned my face. The thick walls prevented us from leaving, nor were we permitted to cross the gate whose angled entrance impeded the passage of invaders and inhabitants alike. Strategically posted guards observed our movements. Hunched under the seething noonday heat, a water bearer crept forward beneath the light-crazed palm trees. Not far off, Abd Allah was squashing black ants, which clustered round his feet seeking death.

Abd Allah and I often went to inspect the place where the retinues of foreign kings set out to be received in the East Hall by the Commander of the Faithful. We followed the visitors from nearby and afar; we climbed walls and got lost in corridors, pavilions and bedrooms, until nobody knew where we were except the gardeners, who gave us the flawed roses. In exchange, my brother gave them lizards we had killed and ants.

The Caliph, who seldom let himself be seen, was often observed by us. We espied him in the basilicalike hall, seated at its center on his celestial throne, his face hidden behind a veil that blurred his features. We stared in fascination at the carvings of the tree of life on the wall panels. At other times, crouching in the grass, we surprised him in the garden in the company of a concubine and a eunuch, admiring the colts raised in the salt marshes of Seville and Niebla. What most astonished us about him was how many bedrooms, beds and women he had, since he could be in only one bedroom, in one bed and with one woman at a time, no matter how great his desire.

Whether it was rainy or hot, my brother and I played and fought all over the streets, stairways and patios. When we passed the jail, the eunuchs threatened to lock us up in the underground dungeon if we did not behave ourselves. We fed bread to the fish swimming in the pools, but we were happiest, especially on scorching summer afternoons, visiting the two fountains whose bronze animals spouted water from their mouths.

We used to wait for al-Mansur, then known as Muhammad ibn Abi Amir, to go by on the ramped street that led from the northern gate to the terrace on which the army headquarters stood, its columns supporting horseshoe arches. The future prime minister made his way down surrounded by Berbers, his helmet striated by the heat.

It was in a nearby garden that I chanced upon al-Mansur. I was holding an apple too big for my mouth. As soon as he noticed me, he came over, grabbed the fruit, put it in his own mouth and broke it apart with his teeth. He gave me back the pieces, sneering at my surprise. By the familiar way he looked at me, he appeared to know me well, but he was surely mistaking me for my brother, who had just begun to receive military training in his army. When I, too, began learning how to use weapons, it was from the commander-in-chief of the central marches, Ghalib Nasiri. Al-Mansur had been with his daughter, whom I had furtively glimpsed in the palace prior to this encounter.

Later on, in the month of September of 971, I watched al-Mansur returning at the head of the troops that had defeated Ziri ibn Manad. They had ridden out from the Alcázar of al-Zahra, where they had occupied the plain, until they reached the Gate of the Pavilion, where they had skewered the heads of Manad and his hundred companions on long lances and pikes. These heads were taken later by the mutes, who held them aloft in the forefront when the parade began through the streets of Córdoba. Surrounded by officials, who had swarmed out to welcome them, and followed by the dignitaries of the city, they rode as far as the Gate of the Dam, where armed contingents and people from the outskirts awaited them. Armored horsemen and archers in white capes with bows slung across their backs converged from several points on the Gate of the Statue. Waving banners emblazoned with yawning lions and leopards and eagles tearing apart their prey, they entered Madinat al-Zahra between two rows of horses, the pikes with the heads bristling in their midst. The Caliph received them on his throne.

In those days of lightning and winds, copious rains and earthquakes, the child giant Umar ibn Araqin was brought before al-Hakam II. His grandfather explained that the prodigy, whose flesh was flabby and lacerated, had grown with monstrous speed to his present size. To demonstrate his appetite, the boy, who spoke despite having only half a tongue, set to work devouring pomegranates and quinces, acorns and chestnuts, grapefruit and walnuts, and all the fowl, flesh and fish they put before him.

A few weeks after this event, an animal was brought to the palace garden; it was like a cat but much bigger, with black-striped yellow skin, a long tail and yellow eyes, sharp claws and teeth. The Caliph and his children, the courtesans and the eunuchs, the favorite and several veiled women, and my brother and I went to see the beast, which had been captured in Hircania and was exceedingly fierce and voracious. It downed whole slabs of meat, crunched bones and tore apart small live animals, which it swallowed rapidly on account of the heat of its breath. The Berbers, who had found it, said it could defeat an elephant and was afraid of the sound of bells, shrinking from their reverberations. If it couldn't escape the ringing, it killed itself, for it abhorred music. The instruments it most hated were the tambourine and the flute. Men captured it with a mirror because it became hypnotized by its deceptive reflection. It was called "tiger."

No matter how much it rained, Abd Allah and I never shielded ourselves from the water. As offspring of the desert, to us the rain's existence seemed a kind of miracle. During a storm we remained outside in the palace garden and let the abundant water drench us. Watched by the eunuchs, Adosinda called to us from the other side of the window screens of a pavilion. We ignored her, not budging from the spot where we were standing.

The afternoon of November fourth, the day the Christians celebrate the feast of Saint Zoilus Martyr and the Cordobans pick carrots and gather acorns, chestnuts and myrtle berries, a white horse galloped across the palace garden. It was one of the Caliph's favorite chargers. When it was gone, Abd Allah and I stood for a long time staring at where it had passed.

On another afternoon, the eighteenth day of the same month, when the Christians were celebrating the feast of Saint Acisclus Martyr in the Church of the Prisoners, my brother and I took a ride on the white horse. We were mounted bareback when the stablemaster came to scold us. First one of us dropped the reins, then the other. First one slid to the ground, then the other. And no one could tell which was Abd Allah and which Alfonso.

"The mules who rode the horse are plump, shapely and of good stock; they could fetch a price of two hundred dinars," a eunuch said, taunting us.

"Everything people think they know about us is false. Nobody will ever know what goes on between us and who we are. Nobody knows us better than we ourselves do," Abd Allah said to me one night, making unaccustomed use of speech. "I never want to be separated from me, from you. Not in this life or the other. If anyone tries to separate us, if hatred separates us, we will find each other again. We are fatally joined."

But as of that night, we began to drift apart, to become independent of each other and to disagree. We wanted to show the world, and above all ourselves, that we were not so alike, that we were completely different persons. Abd Allah chose to dress in black, I in bright colors. He took on an air of death, I, of life. The fifteenth of July, at noon, he attacked me. Before lunging at my chest, he glared at me so wrathfully that I thought he was a demon out to destroy me. I was not afraid of him.

He screeched horribly to frighten me. Digging his knifelike nails into my breast, he tried to gouge out my heart. The more he punished me, the more frantic and furious he became. I felt his pain, he felt my agony. The shreds of skin scraped away by his nails stuck to my fingers. His hands hurt me from pummeling him so hard on my body. He was so like me that for a moment I thought it was I who was savaging him. I read the horror he provoked in me on his face. Suddenly he burst out crying from his uncontrollable fury.

"You are Abd Allah, I am Alfonso, and I hate you with all my soul," he exclaimed, punching me in the face.

"No," I shouted at him. "I am Alfonso, and you are Abd Allah. We will both be what we are for all eternity."

"You're a lying pig," he replied, with renewed violence. "You are Abd Allah, and you've been deceiving me since the day we were born."

When the black eunuch, who was a friend of my mother's, pulled him away before he could kill me, he stood still beside the wall, his eyes vacant. Afterward I learned that his fingers were smeared with stinkwort, the plant warriors use to poison their darts. From then on, Abd Allah devoted himself to weapons, seldom speaking. If someone addressed him, he shrugged his shoulders in response.

Ualada, Adosinda's mother, died old and Christian. Adosinda decided to instruct me in the true faith. She sent me in secret to the basilica of San Acisclo—beyond the walls of Córdoba, on the road to the town of Cuteclara—to study theology, scripture and divine writings. There I met Christian boys who were learning Arabic in the parochial school of San Cipriano. Meanwhile, the beardless scions of the Caliph, sons of their father's favorite slave women, were amusing themselves with adolescent slave girls recently brought from the Christian kingdoms.

My mother, who was no longer called upon in the harem, was unexpectedly banished from the palace without so much as a necklace or a gold coin, stripped even of the earrings she had been wearing in her lobes. Her son Abd Allah had denounced her to the theologians for practicing Christianity in secret.

It was nighttime when I saw her cross the bent passageway, go past the caliphal guard and step over the marble threshold of the North Gate. I remember it was the month of *Shatanbar,* September. The Christians were celebrating the feast of Saint Michael Archangel, the peaches, pomegranates and quince were ripe, the swallows had returned to the seashore, and the so-called Niebla vultures had flown in from the ocean.

Adosinda de la Vega took refuge in the monastery of Tabanos, which was strictly governed according to the rules of monastic life. The abbot attempted to make her a virgin consecrated to God, who would mortify her body with iron fronds and then display herself in the window, as the sainted women Artemia of Cuteclara and Elizabeth of Tabanos had done. Adosinda wished neither to be a virgin consecrated to God nor to mortify her body, but she confessed to one infidelity: Abd Allah and I were in reality the sons of a Jewish physician named Yehuda ibn Ishaq, one of the followers of Rabbi Mosé Hanok. Yehuda, who used to come to the caliph's palace every day with hundreds more Jews in hundreds of carts, all of them dressed in regal clothes and the turban of Muslim officials, had loved her madly. Denounced by a eunuch spy, he had been thrown alive in a basket into a well.

After a few months in the monastery, my mother married a young freeborn peasant by the name of Sendamiro, to whom she was wife and companion, not slave or concubine. Bishop Juan blessed their union. Her dowry, which I surreptitiously furnished, consisted of ten oxen, twenty cows, a necklace, five rings, a silver porringer, a horse, a bed and a maidservant.

Abd Allah found out about the wedding, followed them to their hiding place and denounced them. The punishment for *muladies,* Spaniards turned Muslim, who returned to Christianity was death, and so Adosinda and Sendamiro fled to Barcelona, making twelve stages from Córdoba to Valencia alone. Afraid of being captured during a Moorish foray into the Christian kingdoms, they departed from there for France.

Abd Allah and I were banished to a gallery of rooms with adjoining latrines ranged around an arcaded patio. The gallery was meant for demoted palace residents and for repudiated women or domestic servants. We were treated as brothers, although we no longer spoke to or greeted one another.

Abd Allah would never know that among the herd of Jews he forced to convert to Islam years later was his real father, Yehuda ibn Ishaq, who had managed to escape from the well. I never had further news of Adosinda. I think she died decades afterward near the monastery of Cluny. Or she may still be alive, burdened with days and tribulations.

VISION VII

When I was still beardless, the harem became my church. In its multiple beds I began to love God through the favors of the young slaves and the pleasures of my own flesh.

Hiding in the recesses of the seraglio, I surprised the Caliph in the arms of his favorites or of his eunuchs, and I learned about fondling, kissing and cruelty. My brother, more precocious than I in the vices of the body, used to accompany the monarch during his orgies with slaves, and occasionally received pubescent African girls as gifts.

I spent my days surrounded by al-Hakam II's women, besotted with the smell of their flesh and their perfumes, fascinated by the strangeness of their features and the unintelligible music of their tongues. Sequestered females continually loomed in my path, looking neglected by their proprietor, a man who gave no thought to satisfying his concubines; rather it was they who had to be at his beck and call.

I remember one warm morning toward the end of June, when juice is pressed from green grapes, and goat horns and deer antlers are sawn off to make into bows, that a Greek slave, whose name does not matter, after a brief exchange of words initiated me into the secrets of her body.

I thought about her in the days that followed. I reminisced insatiably, I re-created her nudity, I stroked her thighs, her mountain of Venus, smooth and hairless as a child's, the narrow channel of her sex, which grew more spacious within; I evoked the blind, shy meeting of genitals; I felt swept away by my own lust, by the slipping of my semen into her exposed carnality.

It was very hot in Córdoba. Melancholy and lustful, I was bathed in sweat wherever I went. The sun in my eyes, which sought a glimpse of her, was a wounding furrow, a panting tongue. I still remember it. My desire mingled with the sultriness, and above the city the sky, intoxicated with light, starkly white, seemed to come crashing down onto the dazzled walls of Madinat al-Zahra.

Gradually I forgot her. Her features, which had been unveiled to me in secret, merged with the features of other veiled maidens, and I stopped looking for her.

One afternoon—this time in August—Fronilde, a Basque woman and servant of Subh, bathed me and seduced me while she spoke of watermelons ripening, of ostriches in heat, of sardines abounding, and of jam being made from sweet pears.

When my brother found out about my dalliance with Fronilde, he climbed into her bed and passed himself off as me many times. I don't know whether he did it to cheat me or to feel what I felt at her side, to enjoy the love meant for another as if it were his.

When she mentioned having lain with me on such and such an occasion, I told her she had done so with another, identical to me, in the belief that he was I. Fronilde didn't believe me, or didn't want to believe me, because when Abd Allah dressed as I did, and undressed as I did, he turned into me, and it was virtually impossible for anyone besides us to detect the differences between us. Moreover, Abd Allah did not give her time to notice our minute dissimilarities: a way of looking at certain things, the frequent use of some words, the length of our silences, a mole on the back. When I repudiated her, he lost interest as well. Thus the Basque woman lost two lovers in one.

Luna, my mother's black eunuch friend, interfered with my love for Fronilde. Seeing me much weakened for studies and for war, he said, "Whoever becomes overly used to women's navels won't find the way out to himself or to the world. Too much sweetness and the fly stays stuck in the honey."

Crepúsculo, the young eunuch who had also been a friend of my mother's called me aside to contradict him.

"Secrets which can't be hidden in a woman's breasts are no secrets. Life's pleasures are animal pleasures, not the ones the *ulamas,* the Muslim theologians, recommend. From now on, my scabrous jests will be your instructions."

"Which instructions?" I asked.

"According to the *istibra,* after urinating you must clean yourself by rubbing the penis several times with the left hand against a wall or a stone. . . . According to the *janaba,* if a chaste youth couples with a pubescent woman, it is she who should wash herself, not he," Crepúsculo explained.

"A chaste youth may enjoy a woman's body during her menstruation, except from the navel to the knees, because menstrual blood frustrates a man's intentions, curdles milk and spoils food," Luna affirmed.

"No more than three fingers should be used for cleansing of the anus. According to Salman, the Prophet has taught us everything, even how to defecate," Crepúsculo added.

"The inhabitants of paradise have no behinds, because behinds were made for defecation, and there is no defecating in paradise," Luna protested.

"He who knows says that paradise is full of houris with lustrous black eyes, that these creatures' faces are yellow, red, white or green, and their bodies are made of saffron, ambergris and musk, or are so transparent that the bones and spine show through the flesh," Crepúsculo declared. "On the houri's bosom is written the name of the husband she belongs to and of whom she is enamored. The houris, who are covered by seventy veils, have hair only on their eyelashes, eyebrows and tresses, which are made of raw silk."

"My mother told me that the houris in paradise have converted fervent Christians to the Muslim faith by appearing in their dreams," I stammered.

"He who knows also says that each man has seventy bedrooms, in each bedroom there are seventy beds, and in each bed there is a houri," Crepúsculo went on. "Each time a man makes love to a houri, she is virgin. The man's erection is eternal. The couples' bodies are always young and beautiful, and there is no urine in them, no defecation, no menstruation, no semen. Allah, who prohibits certain kinds of pleasure on earth, allows them in heaven."

"I have been told that in the privacy of his seventy bedrooms, the Caliph is more modest than a virgin, and that his likes and dislikes can be read on his face, without his uttering a single word," I said.

"I would not mind lying in bed with Caliph al-Hakam, even though he is old and decrepit. I know someone who took a blind man's senile virginity and bragged about it," said Crepúsculo.

"Poor us, who are neither male nor female and have been locked out of paradise, both earthly and celestial. Guardians of others' beds, we are in no rush to live or to die," Luna lamented.

"Remember that there are seven categories of people whom Allah will ignore on the Day of Resurrection, and the sodomites are among them," Crepúsculo reminded him. "The Prophet himself cursed those men who assume the position of women during fornication, and those women who behave like men. Remember that the throne of Allah trembles each time a male mounts another male. Remember that they are condemned to suffer endless humiliation and torture in the next world, and that they will come back as pigs or monkeys."

"On second thought, I think it's better to kill the animal of my desire rather than perish under such frightful conditions," Luna conceded. "I do know that a distance of five hundred years separates paradise from hell, and that I will never be able to enter any of the eight gates which admit the blessed to Eden."

I wondered at the eunuchs in Madinat al-Zahra, those creatures with muscular bodies and effeminate voices who were in charge of the harem and always surrounded the Caliph in his public as well as private acts. Many had been gelded in al-Andalus as children, or were youths purchased in the port of Pechina by Jews who brought them to Lucena for the operation. The slaves tried to learn Arabic and the Romance tongue, and some converted to Islam, receiving neuter names such as Hyacinth, Full Moon, Deliverance and Happiness. Ever vigilant, they guarded the doors of the seraglio and the beds of the women, observing their conduct and supervising their chastity. What struck me was that they were neither man nor woman; some were jealous, irascible and greedy, quick to squeal when contradicted or when their food was taken away. The youngest, beardless and delicate, were beautiful and had the bodies of fourteen- or sixteen-year-old girls. During the Caliph's life, or after his death, some were able to obtain their freedom, becoming *mawali,* or converts to Islam, and even owning slaves. When I heard them speak and watched them walk, I wondered: Did he, or she, have the ability to make love as a male or female? Where did they pray, among the men or among the women? Were they like this from birth, were they castrated by other men or did they geld themselves out of perversity? Would the ones who were still boys grow beards or menstruate, would they bear arms or wear silk, jewelry and a veil?

"All the women are yours. Go graze in their field as you please," the eunuch Crepúsculo said to me one day, and he let me peek through the window screens, he guided me to the rooms of those women whom the Caliph no longer frequented, those rooms where neither his favorites nor his preferred eunuchs were to be found. "Whoever does not cast a gray hair into the wind now and then is not a real saint," he said, quoting a poet close to the throne.

"Furtive coupling is as dangerous as wandering among the dunes in the desert; a man is bound to become lost," Luna warned me, for he noticed that I had a penchant for lechery.

"To prevent the semen from rising to your head and turning into putrid matter as a consequence of abstinence, we can make you a present of a slave girl from the market," Crepúsculo suggested.

"Al-Hassan ibn Dhakwam has said: 'Do not sit near the sons of the rich and noble, for they have faces like virgins' and are more tempting than women.'" Luna gave Crepúsculo a meaningful look and led me by the hand to the place where the books were kept.

From the moment I set foot in the caliphal library, I began to distance myself from the temptations of the harem, and I learned to read the secrets of the world in the rare and ancient volumes al-Hakam II had found in Damascus, Baghdad, Cairo and Alexandria. The list of titles filled forty-four notebooks, and 170 women in the city were engaged in copying the manuscripts.

Then, with my own eyes I discovered that Abu'l-Qasim, "Abulcasis," the Caliph's personal physician in the *medina,* and Arid ben Sa'd, the expert on Cordoban plant species and author of *The Calendar of Córdoba, The Book of Generation of the Fetus,* and *The Treatment of Pregnant Women and Infants,* came to the palace library to study. On occasion, the grammarian al-Zaubaydi, who lived in a house in Madinat al-Zahra, and Umar ibn Yunus, who on his return to Córdoba after an absence of two decades, established a pharmacy, sat near me. The lines of Abd al-Rahman I were famous among the readers: "You too, oh palm tree, are foreign to this soil." During those years Ibn Alcutia instructed me in grammar, Abu Ali Khalib in poetry and Arabic proverbs, while al-Hadrami showed me how to make parchment.

In the library I learned that a man some twenty-five years of age, a native of Aurillac called Gerbert, who had studied the *quadrivium*—the liberal arts of music, arithmetic, geometry and astronomy—in the monastery of Santa María de Ripoll under Bishop Vich Hatón, had arrived in the year 971 with the envoys of Count Borrell II of Barcelona. When Borrell's envoys departed, he remained in Córdoba to learn the magic arts, the science of the astrolabe, the uses of the abacus, and the new Arabic numerals. It was rumored that he had really stayed on to study astrology, divination and the incantations of the Egyptian magus Neptanebus, with the intention of becoming a necromancer himself. Years later, he could still be seen strolling in the gardens of the city, brushing the dust off the tablet that an armorer had made for him, which was divided into twenty-seven parts on which he could divide and multiply an infinitude of numbers. Abbo of Fleury, an adept of the *trivium*—the arts of grammar, rhetoric and logic—who had heard in a church in Paris about the coming of Antichrist and the Last Judgment in the year 1000, accompanied him.

It was then that I met Jonás ibn Gabirol, whose parents were born in the quarter adjoining the Gate of the Jews. Jonás wrote verses in Hebraic meter adapted from Arabic poetry and studied grammar, philosophy and medicine. One of his teachers was Rabbi Mosé Hanok, who had come to Córdoba as a slave and now led Talmudic studies in a Jewish school founded during the rule of Abd al-Rahman III.

He and I often walked together around the circular walls of the city. Between their seven iron gates he told me about Ibn al-Farabi, who was planning to write a history of the Andalusian poets.

The Jews of Córdoba corresponded with the Babylonian *geonim,* or scholars and judicial authorities, consulting them on questions concerning the Talmud, the Halakah and their own origins. In time, the Responsa came: "He who reads the Torah must read no fewer than three verses. There are some words which are read and translated, and others which are read and not translated. Ever since the time of the First Temple, from the exile from Jerusalem up to the present day, Sepharad has been the place for disseminating the Torah." Every Saturday, from sunrise until nightfall, Jonás ibn Gabirol met with the *gaon* and his disciples to study it.

Among them was a woman in man's clothing, not yet twenty years of age, of medium height and shapely limbs, pale complexion and large almond eyes, whose beauty caught my attention. It was Jonás's betrothed, Oroceti ha-Leví.

In those days, Jonás ibn Gabirol used to visit Abu Yusuf Hasdai ben Ishaq ibn Shaprut, the personal physician of Abd al-Rahman III and his son al-Hakam II. He was also the person who, as inspector general of customs, supervised transactions in merchandise arriving from the four corners of the earth and, as royal councillor, received the gifts made to the Caliph by the kings of other nations.

In the year 949, the Byzantine emperor Constantinus VII Porphyrogenitus, or "born to the purple," sent a diplomatic delegation bearing gifts of books to the Andalusian Caliph, among them Dioscorides's *De materia medica,* which had excellent pictures of plants. As there was no one among the Christians or Saracens who knew ancient Ionic Greek, the emperor sent a monk named Nicholas to translate it. Hasdai ibn Shaprut worked closely with Nicholas, translating the botanical terms into Arabic. He was also the inventor of the curative medicine *faruq,* a kind of theriac, or antidote. His fame became so widespread that, at the behest of Doña Toda, the queen of Pamplona, he went there to cure her grandson, the deposed Sancho I of León and Navarre, of his extreme corpulence. He succeeded by prescribing herbs and ordering him to walk from Pamplona to Córdoba.

With the books, Abd al-Rahman received a Greek funerary vase with a painting of Charon piloting his ferry, surrounded by winged shapes representing human souls, and Hermes stretching out his left hand to touch the fingers of a deceased woman. The Caliph stared for a long time at the figure of the corpse, unable to comprehend her misfortune.

One day Hasdai ibn Shaprut received news of a Jewish kingdom named al-Khazar. Two men from the land of the Gebalim, Mar Saul and Mar Yosef, told him of meeting with a blind Israelite, Mar Amram, from the country of the Khazars. Hasdai, excited that a kingdom governed and inhabited by Jews existed in the world of the Diaspora, sent Jonás ibn Gabirol with a letter addressed to Joseph, the Khazar king. Ibn Gabirol had only to travel 270 miles between Córdoba and Constantinople and sail over the water for fifteen days to Khazaria.

In his missive Hasdai told the king of the Khazars that he lived in a land known as Sepharad, whose capital was Córdoba and whose caliph was Abd al-Rahman III. He inquired about the size of his country and his walled cities, the number of his soldiers, the amount of tribute he received, and the administration of justice. He also confessed, "We have lost our glory. We are submerged in exile, and we can make no reply when daily we are told, 'Each people has its own kingdom, but of yours there is no memorial on earth.'"

Ibn Gabirol set out one morning in the month of April. Along the way he noticed melons in the fields of Córdoba, grapes and figs, brooding storks, hawks hatching, peasants sowing cucumbers and rice, transplanting squash and eggplants, pruning palm trees and setting jasmine in the earth. Two years later he returned, haggard, weary and prematurely gray. It was the month of *Dayanbar,* or December, when almond trees, pepper plants and narcissi are in flower, cisterns brim with rainwater, and in the manured gardens, leeks, garlic and white opium poppies are being planted. He had been unable to find the legendary realm. When he reached Constantinople, he learned that the emperor had died of typhoid fever or from poison administered to him by his daughter-in-law Theophano. Romanus II now ruled, a comely youth married to a dreadful woman. He also learned that Constantine had been sickly and led a withdrawn life, devoting himself to writing, painting and building a magnificent library, spending thousands of gold pieces on manuscripts, reliquaries, pictures and mosaics. Two of his books, *De cerimoniis aulae Byzantinae* and *De administrando imperio,* were widely renowned.

Hasdai sent the letter again, this time with a Greek merchant, Nicias Melisourgos, who availed himself of the ambassadors of Emperor Otto I and of Berengar, Marquess of Ivrea, to deliver the epistle to the king of the Khazars. Jonás ibn Gabirol referred to the Muslim Ispamia, Hispania to the Christians, as Sepharad, and to the Christian north as Edom. He was especially intrigued by the Messiah of Crete, called Moses, about whom Nicias Melisourgos had told him.

"The Messiah Moses claimed he was sent from heaven to lead the Jews out of Crete. To convince them, he asserted that he had led them in a past life across the Red Sea," ibn Gabirol recounted as we were strolling along the banks of the Guadalquivir River. "He asked his followers to give up their properties and belongings, for in the Messianic era, money would be of no use. The day came when the men, women and children set out to reach the promised land through the dry sea. From a lofty promontory they hurled themselves at the rocks and water and were dashed to pieces or drowned. Some fishermen and Christian merchants who witnessed this madness were able to save a few and to warn others of the fate suffered by those who had jumped. The Messiah, whom the survivors wanted to put to death, vanished."

"Among the books in the library of al-Hakam II there is a copy of the *Commentarius in Apocalypsin* by Beatus of Liébana," I told Jonás one night. "This monk affirmed that the ages of the world are six in number, and that the sixth age would come to an end in the Spanish era 838, but that year went by without the world being over. In a later explanation, Beatus warns us not to heed those who claim that there is a span of a thousand years between the Nativity of the Lord and the Second Coming, because these people think like the heretic Cerinthus."

"Who was this Beatus of Liébana?" Jonás asked.

"According to Paulus Alvarus, a monk from Córdoba, Beatus was a cleric in San Martín de Turieno who wrote commentaries on the Apocalypse, believing that of all books, the Book of Revelation holds the key."

"What else do you know about him?"

"Don Juan, the bishop of Córdoba, says that Bishop Elipandus of Toledo, who was a mortal enemy of Beatus, spread the word that he had prophesied the end of the world to a man named Ordoño and had struck fear into the people. After a brief fast, Ordoño, feeling the pangs of hunger, exclaimed, 'Let us eat and drink, for if we must die, let us first gratify ourselves.' "

"The Book of Revelation fascinates me. I intend to reconstruct the life and acts of the Greek Jew who wrote it down, because he, like me, was a Jew of the Diaspora, and because he lived, as I do now, in an era in which a man is worshiped," Jonás declared.

"John the Theologian disappeared during the first century of the Christian era. The echo of his seven trumpets is still audible and will resound in history yet to happen," I said.

"This era will end with the beginning of the millenary kingdom, revealed directly to John by God," he stated.

"Only a few more years are left before we enter the kingdom of God," I said.

"I am studying the meaning in the book of the seven seals, the seven churches, the seven plagues, the seven bowls, the seven unnumbered visions, the seven-headed Dragon and 666, the number of the Beast, which in Hebrew corresponds to the name of Nero, who will return from death as Antichrist," Jonás confided.

"For the Christians of the North, Antichrist is al-Mansur," I said, half in jest. "During his reign the martyrs will mingle their blood with the blood of Christ."

"The story goes that John was a member of the prophetic circle of Ephesus, but if the disciple of Jesus and the prophet of the Apocalypse are one and the same, he must have been very old when the end of time was revealed to him," he went on.

"The ancients say that after the Crucifixion, the Virgin Mary lived under the care of Saint John in a small house in Ephesus," I explained, "and that

Saint John was exiled to the island of Patmos by Nero or Domitian, emperor of Rome, the Whore.''

"The earth is full of holy bodies and John the Theologian's must be somewhere. Starting today, I will search for his remains in graves, sepulchers, walls and crypts. When I find them, it will be a sign that the end of time is nearing,'' Jonás affirmed.

Some of my Mussulman fellow students wore their hair long and parted on the brow and drank water from golden goblets off linen tablecloths; others wore their hair close-cropped and drank from crystal goblets off leather cloths, in the fashion of the musician Ziryab of Baghdad, the "black bird." A scholar discoursed on the triangular shape of Hispania, now called al-Andalus, surrounded by three seas, the Mediterranean, the Pitchy and the sea of the English; he told us that the earth extended from the church of the Crow, situated on the ocean, to Cádiz, where the mountain of the temple of Venus is, and from Santiago, the city of the temple of gold, to Almería, the city on two hills.

We dined on flour soups, meat, fowl and fish, vegetables and fresh fruit, depending on the month of the year. During spring and summer we had apricots and peaches, oranges and lemons from Almuñécar, apples from Granada, and figs from Raya and Málaga. At night we supped on melons. My mother's favorite dish had been *asida,* a stew of wheat flour boiled in a pottage of seasonal greens, and I looked for it in the inns of Córdoba.

At that time al-Hakam II, the Commander of the Faithful, was seeking a tutor for his five-year-old firstborn son, whom he had begotten on Subh, the young Basque captive who sang and dressed like a youth of eighteen and to whom he had given the masculine name of Dja'far, or Dawn. He finally engaged Muhammad ibn Abi Amir, the future al-Mansur, for a monthly salary of fifteen gold coins.

The palace had five doors that led to the world but prevented the harem women from going out. Water came from the mountains to the palace through lead pipes, and in vessels of gold and silver to Subh's lips. I quenched my thirst at a fountain. On Fridays the caliph walked over a carpeted path through the Bab al-Chami into the Great Mosque. Al-Hakam used to pray there, occasionally accompanied by his children. The Great

Mosque rose on the site of the principal Christian church, and successive emirs and caliphs had enlarged it until it achieved its present splendor. All had expended hundreds of thousands of gold pieces on its structures and additions, because its sanctuary and one thousand marble pillars, its admirable arches resting upon the columns, rose from a foundation of piety.

Long, thick walls circled Córdoba, enclosing gardens, palaces, mosques and houses built along the banks of the Guadalquivir River. The twenty-one suburbs all had their own mosque, market and bath. The Saracens lived within the walls, the Christians in districts apart. At the center stood the Qasaba, a fortress defended by high, substantial walls. Seven gates allowed the armies to issue forth on their forays into the Christian North, seven gates gave entrance to the city, one of them the Gate of the Jews, about which the poet Abu Amir ben Xuhayd wrote: "Near the Gate of the Jews they saw the star of Abu'l-Hasan darken, then disappear. When the Jews saw him giving orders outside their gate, they took him for Joseph."

The common folk of Córdoba took walks in the public orchards. Among the trees and plants brought from elsewhere, the people first saw pomegranates. But no garden in Córdoba could compare with the garden in the palace of Dimaxq, which was perfumed at night by black hyacinths and in the morning by other flowers.

The city market was supplied with the fruits of the earth as well as those fashioned by the hand of man. Some arrived on muleback from other parts of al-Andalus or from distant lands, and conquered and conquerors met in the market.

"The Guadalquivir flows as smoothly as a stream of milk," my Muslim friend al-Razi remarked one afternoon as we stood admiring the river from the bridge of seventeen arches, which al-Samh ben Malik al-Khawlani had built.

"How did he do it?" I asked.

"Only Allah knows," he answered.

"How does Allah make himself known?" I asked.

"By thwarting my plans," he replied, "unless your mother says to the contrary."

"What do you mean by that?" I countered. "My mother says nothing, she's far from here."

"What I mean is, if your mother's Christian saints do not condemn the Mussulman paradise, which they called a brothel. This paradise, full of endless pleasures, of houris with shining eyes and young men beautiful as pearls, obviously troubles their souls," he answered. "Your mother detests harems and the muezzin's calls to prayer."

"My mother is surely dead." I reproached him.

"She lives on in your heart," he insisted.

VISION VIII

The story goes that when King Rodrigo ruled in Toledo—before he was maddened by his own lust, vanquished by the treason of Don Julián, slain by the sword of Allah, and his corpse whisked away by the arts of Satan—there was a house made fast with twenty-four bolts. It was customary for each Visigothic king to add another one. But Rodrigo refused to do so until he had seen what was inside. He ordered the house opened. Within he found a picture of the Arabs, with a sign that read: "When this door is opened, those who are portrayed here will come into this country."

Another chronicle recounts that the kings had a house in which they kept an ark, and in the ark they kept the Gospels, which they used for swearing oaths. Whenever a king died, the house was opened so as to inscribe his name inside. But Rodrigo first put the crown on his own head, then opened the house and the ark, and in it he found Arabs depicted with their bows slung across their backs and turbans wound around their heads. On the panels was written: "When this house is opened and these figures are taken out, the people painted here will invade and dominate Spain."

After seven hundred Saracen horsemen under the command of the renegade freedman Muget, or Mugeid, or Moquits ar-Romi, easily took Córdoba, the Christians who stayed to live among the Mahometans enjoyed religious freedom and kept their churches, their ministers and their rites. Cantors, psalmists and the faithful attended divine offices as always; the bishop, archpriest and other clergymen retained their ranks. In tranquil times nothing prevented them from bringing out the bodies of their dead and parading the relics of their saints in public procession. Nevertheless, many Goths, both nobles and slaves, embraced the religion of their conquerors in order to prosper or to obtain their freedom. The most learned Christians served in the court or the army, or were magistrates, master builders and inspectors of markets, weights, and measures, police and trade; once they were able to speak and write the language of the invaders, they scorned both Latin and their own tongue. Some of them emulated the customs of their lords and kept a harem of Christian slaves or indulged in sodomy.

There was a period when, since Christians wore the same clothing as Moors, the entrance of a Christian into a mosque, like blasphemy against Allah or Mahomet, was punishable by death, or the loss of hands and feet, unless the transgressor turned Mussulman. This held true even though, under the Pact of Omar, which governed the relations between Muslims, Christians and Jews, the latter two undertook not to teach their children the Koran, not to imitate the Muslims in their style of dress or parting of hair, not to ride using a saddle, not to bear arms, not to display the cross on churches or in the streets or markets, not to carry palm fronds or images in procession, not to sing loudly when burying their dead or carry lighted candles. Those who complained most bitterly about this treatment were the muladies, or renegades. Some of them, *christiani occulti,* or secret Christians, despite regretting their apostasy, could no longer abandon the law of Mahomet without losing their lives. Scorned and insulted by the Muslims—who mistrusted their conversion—as if they were slaves, they survived by working in the court or tilling the fields as day laborers.

The Christian priests obstinately opposed the Mussulman religion and invoked Bishop Eulogius, who had divulged the contents of a manuscript from a monastery in Pamplona, which stated that when Mahomet was about to die, he predicted his own death, promising that three days later angels would descend from the sky to resuscitate him. But his disciples waited in vain. Dogs came and set about devouring the cadaver. The Muslims killed the dogs, and ever since, they do so every year.

The priests were also outraged by the conquistadors' polygamy and their paradise of virgin concubines. "This enemy of our Savior has consecrated the sixth day of the week, which should be devoted to mourning and fasting, to gluttony and lust. Christ preached chastity to his sheep, Mahomet preached coarse delights, sordid pleasures and incest to his," they complained, quoting Paulus Alvarus, a follower of Eulogius.

I will never forget the night I first went to the church where Bishop Juan II was officiating and heard him read the Gospels aloud. I left the temple of Lord Christ brimming with faith, and I distributed my clothing along the way among the needy. I made for the cemetery of the Christians, bitterly lamenting my sins, so ashamed of myself that I dared not utter the name of God.

Thanks to Juan II, I learned about Bishops Fósforo and Mumulo, Saulo and Valencio, about the martyrdom of the saints who lived before the Moors came, and about others who suffered Saracen persecution, about Isaac the monk, whose throat was slit before they hung him upside down from a gibbet, his feet bound together, facing the city from the far side of the river.

Isaac's body was burned, his ashes thrown into the water, and his relics scattered, but not the details of his martyrdom. The monks from the monastery of Tabanos promptly numbered him among the saints, and it was recounted that he had begun to perform miracles not only as an infant, but from his mother's womb. The first miracle he worked was to produce another martyrdom: A Frenchman named Sancho, a member of the caliphal guard, blasphemed Mahomet and was decapitated. The following Sunday, six monks appeared before the *qadi,* or judge, blaspheming the Prophet and loudly affirming that they were saying the same words as their brothers

Isaac and Sancho had said. They, too, were beheaded. The cleric Sisenando, from San Acisclo, Pablo the deacon, and the monk Teodomiro followed their example and were slain in similar fashion. The relics of these saints were zealously guarded by the faithful.

There was a virtual carnival of martyrs in those days. Feigning illness, the priests were finally forced to take refuge in their houses to escape the Muslims' hostility and to avoid paying the harsh tributes demanded from them at the end of each month. Once the sun had set, they ventured outside, seething with hatred and resentment, or stayed indoors reading the Bible or the *Lives of the Saints* by the light of a furtive lamp. In morbid apprehension, they thrilled over another's martyrdom and concluded that the surest and most direct path to glory was through persecution and a holy death. If they did not die, they complained that no one persecuted them. When they were sent to jail, the tabernacles were abandoned, spiders spun webs on the walls, the divine canticles were no longer intoned, incense ceased to waft over the altars, and heresies prospered.

One night, in memory of my mother, Bishop Juan sent me an old Andalusian woman who knew her way around the back streets. In a message recited in Arabic and Spanish, she asked me to meet the bishop in a suburb to the west of the city known as the Baths of al-Anbiri.

I went in secret to the appointment. Seated in one of the baths, Bishop Juan questioned me about Abd Allah and asked if I could bring him so that he might save his soul. I replied that my brother was a Mahometan and had denounced my mother; since then, we had not spoken. Then I learned the reason for this meeting: He asked me to deposit the relics of Saint Eulogius in a safe place by transferring them from Oviedo to Córdoba.

"The bones of the martyr," he said, "are in grave danger of being profaned by al-Mansur, who plans to sack that city. By this act you will give proof of your faith."

"What is a martyr?" I asked.

"Martyrs are those men and women who have died in the name of Our Lord at the hands of the Saracens, as Saint Eulogius did. Martyrs are also those who, had they lived in times of persecution, would have died for the holy faith; although they did not put on the crown of martyrdom, they would have worn it in their hearts out of their infinite love of God, since they did make a living sacrifice of themselves on the altar of their bodies," Bishop Juan explained.

"Are there martyrs whose names are not known?" I inquired.

"No," he replied laconically. "Would you like to become one of them?"

"No," I answered.

Ignoring my reply, he began telling me that Saint Eulogius had been born in Córdoba in the bosom of a most Christian family. Anulona, the second of his two sisters, had consecrated herself to God. Small of stature but great of soul, from early in life he had devoted himself to the study of the Holy Scriptures and become a deacon.

"The saint traveled throughout Catalonia, Pamplona and Saragossa in search of his lost brothers," he continued. "Upon his return to Córdoba, the city of Seneca and Lucan, he brought with him copies in Latin of three books: Virgil's *Aeneid,* the *Satires* of Horace and Juvenal, and *The City of God*, by the blessed Augustine."

"Eulogius was put in the jail where Saints Flora and María were already prisoners. During his imprisonment he taught his companions the secrets of metric verse," I told him, recalling my mother's teachings. "Flora and María were martyred on the twenty-fourth of November in the year 851."

"Bishop Eulogius wrote to Paulus Alvarus," Juan went on, "about their bitter death: 'My brother, our virgins, instructed by us amid tears in the word of life, have just secured the palm of martyrdom. The entire Church rejoices in the victory they have attained.' "

"Paulus Alvarus complained that the Christians in al-Andalus knew neither their language nor their law," I interjected.

"He had exhorted them to make a good death," the bishop added. "He used to seek out those believers who were about to die for the faith and venerate their limbs, which were destined for our Lord. He dubbed them 'soldiers of Christ off to fight the impious enemy.' "

And with that we bade each other good-bye.

Another afternoon we met in the house of María Sabarico, a saintly virgin of agreeable aspect and discreet habits, the daughter of a Mussulman from Seville and a Cordoban Christian mother. Juan told me afterward that she practiced the true religion behind her father's back while ostensibly living beneath the banner of Satan (Mahomet).

"Eulogius was elected archbishop of Toledo, but God prevented him from proceeding to his see: He sought the crown of martyrdom in Córdoba," Juan continued, under the admiring eye of María Sabarico, who was none other than my former friend.

"He gave refuge in his house to the daughter of a Mussulman *qadi,* Leocricia by name, who practiced Christianity in her soul, accompanied by her sister Baldegotona," María recounted. "We will have to rescue Leocricia's relics as well."

"Her father, the judge, found out that the saint was harboring her and sent soldiers to surround the house," the bishop went on.

"Saint Eulogius was scourged with switches, a eunuch slapped him on both cheeks and he was led to his torment," I continued.

"He knelt on the ground, spread his arms wide, crossed himself, recited a brief prayer, bared his neck to the executioner's scimitar, toppled over headless and ascended to heaven in spirit, a virgin, doctor and martyr," María said.

"The Moors threw his corpse into the river, the Christians fished out his head and body and deposited them in the church of San Zoilo. The saint's relics worked miracles. Now, after more than one hundred years, the Moors want to disinter him and scatter his remains over the roads of Christianity," Juan said ruefully.

María Sabarico agreed to go with me to Oviedo. Having fallen into a profound sadness after the death of her mother, she was ready to prove her faith and die for the true religion whenever Bishop Juan might ask it of her. The following night, she waited for me at a basil seller's stall. She looked more beautiful than ever; now sixteen, she spoke Arabic and *aljamia* fluently and played the lute. She was, I remembered well, the little girl with whom my brother and I were in love.

From that day onward, we two met on every Christian feast day during the month of May to plan our journey. The other days, we walked in the fields, picking early apples and pears. I was burning with desire to enjoy the love of the young girl who was within my reach, not to worship the image of the future martyr. But I could say nothing to her, lest I frighten her away. Together we witnessed the harvesting of barley and the birth of turtledoves and storks, and we watched the Cordobans making parchment from deer and gazelle skins. I had the foreboding that I would enjoy her company only during that year of 976.

In the months that followed I visited her afternoon and night, under the pretext of rescuing and translating the relics of Saint Eulogius. But each time I attempted to declare my love, she fled, horrified at the possibility of hearing from my lips words to remind her that she had a body and was human.

"Are you free or a slave? To whom do you belong?" I asked her one morning in the street that led to the bakers' quarter.

"To myself, and to the Lord in heaven," she answered, running off. But she glanced back to see if I was following her or if Muhammad ibn Abi Amir's soldiers, led by my brother Abd Allah, were spying on her.

That very day, I chanced on the Caliph in the garden of the place riding an elephant, which trotted as if dancing. People said it was three hundred years old. It came from a place near the earthly paradise. In order to bring it to Córdoba, the men who put it aboard ship pledged to return it to its homeland, and lavished it with caresses, for the largest animal in the world loves being flattered and made much of. Exquisitely sensitive to cold, the elephant felt at ease in al-Andalus, suffering no ailments save for inflammation of the stomach and fluxes.

Growing from the elephant's mouth were two very long teeth, out of which some men fashioned simulacra of gods, images of saints, ivory crucifixes and chess pieces. Its nose was a trunk, which it wriggled and waved, and at the tip were two holes through which it breathed, drank and sniffed.

Suddenly, to everyone's amusement, it sucked in water from a fountain with its trunk and sprayed all present. The Caliph rode into the palace, indifferent to the delight which the animal of colossal and monstrous shape had excited.

A week after the meeting with María Sabarico, Bishop Juan requested my presence one night in the monastery of San Acisclo. By candlelight and before her, he informed me that it was time to fetch the miraculous relics. I sought María's eyes and promised to rescue the holy bones before Sunday. It was Wednesday. By the look she gave me, it was clear she knew that I undertook the business more in hope of pleasing her than out of faith in Saint Eulogius. A violent event in the city interfered with our plans, however, and changed my life: the revolt of the eunuchs.

On the first of October in the year 976 of our Lord, the year 366 for the Mussulmen, al-Hakam II died at the age of sixty-five. Lying in the arms of his favorite castrates, the brothers Faiq al-Nizami and Chawdhar, he surrendered his soul to Allah.

Faiq al-Nizami, the chief eunuch, was master of the wardrobe and the silk carpet factory; his brother was a master goldsmith and falconer. Both oversaw the Caliph's harem and under them one thousand Slav eunuchs were quartered at the gates of the Alcázar. They also held sway over other palace officials and the non-eunuch bodyguard.

To prevent Crown Prince Abu'l-Walid Hisham from acceding to the throne, the eunuchs concealed al-Hakam II's demise, intending instead to crown Prince al-Mughira, the twenty-six-year-old brother of the deceased and the son of Caliph Abd al-Rahman III and his concubine Mushtak. To further their ambitions, they summoned the vizier, Chafar al-Mushafi, a Berber of cloudy origins.

The vizier feigned interest in the intrigue and offered to defend the Iron Gate of the Alcázar. But he immediately convoked the principal dignitaries of the court, the Berber chiefs of the Banu Birzal, the generals and captains of the Saracen and Spanish armies, and Muhammad ibn Abi Amir, and divulged to them the Caliph's death and the eunuchs' treacherous intentions.

During the meeting it was decided that someone should murder Prince al-Mughira. Ibn Abi Amir volunteered and, assuming that the prince had not yet learned of al-Hakam's death, rode off to find him, accompanied by the *quadi* Badr, one hundred bodyguards, several squadrons of Spaniards and my brother Abd Allah. Once in the palace, he notified the prince of the Caliph's decease and revealed his mission to kill him.

Seeing the sword suspended over his neck, the prince swore loyalty to the caliphate and begged for clemency. The future al-Mansur took pity on his youth and sent a letter to Chafar al-Mushafi asking pardon for his life. The vizier replied that he must execute him.

Muhammad ibn Abi Amir showed the prince the answer, and he left, so as not to witness the murder. His soldiers strangled al-Mughira before his women and Abd Allah. Then they strung up his corpse in an adjoining latrine and told the servants that the prince had preferred to hang himself rather than pay homage to his nephew. They buried him in the hall where they had killed him and bricked in the doors.

The next morning, Hisham II was crowned with the title of al-Mu'ayyad billah, "He who receives the victorious assistance of Allah." Ibn Abi Amir staged the act of investiture of the new Caliph, a child of eleven with white skin, deep blue eyes and stubby legs. Flanking the vizier, the two eunuchs swore an oath to the new Caliph. Subh, the sultana mother, was present.

Afterward, Ibn Abi Amir showed the Commander of the Faithful, mounted on a richly caparisoned horse, to the people. The first measures of his reign were to appoint Chafar al-Mushafi as *hajib* and Ibn Abi Amir as vizier, and to abolish the tax on oil.

The eunuchs still conspired. Al-Mushafi learned that people close to them came and went in secret, carrying messages through the Iron Gate. The gate was walled up, the eunuchs were dismissed and Faiq al-Nizami was exiled to one of the Balearic Islands, where he died soon afterward. Durri, the lord of Baeza, one of the more violent leaders of the rebellion, was slain by the men of the Banu Birzal tribe. A massacre of the castrates ensued. Crepúsculo was thrown alive into a well, where he remained until he perished of hunger and thirst. Luna's eyes were gouged out, and eventually he was permitted to beg for alms in the markets.

Within and without the palace, the eunuch hunt continued. Many veiled their faces and tried to hide in the seraglio dressed as women. They were discovered and made to enter the Alcázar by the back door, where, as each crossed the threshold, a blade fell on his head. The Mameluke guards, called mutes because they spoke no Arabic, witnessed the slaughter but could say nothing.

The number of eunuchs who died will never be known. Armed surveillance of the city's Christians so intensified that it became perilous to carry corpses, no matter how stealthily, in and out of the churches. María Sabarico was arrested near the Mosque of Rejoicing and executed the following day as an apostate. Later I learned that the Berbers of Muhammad ibn Abu Amir, commanded by Abd Allah, had beaten, torn with red-hot pincers and stabbed her to death. Bishop Juan's messenger, dressed as an elderly matron, took advantage of the muezzin's call to prayer from the summit of the minaret to meet me behind some trees in the garden of the palace of Dimaxq and tell me what had happened.

When they heard about the capture and martyrdom of María Sabarico, the principal churchmen of al-Andalus hurried to kneel before the *hajib* of the Commander of the Faithful and beg his mercy. They denied knowledge of her and, to keep their privileges, offered total submission and obedience. I saw them returning from their audience, satisfied with the arrangement, riding mules beneath the sultry sun through the Gate of the Bridge.

With my heart reduced to a burning ember, dressed in mourning I picked up a decapitated body and a head—both María's—which were lying on the riverbank and fervently joined them together. The grace of martyrdom had rendered her even more lovely than when she had lived; she radiated gladness, not merely externally, but also from within, from the depths of her soul. When night fell I gave her Christian burial beside one of San Zoilo's walls.

For the last time I returned to the new Caliph's palace. From my bedroom I could hear the sound of lutes, drums and singing. Wondering that anyone dared amuse himself at a time of such anguish, unless it were Hisham himself, I went toward the place, whence came the music.

In a hall lit by round windows, Muhammad ibn Abi Amir was celebrating his victory over the eunuchs. He and other captains were helping themselves to the delicacies of al-Andalus, and to the women of the harem, off leather tablecloths and carpeted beds. An Andalusian slave, still a child, was singing verses so vibrantly that her voice was like an arrow piercing space. The sound made me forget my sorrow for a moment.

The hardened men present, naked swords within reach of their bloodstained hands, listened to her, enraptured. The chief *qadi,* Muhammad ibn al-Salim, an ardent enthusiast of sodomy, was among them. Subh, the emir's mother, spied on the proceedings from behind a marble screen. She herself was the subject of certain mocking verses inspired by her voluptuous excesses.

"Who's that singing?" I asked a eunuch called Lucero.

"The slave does not yet have a name, the new Caliph gave her to the *hajib;* she belongs to him," he replied.

"To Chafar al-Mushafi?"

"No, to Muhammad ibn Abi Amir. In the years to come—although Allah knows more than I do—the present *hajib* will be arrested and strangled in the jail of Madinat al-Zahra."

"What else do you know?" I asked.

"I know—but Allah knows more than any creature in this world—that . . ." The eunuch fell silent, frightened by his own words.

"Lucero sees the Caliph Hisham II besotted by the pleasures of the harem, with which Ibn Abi Amir will undoubtedly overwhelm him in the palace, starting today," said Jonás ibn Gabirol, who was suddenly standing next to me. "Lucero sees that child, smothered with delights, become impotent and effeminate. Of course, to his people he will be an idol, but to the man who weakens him through the brutish love of women and men, he will be an empty husk."

Suddenly we saw a veiled woman approaching through the garden.

"Who is she?" I asked my friend.

"Asma, the learned daughter of General Ghalib. She's going to marry Ibn Abi Amir."

"There are things it is better neither to see nor to know," the eunuch said.

"After the wedding, father and son-in-law will abhor each other, and in a battle between the two, Ghalib's horse will stumble and the pommel of his saddle will pierce his breast. As a macabre gift, Ibn Abi Amir will deliver to Asma in Córdoba the hand and head of her dead father," Jonás ibn Gabirol continued.

"I am thinking of leaving," I replied.

"Do you want to abandon Córdoba, 'the city of diverse hearts'?" he asked. "Are al-Barbar, Barsiluna, Ruma, Ifranya calling to you?" he went on, referring to Barbary, Barcelona, Rome and France.

"It's a four days' journey from here to Granada," I murmured.

"It's a two months' journey from the place where you are to your death," he replied.

"What will you do?" I asked.

"I'll go to Byzantium to search for the body of John the Theologian. It is somewhere in the empire, still uncorrupted. I must leave now. Plague, famine, war, death, the riders who roam the world, will come to Sepharad and Edom in a few years. We must be prepared for the end. Words spin into sentences, sentences into visions, the past and the future converge in the present.''

"What will become of Orocetí ha-Leví?" I asked. "She's so beautiful.''

"She will remain here and take lessons in the arts of disputation and the zither from the Babylonian Jew Dunas ibn Labrat in his academy.''

We spoke no further. The time to go had arrived. He wanted to start searching for the relic of the seer; I, with Eulogius's bones forgotten, disillusioned with life in the city of the caliphs, yearned to bury my body in a monastery in the Christian North.

At dawn I set out on horseback for the land of the Asturians.

VISION IX

Wednesday I strode through León like a messiah. I walked its streets as Lord Christ would have done in his second coming. I sought among its thousand inhabitants the blessed ones who should follow me.

Two angels, Guiberto and Norberto, accompanied me. One held the key to the abyss in his hand, and the other, the chains to bind Antichrist, in case we found him. No one saw them or heard their voices. Invisible, they answered only to my summons, to a brief incantation known only to myself. So luminous and transparent are their bodies that human eyes and ears can neither perceive nor hear them.

Wielding swords of light, Guiberto and Norberto have protected me from the snares and onslaughts of the ancient Enemy and present-day instigators of evil, from the other world as well as from this one. Both have proved to be worthy servants, good at chasing away spirits of harmful invention, whether my own or those my brother Abd Allah sends to trouble my sleep in the monastery of San Juan el Teólogo.

My keen eyes can discern demons in both their natural shape and their human guise as they accompany the Leonese, always one step ahead of their feet and their malevolent thoughts, straddling their backs or perched on their shoulders like monkeys or cats. Scorned or lagging behind, the guardian angels vainly try to warn ingenuous souls against the traps and temptations with which the adversaries of humankind, captained by the devil, seek to send them to perdition. Every war, every plague, every famine, every madness is due to him, and him alone, because to none of us does it occur that the calamities, the discords, the evils that transpire in the world, which are blamed on supernatural forces, spring from our own hearts.

After the hour of Nones, I strolled past the principal church, the venerable Santa María. White storks were building their nests in the ramshackle ruins. I did not go in. Shortly afterward, I passed the monastery church of Santiago, founded by Yquila in the year 917. This convent, razed in 987 by the Saracens, also admits women. Abbesses like Felicia, Imilo and Senduara, who was much beloved by Bishop Froilán, forged its history. They are responsible for the *collegium mulierum* and the care of the ritual objects: chalices, crosses, censers, candelabra, processional candlesticks and books.

On my way from the Carral de Santa María to the Cauriense Gate, I encountered Flora, who had been consecrated to Christ and was a survivor of the convent of Santa Cristina. It is common knowledge that its builder, Arias, put his daughters Justa, María, Domna Infante and Granada, and his granddaughters Honoria and Flora in it; he donated villas and properties to it, and at his death he was given burial on its grounds. The monastery remained in the governance of his family until al-Mansur's hosts arrived, laid waste to the countryside and took captives. Among the prisoners were the four daughters. Two returned from their captivity, the other two remained chained in the dungeons. Flora collected all the mortal remains of her relatives that she could find in Santiago. Honoria was lost to memory.

The sisters Casta and Larga met me on the street leading to the Count's Gate. They have resolved to lead a holy life in the monastery as slaves dedicated to God, following the Rule of Saint Benedict and his divine admonitions regarding hospices and caring for the poor.

From the castle of the city's governor, I contemplated the mills on the Bernesga, the compassionate river that provides us with water. In the distance I was able to make out four Jews tending their vines and tilling the soil. Sampiro, who was also the royal priest, emerged, opulently dressed, from the castle gate on his way to one of his many properties. Above his head the branches of the poplars moved imperceptibly, like time itself.

I retraced my steps, passing the monastery of San Juan Bautista, with its church of earth and brick built into a tower of the wall where it faces east. Here I encountered many women: Salamira, Rodriga, Sobrada, Betote and Elvira. Every one of them leered at me. I lowered my eyes, especially when I caught sight of Froila, the beautiful nun-concubine of deacon García Cabezón, by whom she became pregnant, and to whom, it was said, she had borne a daughter who had disappeared.

Farther ahead loomed buildings destroyed by al-Mansur's Berbers and mutes. Everywhere repairs were being made. Don Alfonso V had undertaken the rebuilding of the walls, churches and monasteries. In the innocence of his zeal, he aspires to increase the population of the city with houses and churches.

In the course of my wanderings, I encountered Doña Especiosa, Doña Mumadona, Semeno, the victualer of the monastery of San Lucas, Doña Flora Lunbroso, Gómez Díaz and Gutierre Alonso, who were visiting vineyards, orchards and houses. Later on I greeted the bishop, Don Froilán, deacon García Cabezón, and the nun Ello, his sister. All those people bowed before me to receive my blessing, except the stubborn and irreverent García Cabezón and Don Froilán. No one discovered the presence of Guiberto and Norberto, although Cabezón stared at my feet as if he had noticed something peculiar about me.

Outside the walls I saw Doña Salomona, who was already considering using her worldly goods to found a convent dedicated to San Vicente and becoming its abbess. The ruined monastery of San Miguel came in sight near the Cauriense Gate, a short distance from the monastery of Saints Adrián and Natalia. Between them stood the church of San Marcelo. To the east the convent of the apostles Pedro and Pablo was a mound of rubble.

Inside the walls I came face-to-face with Doña Urraca Fernández, known as The Shadow because she had made a shadow of her corporeal existence. After her aunt and cousins were slain and her sisters in Christ captured during the Saracen attack on León, she had resolved to emulate the lives of female saints in the Dark Ages and to be like one of them. She passed by furtively without seeing me. The brilliance of her blue eyes remained with me with a curious insistency.

The Saracens set fire to the city, but they could not destroy its thick walls. Ordoño, who restored the battered walls, could not make the inhabitants forget their dread of renewed assaults, and so they raised towers and fortresses in the countryside, built dams and mills on the rivers, and left to populate villages in the valleys of the Porma, the Bernesga and the Torio, unaware that fear and death come from within, not without, and outlive time and cadavers, that life is fear fulfilled.

The walled city of León stretched northward from the market opposite San Martín's as far as the castle, and from the Bishop's Gate it spread toward the Cauriense Gate. Four gates gave access to its interior: the Arch Gate, which led to the market and opened into the street where the king's palace stood; the Bishop's Gate; the Count's Gate; and the Cauriense Gate, which faced San Lucas. All those gates and avenues ushered the Lord's sheep into my hands.

In the vicinity of the public market where the faithful trade their wares, clasping the cross beneath my cassock I roamed the streets and avenues in search of disciples, gazing upon the populace with pity for the present and compassion for the future, as I already divined in them their carrion state. The first person to cross my path, near the monastery of San Lucas, was a partridge hunter, crying copiously because of an eye ailment.

I glimpsed behind him several shapes, which gradually became Munio and Rabiesa Ferrúz and four mules laden with salt, which the two had led all the way from Salinas de Añana.

"Cheeses, I have cheeses that Brother Semeno brought for the brothers . . . cheeses from Sancte Juste, from Kastrelo, they brought them to Lejone . . . cheeses," a friar was crying, when the mute child Gómez pushed him against the table and the cheeses fell to the ground.

"The child upset the table of cheeses," another friar exclaimed as Gómez disappeared among the women. "The devil has kissed the cheeses which the brothers brought to León."

Patiently, I sought the elect inside and outside their adobe houses, beyond the old walls and in the recently erected churches and monasteries where the rules of Saint Fructuosus, Saint Benedict and Alfonso de León are followed. They will follow mine until the end of time, because as of the first day of the Second Millennium my instructions will enlighten the lives of the monks of Santiago, El Salvador, San Marcelo, San Adrián, San Pablo, San Lucas and San Juan el Teólogo. Every one of them owes me complete obedience.

To the left and right of the road I saw the adobe houses, the plowed fields, the yokes of oxen, the yellowy stubble, the rolling meadows and the barefoot peasants in their shirts, earthen as the earth itself. I espied the poplar and willow groves lining the riverside, and the shepherds counting sheep, goats and groves of trees, groves measured by how many pigs could crowd into and feed off them. In the distance I saw six scrawny peasants, who, by their labors, filled the granaries of Santa María each year.

Two men leading an overburdened ass entered through the Bishop's Gate. Whenever the ass paused, they belabored him with sticks. A stone's throw away, a peasant was carrying a live vixen and two headless hens. A pair of villagers passed me, holding a fattened goose with which to pay their lord, Abbot Sabarico of the monastery of San Lucas. At that moment, the indiscreet eyes of a man on horseback came to rest on a peasant woman. Alarmed, a matron drew her mantle over her daughter, like a hen sheltering her chicks when she spots a kite.

I did not choose any of these creatures to follow me. I walked past those men and women, who were simple but unworthy of salvation. I contemplated the distant mountains to the north, the rugged barrier that guards our kingdom from the sudden onslaughts of Antichrist and of his human personification, al-Mansur.

Down Porta Episcopi Street, past the monastery church of Santiago, a cleric was leading a reddish-black horse worth one hundred solidi; a yoke of oxen, one white, the other mottled, costing twenty solidi; and an animal midway between an ass and a gelded goat, ugly and huge. He had just acquired them, and two menials, servants of the Leonese court, were driving them.

Near the cruciform church of San Salvador, built next to his palace by Ramiro II as a convent for his daughter Geloira, I greeted the count who governs the city. Surrounded by his retinue, he was confident that the power of the century is measured by the number of villas, armed men, servants and horses owned and flaunted before the common people.

The count told me that he had already reserved the plot where his body would rest, alongside the monarchs in the nearby cemetery of the kings, where the bones of Don Sancho the Fat lay. Although unable to govern itself, the council of residents meets under his leadership to mete out injustice and to put donations, wills and contracts into effect, to fix weights and measures, liquid or dry, the wages for a day's work and the tax on merchandise, and to elect the overseers of the market. They meet at nightfall to discuss the future and others' misfortunes, blind to the imminent end of their own lives.

A muleteer suddenly appeared between the castle and the market, approaching me with these words: "Oh sir, you who give succor to men, help me. This morning, my male beast of burden fell dead into a ravine. Unless you bring him back to life, men and wild animals will carry him off as carrion."

"How do you know I can revive him?" I asked.

"I can tell by the light hovering over your head," he replied. "When I saw that crown, I said to myself, 'Only a saint can have that.' "

"You believed in me, now return to the road: You shall find your mule restored to life. Then, filled with faith in me, you shall go back to your village in the mountains. There you shall tell all the world what you have seen here."

The muleteer walked off alongside the Bernesga, a river that flowed away through time faster than the eye could follow. The sky clouded over. Swallows flew by. Four storks rose from the towers and walls. That day in May would never come again.

The populace was more interested in buying turnips, onions, garlic, pigeons, geese, cheese, suet, pepper, honey, bread, chestnuts, oil, wineskins, twigs to light up darkness and sacks of wheat than in its own salvation. I took the narrow path paved with cobbles and ruts, which is the road to saintliness. I found no soul worthy of summoning to my side.

Two Jewish merchants entered León through the Bishop's Gate with a drove of mules laden with textiles and jewelry from Byzantium, cloth and Spanish blankets. Women dressed in colorful skirts clustered round them, paying with Galician solidi or Cordoban dirhams. A man who resembled my brother Abd Allah passed me with no sign of recognition. The bailiff appeared, to collect the tax imposed on vendors of ox and horsehides, earthenware pots and wooden dishes, scissors, sickles, wire hooks, table knives, padlocks, hoes and tongs.

Suddenly I became aware of a woman whose head was veiled in black looking at me from the barely noticeable window of an adobe house; a youngish, comely woman who had been spying on me while I, believing myself alone, was observing the others. I motioned her to come down. She twisted her mouth, as if to say she couldn't because she was a deaf-mute.

She wasn't. She was a widow, Heldoara by name, who had not left her walled cell since the death of her husband, Eutropio. Though childless, she could not remarry, for it would be only to fornicate, the Church would frown on her, and she would be barred from receiving communion, even at the hour of her death. "A widow is a woman who has not had two husbands," Saint Isidore had decreed.

"Heldoara," I called, receiving no answer.

It began to drizzle and grow colder. All I wore over my tunic was a threadbare cape. The sole light came from the brief blaze of the sunset. I started back to the monastery of San Juan el Teólogo. The street was long, winding and narrow, full of puddles and mud. Several townspeople were throwing ordure out of houses built against the old wall. Roving pigs and donkeys rooted in the sewer.

The grayish firmament on the horizon did not herald the dawn of the new millennium. In the year 1000, man's humors could be observed, materialized in the state of the wind, the water, the earth and the creatures who share terrestrial space with us. The havoc wrought in the Christian kingdom by the Saracens' forays could be interpreted as a consequence of our century's imbalance. It was up to me, a monk schooled in the arts of the *quadrivium* and the *trivium,* to scrutinize the visible world's disarray in order to prevent temporal conflicts from ultimately upsetting the stability of the invisible universe.

Upon my return to the monastery, I discovered that Gómez had been following me the whole time through the streets of León. But even though he saw my body and stalked my shadow, he knew nothing of Guiberto and Norberto, nor could he perceive the halo encircling my head. If this mute son of base minstrels is still alive and does not come to grief, he may well be useful one day to that as-yet-unborn author of saints' lives who will compose monodies about me.

VISION X

Stunted, short-lived, haggard, flea-ridden men and women—my sheep—came to the little church of San Juan el Teólogo to confess. Bodies bent and hearts contrite, one by one they knelt to rehearse softly the transgressions they had committed and to receive the medicine of penitence prescribed in accordance with their trespasses by the canonical authorities.

These unshod faithful, clad in shirts, swaddled in ashen sackcloth, their feet muddied, their eyes worried or downcast, declared themselves guilty even before confession. Guilty of everything, of what they had done, of what they had desired, of what they had imagined; guilty of being born and of belonging to the human race, whorish and mortal.

They had been waiting there since the hour of Terce, waiting as always for feasts to come, for feasts to go: Epiphany, the Purification of the Virgin Mary, Lent, Palm Sunday, the eve of the Assumption of the Virgin Mary,

Saint Stephen's Day, unaware that life was passing with the days. There was I, close at hand, judge of their acts, words and thoughts, stern-faced, suffering not only for my own frailties, but for those of my brother sinners as well; ready to listen attentively to the revelations of gentlemen and rustics, matrons and servant girls.

I warned them all to abstain from lying to me and to themselves. Just as Adam and Eve were expelled from paradise when they lost their innocence, they could be ejected from the bosom of the Church for their mortal sins. Needless to say, the parishioners who came to confess always tried to overhear, or read on their faces, the sins of others. To impress them, I pointed to the devils on the capitals of the columns devouring wrathful, envious, lecherous and gluttonous humans.

They peered fearfully at those figures. And then, seeking hope, fastened their gaze on the votive cross with the Alpha and Omega dangling from its arms, and on the Virgin Mary of painted wood that dominated the nave. She, crowned and enthroned Mother, her eyes large and kind, with the Child seated on her left knee, blessed them with her hand.

Time and time again I had tried to teach all these people the concept of the Incarnation, the humanization of God and the deification of man in Jesus. I attempted to explain to them that men and women were revertible, that they could die and return, be alive and journey to the world of the dead, be buried and resuscitate. But when I showed them the image at the rear of the church of a laughing Lord Christ, they took it for the devil's tricks because the Savior could be portrayed only in the Passion and the Crucifixion, as on the processional cross to which he was nailed.

I revealed to them that the worst torture demons could endure was their own nonexistence and our not believing in them. To materialize, they were obliged to assume the loathsome shapes of monsters, grotesque humans and filthy beasts. When they retreated, they cast no shadow or were transparent. I also warned them about those demons we create inside ourselves, the most insidious of all, since they are the product of our evil thoughts and our perverse intentions.

"The devil appears when he is invoked and named, otherwise he does not exist," I told them. "Demons are afraid of light and bump against it as against a shield. In their blindness and bewilderment they often mistake the body, place and time and attack innocent creatures. Each man and woman has been assigned two angels, a good one to save him, a bad one to put him to the test. Both are invisible to the eye, but I can see them, and when they sense me, they flee from my presence, my voice, my footsteps. An angel is itself, a demon is an abyss."

Before hearing confession, I wished to receive the anguished parents of several prodigies who had appeared in the kingdom of León during the year 1000. The first to enter were the servants Pelayo and Paulusa, who had been donated by Abbess Rubina to the church of San Juan de Lairones. In their arms they held a son born two months before term one Friday toward Vespers. They showed me the child and asked me for an explanation, as if I were responsible for their descendant. Its head was sunk on its breast, goatish ears sprouted from its flanks, its eyes protruded from their sockets, its nose was perforated. Two horns jutted from the amorphous forehead, the navel extended down a hairy channel until it became a human mouth, all kisses. Although barely months old, the creature could already walk.

"He screeched so when he popped out between Paulusa's legs that the midwife took fright," Pelayo stammered.

"The midwife foresaw that with this creature the human race would increase, notwithstanding he was a monster," the mother declared.

"Father, we have sinned," Pelayo exclaimed.

"He has a handsome profile," I remarked, but my flattery was no consolation to them.

"Now that I look at him, I see that he resembles my husband," the wife observed.

"Don't praise him anymore. The more charming you find him, the more miserable I feel," the servingman wailed.

Before leaving the church, Paulusa commended herself to the three saints kept in the crypt, Cecilia, Columba and Marina, and lit candles before the Virgin Mary.

Donato and Corvasia, residents of León, whose grandparents and parents, like they themselves, had belonged to this parish since birth, came forward. Here they had been baptized, here they had attended religious celebrations and divine services, here they had been married, here they would grow old, and here they would be buried. In the sixth month of her pregnancy, Corvasia had given birth to a son with two separate heads, two joined chests and a single heart. Donato asked me if the creature was a single person, as it had only one body, or two persons, as it had two heads, and which predominated, the heart or the brain. Corvasia inquired whether the creature had two souls, and what would happen if one were good and the other evil, and when the Resurrection of the Dead came to pass, how could one be saved and the other damned.

I told them both to concern themselves with their son's present, because he didn't look as if he would outlast the week.

Donato became jealous when I stared at his wife's naked flesh beneath her ragged dress. I could not help noticing that she was beautiful despite her tribulations, and desirable despite her despair. He waxed even more jealous when the color rose to her face and she looked at me tremulously, her quick, scared, sincere eyes gazing into mine.

"Were I alone with her body, I would sate myself loving her, even though she bore me a monstrous or androgynous fruit," I thought.

Next, the nun Spasanda appeared before me, having procreated a creature without the help of a man. She had been confined to the convent of San Lucas since childhood, and in the year 999 of the Incarnation of the Lord, her belly began inexplicably to swell. One day in February, on the feast of Saint Eulalia Virgin, she brought forth a person already ten years old, whom she called Vilocia. To her surprise, within a week she discovered that the girl understood all the languages on earth.

Sister Spasanda came to me to learn the reason why Vilocia was tormented by malevolent spirits who turned her nights into a frenzy of whippings and ghastly dreams. I asked her if she had not indulged in clandestine lechery with the devil while the abbess and the other nuns were sleeping, and had unwittingly conceived from him.

She said no.

I inquired if she had done bad things at the instigation of the Great Seducer, and if she had sung and danced, alone or with other women, diabolical songs and dances for the delight of the Enemy of the human race, either in the dormitory or in her head.

She denied it.

I examined Vilocia. Her radiant features and shining eyes were to my liking. She was by no means ugly, and her childish body had womanly curves. To my questions of who she was and where she came from, Vilocia responded that her name was Astragundia, she resided in Rome and had come into the world to be the mistress of Gerbert, Pope Sylvester II. She declared that she would grow up rapidly to witness the end of time, this year 1000, the year when the maleficent angel chained in the abyss would be released.

Sister Spasanda disclosed her daughter's peculiar habits. The girl nodded at her mother's every word and swiveled her head to look over her shoulder, as if there were someone behind her. She kept smiling grimly to herself. I followed her nose's shadow on the wall as it lengthened, shrank and curved into a hook.

Vilocia was stronger than was seemly for one her age. She glibly repeated any word she heard in a foreign tongue. I wanted to know which words most troubled the demons, the number and names of the spirits inhabiting her, the moment when they had entered her person, and the reason for their dwelling inside her. Vilocia answered me with lies, laughed outlandishly and began to caw. I made the sign of the cross over her and sprinkled her with holy water.

I ordered her to receive the Sacraments of Penance and the Eucharist regularly and cautioned her to entrust her heart to God while she was being exorcised and to implore Him for health with deep faith and humility, all the while clasping a crucifix in her hands and with relics of saints bound to her head and breast.

I advised Spasanda to watch for Abbot Andrés's return so that the exorcism could take place soon. No one but he, by virtue of the power which the Church had conferred upon him, would be able to drive the demons that troubled Vilocia from her body.

"When Abbot Andrés sets the bells a-tolling, he can exorcise the clouds themselves," I told her. "We need only wait until he comes back."

Next, the peasant Spernicius, an inveterate sinner and incorrigible confessor to the most atrocious deeds, prostrated himself before me. Wearing a maudlin expression, he professed his belief in the Trinity and blurted out a stream of sins. The first was having fornicated with his brother's wife, a wayside whore he had inherited after his brother's death.

I asked him not to rush the confession; gasping and eager, he lacked sufficient tongue and time to recite his errors. I warned him, quoting Saint Paul, that he who is joined to a harlot is made one body, for they shall be two in one flesh.

Before I was through, he was already bawling that he had violently slain his neighbor and friend, although without hatred or premeditation, for he had been hoodwinked by the devil. He had managed to beg the dead man's pardon for having beaten and stabbed him.

I ordered him to lower his voice. But he stuck his face in mine until the stench of his mouth nauseated me and his heavy breathing exasperated me. He stammered out his excesses: He had stolen sheep and other animals from peasants who had fallen asleep on the hillsides; he had committed sodomy with beasts and with a young boy; on the night of Saint Fructuosus the Bishop, he had carnal knowledge of a young slave girl, because of which his wife sold her on the day of Saint Agatha Virgin Martyr. Weeks later, he came upon the slave in question wandering ragged and hungry in a field, and again he had lewd couplings with her. Then he added that he had lain in the same bed with his mother Subildi, with his brother Vicente, who had since been murdered, with his sister Severa and with his daughter Kintila.

I had not finished assimilating his errors when he started off about drinking cat's blood, human urine and water polluted by a dead mouse; about eating the flesh of a horse torn apart by dogs, and loaves of bread smeared with bird dung. Moreover, he had dared to take communion without having confessed and, feeling queasy, had vomited up the Host. All this he had touched, done and perpetrated with his bloodstained, filthy fingers.

With a blast of vile breath, he conveyed to me his wish to intercede through prayer on behalf of the souls in purgatory. Dingy from lack of bathing, he looked as if he had spent centuries in a grave. He stank of clothes baked dry on his skin, of scabs crusted on his scalp, of lice squashed behind his ears. When he admitted to gorging on carrion, he opened his mouth to display snaggle teeth punctuated by gaps. A habitual sinner, his foulness was more offensive than his faults. Finally, I tired of his stuttering, his stench, and his aberrations, and I ordered him to be quiet.

''Spontaneous frights overcome me in broad daylight, in mangers and in fields,'' he said. ''A procession of black deities follows me, carrying a pale and transparent maiden on a bier to nowhere.''

He claimed that a bald, menacing dwarf riding sidesaddle harried him with a lance. He wasn't sure if the dwarf was female. He thought the ghostly cortege was headed for the monastery of San Lucas, or coming from where al-Mansur's hosts had appeared before attacking León and its marches, when the Caliph took away his wife's father, mother, brothers and sisters to Córdoba.

I gave him penance for ten years and one hundred days of fasting. I commanded him to make one thousand genuflections, to stretch his arms in a cross one thousand times, and to recite one hundred and fifty psalms. I ordered him to deal himself one thousand honest blows on the back with a scourge, although for his horrendous and heinous crimes I should have denounced him to the count and the lord of the manor so that they might hang him. The secrecy of the confessional prevented me from doing so, however.

Spernicius stood up smugly, his hair shaggy, his laugh foolish, his eyes crossed. Then he prostrated himself on the ground and in a mournful voice, with tears in his eyes, brayed out the seven penitential psalms, clamoring for absolution of his shortcomings. I said to myself that if I were God I would send him to hell, but being merely a humble confessor I was obliged to take pity on his frailties.

He rose from his prayer, and in accordance with canon law laid his grime-furrowed hands on the holy book and sprinkled his haggard face with holy water. I thought he would leave, but he drew a bag of ashes from a leather pouch he carried concealed among his clothes, which were so torn that his buttocks and skinny legs peeked through. Ash Wednesday had passed, but he gleefully tossed the ashes on his head and, groaning and sighing, covered himself with sackcloth. He turned to give me a look of self-satisfaction and strode out of the church.

I glimpsed Jimena and the nun Froila between the saintly women Begga, Balda and Betote, who had been so devoted to God since their infancy that before they reached twenty they were already deadened by abstinence. The three sisters, who lived in separate cells in the monastery of San Lucas and, as if they were strangers, never looked each other in the eye when they met in church to say their prayers before the altar of the Blessed Virgin Mary, stolidly watched Jimena approaching me. Froila did not move. She had no intention of confessing.

Jimena stopped before the confessional and knelt humbly, her long black hair partially veiling her face. I examined her at will through the window screen. Froila examined me. Jimena looked listless, as though she were ailing. The brilliance of her black eyes contrasted with her dejection. She brought her face so close to mine that I smelled her firm flesh and could see that her breasts were erect; her white bosom was undoubtedly brimming with venial sins.

"Do you believe in the Father, the Son and the Holy Ghost?" I asked her.

"I believe," she answered.

"Do you believe that those three persons are one God?"

"I believe."

"Do you believe that after your body has died you will arise on Judgment Day in this same flesh which I see before me now, to receive retribution in accordance with your deeds, be they good or evil?"

"I believe."

"Will you forget the sins of your neighbor against you, because, as the Lord said, 'If you will not forgive men their offenses, neither will your Father forgive you yours'?"

"I will."

Then I asked her if she had had incestuous relations with Abbot Andrés, or sinful ones with any other monk in the monastery of San Juan el Teólogo, and I warned her that if she did not forsake incest I could not give her penance or absolution. I saw that she wavered, and I rebuked her. "Sister, do not hesitate to confess your sins. I, too, am a sinner, and my faults are worse than yours. Let us freely declare those injuries which you have done to our Lord Jesus Christ, because, as the apostle Saint Paul said, 'But if we would judge ourselves, we should not be judged.' "

"Yes, Father," she murmured.

"I am listening to you, daughter."

"By my own fault, Father, I have profaned the Host. One day I inadvertently let a mouse eat it. Another day, I absentmindedly dropped it on the floor, and yet another day, I forgot and let it dry out, become discolored and lose its taste."

"What else do you have to confess, daughter?"

"My mother and I have found mites in the flour, the soup and the curdled milk, and we have given them to the monks in the monastery—including you, Father—to eat."

"What further wrong have you done, my daughter?"

"I have often shouted at Gómez, who is deaf."

"Have you had lascivious embraces, cohabitation or any sort of carnal coupling with youths from León or its surroundings? Has any member of the clerical orders fallen miserably through fornication on your account, committing lecheries with you which cannot be expiated through penance and mercy?"

"I do not recall having sinned that way, Father. All I can remember is that Gómez asked me to climb up the tower with him and there beneath the bells . . ."

"Did he touch you on the penetralia of Erebus? How far did he do it, and what did you feel? Afterward did he ask you to copulate with him?"

"No, my lord, he pulled out my pubic hair at the place where groin and thigh meet, and I wondered whether I was going to consecrate my virginity to Lord Christ."

"What did you answer yourself?"

"I said no."

"No to what, the caress or to chastity?"

"I told myself I would not consecrate my virginity to Lord Christ."

"What else did he do to you? Did he lay his wicked hands on you? Were you penetrated by him or any monk in any way?"

"No, my lord, I don't remember that."

"Most beloved sister, the *Penitential of Saint John* says that if a presbyter or deacon commits natural fornication after having taken the vow of chastity, he shall do penance for seven years, he shall ask forgiveness every hour, even when asleep, and he shall make a fast every week, save during the time between Easter and Whitsunday. A heap of straw shall be his bed," I spoke in a tremulous voice, which I slyly lowered so she would bring her face closer to mine in order to hear me. "If the monk sins with a beast, he shall do penance for one year. If he masturbates himself, desiring another person in his mind, as I desire you, two years; moreover, if he is assailed by a violent desire of the imagination, such as mine is, he shall do penance for seven days. If this desire is accompanied by a lubricious word or look, twenty days. And if it transpires during a sinful dream, he shall sing fifteen psalms."

The more I recited to her the years of punishment I would impose on my soul should I possess her, the more her cheeks burned, and the more my eyes flashed, the more nervously she twisted her fingers.

"The monk shall do penance for four years if he sins with his lips, but if kissing and licking become a habit with him, he shall do it for seven years. If he defiles a virgin and sheds blood, his sentence shall be three years on bread and water. If he begets a son with her, he shall be exiled for seven years. If he commits the sin of sodomy with a young girl or a youth, seven years. If in a fit of madness he violates his mother, he shall be a pilgrim all his life. Oh, the more I tell you about the penances for punishing a monk enamored of you, the more aroused I become to love you."

Jimena remained silent. I continued.

"My child, perhaps not everything you have done comes to mind. I will question you, and you will answer me. Try to keep the devil from tricking you into hiding something, or from tricking you into tricking me."

Jimena told me her sins. She said she had watched Gómez in the cloister mimicking acts of fornication, that she had seen him in the latrines touching something between his legs, and that when he saw her looking at him he had invited her to masturbate herself and to eat skin and lice from his body. She had refused, not from lack of desire, but out of fear that Doña Miguel might catch them. She confessed to finding this boy using a peasant child smaller than himself in the fashion of dogs by the wayside. The buttocks of both were cold and muddy.

She expressed her wish to be baptized anew to wipe out her sins. I replied that for merely wanting this she would do penance for three years, in addition to the other penances I would impose on her for having sinned with Gómez in word, deed and sight.

The sisters Begga, Balda and Betote gloated at her. Froila didn't move. Jimena smiled to herself. She refused to confess any more sins. Kneeling before me, she awaited absolution.

I gave her a penance of one hundred Ave Marias and directed her to fast on bread and water all the Fridays of the year 1000. I was curious to see if the Hail Mary would cure her of her evil thoughts.

She sought my eyes through the window screen.

I inaudibly declared my carnal desires to her.

"I love you," Jimena whispered and ran off.

VISION XI

Abd Allah did not return to Córdoba with al-Mansur, nor did he follow him on his campaigns throughout the Christian North. He remained camped near León with enough Saracens to take the city and ensnare me.

I met him one morning in June, on Midsummer Day, on my way to watch the barley harvest in the fields. The encounter took place in the monastery's churchyard. He was sitting on a grave between a crumbling wall and a tree bereft of branches. The grave belonged to a newly buried boy, so poor that he had no tombstone. My brother's rugged shape loomed among the sepulchers. The clods of earth on the boy's grave were still so loose that his feet sank into the ground. The clumsily buried child thrust his stiff hands between the rough stones, his exposed face stared at the sky.

Abd Allah glanced sideways at me. His whole body, still as a scorpion poised to sting, followed my presence as I, the intruder, appeared beside

117

the old stone staircase that descended outside the church from the bell tower and disappeared into the crypt where the saints' relics were kept. What he saw was a man of distinction and measured step, self-assured, with a beatific aura circling his head. Each stair was a descent, not toward the crypt but toward the death that he was readying for me.

He felt the irresistible force that drew him to me, the fascination my person held for him. He was incapable of turning his face away from mine. Visibly troubled, he was afraid of losing himself in me, of being swept away by my strength. Such extraordinary emotions flooded both of us that we could hear our hearts beating in our respective breasts.

The closer he and I came physically, the farther apart we grew in spirit; the more we found ourselves alike, the more different we really were; the more we wanted to unite, the wider yawned the chasm between us; the more distant we were from each other, the more we shared a common destiny.

The pale sun shone. Neither of us moved, bewitched by our appearances. There was no one as handsome as he with his black eyes and hair, his fine raiment with bands of black silk crossing his chest. When I looked at him, my own death did not matter, because I could live on in his life. Nearby, his black mare eyed us as if she understood what was happening between us. She was so swift that it was hard to catch her standing still. I can remember her clearly now, I can see her panting, her icy sweat, her almost human fury.

"Wicked men travel in pairs, like scorpions," I said finally.

Abd Allah made no answer. He had come to see me without his army, but armed. He had left his helmet among the stones.

"You and I are digging the same grave; it doesn't matter if we do it alone or together," I added.

He looked me up and down. He still denied me the sound of his voice, which I expected would resemble mine. He found out then that his gaze gave me gooseflesh. He realized that his malevolent power made me want to scream silently, as if I were trapped in a nightmare. He discovered I would have kissed his lips to wipe off that perverse smile that had terrified me since childhood, that I held myself in check to keep from embracing him, as I had always done after we fought. He saw that my cowardice embarrassed me.

He scrutinized me hatefully and said, "Alfuns, how surprised I am that you're afraid of me. Don't worry, I only want to kill you."

"Abd Allah, I am bewildered. I see someone just like me threatening me with death," I said.

"Sir, before the year 1000 is over, one of us two will rule the earth. I don't want to fuse or confuse myself with you, lest when we leave here we no longer know which one goes and which one stays behind."

"Abd Allah, tell me the truth about my mother and about María Sabarico; we'll make peace in this world and in the other."

"Adosinda betrayed us both."

"Both of us?"

"My father and I."

"She betrayed your father, when he had hundreds of concubines in the harem? Only women can be unfaithful?"

"Two souls join together in one when a child is born. The begotten child spends his whole life struggling against those two souls, which are contending in his breast, against those souls which at every moment try to dominate his words and deeds, try to take over his gestures and his eyes. I decided to be my father the Caliph's son, not the Jew's. I have had no mother since the day I was born." I sensed the ghost of a smile behind his words.

"Two from the same species don't have to get along, sometimes they're enemy likenesses. Anyone who sees you and me will conclude that both our existences are valid. All we need to know is which of the two creatures is the real one, and which the false," I declared.

"Time will tell which of us will prevail and endure. I don't mean by this that you or I should lead a double life; we are two equally different persons."

"You're saying what I'm thinking; I've already thought what you believe you're thinking."

"Do you know what? Along the road of years I met a devil who looked like me," he interrupted.

"I am that devil," I murmured, "if I do not mistake your words, which are my own."

"Alfuns, you are an old man now and your sight is dim. With those eyes you couldn't shoot an arrow into a dead body lying at your feet."

"Abd Allah, don't think I'm any less strong than you. I can see well in the dark and fairly far on earth," I said.

"Despite your years, I haven't lost the appetite, twenty women are well served by you in my harem in Córdoba," he exclaimed.

"Despicable things happened when you went to León, when I stayed in Córdoba: You denounced my mother, you arrested María, and you caused her death. I shall never forgive you for it."

"In your world the dead are more alive than the living. So many have been murdered, just forget them. Let dead time stay dead," he replied. "One day, a man used to dreaming pitches into his own night and sees the inventions of his dream so close up and substantial that he comes to believe that they really exist, and the more real they seem inside him, the more he himself becomes unreal, the more he himself turns into a dream."

"The capacity to dream, which is the greatest thing we possess, and don't possess, which makes us human, and inhuman, ultimately drowns us in a sea of images," I told him.

"Wipe that dreamy look off your face," he snapped.

"Where did you learn to look so gloomy?" I asked.

"I learned it in the battle of Simancas."

"How?"

"By letting myself get killed."

"You never took part in it."

"I learned to look dead in the monastery of San Juan el Teólogo, and in the battlefields of Simancas."

"Where have you been all these years?" I asked.

"When I escaped from Córdoba, I went to find Saint Genadio, who years earlier had founded the monastery of Santiago de Peñalba and dwelt in the caves of silence," he began to explain, as if he were me.

"You're lying. It was I, Alfonso, who scaled the mountain in search of the monastery, I who descended to the valley where the cave was, I who followed the path with the yellow flowers and the murmur of the brook. Once I found the cleft crag, I sat down on a stone and looked around me, and I saw that my body was insignificant.''

"There was the cave, its stony mouth gaping open to swallow me, Abd Allah. The gusts of wind outside pushed me backward. There was no one inside. Genadio had died long ago, Genadio was a relic kept in the apse of the church. Standing before the altar, my feet grew cold.''

"The walls of the cave were rough, like the hide of some ancient animal. Water was dripping inside. I, Alfonso, went out, the wind was blowing, everything around me was pleasing: the rocks and the plants clinging to the slope, the gray cenoby in the distance, the holiness which rebuffs the devil as light does bats.''

"I sojourned for several months with the monks of Peñalba. Then I departed, fleeing from myself,'' he stammered, as if he were I.

"You're lying,'' I retorted. "You came with al-Mansur, and you hid with your hosts in the vast cave in the region of the Torio River, there where mist enshrouds the mountain peaks. Now you have emerged to lay siege to León.''

"You hid in the bowels of the vast cave, there where the waters of the Torio gush out between the rocks, there where the waters plunge in an underground cascade into the abyss of yourself.'' He fell silent. Then he said, "I am weary, the world I must rule for the next thousand years tires me.''

"Trying to rise above ourselves, we invariably fall; trying to become gods, we revert to our animal state. What difference does it make if gods live in the momentariness of the eternal and animals in the eternity of the moment?'' I cried.

"Let's leave it like this, let's part here. Life has no end, we can be two in one, or one in two,'' he suggested.

"Escape from me if you can. My breast will not and cannot contain the violence which I am.''

"Free of you, I shall be the other. No atrocity will be spared my enemies. I shall glorify terror.''

"The moon made its way into my doorless cell last night. You were there outside. You were cold and had lost your way."

"The way was lost, not I. Somebody who never takes it, the sedentary one, knows it well."

"You are in hell, and he doesn't know it," I exclaimed.

Speaking to each other thus, we no longer knew who said one thing and who the other. A confusion with the stranger who was my brother welled up in me. The familiarity that exuded from me, from my past, curled around his body and his face. The unwelcome sensation of being and existing alike, which I had not felt since our infancy in Córdoba, returned.

Standing before him, I discovered my own otherness. I observed, as if on my own person, the wrinkles on his skin, the white hairs on his head, and I smelled the odor of his rib cage, the breath from his mouth. I felt the touch of his clothing on my chest, the sweat and grime on his feet. I clenched his jaws, I pressed his lips together.

Suddenly I noticed that he was staring at the spot between my eyebrows. He meant to shoot his crossbow at me.

But first he examined me, he recognized me, as if in a duplication of my gaze, of his gaze, which surfaced from the remote depths of a childhood made of lies.

Abd Allah hated me for certain; never before had I been so sure of it.

"Abd Allah," I admonished him, "forget the evil you're after, go back to being who you were."

"In your madness, you search for me in the past. There's no one there anymore. Abd Allah is dead," he replied.

"Get away from me," I said.

"Getting away from me or getting closer to you is the same; there's no middle way out. Wherever you go, you'll find yourself with me."

"Don't worry anymore about occupying my body. Do it whenever you want, all the death here is yours!" I shouted.

"There's no other way of dealing with you!" he cried and rushed at me, attacking savagely, his face convulsed with rage.

I covered my chest with a shield I had beside me.

His lance splintered.

I was knocked down.

His armed left hand trembled with rancor.

On the ground, I realized that once I was dead, my soul would disappear into his. In a bound I was on my feet, my sword drawn.

A bitter fight ensued. Never before in my life had I felt such strong blows against my shield, such a powerful arm. With each swipe of the sword, his helmet crumpled, his courage redoubled. But his resistance was ebbing. My experience in al-Mansur's army gave me considerable superiority over him. But I took all that he received as well. Determined not to die, he defended himself strenuously, severing the links of my chain mail. Blow by blow, I made him retreat to the wall, stumble over a grave. I wanted to lop off his hands, to slice his shoulders, to gouge out his eyes. He fought back desperately. Little by little my strength increased, his waned.

Tired and weakened, I pushed him toward an open grave. He was barely able to get a grip on the edge with his heels. Standing on air, he managed not to fall in. The yellow light blinded us. After all this time, I knew even less who was winning. We were both losing, for this struggle was like smashing his image in a mirror, like muddying my reflection in the water.

Sancho Saborejo appeared on the bell tower. He looked in our direction but failed to see us. Doubtless he heard the singing of the birds, but not the noise of our weapons. Tranquilly he scanned the horizon, carefree and gay. In the thick of that battle I was still afraid of losing my bodily existence, of being invisible to others.

While we were fighting, me against me, two heavily armed Saracen warriors rode in from the right. Abd Allah let them approach, not turning to look, but sensing they were there. Once they were before me, I could tell they were seasoned soldiers by the scars on their cheeks and their nicked shields. Their hands were crusted with blood.

They hesitated upon seeing us so alike. No matter how hard they tried to tell us apart, they couldn't determine which was which. Only our garments differentiated us. But they could make a mistake, and so they awaited their chance to take sides.

Abd Allah signaled them with his hand not to intervene, nimbly sprang upon his black mare and turned his sword toward me. In his eyes I saw death. I saw my silence and my skeleton. I yearned to kill him immediately, to free myself forever from his person identical to mine. But I made no move toward his body, afraid of spilling my own blood when I wounded him.

I circled on my horse and rode away from him as fast as I could. He remained there among the graves, waiting for me to disappear in the distance. I kept to the shade. He spurred his mount and rode across the cemetery, trampling the graves. The other two followed me at a gallop, yelling and beating on their shields with their lances.

He, supernatural, rode into the wind.

VISION XII

Last night I fell asleep in the scriptorium. I was looking for a name in the labyrinth of letters I had made the day before.

I dreamed I was John the Theologian, and that I was making a book about the year 1000. In my dream the voice of the Lord did not order me to write what I saw, nor did it command me to send my revelation to the seven churches. Neither did I see the seven golden lamps, or the Son of Man with seven stars in his right hand and the sword in his mouth. In the dream I saw myself, my body glowing, my eyes flashing rays of light. The letters, set in white squares as in a mosaic, memorialized an illuminator and scribe, Alfonso de León.

In the manuscript my form appeared facing the monogram of Lord Christ; he and I were drawn with equal artistry and wealth of detail. The words asked the future reader to remember me, and they were arranged in such a way that they repeated the request vertically and horizontally, beginning always with the letter *A*.

This labyrinth commemorated me in secret, just as in his day Florentinus commemorated himself in the monastery at Valeranica. And before him the monk Maius from the monastery of San Miguel Arcángel, a painter and scribe of the *Commentary on the Apocalypse* by Beatus of Liébana, had asked in an acrostic at the end of his illuminations not to be forgotten. It's easy to deduce that for them, as for me, there is no death worse than oblivion.

The monk Maius, impelled by love of Saint John the Theologian's book of visions, limned the words of its stories to instill fear in the wise of the coming of judgment at the world's end, when the dead, great and small, will stand before God to be judged according to their works. Emeterius, the miniaturist of San Salvador de Tábara, taught me the craft of painting the phrases and personages of the Book of Revelation. He learned it from Maius, alongside the presbyter Juan and the nun Ende. After his monastery was burned and razed by al-Mansur, Emeterius made his way to León. His words from the time when he was working on Beatus's *Commentary* are preserved: "Oh lofty tower of Tábara, made of stone, where I sat for so long bent over the parchment, simultaneously straining my pen and my limbs."

When they copy the sacred manuscripts, painters and scribes of the monastery of San Lucas, cannier than I, avail themselves of the apostles' faces to introduce their own features and in colonnettes of words, they have inserted their own reasonings so that the Word, which the Evangelists spread to the four corners of the earth, is their Word, the Word of the deranged monks of San Lucas.

If we look closely, it's plain to see that the faces of the Evangelists are self-portraits of the painter. In his portraits all four have open mouths from which a flowery tongue protrudes, and from the tongue dribble the words attributed to Matthew, Mark, Luke and John. Also, the symbols belonging to each one are placed above the head of another. On one page, two different Evangelists wear the face of the artist. It is the same on the next page. And thus we regretfully discover that the shameless painter from San Lucas was not satisfied with bestowing his ephemeral features on one saint, but gave them to all four.

Other artists, like the deacon Ioannes from the monastery of Santos
María y Martín in León, framed the painted figure with colored circles,
perhaps hoping to imprison time, which seeps incessantly from the pores
and orifices of corporeal creatures.

This morning, after Prime and after uttering the requisite *oratio in scriptorium,* I began to paint the page about the Whore of Babylon in the Apocalypse. It was raining outside and the poplars swayed in the wind, lightning
silvered the gloom of the scriptorium, and the peals of thunder weren't
scaring anyone except me.

Before the midday meal, toward the hour of Sext, it stopped raining,
the stones and fields were bathed in damp light, and the road to León
became a quagmire. I finished illuminating the passage that declares: "And
there came one of the seven angels, who had the seven vials, and spoke
with me, saying: Come, I will shew thee the condemnation of the great
harlot, who sitteth upon many waters, with whom the kings of the earth
have committed fornication; and they who inhabit the earth, have been
made drunk with the wine of her whoredom."

Doña Miguel came to the door to tell me that she had left my daily
ration—a piece of cheese, a loaf of bread and an egg—on the kitchen
table. I told her I would go down afterward. Then, hunched over the
lectern, pen in hand, I outlined on the parchment the serrated border of
the dress worn by the figure of the whore enthroned on the waters. Beatus
of Liébana identified this harlot, on whom I placed a Saracen crown with
a crescent at its center, with Iniquity. The two royal personages who assist
her in raising the goblet filled with the wine of fornication, although drawn
facing forward, are looking sideways. I drew hybrid monsters and malignant
powers around them. In an earlier dream, the ghostly figure of Saint John
the Theologian had warned me about the presence on earth of the triad of
evil: the Dragon, the Beast and the False Prophet, a triad that countered
the Holy Trinity: the Father, the Son and the Holy Ghost. In another part
of the miniature, I painted the figure of Lord Christ holding the world in
his right hand. In the middle of the world, I placed an eye looking out at
whoever looks at it, my own eye.

It was almost dark when I put the Son of God into an *O,* the *O* into a
diamond, the diamond into the keeping of the four winged Evangelists. To

the illuminator and the scribe—I am both—I gave an elongated profile, large eyes, delicate ears poking out of long hair, a sharp chin, cruciform mouth, a short skirt and bare feet. Not far off I introduced the presence of the black Raven who, according to Saint Isidore of Seville, feeds on corpses, starting with the eyes. To thwart the grim figure of the Raven, in front of a blue tree filled with birds I placed the lion and the ox, animals who Isaiah says will eat straw together in the millenary kingdom. Lion and ox fill the circles of the letters O and B.

My bodies cast no shadows; they are hands, feet, heads and colored garments in an imaginary space. By the time I finish the book, I will be an old man. Moreover, like my master and brother Emeterius, disciple of the great painter and scribe Maius, I hope that death doesn't surprise me until I have reached the book's harbor.

Martín Meñique, the cleric who accompanied Abbot Andrés in his mission on earth, used to prepare the parchment leaves the Mussulman way, in the adjoining room, so that I could illuminate them, but ever since he left I must do the work myself. He, who also helped me to rule the lines and lay out the columns, used to write the words of the manuscript on a tablet resting on his legs. His writing was so regular that no interruption or pause between one day and the next was noticeable, despite the months and years gone by.

Also in charge of recording episcopal obituaries, the genealogies of kings, and the dates of construction and dedication of churches and monasteries, Martín Meñique tried to keep abreast of the almanac, although he had forgotten the day and the year of his own birth. His style was unmistakable: When he was inspired, he made tall, svelte T's and L's; when he was tired the B's and F's were ungainly and squat. He often left blank spaces on the pages, undoubtedly intending to add the names of Abbot Andrés, who had commissioned the book, and his own, adorning the initials with intertwined figures of birds and fishes. In the M I drew to tease him, I dangled a scribe from the tails of the letter S above it.

The future is clear to me now that I am embellishing the sacred text. In the labyrinth of letters decorated and yet to decorate, I discern the end of the world and the doom of its creatures. Here in this monastic precinct, which since its founding and dedication has followed the Rule of Saint Benedict, I see the end of time.

Until it happens, I will celebrate the liturgy of the Last Days, coloring the figures in the book with green, black, red and blue inks. Before my eyes the light becomes image, and the image, a body. Using inks which I alone know how to prepare, I paint beasts and foliage, tightly entangled curves, contours that twist and twine into one another. I spurn gold—the radiance of noon suffices me.

I, who ornament the initials of the words and the spirals of the letters with the tail of a fish, the wing of a bird, and the blind stare of an eye, cannot draw my own face, the face of the Lord of the Last Days. To all appearances, I do not know it yet.

While I am painting the path, the tracks of the walker disappear. While I am doubled over the lectern, I already see the scriptorium, the church, and the rest of the monastery in ruins, my body stripped of flesh and my skeleton an alien thing; I descry future visitors searching among the stones for the acts they believed were mine, but which never belonged to me. Because the moment my life happened, life went up in a flash of oblivion. Because this light of Virgins and Christs, this light of intangible blackness which it has been granted to me to see is not the Light, but merely the shadow of the Light. Because this light, which drowns in my eyes, is not the Light we dreamed about as children; we have never seen that Light again on earth.

My end is the beginning of metamorphosis, my beginning is the transformation of bodies, including my own. My words, like bodies, shrink in size with use; they acquire a dual nature, no longer what they were, never what they want to be, until they merge and vanish in the unexpected and alien form that time vouchsafes them. As we advance toward death, moving farther away down the unfinished road, there is a decrease in the magnitude of the figure and a fading of color in the letters, letters that are windows through which the poverty-stricken, the ignorant and the wretched—who don't know how to read—might one day glimpse the Creation, be amazed by the Incarnation, and grieve over the Passion.

Now that the world is coming to an end, I am determined to find the secret Name of God by making visible the inner letters of my own soul, because I know that no word, sentence or book exists that does not manifest and express, in whichever of its infinite combinations, the presence and absence of the Divine Word.

In the *O* is encoded the universe of the human head; the figure of Eve is not confined to the *E*—her history is to be found in the carnality of the generations and degenerations to which she has given birth. The *V* is the Virgin, a *V* that turns into the *N* of the Nativity and the *A* of the Annunciation and the Assumption. The *D* contains a figure, that of David, which escapes from the sphere of the letter to climb over it and into the foliage adorning it, as if the psalmist were trying to reach the limits of his own corporeality.

The Virgin is embodied in several letters: In the *T,* she holds a cross in her left hand; in the *C,* ashes in her right hand; in the *I,* she is an initial; in the *B,* she begins the sentence ''Blessed is the Man . . .''

With the onset of night, I retreat to the dark leaf where I am portrayed. But before doing so, I remove my eye and hand from things; I store in myself what surrounds me. Because, to fashion my figures, I have made a mix of everything: powder, bones, stones, memories, flesh, rags, glass, teeth, hair and ashes.

In the war of the end, I will carry the book under my arm as a talisman. In the millenary battle, the illuminated figures and the written words, the scribe and the artist will be one and the same.

VISION XIII

From outside, the adobe house was shaped like a circle. At first, it didn't seem to have any doors, but I found a small one, hidden in the wall. It had been set below ground level, and I had to crouch to pass through it.

A lame, toothless peasant who was working in the wheat harvest came to tell me that he had heard a woman's cries on the road to the monastery of San Miguel de Escalada. He thought she was being murdered. Moments before hearing the cries he had seen a man dressed in Saracen fashion, very like me in face and body, go into the house. A pale matron in black accompanied him. Fearing the worst, we hurried together toward the spot.

The peasant dared not enter the house and hid with the mules by the river, near the poplars, among the gorse.

A plant, dusty as if with ashes, guarded the entrance to the house. Sprung from debased soil, its leaves, covered with prickly down, tapered to a point. Its mouthlike flowers drew back to lunge and bite. I pretended to turn my back to it, then whirling suddenly, I sliced it in two. A viscous liquid oozed from all its mouths.

The door was bolted from within. I pounded on it softly until the bar gave.

I groped my way along a dank, chilly corridor with a dirt floor. The corridor dipped sharply, then climbed through steep, narrow darkness. Silently, I approached a room. Two people were leaning over a table. Each held a knife dripping with fresh blood. The lingering light filtered in through a tiny unglazed stone window. The two figures' gestures were repeated on the wall. Beside the table legs, a black dog was lapping up the blood.

On the table lay a woman's naked body. I could see by the size of her belly that she was pregnant. Though still alive, she had no tongue left to scream, no strength to move; she could only watch with eyes aghast what was happening around her, on her, and inside her.

The man, very like me in face and body, dressed in Saracen fashion, raised his hand and let it fall, inert. The evil-looking matron skillfully thrust a curved knife into the woman's belly and withdrew it, just as Doña Miguel would cut meat in the kitchen of the monastery of San Juan el Teólogo.

Suddenly aware of someone standing there observing me, I felt like a drunkard seeing double. I was Abd Allah.

Behind me, the matron in black was so intent on my every move that the woman stretched out on the table could hear her breathing and was terrified by the wicked gleam in her eyes.

"Almarada," the man with my voice, my face, and my body hissed. "Help me."

From my hiding place, I could see the woman trying to learn from the expression of the matron dressed in black what awaited her next, where she lay inert. Almarada was the female who accompanied Abd Allah. She wore a shabby, faded black gown. Her long black tresses hung down to her hams and snaked up above her head. Her finger- and toenails were bluish, and she was barefoot.

His hands were swarthy and sore. A dented helmet barely covered his ashen hair. His clothes were as stiff as if they had been made out of the pieces of a steel cuirass. The wounds and bruises of war mottled his face.

The victim rested on a narrow, rectangular table that reminded me of a coffin or a boat. Now her legs were hidden by a black cloth, her hips uncovered, her breasts mutilated. She had already died, her eyes frozen with terror, her mouth agape in a mute scream.

"Don't worry, I will be father to your son," he whispered, for Almarada had taken an infant out of the woman's belly. I don't know whether it was alive or dead. They tossed it into a black cradle, and there was no sound of movement or crying.

Then he plunged in his hands to rummage in the woman's womb. No doubt he was looking for the second creature, because he jabbed furiously at the placenta. He didn't find the other one, the twin.

Almarada had blood on her lips and fingers. A sword, a dagger and a lance were propped against the wall—Abd Allah's weapons. Once again, I heard in an adjoining room the steps of an intruder coming closer. I turned hesitantly to look at him, who was similar to me, who was spying on me. When they discovered I was there, the face that looked at me was my face. In Abd Allah I found what I hated in myself. Surprising him in a crime, I doubted my own goodness.

I quickly saw the stranger identical to myself, who not only shared a past but perhaps a soul with me, was glaring at me spitefully out of his jealous eyes. I could not bear this odious resemblance. He had no right to be my twin. I had to get rid of him, to bury him in myself.

"Who goes there?" a voice asked, sounding like mine.

"I do," I said.

They both ran away. I couldn't tell if they took to the roof or ran out the hidden door. He snatched up the weapons in passing. The black dog followed them. The woman's corpse remained on the table, the child's in the cradle.

I went outside, and I pursued them among the poplars and oaks. I could still see Almarada in the distance; she hurried toward another Almarada, who awaited her, motionless, beside a bare tree. The peasant cowering among the gorse looked at me perplexedly, wondering whether I was the ghost who had fled or the man standing before him. That's how spectral we were.

I went back to the house to cover the dead woman with my cape. With some repugnance, I closed her eyes. It was Corvasia, Donato's wife, who lived in a street near the monastery of San Lucas. When her two-headed son died, she had become pregnant again.

After I returned to León, Bishop Froilán told me that that afternoon he had ordered the arrest of a vagabond who claimed to have attended a dinner of spirits with a gentleman dressed in black and his wife. During that banquet he had gorged on human flesh and blood. In subsequent interrogations the vagabond confessed to having fornicated the previous night with a matron who he suspected had already died. But he did not know it for sure because the gentleman dressed in black and his companion had covered the body with a black cape. What he knew for certain was that she had not responded to his caresses.

VISION XIV

"Sancha Ruiz, Elivira Meñique, Froila Vigilaz, Vita Cabezón, Oroceti Velasquiz, Helizabet de la Vega, Dominga Turrado, Azenda Sobradelo, Fredenanda de Monzón, Gondesalva Gudestioz, Heldoara de la Mata, Beila Beilaz, Giloira Rudríguis, Quintela Dávila," the minstrel introduced me to the women he was harboring in the monastery. "They are all pious ladies who will await the end of time with us."

"If you could see what these ladies have under their skin, the mere sight of it would nauseate you," I said to him. "They are the door to the devil."

"Don Alfonso, my master, by the centuries upon centuries, do not be angry with my Sancho," Oro María pleaded.

"The people hereabouts will gossip about the presence of nonreligious ladies in the monastery," I explained to them. "They must leave tomorrow at dawn."

"Heldoara, Vita and Dominga have left their fathers and husbands; El-

135

vira, Helizabet and Oroceti have relinquished their jewels and fancy clothes, Gondesalva, Fredenanda and Azenda have abandoned their homes to come here and wait for the Last Judgment. The others have done as much," Sancho declared. "But if you so order it, they will abandon this refuge as well."

"Nobody saw them come in, and nobody will see them go out," Oro María assured me.

"I hope so, and I don't want to know any more about them," I said.

Ever since morning the spectacle of the minstrels' wantonness had shocked me. I had stumbled onto Sancho Saborejo, Oro María, Jimena and their lady friends in the cloister, their hands smeared with blood and black feathers.

"What mischief are you up to?" I asked them.

"Oh, master, sir," Sancho and Oro María answered in unison, "it's the fear."

"What does fear have to do with this carnage?" I asked.

"The fear of the end of time, the fear of the end of us, the fear of fear," Sancho Saborejo replied, holding the huge leg of a monstrous fowl in his hands.

"Where did you get that prodigious bird?" I inquired.

"A bald, ugly she-dwarf dressed in yellow, who was passing by, gave it to me saying, 'With this flesh you can sate your hunger,'" Oro María stammered out.

"She could have been the devil," I warned.

"She was in too much of a hurry for me to find out who she was or where she came from," the minstrel said.

"Since Sancho Saborejo and his wife came to the monastery of San Juan el Teólogo, there's been a stream of charlatans calling themselves Mary who follow in the misguided steps of other charlatans who call themselves messiah," I rebuked them.

"That's not true, Lord. We've only helped widows terrified of the year 1000, maidens fleeing from the hosts of al-Mansur, and crazy virgins from the monastery of San Lucas."

"Your son Gómez makes obscene signs with his hands and lewd grimaces with his mouth at these foolish women, which they take for prophetic gestures,'' I scolded them.

''We take for truths the signs and grimaces that Gómez makes,'' said Sancho Saborejo.

''The desire to couple and become drunk with those strayed sheep while the Saracens are surrounding us, while the world nears its destruction, and the living and the dead advance toward Doomsday strikes me as senseless,'' I continued.

''But they have come here to commend themselves to the protection of our Glorious Mother, not to wallow in fornication or hasten to perdition,'' Oro María protested.

''I can save the women; they have only to follow me, obey me and worship me,'' I told the minstrels.

They looked at each other in surprise. I looked at them. I was afraid that with so many strumpets at hand, my head would swarm with indecent images, and the temptation to propagate my sacred progeny in Jimena would come to me; for I cherished the hope that, through the conjunction of contrary seeds, the legions of saints would increase and prosper on earth.

All three of us knew that on the Sunday before Sancho had not been sober enough to serve me in the celebration of holy mass and had not come to the church when I sent Jimena to bring him to prayers and the divine office. He woke up drunk and confused between the hours of None and Nocturn, believing it was Monday. He confessed to me then that he had spent the day of obligation asleep in Oro María's arms. When I learned that he had also had carnal copulation with Beila Beilaz, who had been a nun, I threatened to oust him from the monastery and commanded that he do penance and scourge himself. I was not stricter with him because he promised to mend his ways, but soon afterward, he went drinking in Shaky Ramiro's tavern with the ex-nun.

On Monday I waited in vain for him to assist me at the canonical hours. Stupid with sleep, at Matins he rang the bell he should have rung at Lauds. Looking grave, he later assured me that he'd done it on purpose because Beila Beilaz, naked and befuddled, was coming down the stairs of the choir holding a lighted candle, and he'd meant to warn me with the ringing. I should, he said, guard myself against the nakedness of Beila Beilaz, and other nakednesses no less enticing than hers. And I should keep in mind that the ladies he had brought to the monastery of San Juan el Teólogo were far from negligible; they were shapely and handsome, ranging in age from fourteen to twenty-five years.

Tuesday night I was awakened by Sancho Saborejo's shouting. Beila Beilaz, breasts bobbing, was trying to kill him with a Moorish dagger. With each stab she aimed at him the minstrel shouted, "My heart's not in my chest, my heart is here, on my back. Even if you wound my body, you won't hurt me, because I'm not home." Terrified, Gómez came to get me in the scriptorium.

Early Thursday morning there was a robbery in the monastery of San Lucas; the thieves took a mule with its bit, a lame horse, two blind asses, five oxen with as many calves, eight hens, a goose, a she-goat and a lamb, a mantle and a table knife, a load of salt, barley, bread, and an indeterminate quantity of wine. Many of these animals and things later appeared in the monastery of San Juan el Teólogo among the graves, the cells and the clothes of minstrels and ladies.

I called Sancho Saborejo aside. "The church of God was made for praying, not for larceny." I reproached him. "It's a house of prayer, not a den of thieves."

Seeing how angry I was, he gave me an account of the orchards he had visited, all far from the monastery of San Lucas, during his labors yesterday.

"I can give you news of the orchards and vineyards along the wayside," he said. "*Ego,* Sancho Saborejo, went past the orchards belonging to Domingo Bazolin and Micael Pie Esquierdo, Johan Roca and Pedro Nariz, Pedro Ferrero and Pedro Pérez, and María Pelaez's sons. Following the path which leads to the principal valley, I passed Cibrian Calvo's son Joanin's vineyard. When it was almost dark I cut across the vineyard belonging to Durant Elegano and Fernán Pelegrino."

"Enough of orchards and vineyards. You'll drown in the well of hell's orchard," I interrupted. "Give me some news of the animals from the monastery of San Lucas which you and the concubines brought here."

"Master, Lord, I swear by our Glorious Mother that I have never set foot in the monastery of San Lucas, except once with Beila Beilaz, to glimpse from afar its holy abbot, Sabarico by name.''

"Then it was your sinning shadow that went up to the altar; you and it must return what was stolen right away," I told him. "The disciples of our Lord of the Last Days are not allowed to fornicate with nuns or to rob churches."

"I swear not to lapse again. I confess that a horn of twisted silver we were carrying off began to moo without anyone blowing into it. I confess that two psalters burned up in our arms in protest because we had removed them from the holy place where they belonged," he said, kneeling.

"This ill-gotten prosperity will help you to lose a hand, a foot or both eyes, and, at worst, to swing from the gibbet," I warned him.

Sancho left in haste, both he and I aware that the minute he saw any coins left lying around he would pocket them, because no one can say who owns money or where it comes from.

I headed for the kitchen. Jimena was sitting on a wooden bench in her furry shoes, her hands sheathed in rabbit-skin gloves. Onions, garlic and wheaten bread were on a table. A mouse had gotten into the provision box and eaten the cheese. Smoke twisted up from the fire to the roof. Near the fireplace stood tongs for stirring up the logs, trivets for casseroles and wooden pipkins, and the pothook on a chain. Doña Miguel had gone to the latrine near the stable. A donkey worth four solidi gazed in through the window facing the orchard.

"Isn't it time for supper?" Jimena asked.

"I'm not hungry; I want you to come with me," I said, taking her hand and giving it a squeeze.

She turned red.

"I must put away the soup pots, the plates and the spoons, and then I must make the beds," she said.

"The beds are made," I murmured. "They need warming."

She did not seem to understand what I wanted, so I ordered her to leave the kitchen with me. I meant to keep her by my side, far from the others, until sunup. As soon as she seized my meaning, she broke into a smile.

"Jimena," I said to her in the refectory, "tonight I want us to do what we're going to agree upon now. I'll leave open the door to the room where nobody lives, the isolated one with the small wooden window you sometimes look out of. You'll come to me once everyone is asleep. I'll give you whatever you want.''

"Will you give me a smock with a collar?''

"I'll give you a green smock and a gown from the Orient and an ermine cloak,'' I told her.

"And a girdle of scarlet wool, so you won't have to flog me with leather straps.''

"Maiden, tell me what you learned from the minstrels,'' I asked, thinking I heard Doña Miguel's steps in the corridor. But it was only Gómez, wandering like a lost soul from dormitory to church and from church to graveyard.

"Sir, I learned the names of the four winds and the seven planets and the commandments and the promises of God, and I learned the speech of birds and beasts. And I learned to sing and play the drum.''

"Maiden, what are the signs for telling if a woman is beautiful?'' I quizzed her.

"I learned from Oro María that a woman is beautiful if she is mistress of eighteen signs.''

"Tell me what they are.'' The steps died out in the corridor.

"She should be black of eyebrows, hair and eyes; long of body, neck and fingers; broad of hips, back and forehead; rosy of lips, cheeks and gums . . .''

"And what is a man's greatest pleasure?'' I asked, interrupting her.

"That of lying with a woman for two days.''

"And why two days?''

"The first to know her, and the second to repeat her.''

And so we walked and talked as far as the room, for I decided it was best to bring her with me once and for all, lest her mother, Oro María, or Sancho Saborejo appear and dissuade her from my purposes.

"Tell me, sir, where is the bed in which we are to sleep tonight?'' she asked.

"There.'' I pointed to the cold, thin mattress awaiting us. Then I fell silent.

She broke the silence. "I beg my lord that should you vanquish me in our questions and answers from now on, I will give you my clothes just as I am wearing them, and if I should chance to win, you will give me the clothes that you are wearing.''

"I grant you all that you have requested," I vowed, admiring the flash of her eyes in the half-light.

"Remove your clothes, for you have been vanquished with the help of God," she said boldly. "Is this the grasshopper which gambols among the hills?"

"It's the snake's tail," I blurted out.

"What a big pest it is," she replied. "Now lie down so I can perform the loving I promised."

"Take off your clothes," I ordered her.

And as the noise of the departing ladies faded away in the monastery, I took Jimena naked, just as she was, and I stroked her body from feet to breasts. My cold hands ranged over her and she shivered. Clad only in her hair, she let the moon turn her brighter. My legs were trembling.

"Jimena, my life, linger here until dawn, do not leave me for any reason, and I will give you whatever you please," I coaxed. "The man who will have you tonight was born at a lucky hour. I will light the fire of the torches to admire in your person the beauty of the world which has amassed in your body. Madam, I shall quicken your vitals."

"Your love will undo the bonds of my honest life, and from today onward I shall be a matron. I beg you not to forget this place, for you will be very satisfied with your friend."

"The abomination of plucking the stem of a virgin's flower makes me shudder," I whispered.

"By grace of the Holy Ghost, I will love you and I will beget your child."

"Your vulva and your womb will close again, as did María's after she conceived," I assured her.

"My lord, in my heart I believe what you say to me, for if you are not the light, you have come to be witness to that light," she said, her cheeks glowing.

"I am the light," I sobbed in the midst of her body.

I sobbed because I saw hovering above her flesh the funereal shadows that man will touch in days to come, the fish that will cry out from the leafless trees, the buildings that will kneel on their foundations, the quarrelsome rocks that will smash against each other as men have taught them to do, the hills that will flatten into valleys, the graves that will gape open with the bones of so many resurrected sons of God. I will hear the herald angel blow the trumpet of twilight, and I will watch all those who were born and engendered rise up at my side.

"I, Lord Christ," I told her, "will be at the center of the golden armies, and I will put the minted gold into the mouths of the covetous. I will fasten the foul harlot to the lewd monk's anus. Beneath the holm oak I will deny charity to the haughty who rob the wretched, I will ram the teeth of the violent into their guts, I will tie the demons down with candent chains and give them one thousand lashes with my astral eyes. They will look from where their eyes were into the hell taking shape within their bowels, and never, ever again will they lead us astray. Then I, King of Kings, leading the way and with righteous arm, will enter into the glory of the true Father."

VISION XV

"Antichrist will be born from the sin of a human couple. At the moment of conception, the devil will enter the belly of the whore to become flesh inside her. Like the Mother of Jesus, the mother of the Beast will require her own unholy spirit, her prophets and her messengers. The fruit of this abominable fornication will be called a son of perdition, a damned man, a man inhabited by Satan, an instrument of the devil. Necromancers and wizards, sorcerers and seers will educate him in the malefic arts, and noxious spirits will be his guides. On the day of his glory, he will sit on the divine throne in Jerusalem and pass for the son of God. The power of this spawn of evil will stretch from sea to sea and from east to west," Doña Urraca the Shadow said, showing me a Latin manuscript entitled *Adso Dervensis.*

"This historical darkness began when the Muslims cut off our trade routes and seized our lands. Separated from each other and forced to provide for their own needs, the Christians sank into poverty. According to Eulogius and Paulus Alvarus, Antichrist is Mahomet; according to Don Froilán, he is al-Mansur," I declared.

Doña Urraca looked at me and proceeded. "Antichrist will beguile the simpleminded with miracles and artful prodigies; he will strike at the wise and the righteous with terror, tribulations and corruption. Unscrupulous lecher that he is, he will debauch the sons and daughters of man as children, so that they will grow up flawed and perverted. He will resuscitate corpses while exterminating thousands of animals and plants. He will speak of saving the earth while he burns forests, fouls the air and poisons the waters. Armed with an ass's jawbone, invoking peace he will fill the world with the dead. Wherever he walks, rivers will die, trees will topple, youths and maidens will wither. He will convince with wiles, he will be dressed in radiant clothes, while the people perish from hunger and thirst beneath the sullied sky. Antichrist will promise light; he will affix false suns in the firmament. He will be exalted; he will possess women and sackfuls of gold. He will be king of greed and pride. The legion of his followers will wear the mark of his power on their brow. But the true Messiah will slay him with the sword from his mouth, which is the Word."

"There have already been Antichrists in the world: Antiochus, Nero, Domitian, al-Mansur. And others will be born," I said.

"Whoever leads a life parallel but contrary to Lord Christ's is an Antichrist. Whoever comes to uncreate the kingdom of nature created by God is an Antichrist. Thus says the apostle. And thus say I in the marketplace and outside the church of San Juan el Teólogo," she asserted.

Doña Urraca the Shadow was fair of face and small of body. Gracious and discreet, difficult to gladden, she was melancholy and mournful. Gifted with the spirit of prophecy, she divined what had taken place in the past, and what would occur after her death. Her mother, Gontruoda, and her father, Gonzalo Fernández, ushered her into the century in a nameless region near León, and nobody knew how old she really was. Sometimes her face shone with youthful sprightliness, sometimes it was lackluster and drawn.

They tell how when Cardinal Raymundo came from Rome laden with relics and the peasants crowded to seek his blessing, he noticed Urraca and requested that she be brought before him. He kissed her on the forehead, asking the clerics clustering round him who her parents were and what her name was.

"She was baptized with the name of Urraca Fernández," one replied.

"Is this child your daughter?" Raymundo asked Gontruoda and Gonzalo when they were led into his presence.

"Yes, my lord," they answered.

"Happy are the progenitors of such a holy creature, for on the day of her birth there was rejoicing in heaven. She will be worthy before the face of the Lord. I, who roam the earth in search of virgins, am certain that here I have discovered a most wondrous one," the cardinal exclaimed. And turning to Urraca, he said, "My daughter, promise me that you will keep your body intact and will consecrate it in holiness as a bride of Christ."

"Blessings upon you, Father, for this is what I most longed for in the world. I was only waiting for the Lord to deign to answer my prayers," she said.

"Have faith, my daughter, and the Lord will satisfy your soul's desires."

"I only hope, Father, that I will have the strength to endure the horror of virginity," she replied.

"Oh," he murmured to himself, "the mere thought of this immaculate maiden troubles my sleep. I can already see the skull beneath the skin of her face, I can already touch the bones beneath her flesh, and while I am standing before her living body, I am already kneeling before her bony relics."

Soon afterward, Cardinal Raymundo, feeling weary and disinclined to return to Rome, asked Queen Teresa to allow him to spend his last days in a church in León with his relics, and to give him leave to continue his search for virgins among the Lord's sheep. It was then that he encountered Urraca Fernández again.

"Daughter, do you recall what you told me the other day about your virginity?" he asked her.

"I remember, Father, that I promised to dedicate it to God and to you," she replied, her eyes downcast.

"Take this silver coin and bore a hole in it so that you can wear it around your neck all your life. That will remind you of your promise. The twelve spiritual virgins will be with you always. Their names are Innocence, Harmony, Patience, Faith, Simplicity, Charity, Chastity, Truth, Generosity, Abstinence, Discipline and Prudence. From now onward we will instruct you in the sacred writings.''

"Because all virile flesh has its origin in female bodies, physical copulation must become spiritual copulation, so that holiness may be born from this nuptial union,'' said the monk Andrés, who was not yet abbot.

"My God, confer on the corruptible Urraca the grace to one day receive your Son as her holy husband,'' Cardinal Raymundo exclaimed. "Give this wretched, ruined man that I am the strength and words to narrate the life and deeds of the virgin whom Urraca Fernández will become in the future.''

"May she be a living paragon of chastity for all the virgins of the realm. She, who was born of a woman of clay, whose distant mother is Mary, the Glorious Maiden, who conceived without help of man and was virgin during the birth, before the birth and after the birth,'' Andrés added. "She, a descendant of the sealed fountain, which as the blessed one says, is loftier than the heavens and deeper than the abyss, for it is the temple of the Lord and the terror of hell.''

"Let us put her fortitude to the test right now,'' Cardinal Raymundo suggested. "We'll lock her in a cell and send guards to her door who will use deceit and violence to assault her virginity the first chance they get. If she is not weak, Urraca Fernández will abhor the coupling of the flesh.''

"The enemies of chastity will endeavor to corrupt her, luxuriating in their desire like dogs in their own vomit, and they will seek to transform her into worms and dust through contact with their lust,'' Andrés the monk continued.

"The mere thought of it excites and disturbs me,'' Raymundo declared. "If a man deflowers a virgin consecrated to God and causes her to lose her honor, the seducer shall receive a penance for three years, and during the first year he shall be given only rations of bread and water.''

"The Canons of Saint Patrick stipulate that if a monk and a nun travel together, they should not spend the night in the same inn, nor go from town to town in the same carriage, nor chatter incessantly with each other,'' the future abbot of our monastery recollected.

"A virgin who has made a vow to God to remain chaste all her life, and afterward knows a man in the flesh, will be excommunicated until she desists from her adultery and fulfills her penance," the cardinal affirmed.

"And whoever is excommunicated may not enter the church, even on the eve of the days of the Passion," Andrés exclaimed.

"A virgin who believes that there are vampires in the world will be anathematized," the cardinal concluded with a sinister laugh.

Together they clapped Urraca Fernández into a cell and stationed brawny men at her door. Together they positioned themselves in the cloister to observe the tempters' movements.

"The devil is helping them; he has snuffed the flame of the candle and filled the cell with fog," Cardinal Raymundo murmured.

"Oh, Redemptrix, persevere, because she who perseveres until the end of her days will be saved!" the monk Andrés shouted at her through a hole in the wall.

"Chaste sister, the Mother of Lord Christ has sent me to put you to the test, open the door for me," one of the tempters called to her.

"Why are you so surprised at my love? I'm the apostle Peter, open up for me," the other cajoled.

"What's your name?" the first one asked.

"My name is Gloriosa," she replied.

"Your name is Harlot, you can't fool me," the second one sneered.

By the time it was almost Matins, when their expectation of sinning with Urraca Fernández had come to naught, the tempters began simultaneously to insult and extol her. They told her there was no whore or virgin in the realm more beautiful than she, that nowhere had they met a maiden or fornicator like herself.

Inexorable and resolute, the peasants' daughter barred the door. She made her face ugly, smeared her forehead, cheeks and mouth with mud, cut off her hair and set to praying. The Holy Spirit shone his rays around her head, and she fell to her knees, stunned by such splendor.

When the tempters saw that their own features were grimier than the virgin's muddy cheeks, they began abusing her with cruel and lewd insults. But singing wafted through the walls of the cell. The monk Andrés and Cardinal Raymundo distinctly heard the words: "My God, thou shalt sprinkle me with hyssop, and I shall be cleansed; thou shalt wash me, and I shall be whiter than snow.''

"Have you noticed something?" Cardinal Raymundo asked the monk Andrés.

"No, except that our virgin is in grave danger," the future abbot replied.

"She is burning for Lord Christ. After Matins she dressed in white. Oh, how I hate her virginity, and how many times have I conspired with myself to deflower her," the cardinal groaned.

Some say that as they spied on her through cracks in the door, the two clerics saw white rays shining from her mouth; that once they were convinced that her virtue was protected by the angels in heaven, they prostrated themselves before Urraca Fernández to beg forgiveness for having doubted her integrity.

"To be sure, this virgin is fair of face and of form, but she is even more lovely in modesty and chastity," Cardinal Raymundo avowed. "Her eyes are like gems sparkling with supernatural passion."

"Henceforth we may say that in her soul this virgin has put on the ring of faith, that she has drunk the wine of eternity from the chalice of time," the monk Andrés said.

"I humbled my body with fasting and prayer," Urraca Fernández revealed when the day dawned and the men fled from the light. "A dazzling flame descended onto an invisible altar and penetrated my brow."

"After His Ascension, the Savior of the world chose a few just men to show the faithful the road to eternal life. For the same reason, the deeds of dead saints must be written down, as a perpetual stimulus to the living, but as for me, there's nothing worthy of remembering, so it's all the same whether I live or die," the virgin-hunting cardinal confessed, and a few days later he did die, of old age.

Here the story goes that, on Friday, the twenty-ninth of May, of the year 980, the parents of Urraca Fernández forsook the light of this earth outside the city walls, victims of the burning disease. Urraca and her seven younger brothers and sisters were taken in by their aunt Austreberta, a widow of almost monastic habits who had lived in León for the past five years. The orphans lived happily there until, on Thursday, May 5, in the year 987,

Urraca's sisters and brothers were conveyed to the monastery of San Lucas to their uncle Leodebodo, an elderly man of some forty years, also a widower, who belonged to Abbot Sabarico.

This was when al-Mansur launched his campaign of pillaging and made ready to attack the city. King Vermudo II fled to Galicia, and a Christian rebel, Conancio by name, spread the news of his death. A number of Leonese, fearing the Saracens, took their wealth and their children and sought refuge in distant parts; others, like García Gómez, count of Saldaña, rebelled against the king and, allying themselves with al-Mansur, seized power and marched against the Christians. It was under these circumstances that Urraca Fernández persuaded the clerics and nuns, who were about to set out on horses and mules for Santiago, not to abandon the sheep of Lord Christ, leaving them at the mercy of the Saracens. Many went; a few paid heed. These faithful few began fasting and praying at her side in Santa María de Regla.

"Under the protection of our Lord, who has never forsaken his creatures, León will not be touched by the Muslims nor by the renegades who ride with them," she said encouragingly.

Goaded by the Enemy of the human race, who since the world began has opposed the good works of the righteous, a friar by the name of Cariveo and the aforementioned Conancio, concealing his treachery, declared that Urraca Fernández was a false prophetess, and that the best course of action for the Leonese would be to hide the treasures of their churches and monasteries in secret places in the city. These riches would be defended by Count García Gómez, who then ruled in León, and by themselves, with their weapons, which were the only relics that performed real miracles. Cariveo and Conancio argued that there was no safe place in the kingdom to hide from al-Mansur's siege. In addition, as Urraca Fernández was possessed by the evil spirit, they should rid themselves of her once and for all. The best way to do it would be to stone her or throw her into a bottomless pit they knew of, in a cavern near the river Torío.

At the instigation of the Ancient Seducer, they did not wait to hear testimonies to her innocence, they condemned her to death. Armed with swords and lances, they went looking for her in the church of Santa María de Regla. Cariveo, who had been a hermit and was maddened by the demon of noontide, urged Conancio and his cohorts to stone her then and there. But God, who protects those who place their hope in Him, made it come to pass that at that very moment the Saracens poured in on horseback and on foot through the gates of the city and spilled over the walls that protect it, wounding or killing with lance and sword every person who crossed their path.

As she knelt before an image of the Mother of God, Urraca Fernández saw rushing toward her, in pursuit of a beautiful nun named Froila, a half dozen ruthless, enraged Moors with bloody hands, howling and screeching "*Luyun, Luyun!*" ("León, León!"). At the sight of them, Urraca, tranquil between two tapers, began to pray: "*In nomine Sancte Trinitatis. Ego Urracha Dei gratia totius Spanie Regina vobis Sancte Maria . . .*"

The Saracens barred the doors to prevent the nuns inside from escaping. A number of Muslims who had surrounded the church began kicking and battering them to break them down. Others climbed with their weapons to the roof and jumped into the nave. A crossbowman, catching sight of the kneeling Froila, drew his bow to shoot her in the back, but as swift death flew toward the nun, Urraca Fernández caught the arrow in the air. Moreover, when the bowman made as if to attack Froila with his lance, Urraca Fernández covered her with her mantle, so the church would not be defiled by the sacrilege of such a crime.

When the nuns Sancha and Vita saw the armed men milling about on the roof, they mussed their hair and raked their faces with their nails to make themselves ugly. Sancha tolled the bells, whose sound the Muslims detested. Prostrating themselves before the altar, the women recited psalms and litanies, singing and praying, anguished and sobbing.

Once the doors had been forced, al-Mansur himself rode in on horseback as far as the altar, onto which one of the Saracens had flung a muddy, paint-smeared pig for him to stab, if he so wished. Al-Mansur on his white mare, sword in hand, first saw the pig, then the altar, then Sister Froila, whose flesh gleamed through her torn clothing.

The pig squealed, scenting death. Sister Froila, afraid that violence would be done her, swallowed her tears in silence, for she had already escaped from the monastery of San Lucas, where the infidels had fornicated with the nuns.

"I care not what my troops do with these whores," said Count García Gómez.

Urraca Ferández stood beside Sister Froila to protect her. Al-Mansur became aware of the saint's presence and swept his eyes over her. The count raised his sword to behead her. Al-Mansur, struck by Urraca's serenity, checked the count with a movement of his hand. Then, without a word, he spurred his mare and galloped out of the church. The count and the other Saracens followed him, dragging the pig by its hooves, exhilarated by their own fury.

Three Berbers, who had been crouching behind the altar, emerged with the ornaments of the church: silver goblets, vestments, weapons, caskets containing relics of saints, and a particle of wood from the Lord's cross. They had taken Abbot Sabarico's mules and horses. In their irreverence, they paraded up and down, clutching their sacred booty in their blood-stained hands. Other Berbers captured the nuns Sancha and Vita in the church.

Outside, dozens of eunuchs were chasing friars, townspeople and peasants, who called in vain on Saint James the Apostle for help. Some tried to get into churches and monasteries to escape death or captivity, but the doors were blocked or bolted. Other unfortunates were dragged through the streets in chains or carried off in carts, to be sold afterward as slaves. The deacon García Cabezón ran frenzied into the church, looking for Sister Froila.

I was passing by the monastery of Santa María y San Martín when I encountered al-Mansur. The Saracens had just sacked its treasures and set fire to the scriptorium. The library was in flames; the fervent words of so many wise men who had existed in the world were going up in smoke. My despair increased when I saw León's Bible threatened by the fire. Written for Abbot Maurus under the direction of the monk Vimara, the work had been executed by the scribe and painter Ioannes in the year 920. Nearby, the leaves of a *Commentary on the Apocalypse* by Beatus of Liébana were burning.

"And the woman was clothed round about with purple and scarlet, and gilt with gold, and precious stones and pearls, having a golden cup in her hand, full of the abomination and filthiness of her fornication."

Not only the letters were disappearing; the fiery ball enveloped the whore, crackling its way up her legs and garment until it reached the hand holding out the goblet to the fornicators. The eyes in her face became bluish globes. The other figures in the book writhed as if suffering. Now they turned blue, now red, so that for an instant the fire mimicked the forms of the Revelation and depicted the hosts of Antichrist, and then, captive in the flames, the avenging angels who will mete out judgment on the last day complained.

Raging unbridled, the fire now assailed the figure of Saint Luke, licking at his feet, which curved like hands. The Evangelist, staring out of the book both full face and in profile, seemed unaware of any threat, safe within the frame of circles in which the following inscription could still be read: "OLectorumLegis . . . pray for the scribe . . . Ioannes deacon executed it."

As the leaves burned, flames flared from the ashes, flames wreathed in smoke, which took the illuminated figures by surprise and devoured them. The blazing figures appeared to be moving, to be fending off with hands and feet the hot tongues that lapped at them from all sides. But to no avail, for the flames rose around them and died out only when the books ceased to exist.

The Saracens had seated a friar, who was both scribe and painter, in the center of the library amid the manuscripts. In their extreme cruelty, they had swathed him in heavy garments and fettered his limbs.

Although I was unable to save the monk and all the ancient tomes from the fire, there was one book I had to rescue, the Book of Revelation, because its sacred matter was akin to the century I was experiencing. Surrounded by Saracens, I quenched the flames with my bare hands and hid the book inside my clothing.

When he saw me, the chained friar hopped to the pyre, trying to deliver the León Bible from the flames. His body burning, he managed to push the book with his fingers against the crumbling walls. García Cabezón snatched it up and smothered the fire with his cloak.

Frightened by what he had done and what he saw, Cariveo let himself be caught; he had angered God by seeking to wrong Urraca, the holy virgin. Conancio joined a band of Berbers and rampaged in the city and the countryside. Later it was learned that he purchased miserable captives cheaply and redeemed them to their families for twice the price.

On his way back to Córdoba, al-Mansur set fire to churches and monasteries, captured abbesses and nuns, razed fields and peasants' huts. The traitorous count, García Gómez, remained behind to oppress the region, abetted by the Andalusian troops.

Once the danger was past, Vermudo II returned and punished Conancio, sending him to prison and confiscating his villa at Oncina and other property. In time, the abbots and anchorites, presbyters and nuns also returned to León.

VISION XVI

The Muslims departed after two days of looting, rape and criminality. León was left destroyed, burned and full of corpses, among them those of Aunt Austreberta and her young daughters Blanca and Elvira, holy virgins whose bodies surfaced with matted hair, torn clothes, and bare breasts. Urraca had once found solace and companionship with her cousins, who were mischievous and affectionate by nature.

"When they see these dead girls, all the virgins of Lord Christ will be saddened," she said to herself, mourning for the second mother she had lost.

The story has it that when the Moors went back to Córdoba, the Leonese buried their dead, tended their wounded, grieved for their captive relatives, held processions, celebrated masses and began to rebuild the ruins. Urraca Fernández set herself cruel fasts and continuous prayers; she remembered Job and accepted her misfortune as God-given. Exchanging her mourning garments for those of a bride of Jesus, she vowed to succor the destitute and starving, to comfort pilgrims and prisoners, and to delouse the heads of children orphaned during the Saracen expedition.

Though she wore secular clothing, Urraca resolved to lead the life of a religious; she spent the night hours reciting psalms and prayers. Always humble, during divine offices she knelt or sat at the rear of the church, next to the door, manifesting the insignificance of her person. In the house of her deceased aunt, she prepared a small cell with a tiny window to admit light. Her bed was of straw, her pillow of stone. She had a serving-woman with thick hair, who was named Balda and who came every morning and brought her barley bread and water, which she sipped, mixed with ashes, and distributed the leftovers among the neediest.

One day the woman failed to appear. Still a virgin, Balda was seduced by the devil, who was scheming to kill Urraca with hunger and thirst. Before departing, Balda had said to her mistress, "I can't live with a shadow who refuses to eat or drink the excellent fruits of this world. I'm going where they're more abundant." But she did not leave to gorge on the fruits of the earth; she left to wallow in lust, for the Enemy had deceived her.

After her departure, Urraca made no move to seek sustenance; she sat staring at the window, as if expecting revelation to enter through it, reminding herself that, according to Solomon, God does not permit the righteous to perish of hunger. But it was the demon who entered, with flaming hair and slobbering snout. Breathing into her face, he exclaimed, "I concede that the angels in heaven are protecting you, and they've threatened to chain me up for another thousand years if I make you suffer. And so, I'm going."

Enfeebled, prostrate on the ground, before sunup Urraca watched the Ancient Serpent depart, knowing he would be back soon. Contemplating her own misery, she mused, "He who provides for humble folk, for spiders and butterflies, will feed me, the Shadow, with light from heaven."

As she concluded her prayer, rain fell from above and covered the roofs and fortifications of León, filtering in through the walls of her cell so that she could drink.

Although she remained a recluse, her fame as a saint crossed the walls and spread through the streets. One Sunday, at the hour of Sext, a blind woman by the name of Monegunda came to her door to implore Urraca to help her. She had lost her sight and could only go about guided by her niece. But that afternoon, as she was climbing the stairs of Urraca's house, she had felt that she knew the way.

"The light of day forsook me, I live as though dead. I beseech you, Sister, lay your hands on my eyes," she pleaded.

"How do you know that I can cure you?" Urraca asked.

"The shadow of your body appeared to me in a dream, and I said to myself, 'This is the holy virgin who will be able to heal me.' "

"Who took the light away from your eyes and left you in darkness?" Urraca inquired.

"I don't know who did it. One morning I opened my eyes, and I couldn't see my hands. Don't leave me in the gloom, I beg of you."

"By the grace of our Glorious Mother, you shall receive the pristine light," Urraca said and made the sign of the cross, placed her hands moistened with saliva on the woman's forehead, and the blood receded from her pupils, the shadows dispersed, the world took shape again before her eyes. The first thing Monegunda saw was a resplendent face.

"Help me. Save me," implored a little girl with a fatal tumor on her neck who came to Urraca one Saturday afternoon.

"What an inopportune death," Urraca muttered and traced the sign of salvation over the tumor, which burst open of its own accord. Four jets of pus spurted out, and the sick girl miraculously grew sound.

After that, the widow Goda appeared in Urraca's cell with her daughter Rusticula, whose hands had become paralyzed three years earlier. They had heard about the virgin's virtues in Astorga and had come from there to prostrate themselves before her.

Urraca took Rusticula's fingers between her own, stroking them gently, and the clenched hands opened as if to seize the light.

"Why do you come to me? Aren't there greater saints than I on earth, who work miracles and intercede before God to succor the ailing faithful?" she used to ask those for whom she was a saint.

Among the women who flocked to her house was a matron named Dedimia, who revealed that in her belly was a nest of vipers that bit and scratched at her entrails so that she could not get a moment's rest day or night. She could take no water or bread because it so infuriated the reptiles that they flooded her whole body with venom. These snakes with pointy wings and sharp nails tormented her unceasingly.

At first, Urraca declared herself incapable of helping someone so seriously besieged by the armies of the Enemy, but after the poor woman insisted, she agreed to place her hand on Dedimia's abdomen to attenuate the atrocious pain. Urraca squeezed her eyelids shut and placed serpolet, an herb that creeps along the ground and fastens on whatever it touches, on the woman's belly. The herb coiled around the vipers, and with sharp pangs, Dedimia ran to the latrine to rid herself of the beasts.

One Monday, as the day was casting lengthy shadows at the feet of buildings and beings, they brought to her Fernanda, a little girl so consumed by the burning disease that her father had lit a candle as tall as she was next to her, to burn along with her.

The illness had already spread to one limb and was stalking another, when Urraca located the source of the invisible fire and applied the relics of saints, whose names she did not reveal, to the most ravaged parts of the girl. Before the candle went out, a light shone on her feet and the heat disappeared.

As Fernanda's father was taking his leave, he showed Urraca his swollen jawbone, complaining that a rotten tooth prevented him from eating and drinking, and the pain was so excruciating he couldn't sleep and would rather be caught in the jaws of death than endure his own mouth. Urraca asked him to close his eyes, to concentrate on our Glorious Mother and go home, and the tooth would stop hurting. Meanwhile, she placed a damp cloth on his gums to alleviate his agony.

On the feast day of Saint Timothy, a young girl named Dominica, who was possessed by a demon, came to her cell. She had escaped from the chamber where her parents, simple folk who believed her insane, had locked her up. Her body and clothes were infested with fleas. She implored Urraca to free her from the evil enemy whose fury was tormenting her, who never stopped thrashing inside her.

At the sign of the cross and the sound of certain prayers, which Urraca uttered in Latin, blasphemous words poured from the possessed girl's mouth and the greasy body of a black demon in the shape of an Ethiopian dwarf shot out.

At the end of May, Urraca received her most unexpected visitor, Gómez, the minstrels' son. He stood the whole afternoon before her door, not daring to knock or go in. When she finally noticed him, she admitted him at once. He pointed to his palate and awaited the miracle.

"For your tongue to lose the impediment which binds your words, you must wait for your heart to invoke the name of God; that is, until speech wells up from your soul," Urraca explained to him. "The Lord, who opened the mouths of mutes and loosed the tongues of children, will make you eloquent."

As Gómez did not understand, she added, "The devil makes men mute; once he abandons you, you will speak."

Gómez ran off.

"Those are the seven churches of the Apocalypse: Ephesus, Smyrna, Pergamum, Thyatira, Sardis, Philadelphia and Laodicea," Urraca said to me, pointing at a painting on the ceiling of the seven houses of worship, seven façades with horseshoe arches above the doors as in the monasteries of San Lucas, San Juan el Teólogo and San Miguel de Escalada:

"Our Lord, Son of God, allow man, standing on the ashes of his feet, to survive the death of the millennium and of himself," I prayed.

"And guided by your Hand, may he find the grace to enter the millenary kingdom which You have prepared on earth for the righteous ever since the beginning of the world," I heard Urraca say as she knelt before the altar.

VISION XVII

Toward Matins, Urraca the Shadow returned to the dormitory. I thought she had left the monastery after we spoke, but she had only pretended to leave, hidden in the refectory, and reappeared. In the candlelight I saw her stretch and shrink on the wall. At first, when she opened the door, I mistook her for Jimena. "Now that her mother's asleep, she's coming to visit me," I thought.

"Is that you, Urraca?" I asked. "It never occurred to me that since you have a body, you could enter my dormitory as a shadow."

"The shadow is a shape, just like a body," she replied.

"How did you get in? The monastery gates are locked."

"I came in through the cemetery that surrounds the church. I crawled over the graves to reach you."

"The saints who are buried there should have blocked your way. They defend the monks' chastity."

159

"They didn't notice anything, they sleep the sleep of the dead."

"Doña Miguel, the minstrels, didn't they hear you?"

"No."

"If I put out the light you'll be effaced," I warned her.

"When it's pitch black, I turn into a body."

"Why did you come?"

"I am returning to you. I am your soul."

"Do you also speak for me?"

"I've spent so much time on the ground that out of necessity I've learned the words of the living."

"Are you flat and empty?"

"The shadow fills the body it belongs to," she retorted.

"During the day, when you live in your cell, do you also keep silent?"

"The shadow fills the silence."

She embraced me. She wanted to dance, but I freed myself from her arms, recoiling from her body, which was made of live embers. She clasped me again, kissing me with lips as black as coal.

"Who are you?" I asked.

"I am your death," she declared.

At that moment I awoke, not in the dormitory but among the relics of the saints in the crypt of the church. Then I discovered that the lamps and candles had been extinguished. I went up to the cloister. Through a grate-less window, Gómez was spying on my movements. The expression on his sallow face revealed that he knew more about me than I about him, and that he had been following me all night.

I shooed him away with threatening gestures and scowls. His face twisted into a frown, and his eyes flashed with hatred. Once I felt sure he had gone, I went to find Jimena.

She was not in the cubicle adjoining the kitchen where she usually slept, nor was she in the neighboring rooms. I finally found her near the orchard in the latrines, enveloped in her smell. She had left the latrine door open out of fear of the darkness, even though there was a full moon. She had brought no candle or other light. Silent and still, she gazed toward the corridor leading to the cloister.

Tiptoeing down the corridor, hugging the wall to avoid being seen, I reached her where she sat watching me as I advanced. Her legs gleamed in the moonlight like silver fish; her buttocks were creamy white. Her eyes flickered in the shadows, and her black hair covered her back and breasts.

"What is your pleasure?" she asked me. "Has the time come for fattening the pig? Is it October already?"

"Madam, it is as you wish," I answered.

"As you like," she assented, neither turning away nor covering the naked parts of her body.

"You are a young, beautiful woman in your prime." I stroked her cheeks with my hands, which slid down to her breasts, and I bared them to the air like two loaves of bread.

"Say something," she said.

"It pleases me to remain like this."

"Don't tell anyone that you lie with me."

"I won't; not telling is the greatest wisdom in the world."

"When we think we are alone, there are always ghosts spying on us from amid the shadows."

"What a tender, ghostly girl." I looked into her eyes. "The moon becomes you."

"I'm afraid," she whispered, taking my hand.

"What's making you tremble? Did you look death in the eye? Did you see something tonight that frightened you?"

"I fear my mother, especially between Matins and Compline. That is, all day long. I wish she lived far away from here."

"Do her features scare you more than the lightning and thunder did on this rainy night?"

"Even more than the bolts." She nodded.

"If she shows up, I'll send her to San Lucas with a bushel of fleas of all colors and sizes for Abbot Sabarico. Or I'll give her some money."

"She'll want the fleas."

"When I tell her about it, she'll only want the money."

"Hurry, come closer," she said. "I'm cold."

"Don't get dressed yet," I begged.

"Warm me with your desire." She clung to me.

"Lie down on the ground on that white cloth." I gave her a little push, patting the cloth into a pillow for her.

"Wait a bit, let's take all our clothes off and look at our bodies. Let's not act like thieves who run away before they've stolen anything."

"What do you have here?" I touched her.

"Nothing but death," she replied.

"Even here?" I asked.

"Even there, and farther inside."

"And what else do you have?"

"Honey."

"Give it to me."

"Remember how the bees once asked the beetles to dinner, and they got stuck in the hive."

"Jimena," I said, "we construct our life and our work for death alone. We're like the spider who spins her web to trap a fly, and when she's got it caught in her threads and is about to eat it, at the last moment a wind comes and sweeps everything away."

"It's dark, and you're raving."

"You have made me see the light at this hour." I began to kiss her.

Jimena lifted her legs toward the sky. I slid beneath her and she sat on top of me. When I penetrated her, she farted.

"What was that?" I asked.

"The lord of the winds coming out to welcome the gentleman." She grinned.

"Keep him inside," I suggested.

Moving, she farted once more. "The lord came out again. Speak to him."

"If we stab him, he'll be quiet," I said.

"Who will be the murderer?" she asked.

"I will."

"I think the wild beasts already ate him," she murmured.

"I'll kill him."

"Who are you?"

"You'll know soon enough."

"I already know you."

"Turn your back to me, and your delight will come faster."

"You say true, so I shall."

She crouched on all fours and I closed with her silvery buttocks and made love to her at a canter.

"It pleases me," she said. "Now, give me one of your eyes and I'll give you one of mine. If they're alike, no one can ever tell which is yours and which is mine. That's how we'll know we love each other."

"How strange you are." I pushed away her fingers, which were feeling for my eyes.

"What if I were a devil who had turned into a woman?" she asked.

"I would love you."

"What if I should grow a man's member?"

"I would turn into a woman such as you are."

"Four months with child? Or maiden and virgin as I was?"

"As much as I might want to, I couldn't return to your previous condition."

"You would have to be born again to be pregnant like me."

"Who got you with child?"

"A man who is pressing against me."

"Me? Or he?"

"Who is he?"

"The Lord of the Last Days."

"Is he here now?"

"He is, but you can't see him, because it is not yet time for him to show himself to the world."

"Do you know him?"

"He is the father of the child of God, the father of your child."

"I don't understand this."

"One day you will, and you will be glad you bedded with me." But she still didn't understand.

"What are you saying?"

"I'll explain it to you later. I can only tell you now that the fountains and rivers that flow into the sea will come to you, all the birds on the branches will come to your body. You will be a tree of life."

"Your desire has shriveled."

"You want more?"

"More."

"Nestle closer, then."

"Who can that be?" Jimena froze.

"What?"

"I hear footsteps approaching."

"I'll go out to meet them."

"If it's my mother, what will become of me?"

"Hide in that corner, I'll take care of her."

Someone knocked at the door.

"Who's there?" asked Doña Miguel.

"I am," I answered.

"Come out here," she ordered.

I went out and stood in the doorway frowning, my sword in hand.

"You're leaving just in time," she declared, as if it were she who was staying.

"Your mother left quickly," I said to Jimena.

"How was that?" she asked.

"She won't come back unless I call her," I said.

"I hope she's not spying on us from the bell tower."

"Do you want to fornicate?" I asked her.

"Do you know how to play the Game of Not-Knowing?" she asked, ignoring my question.

"How does it go?"

"Lie on your back, don't look, and deliver."

"I deliver," I murmured.

"I command you to drink from my breasts without stopping."

"I will drink the thread of nocturnal light from your two moons," I stammered.

I held her tightly. I made love to her another time, in the manner ordained by Saint Jerome, with serene passion. I sank into her flesh with hot desire, as the saint does not ordain, until I felt old and tired. "There's nothing worse," he says, "than loving your lover as if she were your wife." "There's nothing better," I reflected, "than loving your concubine as if she were your wife." For each position I tried out on her body, I would have to do penance, to fast seven years on bread and water, to pray the Paternoster a hundred times over, and to give alms to the needy, the sick and the pilgrims. First, for looking upon her nakedness; second, for mounting her in the traditional way; third, for having her *in retro* with extraordinary voluptuousness; fourth, for preventing her from conceiving during coition; fifth, for enjoying her wanton embraces, embraces that are reprehensible even with a strumpet, not to mention when they are practiced in the sacred confines of the marriage bed. And, sixth, for seeking pleasure in a religious precinct, for doing so during her pregnancy, and for having preceded the act with prolonged kissing and lewd caresses.

"Who are you?" she asked me in the early morning.

I contemplated her white belly, her firm, erect breasts, her sprawled legs newly awaiting love; I imagined my child in her womb, looking at me with big eyes. Then, naked as I was, I answered, "I am the psalm lips utter, I am the tongue created by the Word to utter the psalms, I am the silence that follows the psalms."

Once desire was drained, I went to the cloister to wash my hands and face in the fountain. No sooner did I get there than I encountered Gómez, smirking and sinister; he had been in the orchard the whole time, staring at the latrines.

VISION XVIII

Isidoro, the Messiah of the Poor, reappeared. Transformed into the prophet of Antichrist, he came to León to announce the coming of the Black Rider and the millenary kingdom of al-Mansur and the Saracens.

"The son of perdition outlived his enemies and is seated in the temple of God in Jerusalem," he proclaimed in the marketplace. "He is not a man of flesh, he is not a man of air, he is body and spirit, and he descends from the tribe of Dan. He is indestructible, and death has no dominion over him."

Shortly before his return, a rabid black dog had attacked a cleric outside the monastery of San Lucas. The cleric, who was strolling among the poplars, was bitten on his hands and legs by the furious canine, which suddenly materialized out of nowhere. The bitten cleric loped away, barking like a madman.

From his appearance outside the monastery of San Juan el Teólogo at the end of April until today, the beginning of September, Isidoro had roamed the lands of Christianity with his hosts of believers preaching the advent of the era of evil. In the forests and among the crags, his disciples had formed communities of the Church of the End of Time, where he was worshiped as a messianic king.

Midway through July, he revealed in Sahagún that he had contracted matrimony with a nun called Aneladgam. In celebration of their wedding night, his followers placed loaves and fishes, inky flowers and jet black necklaces on their table and in their bed.

Isidoro the First, as he now styled himself, no longer made any distinction between Isidore of Seville and his own person. When he referred to the Isidore of old, he claimed that he had preceded himself in the world, that he was the lord of lords and god of gods, and he promised to judge the living and the dead and to scourge the century with fire. Sumptuously attired messengers, bearing banners and crucifixes aloft and crying hosannas, heralded his entrance into a city.

"I have come to free you from the shackles of your beliefs. You are worshiping false prophets, paltry saints and names that never were people," he railed at the rustics who thronged to receive him at the Bishop's Gate.

His black-clad companions brought to León mules laden with caskets containing relics of Saint Martin, whose body was missing only one hand; of Saint Fructuosus, whose corpse was itself the relic, plus one leftover bone that didn't fit anywhere; the head of Saint Victor; a foot of Saint Benedict; a tooth of Saint Faith; a finger of the bishop of Braga. In addition, they displayed tiny bones from Saints Susan, Cucuphas, Torcuato, Engracia, Eulalia, and Basilio, the martyr and bishop who was resuscitated by Saint James the Apostle six hundred years after his death. Socram brandished the ears of Audito, the patron saint of hearing, promising that those who inserted their fingers into the holes and afterward into their own ears would obtain relief from their complaints.

Nauj exhibited the cords that had bound Lord Christ to the column of flagellation; his milk teeth, which his mother, the Glorious Virgin Mary, had zealously guarded; the sponge with which his mouth was refreshed on the cross; and even several bits of his body. These particular relics, culled and purloined from churches and monasteries, were kept in an ark wrapped in black cloth. But the most miraculous relics were the fingernail cuttings and hairs of Isidoro himself.

"Behold, this receptacle for holy relics is shaped like a human figure, to keep in miniature the very body of Saint Eulogius," said the so-called Sacul, who had awakened one day to see the light, after falling asleep in a field, and a swarm of flies penetrated his body between his buttocks and exited from his mouth, forming words. The flies ordered him to become a disciple of the messiah Isidoro and go out into the world to preach the Third Testament. He repudiated his wife and went into a church built on a rock where, in the sight of the faithful, he produced a wooden chalice, drank the wine, and with chalice in hand assured the Christians watching him that if they followed his teachings they would be like monks, and if they dedicated themselves to licentiousness they would become virtual angels of Antichrist. When they heard this, the faithful decided he was a blasphemer, dragged him outside and beat him.

"Here are the relics of Saints Maximus, Venerandus and Bertulfus, stolen by Electus, from whom we ourselves stole them. These are the heads of Saint Vincent, Saint Fausta, Saint Epiphanius and Saint Speciosa, which were stolen by thieving clerics, from whom we ourselves stole them," Nauj boasted.

"Maximus conveyed to Ravenna the relics of Saint John the Baptist, Saint Andrew and Saint Thomas; the body of Mary Magdalene was translated from Palestine to Vézelay. We have brought all these saints, male and female, to León," Socram declared.

"I wanted to steal the eleven thousand virgins of Cologne, so that, like the Saracens, each follower of our lord Isidoro could have a virgin of his own, but their virtue was so ponderous that we would have needed an army of eleven thousand demons to carry them," Nauj explained.

"This is the Third Testament," Isidoro thundered. "The Day of Wrath has arrived. It is not Lord Christ who will come to judge the quick and the dead, but the devil. The sun and the moon will grow dark, heaven and earth will cleave together, the faithless and the unrighteous will live forever. The good will perish in disgrace."

"The Black Rider will reign as judge and lord among his elect. The spiritual capital of the orb will not be Zion but Calatañazor, where, in a fantastical battle, Almanzor will lose his tambor," Nauj foretold.

"Since its beginning, the world has been dominated by the wicked. Until its end, the world will be dominated by the wicked. The common people love cruel men and enjoy being afraid!" Isidoro shouted.

"One day, the poor will be miserly rich. One day, the light of the sun and the moon will be seven times less. One day, the orchards of paradise will become deserts, and there will be droughts and a dearth of wheat, fish, wine and fruit. It is about that day that Isidoro has come to address you," Socram announced.

"He, Isidoro, will prepare the way for the Tyrant of the Last Days, descendant of Antiochus, the horned king," Sacul affirmed near the castle. "He, Isidoro, will raise up the throne of death over all life."

"He, Isidoro, has seen the omens of the second coming of Antichrist in the appearance of a comet in the sky; he has read the signs of the times: evil rulers, civil discord, wars and famines, plagues and assassinations. When the moment comes he, Isidoro, will display the omens on his own flesh, a black cross over his shoulder blades," Socram proclaimed.

A monk turned thief and murderer, Socram had previously lived as a wild man in a hut in the forest. Lying in ambush among the trees, he had devoted himself to robbing merchants and despoiling pilgrims, informing them that he did so for Saint Isidoro, whose life he was writing. "Anyone who robs and despoils pilgrims and virgins, or any person of whatever estate who is on their way to a holy place to pray, is worthy of heaven," he explained to them, while he stripped them bare. Following the Saracens' example, he waylaid villeins, servants, matrons, friars and every other defenseless creature who happened his way, and demanded ransom for them. Some of the men and women who went into his dwelling never came out whole again. He slit their throats, mutilated them, profaned them and ate them in a grisly banquet, afterward hanging the heads and genitals from the ceiling for his own amusement. One Sunday in August he found himself in prison, after attempting to rob an armed bishop who was journeying to Rome with mules laden with gold and silver ornaments. He was arrested by a nobleman disguised as a bishop, but before long he escaped and joined the Messiah of the Poor.

"The messengers of darkness are already here. The future is present in the person of Isidoro," said Nauj, standing in front of the monastery of San Lucas.

"He, Isidoro, will separate the black sheep from the white, and he will be enthroned in the midst of the earth. He, Isidoro, the son of Lucifer," Sacul exclaimed.

"The gates of the North have sprung open, and Alexander's troops have escaped. The people from the North have come to eat the flesh and drink the blood of children who were born dead and who were born alive; they have come to swallow snakes and scorpions and the carrion of animals," asserted Noel, a disreputable *miles,* or soldier, who during the past months had led a gang of thieves dressed as monks, not only robbing merchants, bishops, knights and other wealthy travelers carrying objects of gold and silver, but also stealing peasants' oxen, mules and swine.

"This week the son of perdition will appear in Ioppen and will pass judgment on the living and on the dead," Isidoro predicted, thrusting his hands vehemently skyward.

"Where is Ioppen?" a matron wondered.

"Ioppen is in Ioppen, and you don't want to know more than that, because knowledge is sinful and defiant," Isidoro snapped.

Airam, who served as wife and mother, was by his side, and behind her stood Airam Aneladgam in gold bracelets and jewels, for Isidoro, following the Muslim custom, possessed several wives and had a favorite.

Shortly before Vespers, Isidoro preached at Fronilde's plot of land and then before the church of Santa María de Regla. Surrounded by Noel and Socram and a crowd of the poor, the sick, and the vagabond, he ranted against the venal and libertine clergy, against well-meaning rustics, chaste women with sinful souls, honorable skinflints, scrawny gluttons and humble braggarts, and he cursed hermits and wandering saints who led a life of poverty and privation.

"Survivors of the famines, which scourged the land during the year 1000, my followers have dragged their hunger hither and thither without finding a church capable of succoring them, for all have exhausted their treasuries," Isidoro declared.

"The living dead you see before you were abandoned half-naked in the fields, like carrion for man and beast, or jettisoned by the wayside, which was used as a cemetery," Noel added.

"The chaos of the times entered clerics' bodies and damaged their souls!'' Sacul cried. ''Pay no tithes to those demons.''

''Greed has taken hold of the servants of God. The church has caught charity's cold,'' Noel protested.

''Isidoro, the feeder of souls, gives the wretched and the needy, who were gobbling putrified flesh in the fields, fish and loaves, meat and fruits to eat,'' Socram announced.

''But they are invisible,'' a starving man complained.

''They are made of air and faith,'' Isidoro assured him. ''After ingesting them, you will fly.''

''Immaterial souls nourish themselves on immaterial food, pigs gorge on pigs,'' Socram added.

''When our stomachs are full of air, we will shit wind.''

Isidoro set a gilded coffer before the people, taking from it fine cloths and golden goblets, and he showed them the images painted on the cloths and the fantastic figures on the goblets.

''Take as much air from the sky as you want,'' he said to Sancho Saborejo, who had come to hear him. ''However much fits into your hand is yours.''

The peasant Spernicius grabbed a gold staff, vestments threaded with gold and a sack that clinked as if it were full of gold coins, and hurried out of the atrium. Imagine the poor man's astonishment when he reached the Count's Gate and found himself empty-handed, for it had all vanished.

The sick of León were similarly disenchanted after Isidoro cured them of blindness, lameness and deafness, for no sooner did they stray from where the miracles had occurred than they went back to being blind, lame and deaf.

Nevertheless, at the hour of Compline, the Messiah of the Poor stood on the roof of the monastery of San Lucas, and, prostrating himself before the altar of heaven, gave his blessing to the crowd. Flourishing a black cross, he married prostitutes to their chance lovers and persuaded fine ladies and peasant women to throw their clothing and adornments onto a bonfire, to cut off their hair, and to draw blood from their thighs and breasts. Gómez was there among the faithful.

Standing next to the gallows, from which four kidnappers and thieves were dangling, Spernicius signaled to Isidoro that the sacks were empty.

The men hung close together, rings around their necks, eyes bandaged and hands bound. Save for a piece of cloth covering their private parts, they were naked.

"God has chosen you!" a nun shouted at Isidoro. "Your soul is more precious than gold and silver."

"It is just to torment the destitute, to edify from evil deeds a perverse heaven to replace this heaven, and to establish a wrathful earth on this green earth," Nauj burst in.

"See how I make newborn creatures old and turn the light into night. I possess diabolical healing powers, my presence alone causes plants to wither and ashes to rain down on the fields. My ephemeral kingdom of imperfect harmony and depraved pleasures will be founded on this permanent and tedious kingdom. You who follow me will be the sinners of the Second Millennium; in the black light, your rotting clothes will seem to be made of the finest white linen," Isidoro preached.

Roused by his ranting, a number of his faithful piled into the squares, spilled out onto the streets, or took to the roads, looking for someone to assault, rape and kill. Others, armed with leaden maces, sharpened sticks, knives, axes, mattocks, slings, swords and lances, turned into thieves and murderers; they eventually died of the cold, or of body wounds, or were executed by Moors or Christians. Before attacking, they gnashed their teeth, snarled like wild animals, screeched like birds, all to inspire fear. A wrathful Socram, scythe over his shoulder, rode at their head on a skinny nag.

"The most villainous will be saved in the judgment of evil," Isidoro promised them in the marketplace. "Where are the godless who want to lose their souls? Come with me. Better be damned for committing horrendous sins which gave you pleasure, than to be damned for merely premeditating them. Serve gold as you would an idol, venerate it in place of the Lord."

When someone asked if taking up arms against King Alfonso and our forces, which were readying themselves for the defense of León, did not violate God's decrees, the false messiah answered, "The Prophet said, 'Weapons are part of Allah's decrees.' The Saracens say, 'The sword is the shadow of death, the lance is the rope of Destiny.'

"On the day of the battle of the end, the Black Rider will bear God's greeting, and the saints who stand in his way will topple over like so many clay statues. The Black Rider will conjure up misleading portents and foolish prodigies to deceive the Christian hosts. He will make base blind men see, thieving deaf hear, cutthroat cripples walk, and cure the possessed of saintliness. I tell you truly, brother men, that I am immortal."

Not far from there, Bishop Froilán was thinking just the opposite, and he asked García Cabezón, the bailiff Diego Bamba and two other men to try to arrest Isidoro. The capture took place on Sunday. Isidoro was celebrating mass in Santa María de Regla, the church desecrated and laid waste by al-Mansur in 988, when the four men arrived. His back to the altar, Isidoro was preaching amid the ruins. "This is no good," he said, flinging a crucifix to the floor and trampling it.

Stalwart and circumspect, García Cabezón threaded his way through the multitude of prostrate faithful. Pretending to be a disciple, he knelt as if to worship, clasped Isidoro around the knees and threw him to the ground.

"You whose relic lies in blessed soil, come to my aid on Judgment Day," García Cabezón mumbled as Isidoro fell.

"What's the fuss, if that thing I threw on the floor has no importance whatsoever or any supernatural powers?" Isidoro replied, hitting his assailant on the head with a chalice he was holding.

"So, blasphemer, you have dared to denigrate my body," said the bailiff Diego Bamba in the name of the crucifix, and punched him.

"Why bother with a dead Christ on the cross when I am here and alive?" Isidoro squealed.

At that, the two other men stepped in to overpower him and tie him up. Together they conducted him to prison, prodding his body with daggers and holy crosses. Isidoro squirmed away from the magical stings.

The bishop had him jailed in a tower near the city gates, accusing him of harboring the spirit of the devil, of blaspheming against heaven, and of swindling the populace with promises, impostures and spurious miracles. He also charged him with pillaging the churches and monasteries of León. Two clerics from the monastery of San Lucas reminded the bishop that Isidoro's madness had reached such a pitch that he believed himself to be God and God's envoy. Moreover, he had accomplished his misdeeds with the connivance of the devil, who had enabled him to appear in several spots at once.

Abbot Sabarico said, "In one day Isidoro walked as far as an ordinary man could walk in one month. Abetted by the fiend, he appeared in three places at the same time: the church, the market and the monastery of San Lucas, to attack the bishop and the Church. He vanished as if by magic from all three places simultaneously.

"Each time the king's troops were about to capture him, Isidoro escaped and was nowhere to be found for months. Mortals were helpless against the Evil One's superior powers until today," Sampiro, the royal priest and notary, remarked.

"Who are you?" Froilán asked the prisoner.

"Isidoro the First, the god who will come to judge the quick and the dead and to punish the world with fire," the messiah answered, brandishing a black staff in the shape of a serpent.

"What does the staff in your hand signify?" Sampiro asked.

"It stands for the holy trinity of evil. I am holding up the firmament on the tip of the staff," he answered.

Froilán, Sampiro, García Cabezón and the others present laughed at his lunacy, but fearing that his disciples or the Black Rider's hosts might free him, they took care that he was well guarded.

Diego Bamba waited anxiously for Don Froilán's order to execute Isidoro. The bishop had promised that the messiah and his disciples would have their throats slit before the feast of the Nativity. To our surprise, nothing happened in the days or nights that followed. Neither the Black Rider nor the devil came to his rescue.

"My supreme judge, the author of all evil, knows that I will be faithless," Isidoro said to the bailiff as the latter was positioning him against the wall, prior to torturing him.

Vengefully Diego Bamba tore his flesh with red-hot pincers, and the incarnation of the spirit of evil howled in pain. "Earth, gape open and swallow up my enemies!" he cried out, his face flushed with terror.

Even when he was nearly dead he still believed that he was invulnerable to death.

VISION XIX

On the first Thursday of November, when the peasants slaughter pigs, Sancho Saborejo came to the scriptorium after Compline to tell me that, happening to be with Beila Beilaz somewhere in the monastery, he had noticed that someone had left a dead body in the crypt of the church of San Juan el Teólogo.

"The body is Almarada's, the Black Rider's consort. In León they're saying that she died in childbirth Monday night in the Saracen camp," the minstrel volunteered.

"If it is she, she has no business being in the crypt with Saints Columba, Cecilia and Marina," I said.

Sancho and I hurried to the funerary chamber, descended the stone steps hugging the outer wall of the church and found ourselves before a narrow door, which led to the subterranean room.

Above, the church was girded by the cemetery, below, crisscrossed by a catacomb. An opening in the apse gave access to the nave to the faithful who assembled in the basement on saints' feast days to worship their relics. A semicircular corridor crowded with humble tombs led to the cubiculum of the three martyrs. Uncorruptible, they held out to the congregation the hope of resurrection of the flesh.

A line of urns disappearing into the icy darkness of a cave could be glimpsed through a small window in the wall of the funerary chamber. They contained the mortal remains of clerics who had gone to the other world while illuminating the Book of Revelation. I could not keep my heart from shrinking when I found myself in my future resting place, picturing myself buried in an anonymous stone box.

Candle in hand, Sancho and I stumbled over the sarcophagus of a nameless righteous person, whose skeletal body could be contemplated at will through a hole in the wall of the apse. We went deeper into the crypt, as if descending into ourselves. The corridor sank seven steps beneath the church's floor. A blurred inscription commemorated an abbot of the monastery who was interred there.

As we crossed this uneven basement, we wondered how someone had been able to carry a corpse as far as the oratorium without anyone in the monastery taking notice. "The dead woman was transported here by demons," the minstrel declared.

"She was brought here by Abd Allah, the Black Rider," I replied.

"Who was Almarada?" Sancho asked.

"Abd Allah's concubine," I told him. "Daughter of a Baghdadi slave in al-Hakam II's harem, from adolescence she devoted herself to conjuring spirits. Her specialty was not giving sons to her polygamous husband and conversing with the half brothers and dead offspring of the Commander of the Faithful. 'My father never touched me,' she would avow when anyone insinuated that the Caliph had deflowered her."

"Those who had glimpsed her in León say that she was wanly beautiful, but they had to avert their faces when looking at her, for fear of losing themselves in her flashing eyes," Sancho said.

"She always dressed in black, and in recent years death rose to her face; she turned cadaverous, not from tribulation or sickness, but because she used her face intentionally to unnerve my brother and frighten everyone who met her. In her presence no one could say with certainty whether she was alive or dead," I recollected.

A sound of murmuring came from the oratory where Almarada was stretched out. Sancho blanched and looked at me mutely.

I continued to think about Almarada, who was born in Córdoba and had lost her father at the age of three. ("And I couldn't devour his death with my eyes," she had once remarked to me.)

"At the age of thirteen, she was sent by her mother to Toledo to study necromancy with clerics who skinned cats and sliced up pigeons, read the future in the thumbnail of a virgin boy or on the shiny blade of a sword, and conversed with the departed," I went on to say. "It was she who appeared to the disciples of the black arts, dancing lasciviously when the *magnus nigromanticus,* or supreme necromancer, of Toledo invoked evil spirits. She was the funereal goddess of the night, tempting the apprentice sorcerers, who were forbidden to cross the circle traced on the ground. Their eyes fastened to her body, immersed in lecherous fantasies, they were dragged to hell in pursuit of her flesh."

"What else does the story say?" Sancho asked.

"Returning to the city of the caliphs when she was about seventeen, she became a prostitute, not for money but of her own will and wantonness. She coupled with many men and engaged in perversion for the sheer pleasure of it. One orgiastic night she found herself with Abd Allah in al-Mansur's palace, and she became his lover. 'Darkness has descended on your life,' her mother said when she learned her daughter was living in the Black Rider's harem. 'It descended when I met Master Melchita in Toledo,' she retorted."

"Did the Black Rider ruin her forever?" the minstrel asked.

"Almarada's spiritual possession—her body had been possessed a long time ago—took place one midnight in Córdoba, in a Christian church desecrated by the Moors, exactly six months after she took up with Abd Allah, who was then in the Christian North with al-Mansur. Afterward she was seen wandering in cemeteries at night, muttering the name of Ahriman, and she became enamored of fire, so that dawn would find her staring into the flames of bonfires she herself had lit. She confided to her friends that as she lay naked or beneath a gauzy cloth, Ahriman, tall and muscular, with snakes writhing at his waist, visited her in dreams and made love to her, though she derived no pleasure from it.

" 'Fear not, doubt not,' her spectral grandmother soothed her when she awoke. 'Walk on burning coals and I will give you the tresses of immortality.' 'I'll burn myself, no?' she asked her. 'The fire will gradually come to know you; at first you will feel the heat, but afterward you will feel no pain.'

"One day Almarada conceived, not in her own womb but in the belly of a Cordoban Moorish woman. Abd Allah was shown the child, and he asked her who the father was. 'I know——not,' she answered. At six weeks the creature died.

"The ballads say that Almarada began to eat nothing, to drink nothing, to bathe not at all, and to grow thin, although she was strong and endowed with an amazing vitality. 'I've been playing with Ahriman,' she admitted.

"Moreover, as she was no longer her own mistress, she began going into Christian churches in Córdoba and smashing their religious images. Furthermore, she dared not look Abd Allah in the face for six months. Aware of what was happening to her, he did not protest.

"In the presence of her harem-mates her body was unexpectedly seized by a tremor, which surged from her feet to her hips. Almarada explained that it was not she who had trembled, but the demon stirring within her entrails. She would suddenly break into a dance from the waist down, tingling with pleasure and eager to reveal her visions to the persons around her. But the words she uttered——which issued from her spectral grandmother——were meaningless, even to herself.

"Her hair began to grow very long, and her braids became matted; her head ached and lice infested her hair. Abd Allah insisted that she cut it, for when people saw her with her mop of hair sticking up into the air, they avoided her or did not conceal their fear and disgust. She finally washed it in milk and wrapped it in silk scarves, but that did not suffice. Bartolomea Rodríguez, the dwarf slave whom Abd Allah had brought from Zamora, anointed her hair, armpits and pubis with oil; she cut off one hundred locks to remove the lice. 'Touch them——not,' she warned Almarada and buried the shorn tresses.

"Weeks later the hair curled on her neck and snaked upward. Almarada

said her six braids, or serpents, had been given her by Ahriman and she
would never trim them again. More plaits fell down her back and to her
knees. To keep the lice out, the dwarf bathed and perfumed the braids.

"Supposedly she died in childbirth on Monday. Since then, her custo-
dian, Bartolomea, has been preparing her for her supernatural wedding."

"At dawn today bells swathed in black with muffled clappers tolled
silently three times," said Sancho. "A eunuch divulged that she had expired
without a light or candle, shrouded in the darkness of her own night."

"Perhaps after twilight someone brought her corpse, already washed and
dressed, to the crypt of our church," I speculated. "Now I see that the
woman is naked, and what I took for clothing is the hair covering her."

"What are you spinning?" a dwarf in a yellow smock, head shaven and
eyes sunk behind prominent cheekbones, asked Almarada.

"I'm not spinning, I'm raveling," she replied from the coffin resting on
a wooden table.

"Are you afraid of being laid in a tomb?" Bartolomea touched her cold
hands.

"I fear—not," Almarada murmured. "I felt afraid when my heart
stopped, when my eyes were open and I saw everything go black around
me, and the void had my own shape."

"I knew you were falling by the fluttering of your eyelids." Bartolomea
nodded.

"Plummeting into the abyss, I confessed my sins. Each sin accused me
in its own voice."

"I saw you exit your body, cross the night and meet another spirit who
resembled you," the dwarf said. "Down here we all tried to revive you.
From behind their lids, your eyes looked into mine."

"They declared me dead, and I plunged into a night so narrow and
dizzying that when I emerged from it, I emerged from my own body too."

"What else did you see?"

"Abd Allah and my mother were crying over me. Strangest of all, their
pain touched me—not. I came to a rankly steaming black river where foul
creatures were tormenting souls. I could not go in because it was still
sealed against me with seven seals. Deep green meadows lay on the other
side of a bridge. A voice inside me said that I would not rejoice in them.

I was about to cross the bridge when someone warned me that I should not, because I risked slipping and falling into the mud. A loathsome man came up to me from behind, wound my hair around my hips and started dragging me toward his filthy cave. Then I awoke here on this table.''

"Your clothed body descended, your naked soul arose; your blue body was preparing for a second birth, your soul had nowhere to go," said Bartolomea Rodríguez. "Lying face up, after we celebrated your funeral rites, your hands were uncrossed over your breast, your eyelids shut. When you awoke, you opened your eyes inside. You asked for water.''

"Once I was dead, I forgot I had died. I was blind, but I had eyes front and back which could look everywhere. When I fell into the night, my centuries passed before me for an interminable moment, which stretched from twilight to cockcrow. The dead feed on yesterdays and on the image of things, they embrace and love the semblance of bodies, they are lost in the void trying to reach themselves, because they can no longer tell the difference between what is spiritual and what material, between what is their own and what is someone else's. In that trance I heard Abd Allah ask me to return to his side, I heard an unfamiliar voice ordering me to reenter my body through my head and to live among men until the end of time. I returned, but I never smiled again.''

"Don't think about that. Black maidens are converging on the monastery of Nauj Nas to attend the espousals," Bartolomea Rodríguez tried to calm her.

"Man's home is the grave; that is where he will ultimately deposit all his belongings and all his days," said Almarada. "Tonight will be my funereal wedding.''

"The boy whose birth killed you came out bewitched; he had no chance to suckle death," the dwarf declared.

"Nor the milk of a small woman like yourself," Almarada added.

"She lay still in bed during her last weeks, only moving over when he came to see her," Bartolomea said, referring to Almarada.

"I know. She was gravely ill, and my tongue, ulcerated and swollen, had filled my mouth and refused to speak," said Almarada.

"What happened next? Did you see my father in paradise? Do you need money to live in the other world? What do the spirits think of al-Mansur?''

Bartolomea asked. "What else did you see? Tell me."

"I saw things people see in mirrors, I heard conversations people hear in dreams and don't remember when they wake up." Almarada was becoming uneasy. "I can't tell the illusions apart."

There was a sound of bare feet on the stairs.

"The guests must be demons; mice are sewn into their clothes and spiders imprinted on them," Bartolomea exclaimed. "Nothing or nobody can stop them from reaching Nauj Nas."

"Dress me now for the wedding, it's getting late," Almarada said, stretching out her arms.

"It's good to be young and single again, you get what you want at night. When you're old, you bed down with skinny solitude," the dwarf said, helping her to dress.

Just then a man entered the crypt. It was Abd Allah.

"Oh, my love, everyone is selling their wares in the market, but nobody has days for sale. Oh, my love, what you lost on this earth cannot be purchased anywhere," Abd Allah said to Almarada, who was lying on the table again. His raiment was black, his hat was black. Everything about him evoked the dead.

"Be afraid—not. Although I have really died, I am allowed to be among the living. From now on, you'll have to become used to my spectral state." Almarada got to her feet. Below, her hair brushed the back of her knees; above, her hair stiffened into a snake.

Together they started climbing the stairs of the crypt, pale and solemn. I followed them softly. Sancho remained behind, petrified with fear.

Without a word to each other, they halted before the door of a ruined church, which I had not noticed before. Perhaps it was imaginary. Abd Allah stood on the right, Almarada on the left. A lame priest, whom I thought I'd glimpsed months before among Isidoro's followers, made his entrance wearing a black surplice and stole. He was going to perform the necrophiliac wedding.

Bride and groom moved toward the altar.

The church began to fill with somber musicians and sinister guests. Everyone recognized the Black Rider by his apparel and weapons and by his melancholy mien. The bride glided on bare feet, which disappeared into the floor as she walked. At the sight of the couple, everyone raised their hands in a sign of mourning.

Outside the church servants and slaves in graveclothes prepared inky soups, reeking meats and fish, cakes of ashes and murky drinks. Their faces were translucent, they spoke in whispers.

Bareheaded, the best man unfurled a black flag sewn from scraps of dead widows' weeds. Their faces veiled in black, the bridesmaids appeared, clutching withered flowers. Bushy tufts of hair spotted their cheeks. Their eyes were of two different colors; one was open, the other closed. They had come from afar on horseback. Passing by water, they cast no image.

Holda, her eyes bandaged but all-seeing, was first. Sumptuously un-dressed, her dark nakedness was covered by transparency. Now and then she turned translucent.

"A maiden should not venture out alone in daylight, lest her depravity be corrupted," said the dwarf, her face half eaten by the shadows.

"Lucky you, companion, that so many trollops have come to your wed-ding," a female friend greeted Almarada.

"What will the bridegroom do with such unspeakable beauty?" another friend wailed.

"Almarada, for your wedding I meant to dress you in rich silks and precious jewels, never in tears and yearnings," sighed the dwarf.

Almarada's mother, once fair, now hid her gaunt features behind a black veil.

"When the daughter bloomed in the garden of her house, her mother sold her. My only regret is not asking a higher price for her," she con-fessed. "Once the wedding's over, I'll return to Córdoba."

Black and erect was the bride's hair. The veils were sewn to her clothes with black thread. Her necklaces, earrings and rings were black. She was terribly pale.

"*Mors, morsus, amaritudine,*" I heard the priest intone.

The ceremony began before an empty altar. Night was visible through gaps in the walls; the darkness inside overlapped the darkness outside, and vice versa.

Hidden on the stairway leading to the apse, I strained to see and hear what was happening in the church. What I failed to understand was why

Abd Allah, a Mussulman, was marrying by the Christian rite. He did so, I later learned, because in Toledo, Almarada had been a virgin consecrated to God and had lived in a convent.

The story goes that when she was a nun, she appeared naked and unkempt one June day at noon to a most saintly anchorite by the name of Sofronio the Blind; when Sofronio saw her so clearly, he thought he had recovered his eyesight, but when he realized that she was nude and her posture lewd, he squeezed his eyelids shut to avoid falling into temptations of the flesh. As the dazzling body persisted in his mind's eye, he understood that what was standing before him was a demon, not a woman. Unable to resist the desire burning him within and without, he fled to the mountains howling like a dog.

The groom took a step forward. The bride stood at his left, her eyes blazing, her hair rising from her head like black flames. Her whole body glowed in the moonlight like a ghost's.

The priest asked if any person among those present knew of an impediment to the marriage and, if so, to state it under pain of excommunication.

The godparents, several old people dusted with ashes who were standing behind the betrothed, said nothing.

The priest asked the names of the bridal pair. They muttered them in reply. The best man saluted with the unfurled flag.

Abd Allah and Almarada each caught hold of a corner of the flag. Large quenched candles were placed at their sides.

"Do you take not for wife this woman, in this world and in the other?" the priest asked Abd Allah.

"I take her not."

"Do you take not for husband this man, in this world and in the other?" the priest asked Almarada.

"I take him not."

The priest ordered them to join their right hands.

"I, Abd Allah, take you not for wife, Almarada, from today until dust do us part."

"I, Almarada, take you not for husband, Abd Allah, from the day dust do us part until today."

"In the name of the rebellious spirit, I marry you not, and confirm this sacrament between you," said the black-clad priest, and he sprinkled them with black water, lowering black crowns over both their heads six times. To Abd Allah's misfortune, his crown fell to the ground the fifth time.

"Your kingdom has commenced not," the priest told them.

The bride and groom exchanged scorched rings. Once again the priest sprinkled them with black water and blessed—cursed—them in an unintelligible language. Turning their backs to the cross and the Bible, both invoked spirits and promised to have a hateful union in good times and bad, until the rotting of their carcasses.

Abd Allah made Almarada the gift of a casket containing jet-black necklaces and ribbons. She put black flowers on her hat. At the rear of the church, someone blew out the flame of a candle that had continued to burn.

"You are married until the end of the millenary night," the dwarf declared to the bride from the dark.

"When your life is over, you will be ashes. When you are ashes, you will have been born," her mother exclaimed.

The somber musicians began playing their instruments. Escorted by other clerics, the priest, in his black surplice, stole and cloak of the same color, proceeded to the house of the dead.

Abd Allah took Almarada by the hand while the others formed a circle around them to watch as they did the Dance of the Raven. The couple's feet moved from right to left, as if dancing against time. The best man emerged from the church, waving the black flag.

The ghostly guests waited in the dark for the newlyweds to appear and drank to their unhappiness from empty goblets, which filled with a bloody liquid that did not decrease with the drinking. Spent candles and masks of human faces were handed out.

"*Oremus,*" said the priest.

None knelt.

Verses from the Office for the Dead issued from the church:

. . . *mi-se-re-re*

. . . *mi-se-re-re*

Tu il-le parce

Ad te cla-man-tes, Ex-au.

The phantom congregation responded:

. . . *mi-se-re-re.*

The bridal pair gazed at the moon through the torn clouds.

Everyone began to walk in a funereal procession toward the graveyard. At the head, laymen carried the burned-out tapers. The clerics, two by two, were followed by black women like those who accompany the cortege at Mussulman burials.

Shades appeared behind them, some on horseback, others on foot; some without heads, others missing hands and feet. Several wore masks of the living and the dead. They had come from afar and were leading black stallions. Darker than the darkness, they blended into the surrounding landscape.

Next came six skeletal women representing death. The figures, which danced on the graves, were a queen, an abbess, a horsewoman, a widow, a pregnant lady and a maiden. Their faces were eaten away, their beauty consumed by worms, their eyes unseeing. Whether the women were elderly, youthful or childish, the musicians of death danced with them, and dancing they traversed the night, embracing until they merged into one another.

Six shadows carried Almarada's empty coffin while two cantors chanted the litany for the dead. They went straight past the graves and the monastery, walking in the direction of Abd Allah's camp. There they celebrated the funerary wedding.

VISION XX

"Get up, Sancho, husband, the peasants have already slaughtered the pigs. This is no time for lying down. Disguised as a lady, you must ride this chestnut horse along the river to where the Saracens are watching us. There you will spy on what they're plotting and return rapidly to León. I shall stay here until I have seen my bidding done," I heard Oro María say in the dormitory.

"What are you saying, woman? The hosts of Abd Allah, the Black Rider, the fugitive from the Lord, are losing no time. Yesterday they ravaged the countryside, burned the fields, sacked the villages, ravished every maiden and peasant woman they could find, and from the houses they stole children and beasts, and spread the rumor of our imminent defeat. Do you want me to give up the ghost in this?" Sancho Saborejo rolled over on the bed of twigs as if addressing God, or the wall.

"Some peasants came to seek refuge in the monastery, others went

186

farther on, to Sahagún, Oviedo and Astorga. Still others hid in their own dwellings, afraid the Saracens would find them in the churches and monasteries, which they invariably raid in search of riches and virgins," said Oro María.

"During the night Spernicius came to tell me that three renegade Christians dragged Doña Miguel away, to hang her from a tree near the river Bernesga. Is it true they took her away, is it true about the tree?" asked the minstrel, opening his eyes.

"That's how it was. They hung her by her hands and feet from the branches. 'The Moors are going to kill me,' she screamed when I lowered and untied her. In addition to giving her a beating, the Muslims had sheared her shaggy beard."

"It will grow back quickly. But talk to me about the day, woman. Tell me if it's rainy and chill outside." Sancho Saborejo peered around him.

"Oh, and the Muslims kidnapped Jimena," she added, as an afterthought.

"Where is Jimena?" I asked Oro María, very startled. "I don't see her anywhere in the monastery."

"The renegades carried her off; they sat her on a mule and took her away to sell her in the slave market of Córdoba."

"How did you find that out?" I asked her.

"A renegade Christian let it slip in the new language, Romance. He looked as if he'd just awakened from a bad dream."

"We'll attack Abd Allah's hosts. We'll tear him to pieces," I said, furious. "We'll fall on his men by surprise and kill them all, if the king gives us license."

"We will lift up our voices and blow the horns to summon knights and peasants to war," said García Cabezón, with Sister Froila at his side.

"Yesterday afternoon by the riverside, I spied an enormous eunuch astride a black horse," Sancho Saborejo revealed. "He was leading two Christian ladies, each on a mule, two maidservants on foot, and two elderly squires with bound hands. To the rear, merciless Saracens were prodding the prisoners."

"The Saracens, massed on the outskirts of León for the final battle, have pitched their tents on the far shore of the Bernesga River. Lying in ambush along the roads and among the poplars, they hope to capture us or put us to death. We can see them from the portico of the church, and they can see us," said the bailiff Diego Bamba.

"The Saracens have more than a thousand saddled horses, and on each, a long sword hangs from the saddletree. They wear another slashing sword hanging from their necks," affirmed García Cabezón.

"From the portico we can observe their horses, fiery steeds, robust from exercise, varying in color and build, yellow and silvery whites; light grays, dappled and spotted, jet black and dark green; duns and chestnuts; roans and sorrels, golden and bright yellow; bays with white blazes or stars on their faces," said Sister Froila, whose father had been a breeder of horses in al-Andalus.

The horses sweated under their riders. Now and then a warrior, impetuous and wrathful, broke into a gallop, measuring himself against the Leonese who rode out to confront him. He shouted threats and insults in his own tongue and returned to his fellows, who were making a great din blowing trumpets and shrieking.

"We will all die, they are more numerous than we are," Oro María wailed.

"There are legions of horsemen with two swords apiece, and they're looking straight this way," said Sancho Saborejo, who had gone, in women's clothes, on his chestnut mare to take a look at them near the river.

"Almanzor's troops are on their way to join the battle against us," said García Cabezón.

"After vanquishing Sancho García in Cervera, the Saracens fell to pillaging the fields of Castile. They attacked the city of Saragossa and the region of Pamplona. They're taking captives all over," said Sancho Saborejo.

"They'll carry off our wives and daughters to their harems, and we'll become their slaves," said the bailiff Diego Bamba.

"All the women must tuck their hair inside their clothes or cut it off, so that they will look like men to the Saracens' eyes," Sister Froila suggested.

"We heard that they would attack by night, for the moon is theirs, and the sun ours," García Cabezón declared, flourishing his rusting sword.

"Their jeering and blustering is done to frighten and confuse us. Almanzor, the captain of the Saracens, will lead the battle and he will attack by day," Diego Bamba said in a faltering voice. "Don't think I'm quaking from fear, I'm only sick."

"Which would you prefer: to surrender one hundred of your own and your family's daughters to Almanzor and his lechers, or to lose your life?" García Cabezón asked Diego Bamba.

"I prefer losing one hundred daughters of yours and the Castilians to losing my life," the bailiff replied.

"Almanzor went back to Córdoba, and the Black Rider will captain the riders of the Apocalypse," I said.

"They will wait for the corn to be reaped before invading León," Diego Bamba declared.

"We'll keep watch on them from the mountain passes, from the castle and the walls," the nameless horseman vowed.

"They've surrounded us, and they're only waiting for the order to attack," García Cabezón said. "All manner of Muslims ride with Abd Allah: Arabs, Berbers, Turks and Guineans. The mercenaries from Ifriqiya first wound, capture or behead the Christians, and then they stew, roast and eat them."

"They only pretend to devour the bodies to frighten us. That's how they put fear into the Goths, who when they saw how grisly they were took to their heels and left the villages and castles defenseless," the nameless horseman declared. "Dreading their cruelty, our ancestors allowed them to conquer our lands and lives in no time at all."

"The Christians had no weapons to ward them off, only staves and fear to face them with," García Cabezón recalled. "The king of the Goths was Guitixa, or was it Vitiza, or Uitize, or Uuitiza?"

"They had the king, Don Rodrigo, and the count, Don Julián, to finish us off, the first with his despicable acts, and the second with his treachery," added the nameless horseman.

"We must send messengers to the farthest reaches to advertise the danger hanging over us, so that gentlemen and peasants will unite with us, and together we can take on the might of Almanzor," Diego Bamba urged.

"We'll carry our swords under our cloaks and draw them the instant the signal to attack is given," said García Cabezón.

"Never have I spilled the blood of any fellow creature, but to defend God and our people, I will wield the sword and the lance against our enemies, the Saracens," exclaimed an elderly monk. "The mission falls to us of forging an alliance between angels and men."

"The paltriness of our army obliges men of God to take up temporal weapons," sighed García Cabezón, on whom, after Gonzalo Vermudez's treason, King Vermudo II had bestowed the monastery of San Miguel de Almazcara and the villa of Santa Leocadia.

"In this battle, many religious will die, resorting to secular violence to defend the Christian faith and brotherly bonds between creatures—but not out of pride or lust for power, or for glory," the elderly monk remarked.

"In the year 1000 the Church has accepted the spiritual presence among us of thousands upon thousands of the deceased, whose bodily fate we have witnessed, but whose mortal destiny we are ignorant of," said García Cabezón. "Many of the dead whose death befell them centuries ago, and many of the dead whose death will befall them tomorrow, will receive together the grace of resurrection when time is over."

"You who are such fleshly kin will carve out friendships with your swords," the elderly monk said with a sickly smile, seeking my eyes.

"We will not sleep all night long, to be on the alert for the Saracens," said Sancho Saborejo.

"Men are more afraid of dying at the hand of the Saracens than of suffering everlasting death on the day of dread," said the elderly monk.

"To encourage the villeins in combat, the king will grant them rights and exemptions, which will make them similar to the nobles without being equal to them," the bailiff Diego Bamba announced.

At dawn, prelates from other parts arrived accompanied by people with weapons and a throng of infantrymen ready to fight. Toward noon, we learned that the count had fled to Santiago during the night, taking with him his riches, his holy relics, and his women and children.

VISION XXI

One Sunday in December, before the Nativity of Our Lord, at the hour of Tierce, amid copper and brass censers, Bishop Froilán, staff and lance in hand, traversed the damp streets on his way to Santa María de Regla. During the past weeks he had been in a fever to say mass two or three times a day.

Seven acolytes on foot and seven deacons on horseback, dressed in chasubles and sumptuous albs, solemnly cleared the way for him, García Cabezón going before all the rest. Subdeacons attended the deacons. Other clerics and I followed close upon the bishop along with the principal ladies and gentlemen of the kingdom. We marched in step, singing litanies and penitential hymns.

The bells pealed thrice: first *ad invocandum;* second, *ad congregandum;* and the third time, *ad inchoandum.* At that very moment, the shackles of the prisoners in jail were loosened because their brother, Bishop Froilán, was

191

offering the Sacrifice of the Mass. At the entrance to the ruined church, a bearded priest with black eyes and hair was waiting for us. Yet more clergymen were already seated on the broken benches, in the presbytery and around the altar.

The altar was a plain table, draped with a cloth, which hung over its edges. The nave had been occupied by the townspeople, who had entered carrying the processional cross aloft. Bishop Froilán was escorted to the *secretarium* devastated by al-Mansur. There he donned the liturgical vestments: the alb, the shoulder scarf, the tunicle, the chasuble and the pallium. The Gospels were opened. An acolyte led the bishop to the altar. All rose.

Accendite! sang the two rows of cantors. *Domini iubete!* was the reply.

The bishop stood before the altar, made the sign of the cross, prostrated himself to pray to God, recited the Confiteor, letting everyone hear the confession of his sins, arose and kissed the Gospels. A prayer was said: *Pax Christi quam nobis per evangelium suum tradidit, confirmet et conservet corda nostra et corpora in vitam aeternam.* He kissed the altar. He was heard murmuring, "*Oramus te, Domine.*"

The deacon, García Cabezón, approached, swinging a censer hanging from three chains, while clouds of incense perfumed the nave. Bishop Froilán began to read the text of the Introit from the missal, and a psalm was sung alternately by two choirs, concluding with the Gloria Patri. The Kyrie Eleison followed, García Cabezón singing, and the people responding.

Gloria in excelsis Deo
et in terra pax hominibus
bonae voluntatis.

resounded in the air.

As I listened to the hymns, it occurred to me that this ruined church had been rebuilt from song, with voices for stones. I turned my head to look at Jimena, pregnant, blessed among women. To one side of her stood Doña Miguel and Oro María, to the other, Froila, the comely nun. In front of the four, engrossed in prayer, was Urraca the Shadow, dressed in blue.

The many sons of Don Berto Fernández and his wife, Rigoberta, were in the other nave. Near them clustered the rival family from San Juan de

Lairones, the daughters of Adelberto and Adalberta Gundisaliz, flesh-and-blood creatures of the year 1000, who one day would be reduced to names on a parchment scroll.

The choir sang:

Laudamus te
Benedicimus te
Adoramus te
Glorificamus te
Magnificamus te.

I could not take my eyes off Jimena's body, or my thoughts from the pretty child she was carrying within. Looking at her, I sensed that she would remain behind in the millennium that was expiring, while I, and my chosen offspring, were entering the Second Millennium as lords and redeemers of men and of days.

Jimena tried to conceal her belly beneath her clothes. While wiping the grease off her cheeks the day before, she seemed to have scrubbed the color off with the grime. Her loving eyes shone.

"*Domine, Fili Dei Patris, agne Dei, qui tollis peccatum mundi, miserere nobis,*" Jimena heard the choir sing. Standing beside Sancho Saborejo, Gómez looked as if he knew everyone's secrets.

After the Gloria, the memorial to the Passion of Jesus continued. At a certain moment, the standing worshipers, their hands upraised, turned their eyes toward the east, to the part of the church where Lord Christ was. Clerics, acolytes and the faithful took communion. Urraca was the first communicant, García Cabezón, the second, Froila, the third, and the fourth—though he hadn't confessed—Gómez the Mute.

The celebrant bishop exclaimed, "*Humiliate capita vestra Deo,*" and the congregation knelt, bending their heads.

The deacon García Cabezón sang *Ita missa est,* staring deeply into Sister Froila's eyes.

The congregation responded, "*Deo Gratias.*"

The bishop kissed the altar once more, murmuring, "*Placeat tibi sancta Trinitas.*"

The procession of clerics returned to the *secretarium,* a monk with a censer in the fore. Before dispersing, the congregation worshiped the relics of the saints.

"Didn't you see a demon among the clerics who was tossing the children's voices into a sack?" Urraca asked me. "He thought their voices were corporeal creatures which he could carry off to hell."

"When he's on his way there and takes out the babes' voices, after the grace of the hymns has gone, all he'll hear will be grunts and howls, because he'll be listening to himself. Then he'll try to trample the voices, but they will be invulnerable to his feet and will waft into the air singing Gloria," I said.

I turned to look at Jimena. In another part of the nave, she returned my glance.

VISION XXII

Under a chilly drizzle, twelve boys from the monasteries of the kingdom came at nightfall to the palace in León. They were oblates whose ages ranged from three to twelve years old. A mentor instructed and disciplined the four youngest ones, who were placed next to me. Other mentors took charge of the children who remained behind at the entrance to the refectory.

Newly arrived from Galicia, Don Alfonso V made his appearance. As a child of five, after Vermudo II died, God had elevated him to the kingship on the eleventh of October in the year 999. He made his entrance with his mother, Doña Elvira, the queen; his tutor, Don Menando González; the presbyter and notary, Sampiro; other palace monks, and his retinue. Prelates, archers and lancers stood guard over him.

"My lord, grant me license to captain the warriors who will confront the Black Rider's hosts. My sole honor will reside in vanquishing the Evil One's forces," I implored him.

The king conferred in a low voice with Doña Elvira, then bade me rise, for I had bent one knee.

"I, Alfonso, king by command of God, as was my father, Don Vermudo, seated on the throne of my forefathers, not for my merits but by divine favor, do grant that you bear the cross and the sword during the battle of the Christians against the armies of Antichrist," he proclaimed, handing me the royal weapons.

"Make sure you don't miss when you strike the blow that will put an end to the terror the Black Rider has brought upon us," Doña Elvira added.

"I accept with humility. In God's name I will be captain of the Leonese warriors," I swore.

"Amen. Amen in the heavens and on earth. Hallelujah beneath the Holy Trinity of our Redeemer and Lord," Sampiro exclaimed.

The child king nodded his head at me and touched my shoulder with his hand. Bishop Froilán II raised the golden Visigoth cross, the bells of Santa María de Regla pealed, and *vihuela* and zither players began to play an antiphon, asking God to protect us in the war.

A seated repast followed. The oblates arrived in silence and in line. Two children stood beside the abbot's table, and at each table there was a boy facing his mentor. The other monks sat down, backs to the wall, at successive tables, according to their order, rank and age.

A linen cloth was spread over the king's table, and each of us was given a wooden spoon. By virtue of his primacy, Bishop Froilán was placed near the king. The Moorish slaves, Yuseph and Numara, gifts from Sampiro to the queen, hovered behind Doña Elvira. Those who arrived late had to remain standing at the entrance to the dining hall, although the lesser and younger monks relinquished their seats to their elders and betters.

"I, Sampiro, the insignificant servant of the servants of God, in the name of the Begotten One . . . ," and he blessed the meal.

The servants brought basins for washing our hands. First they served the soup, bacon, bread, onions, garlic and turnips. Then came mutton, goose, chicken, trout from the Bernesga, lamb, cheese and honey. Most of us used our fingers, eating off shared plates, passing a large goblet of wine from hand to hand. The king was moderate in his eating and drinking, his watchful tutor seeing to it that he kept clean and neat.

"I shall eat, so as not to be deemed guilty of overweening fasting," said the bishop, Don Froilán.

"The minute we leave, I vow to go and feed the twelve worst paupers, including Spernicius," promised Abbot Sabarico of the monastery of San Lucas, who was tipsy.

While we were eating, the clerics and principal lords of León discussed the 150 solidi which the queen had paid for the manor of Velasco Aquilone on the banks of the Bernesga, with its fields, mills and fishponds, and how in the year 999, Doña Zida and her sons had sold the land near the Count's Gate to the abbess Senduara and the monastery of Santiago. Then Sister Froila mentioned that, four years earlier, she herself had donated diverse properties to that same monastery.

"In León a plot of land with no houses at all can cost as much as twenty solidi," affirmed Don Fulgencio, a presbyter who helped Sampiro in his notarial tasks. "The city is one great monastery: In every property stands a cloister, and on every street four temples of God are being built."

"Bishop Froilán will cede to Sister Froila an enclosed property with houses already completed, adjoining the bishop's seat at the church of Santa María. But I would sell the properties of my monastery to Sister Froila and charge her nothing, if only she would let me shrive her more often," Abbot Sabarico remarked to García Cabezón, who was leering so brazenly at the nun that she blushed.

"I will donate a villa to San Juan el Teólogo, on condition that one day García Cabezón be appointed abbot of that monastery, so all the inhabitants—the present ones and those who will come to reside in the village—may be subject to his power and pay him twelve bushels of barley each year," said Froila.

"Sinner that I am, when threatened by the sword during the Saracen persecution and pricked on by fear of death, I took flight, escaping captivity at the hands of the Ishmaelites. Even though I did not share the fate of many colleagues in blessing who were mowed down by steel, I did lose all I had," declared Sampiro, who was the proprietor of a number of villas and afterward would be owner of many more, which the king, Don Alfonso, would give him. He wrote the deeds, by the grace of God, with his own hand.

"The Saracens invaded this land and destroyed the city of León. They went to the monastery of San Lucas and sacked it; they demolished it and put it to the torch. We monks were left with nothing, not an ox, not a ewe, not a horse, not a donkey, not a crust of bread to feed ourselves," moaned Abbot Sabarico, who by now was drunk.

"There was no city, no church, no monastery where the servants of God remained," lamented García Cabezón.

"I came to León from Zamora, and I entered service in the palace of my lord, the most serene king Don Vermudo. Blessed be his memory, because while he lived he showered me with properties," said Sampiro.

Sancho Saborejo and Oro María came out to give cheer to the assembly with music and dancing, but just then Urraca, dressed in blue, burst in and they fell silent and still.

"It's Urraca Fernández," García Cabezón whispered to me, as if I didn't know who she was.

The king, Don Alfonso, and the queen, Doña Elvira, and everyone present welcomed her. She was offered chunks of meat, but she spurned them, saying they did not befit her humble and visionary state.

Bishop Froilán took her by the hand and led her toward Doña Elvira, and everyone sat down on the benches to listen. Urraca knelt before an image of the Virgin Mary and began by saying, "*In nomine Sancte Trinitatis. Ego Urracha . . . ,*" and then she said nothing.

Don Froilán went to her side and begged her for the love of God to speak to the king and queen and gentlemen and ladies who were there, crushed by the dread that the presence of the Black Rider had brought into their lives and by the fear of the end of time that had taken root in the land.

"I am no witch or soothsayer, I am a Christian, and a disciple of the Mother of God," Urraca broke her silence. "A wise Jewess by the name of Mioro de Alija del Bernesga taught me to read the signs of the future in the clouds of the present. By the omens which have appeared these days, I see atrocities and dire calamities approaching. The hosts of Antichrist will

soon make war in our lands, and if we do not stop them at the gates of
León, they will annihilate all Christendom before the year 1000 comes to
an end.''

"We who are here know all too well that we risk losing our souls and
our bodies to Antichrist's hosts if God does not come to our aid," Bishop
Froilán said at once. "I beg you, oh chaste one, interpret for us this dream
which we all dreamed last night: the dream of our death at the hands of
the Black Rider and his armies.''

"Throughout the days and nights of this year 1000, evil spirits have
appeared who roam the land, bent on sowing terror and shaking our faith
in God," said Urraca the Shadow. "Alfonso de León, the Lord of the Last
Days, the man chosen by the Divine Will to save Christendom, is here
among us and will help us. Many are the things that were hidden and are
now revealed.''

"In truth I tell you," answered Doña Elvira, "that the Leonese will
emerge unscathed from the battle against the Black Rider's hosts.''

"Only yesterday, I dreamed I saw in the sky the nine bloody suns which
the Tiburtine Sibyl explained to the one hundred senators of Rome. The
nine suns prefigure the human generations yet to come. This means that
man will not be annihilated by Antichrist during the battle," Urraca declared. "Alfonso de León, the Lord of the Last Days, will save us from
death and from the hell that follows upon it.''

"Friends and kinsmen, great is the responsibility that you place on my
shoulders. I beg you to give me counsel as good soldiers and Christians,
which you are," I began, when I saw them all clustering around me.
"When it is known throughout Spain that we have risen up with the land
of León against al-Mansur and his army, all the good works we have done
will be for naught, and our very lives will be menaced by death or captivity.
I promise you invisibility in combat, and should some unfortunates among
you meet with death, I can assure you of resurrection in the flesh on
Judgment Day, which is not far off. Friends and kinsmen, I invite every
one of you to fight blindly in the war of the millennium alongside me,
your redeemer. You have already heard what will befall us if we do not
battle with all our might for God and Christendom.''

"The queen has heard, Alfonso de León. Rest from the fatigue of today's toils so that you may find yourself in good spirits and refreshed for the battle," Doña Elvira exclaimed.

"The Lamb of God has metamorphosed into a brave chief of the Christian armies. I doubt he will save us from evil, but he will protect us from the devil," the bishop opined.

"God willing, tomorrow Sunday, before the day is over, we will be free of the Black Rider and the Saracen threat and from al-Mansur's continual harassments," I affirmed. "If God is not willing, we will have to endure further days in anguish."

"If it is Antichrist you fear, fear no longer. I will be near to defend you from his venom," said Urraca. "And I do not say this to discredit your valor, for throughout León you are held to be a courageous knight in arms."

"Sister, give me faith in the Lord because I sorely need it, but if it is necessary for my body to perish in battle, I am disposed to accept my corporeal death to save my soul and·the soul of my brothers from the promise of hell," I said.

"Did I hear aright, you have said brothers and not brother?" she asked.

"You did, Urraca, and I uttered what I said in my soul, and God listened."

"We wish to salute the one who does not allow our souls and swords to grow rusty," the deacon García Cabezón intoned.

"And the Lord who will permit us to avenge the tribulations which our king, Don Vermudo—at whose side I yearn to lie the day of my death—suffered at the Saracens' hands," Sampiro added.

"Your wishes will be fulfilled: You will become bishop, old, blind and dead," Urraca promised him.

Then I swore an oath on Saint James's arm, the relic that Bishop Froilán thrust at me.

Queen Elvira deemed the audience to be over. Each of those present took leave of Don Alfonso V and kissed his hand, crossing themselves before a holy relic, a splinter from the cross on which Lord Christ was crucified, brought here for the occasion. Each one of us made a bow to Doña Urraca and retired to his inn or his tent, according to our rank.

The queen asked to speak privately with Urraca. We all left the palace. Noblemen and squires protected us from dangers in the street and brightened our night with torches. Outside, the townspeople and clergy of León were waiting to witness our exit, and they accompanied us as far as Santa María de Regla and the Bishop's Gate.

My way lit by glass lanterns, I continued thence to the monastery, escorted by Sancho and Oro María, García Cabezón and Sister Froila, as well as riders and armed peasants.

Alone in my cell after Compline, and curious about the enterprise entrusted to me, I drew out the royal sword. I examined the crossguard engraved with the words *Ave Maria gratia plena,* the wooden hilt, the silver blade. I begged the true God to grant me victory so that the land would not fall into the hands of my brother's hosts. García Cabezón and I played chess until Matins. The ivory pieces, which had belonged to Saint Genadio, were large, with rectangular sides and incised circles. Sister Froila sat down beside the deacon, occasionally watching him play, occasionally dozing.

Jimena appeared at dawn, her hair disheveled, her clothing torn, and her face awry.

"Sir," she said, "do not come near me, for this night Abd Allah, called the Black Rider, coupled with me, and then he gave me to his hosts so that they might ravish and humiliate me. He believes this deed will kindle a great anger in you, and then Satan will make his way into your breast, for you will think to kill your brother."

"Give to me, oh Lord—and not to any other—strength and sense to be avenged on the unbelieving brother," I said, borrowing words from a future ballad, as I squeezed a chessman in my left hand, my breast swollen with rage.

VISION XXIII

Saturday, toward the hour of dusk, two haggard, bearded men, shabby and unshod, were seen coming down the road to Santiago, one on muleback, the other on foot, staff in hand. It was Abbot Andrés and Brother Martín Meñique, who had left the monastery of San Juan el Teólogo at the start of the year 1000 to go into the world and broadcast the signs of the last days.

Both abbot and cleric gave the impression of being used to emaciation, as if they had managed to be gaunt and thin only after much perseverance, work and discipline. All they lacked to satisfy their expectations of complete mortification was the crown of martyrdom. Otherwise, they were a pair of walking relics.

Their bodies had been branded by mishaps, mistreatment and misadventures. In others' bodies they had experienced maladies, meanness, sorrows, deaths and horrors, through their vocation of suffering the misfortunes of others in their own flesh. At first glance, their manifest chronicle of the earth was an interminable succession of afflictions and tribulations.

"Why are you in such a disastrous state and so fewer in number than when you departed from San Juan?" I asked them, unable to discern which of the two had his eyes open wider, for their lids were closing with sores and exhaustion.

"The Moors took our strongest brothers captive; they subjected the oblates and the youths to castration and sodomy, and they carried them away to Córdoba dressed as little girls and maidens," Martín Meñique said, barely parting his lips.

"Others could not withstand the journey and succumbed in different parts of the land," Abbot Andrés mumbled, squinting as if sleep were overcoming his eyes or the light were wounding them.

"During our pilgrimage we were stricken by the arrows of criminals and thieves. Here and there they despoiled us of our monies, animals, clothing and provisions. In the month of December, we had such a wealth of rags and hunger that no one could take them from us."

"We two survived," said Abbot Andrés. "The rest were blown by death to the other world, like bird feathers."

"The demon of envy, which we all nourish inside ourselves, coaxed the enemies from our bowels, and our road swarmed with vipers," said Martín Meñique.

"It was this enemy, more than privation, more than the rains, more than the cold, more than the heat and the wind, more than the wrongs, more than the Saracens, that brought us to our present misery," Abbot Andrés added.

"As you well know, Alfonso, all those sufferings, joined with the on-slaughts of death, will contribute greatly to the perfection of your virtue," Brother Martín Meñique reassured himself and me.

"You have arrived in time for the battle of the millennium, of the forces of good against the hosts of Antichrist," I told them.

"We saw al-Mansur's armies in several places near León, but unless my eyes deceived me, we have yet to catch a glimpse of him," the abbot declared.

"Soon enough he'll be on top of you in all his wickedness," I warned.

"Though I am very old—I have already passed sixty—I can be of use tending the wounded, giving absolution to the dying and burying the dead," Father Andrés volunteered.

"I shall bear arms until I die," Martín Meñique vowed.

"Since the beginning of time, we have never stopped dying," the abbot remarked.

"And imagining," Martín said.

"If we do not defend the earthly paradise which God created for our enjoyment, we won't be worthy of calling ourselves men," I added.

At this point, Abbot Andrés asked about his friend Don Pelayo, a monk from the monastery of San Lucas. I told him the monk had died and was now underground. He asked when the death had occurred. I replied, in May, when the storks build their nests on the roofs.

"Who else has died?" Martín Meñique inquired, his hair bristling.

"Doña Sancha's youngest son died, the one who used to come to the monastery of San Juan to take divine instruction with the oblates. Gabriel died, the poet monk from San Miguel de Escalada . . . he died happy. Two nuns from Santiago coughed themselves to death on Palm Sunday; on the eve of the Ascension of the Virgin, two clerics from San Lucas slew each other because of slave girls that had been donated to the monastery by a renegade Christian; Corvasia, Donato's wife, was murdered; Abbot Andrés's bitch watchdog died before Epiphany," I replied. "This summer, the sultry season was short, and the Saracens came to burn the crops of already hungry people, to take away their wives and daughters."

"That's why this war?" the priest asked.

"The war is because al-Mansur wants it," I said.

"After the battle, we will return to the monastery of San Juan and rest from our weariness for one thousand years," Martín Meñique sighed. "Doubtless tonight we shall sleep armed and afraid."

"That's so," I assented.

"Now we will make our way to the convent of San Salvador, where our sisters in Lord Christ will receive us with charity and rejoicing," and Abbot Andrés set out, starved for food and slumber.

"By Matins we will be fit for the battle of the millennium; now we'd best put a few crumbs of bread in our mouths and console our thirst with a few drops of water," Martín Meñique said, following closely after the abbot, clothed in the weapons of faith, ready to spend the night dreaming about everything that he had not been.

With dragging gait, they stepped into the throng, persevering in the monastic rule that obliged them to emphasize their corporeal insignificance at every moment. The crowd swallowed them up, as if they had never existed.

After Compline, it was rumored that a Jewish man who had found the remains of Saint John the Theologian in distant lands was on his way to León. On the wings of the rumor the man himself arrived: Jonás ibn Gabirol. He brought a casket in the shape of the letter Omega—Ω—which contained the relics of the author of the Apocalypse.

When I went to welcome my friend from Córdoba at the Bishop's Gate, I barely recognized him. His hair had turned white, the skin of his face and hands was dry. Only his black eyes flashed in his aged countenance. He knew me at once. We stood facing each other, taking stock. Jonás was looking at me not from the distance between Córdoba and León, nor from the years gone by between our separation and today, but from across the abyss that yawns between one man and another. Exhausted, he seemed about to fall on his left side. Every fiber of his body revealed the long road in time he had traveled since we bade each other farewell that night in Madinat al-Zahra.

With difficulty, he raised his left arm, from which several tatters hung, and pointed to the casket. "I have scoured the land seeking you. From the Christians of Córdoba I learned you were in León. I have dragged this box all the way from Patmos."

I made no answer, but stared at him, amazed that he was alive, that he was before me.

"The other day when we met, I left Córdoba on a mule for Valencia, where I arrived after twelve stages," Jonás recounted. "I went to Tarragona, beside the sea, and from there to Barcelona, which I reached after walking for two days. In Gerona I stayed a few days with the Jews of the community. Afterward I was in Narbonne, a city renowned for its scholars of the Torah. At Marseilles I took ship. After four days' sailing, I fetched up on the outskirts of Genoa. After traveling many days, leagues, cubits, miles and spans, I found myself in Pisa, Rome, Naples, Melfi, Brindisi. With scant gold and victuals, I crossed the Utmost Sea. I saw Corinth, Thebes, Thessalonica and Constantinople, where Basil the Second reigned. Everywhere the Jewish merchants who knew the roads and the Jews in the cities gave me food and lodging. Amid the hardships of the highway, when I felt most forsaken and lost, someone always came to succor me, and someone always came to aggravate my misfortunes."

"How did you find the tomb of Saint John the Theologian?" I asked.

"John the Seer was arrested by order of the emperor Domitian and banished to Patmos, a rocky, volcanic island. There he was condemned to sleep on the ground, scantily clothed and almost without food. There I went to search for him, although I had heard that there were two tombs in Ephesus that tradition said were his."

For an instant he fell silent, engrossed in himself. Then he continued. "I found the grotto where the Holy Spirit supposedly revealed to him the secret of the end of time. Seized with fear, I went inside, touched with my hands the niche where he was wont to lay his head to sleep and the crevice where he steadied himself to rise from the ground. To the right stood the stone desk on which his disciple Prochorus wrote at the prophet's dictation. It is said that the rock took shape when Saint John heard the Divine Voice saying, 'I am Alpha and Omega.' I, mortal and blasphemous, touched the sacred lectern on which the Seer wrote the Book of Revelation. I touched the stony door on the flank of the mountain where he lay down in his exile and took shelter from the sun. I, like other pilgrims, scrawled my name on the rock, with the following supplication: 'Remember me, oh brother, on the day of the resurrection of the flesh.' I did not find him."

"But if his tomb was not on the island called Patmos, where could it be?" I asked.

"An old monk told me that upon the death of the emperor Domitian, John the Seer returned to Ephesus to govern the churches in Asia. That is what Eusebius says. His body disappeared in Ephesus; nothing is known about his death. Some say that having reached the age of one hundred, he ascended to heaven, still alive."

I looked at him perplexedly, and he continued. "Ephesus was one of the seven churches of Asia to which the Book of Revelation refers. In Ephesus the Virgin was declared Theotokos or the God-bearer, during a great council of the Church in the year 431. It is natural that the mortal remains of Saint John the Seer were to be found in Ephesus."

"So you went to Ephesus?"

"For weeks I hunted down his body in the caves where the Seven Sleepers were raised from among the dead, and in the modest last house of the Virgin where she lived in his company, for Lord Christ entrusted her to him before dying. It was an extremely hot Sunday as, famished and feverish, I was making my way down Hagios Theologos hill, where the emperor Justinian built the basilica of Saint John the Theologian in the sixth century, when I met the Greek merchant Nicias Melisourgos, now grown old, who as if divining my thoughts shouted to me, 'Stop, someone is looking for you.' "

"And then what happened?"

"I turned my head and saw a luminous figure descending through the air. A white garment reached its feet, a golden sash girded its breast. Its locks were woolly white, and its eyes like flames of fire. From its mouth protruded a two-edged sword. It was the Son of Man who, with his presence, was showing me the place where his disciple lay. He came to a halt on the altar where the death and the assumption of Saint John had presumably occurred. When the figure vanished, I knew that my attempt to lay hold of the Seer's historical body was in vain, as vain as trying to lay hold of the absence of things. If the author of the Revelation still existed, he existed only in his words, which were his body. In various places, graves were found that contained him, if not in his entirety, at least his sacred hair and bones. And arks with his supposed relics, which surely belonged to other dead people, were for sale at high prices in churches and monasteries. What is certain is that Saint John the Seer was no longer a Greek Jew or a Christian Greek Jew; he was a person who had perished more than nine centuries ago, and his skeleton was not identifiable. No one even knew whether he had been one man, two men or none at all."

Jonás swallowed and went on. "Nicias Melisourgos showed me a stone door on the hillside. I opened it and descended seven steps. Seven crypts of stone awaited me. In the fourth I entered a room where sepulchers set in a circle shielded a central cubicle. Seven coffins of stone lay upon seven tables of stone, immersed in time, darkness and cold. On the walls were carved seven words from the Apocalypse. I dared not open the coffin in the middle, which had the shape of a cross. By the sweet odor escaping from it, I divined that it harbored the body of Saint John. It was like daring to open one of the seven seals. Only the Lamb, the Firstborn of the Dead, is permitted to see and reveal the countenance of death.''

"What more?" I asked him, my anxiety matching his.

"The other six coffins belonged to faithful who believed that on the Day of Resurrection, because they were neighbors in burial, they would be saved along with him. This subterranean cemetery, which dated from the first centuries of the era of the Incarnation of the Lord, let in the light through a tiny window hidden in the rock. The last rays of the sun crossed the basement, the crypt and the circular hall to rest on the forehead of the body kept in the fourth coffin.''

"How did you dare bring him to León?" I cried.

"I couldn't open the coffin, so I flung myself down next to it. I imagined from the words in his book a new sun and a new earth. According to John, the first sky and the first earth went away, and the sea is no longer. I, in my darkness, saw the Holy City of the New Jerusalem descending from the heavens, arrayed in God, like the bride arrayed by her bridegroom. 'I will surely come soon. Amen, so be it,' a voice said to me.''

"I do not see a coffin of stone," I remarked.

"Because his death and his sleep weigh centuries, and his words, millennia, I left the corpse in its place of repose. I have brought only this casket in the shape of an Omega, with a few of his relics inside.''

On the bottom of the reliquary there was something written in Greek, which the octogenarian Nicias Melisourgos had translated into the Spanish vernacular. One sentence read: "Here lie the relics of John of the island which is called Patmos, by the word of God and the testimony of Jesus the Christ." The others affirmed: "The tower of Babel and the New Jerusalem serve no purpose, because they are works of man," and "The end of history, provoked by man, will be determined by God." There was also a painted tree of life with the letters Alpha and Omega intertwined.

"I know as little about the author of the Book of Revelation as I know about myself," Jonás ibn Gabirol added. "Worst of all, I don't even know if I've crossed half the world carrying a casket that contains only a legend, a miracle-making legend."

As we talked, people began to cluster around us, curious to see the relics of Saint John and to hear our conversation.

"You are in time for the battle of the end," I told Jonás. "We fight against the Saracens, the hosts of Antichrist, who are encamped outside León."

"Here is your white horse, your bow and your crown, so you may emerge victorious, so you may vanquish our enemy," he replied, as if he knew everything.

At that moment, Sancho Saborejo appeared with the horse, the bow and the crown that Jonás ibn Gabirol had just mentioned.

"We should go to the bishop's inn, where you can eat and spend the night," I said to Jonás.

"Blessed is he who reads, and blessed are those who hear the words of this Prophecy and pay heed to the things that are written, for the time is nigh," he muttered, allowing me to lead him to the inn as though he were Saint John in person.

Bishop Froilán II, filled with fervor and fear by Jonás ibn Gabirol's discovery, ordered that the holy reliquary be displayed in Santa María de Regla in full sight of the populace. The nuns of León and its environs brought out in procession relics of their own saints, male and female, to honor him. Psalms were sung as on a feast day, the feast of the end of time.

"I have come to this place to await the night of the world," Jonás ibn Gabirol told me, and he sang a new song that went: "You are worthy of taking up the book, and of opening the seals, because you knew death."

VISION XXIV

Princes and princesses, bishops and abbesses, merchants and monks, blacksmiths, carpenters, tailors, shoemakers, gentlemen and a great quantity of peasants and paupers, each with his vision and his fears of the era that was coming to a close, came to await the night of the world.

Men learned in many and diverse arts and trades were seen on the streets and avenues of León, as well as women from foreign provinces and realms, in clothing, headdresses and ornaments never seen before. Many of these people gathered inside and outside the churches, speaking in tongues novel or known, bringing merchandise from villages beneath the sway of the Saracens or from even more distant lands. The one thousandth year of the Incarnation of the Lord had been transformed into a feast of prodigies and terrors.

The populace became wrought up by the sermons of clerics, the premonitions of charlatans and the birth of monstrous creatures, who were promptly murdered by their parents, who feared they had engendered the devil's spawn. The people imagined earthquakes that fractured walls and churches; foresaw calamities, famines, plagues, the death of powerful personages, and all manner of evils. They took to observing the sky, an indifferent and dreary sky, which could serve equally as the stage for the final battle between the armies of good and evil, or as the sacred space where the Messiah would appear.

To counter the avarice lodged in the hearts of Lord Christ's servants, the pillaging and incest, the robbery, homicide and adultery that occurred each day, the faithful donated their riches to the poor and to the churches. To counter vanity, maidens and matrons cut off their hair, dirtied their faces and hands, and mortified their bodies. Squires and knights went to the city squares and the kingdom's highways to proclaim the signs of the coming of Antichrist and the end of time, and they undertook to lead lives more ascetic than the hermit monks', in penance for their sins.

At dawn, the day before the Nativity, yet another mass was celebrated in the ruined church of Santa María de Regla. Choirs of boys and girls sang. A Frankish musician familiar with the *quadrivium,* who had studied numbers and their harmonies, praised the glory of God, the morning light, the Creation of the world, the course of the planets, and the life of man on earth. But when the celebrant of the divine office wished peace to the congregation, and a peasant woman approached the altar to receive the blessing, everyone realized that the musician was a dead man.

Between the hours of Prime and Tierce, the sun vanished from the sky; some said there had not been such a dismal day on earth since Good Friday, and near the Cauriense Gate a hermit surprised a couple fornicating under cover of night. The hermit, none other than Spernicius, strode up and down on the walls shaking his fist and growling at the naked copulators, who fled in terror.

After Tierce, a fisherman came to tell of having seen a fish off the coast last Monday at nightfall, so huge that it was like a living island. Its mouth was on its forehead, and when it swam, the water billowed and surged in its wake. A smaller animal swam beside it, its offspring, to which it had given birth fully formed and perfect. It was a leviathan, a whale. At dawn on Tuesday it disappeared.

"It is a signal that the tumult of war will begin in this century," said a shabby, sorrowful man.

At the hour of Sext, a nun named Mumadona from the monastery church of Santiago, who was late in going to the refectory to eat, saw the chapel where she used to pray crowded with men and women in white garments with purple lights flickering over them and a man facing them, holding a luminous cross in his hand. It was I, in my capacity as Lord of the Last Days. A celestial melody issued from the lips of the men and women. Upon hearing it, Sister Mumadona knew that the song was not the work of mortal creatures, for it stirred the invisible presences in the chapel.

At the hour of None, the spirit of the Ancient Serpent entered Fulberto, a monk from the monastery of San Lucas. After climbing the wall, he started hurling stones at passersby. When they learned that he was possessed by the Evil One, three stout clerics from San Lucas grabbed him from behind, sprinkled his mouth and hands with holy water and pressed crosses against his chest, intoning prayers and litanies all the while.

"He is my servant in the monastery of San Lucas, where all the monks are mad," Fulberto shouted in a voice not his own as the brothers tied him up and carried him away.

In the middle of the afternoon, a comet with a dazzling tail appeared in the western sky. Its sinister brilliance lit up fields and streets, walls and brushland, groves and rivers, even penetrating houses and caves, and for an instant of dubious splendor the comet took the shape of the Ancient Serpent.

The portents continued. A peasant woman dreamed that a cat with a human face was devouring her bowels and awoke to find the animal rooting lasciviously in her private parts. This was taken as a sign of the presence of the fiend, and as a forewarning of the Last Judgment. During Vespers, while the monks and nuns of San Lucas were singing the Magnificat, a Viking, bound hand and foot, was brought to the gates of the monastery, having been found outside the walls by sentinels. They accused him of spying and would have killed him, but the man, whose wits had obviously strayed, managed to say in a mixture of tongues that he had been abandoned by his companions along the northern coast, and in exchange for his freedom he would show the Leonese the way to reach Constantinople on horseback over frozen rivers and seas. The bailiff Diego Bamba arrived and declared that he would not execute the prisoner, he would only gouge out his eyes, cut off his tongue and leave him blinded and mute on the road to Córdoba. At that, the moon, which had been visible all day, turned red and changed shape.

"A she-wolf will gobble up the moon, and a surfeit of horrors will ensue," Spernicius brayed.

Four aged and infirm men, who had come to be healed and rejuvenated in the monastery of San Lucas, and twelve paupers armed with sticks immediately surrounded Spernicius.

After Vespers, clerics and knights, maidens and matrons scanned the sky in search of portents. Some discerned in a cloud, which obscured the horizon and turned fields and bodies red, two magenta vapors, which congealed into the bodies of wounded soldiers who fought among themselves. At the height of their wrath, they vanished.

The nuns of San Lucas asserted that the cloud was raining blood and prophesied wars with the Saracen caliphs and among the Christian kings.

"The devil's witches are causing this eclipse," exclaimed one of them.

"Witches can't cause eclipses; the moon brings about this phenomenon," Froila replied.

"Then I will give milk to my child," another nun muttered, cradling a suckling pig in her arms.

The knights divided the combatants in the sky into Christians and Saracens, angels and devils, kings and caliphs, Alfonso de León and Abd Allah of Córdoba. They were convinced that the armies of good and evil were disputing the heights, and they believed that the stars fought among themselves like warriors on earth.

A pilgrim from Santiago glimpsed shreds of celestial vestments stained with the blood of martyrs in the southern region of the sky, and two clerics from San Salvador saw a fiery cross. García Cabezón swore he had seen the last Emperor of the World leading the people of God across the sky toward nowhere.

Their strength regained, Abbot Andrés and brother Martín Meñique imagined that terrible faces were striving to grow larger and more defined, so as to invade the entire firmament. A *muladi* from Córdoba, who was staying the night in the monastery of San Lucas, recognized the face of Satan, or the armed figure of al Mansur, in the reddish clouds at twilight. Nuns from San Lucas and Santiago conjured up a vision of angels and saints and the Virgin Mary decked in lights and stars. More than any other apparition, she dominated the heavens at the end of the world. Abruptly, in the middle of the street, the sisters knelt and prayed to her image hovering above the walls.

"That's how female saints reach paradise . . . on their knees," Froila remarked to Abbot Andrés.

"What the nuns take for stars and lights are mothers weeping at the burial of children who died of the burning disease," García Cabezón said to Froila.

"It is not a burial of children, it is a rabble of the ragged and starving. Their feet are wrapped in rags against the cold," Martín Meñique observed.

"Saint Eulogius's staff glows in the sky between sunset and sunrise. This prodigy will cease during the one thousandth year of the Incarnation of the Lord," explained the *muladi,* whose ears had been slit before he escaped from Córdoba.

"Satan will be unchained once the thousand years are over," a French monk about twenty years old predicted, mixing Latin with Romance. "He will plow through the great forest, cutting down trees and poisoning the waters. To protect himself against famine, man will sow fields of wheat."

"Today the monks of San Lucas crossed the river Bernesga without wetting their tunics or their shoes," García Cabezón reported.

"Today the Emperor of the World, Otto the Third, has disinterred the body of Charlemagne, which was seated in the crypt of the golden basilica of Santa María in a perfect state of preservation," said Jonás ibn Gabirol. "When the cadaver was put on public view, a hulking man named Adalbert tried on the king's gold crown, to take its measure, but it engulfed his head; he compared his leg to the monarch's and found his own narrower and smaller."

"If history is sacred, a man's life is a theophany," said the Frenchman, who years ago had survived the epidemic of burning sickness.

"That figure there is the Celestial Dragon," Sancho Saborejo ventured to say, although no one paid him any heed.

"The order of the seasons and the laws that have hitherto governed the world have changed; they have fallen into eternal chaos, and the end of the human race is feared," the young monk revealed.

"Tell me your name," I asked him.

"Rodulfus Glaber," he said and disappeared into the crowd.

Not far away, many people had gathered to dance and sing in a last celebration of life. The Christians with their crosses, the Moors with games of skill, the Jews with crwths and viols, each in his own tongue and his own fashion praised the Messiah, offered prayers to the All-Powerful Lord.

In a procession full of sadness and lamentation, they acknowledged the joy of having lived, and Jewish women sang alongside Moorish women. At their head marched Tubal the Jew, wrapped in a traveling cloak, his *vihuela* in its case dangling from the saddletree of a skinny jennet, which followed him docilely.

The drummer Mahoma Chacho led the group of rebec and flute players, trumpeters, leaping Moors and Christian drummers. Lagging behind came Ismael Cordobés and his wife, Crepúsculo. The dwarf Vitiza Rodríguez carried the chair that King Alfonso V had given him when he married the widow of Count Ramiro Cuervo, who was executed by Don Vermudo the Gouty.

"Matrons and maidens, cavaliers and clerics, squires and servants, wretches and woebegones make up the audience that will hear and witness what I have to say," boasted Vitiza Rodríguez.

"Though we are on the eve of the end of time, the minstrels are still singing and dancing for wages and wear, to be bedded and fed," said Oro María.

"In this assembly there are minstrels who walk the roads bleating the omens of the end of the world. But that blind minstrel, who knows the feats of old, crosses the Spains on a single ballad," Sancho Saborejo remarked to me. "Amid their song and dance, all of them are imploring God's forgiveness for their sins, in the hope of surviving Doomsday and witnessing the dawning of the new millennium."

The sun darkened, a cloud covered the sky, and people, houses and objects were tinged with a saffron light. Then a furious hailstorm broke out, whose like had never been seen before, and the horse belonging to the abbess of San Lucas, which was tethered in the orchard, chewed through its rope and galloped toward the plains.

Night fell. A prodigious silence overwhelmed the world. In San Lucas a cadaverous priest, alone in the church, celebrated an office for the dead. Disguised as a pilgrim, Spernicius presented himself to the nuns at the monastery, insisting that they were obliged to receive him as if he were Lord Christ himself. Fulberto, the monk who had gone mad that morning, chased him away with a stick.

A dwarf dressed in black rags, who was not Rodríguez, came down an avenue in León. Burdened with his own weight and time's, he thrust himself forward as he walked. Despite the hot breath he exhaled through his protruding lips, he appeared to be dying of cold. The sack he carried was full of children's corpses, or gold pieces, for it clinked and clattered like bones or coins. He waggled his bawdy body now like a man, now like a woman, trying to seduce us with his flesh.

He had already shown himself once today, at daybreak, wreathed in the veils and mists of dawn. I had heard him in the latrines of the monastery of San Juan, bawling in Romance and in Arabic, ''In Calatañazor, Almanzor will lose his tambor.'' Armed with my silver sword, I chased him along the monastery corridor until he ducked into his own night.

''We can but recognize the hand of God in all the prodigies, all the portents, all the calamities, and even in the apparitions of the devil,'' said Abbot Andrés. ''By showing us comets and monsters, scourging us with famines and plagues, wars and deaths, our Lord acquaints us with his wrath. We must make a virtue of fear, a penitence of the earth's disarray.''

It was almost midnight when Urraca the Shadow appeared outside Santa María de Regla. Her eyes wild, she began to reel off the deaths that had occurred lately.

''Vermudo the Gouty died, García Sánchez the Trembler died, Speciosa died, the sultana mother Subh died, Sabaricus and Teodaz died. Everyone dies,'' she concluded, ''with property and without property, with solidi and without solidi, with crosses and without crosses, naked or clothed, they perish. The earth dies, the stones die, the trees die, even the light dies.''

"The comet's tail has become more dreadful in the bluish dawn. Its baneful blaze fills the depths of darkness, and thus it will remain until cockcrow," said García Cabezón to Froila, who could not stop looking at him.

"It is a new star that God has placed in the firmament," Martín Meñique surmised.

"It is the eye of Saint James dilating in space," said Froila.

"Only God can know that!" Abbot Andrés exclaimed.

"A mysterious fire is devouring the monastery of San Lucas," Spernicius, limping, came to tell us.

"Because it was built on the ashes of faith, its entire edifice is collapsing," said the shabby man.

"That's one of Isidoro's followers. I recognize him by his flaking teeth and his bloodshot eyes," Diego Bamba cried out, pursuing him.

"It had to be the day that Jonás brought the relics of Saint John the Seer to León, the day that he was received with great honor and rejoicing by King Alfonso and all the nobles of the land, the day they enthroned the prophet of the Apocalypse next to our Glorious Mother in the monastery of San Juan, that so many dire things happened," Sampiro wailed.

"Look, they caught the butcher who was digging up children's corpses in the cemetery of San Lucas to sell them as pork. See, they're taking him to prison," said Spernicius. "It was I who denounced him."

"Now you shall see, Lord, the old and the young issuing from their houses, virgins and matrons rending their clothes and their hair with hands and knives, forsaking everything they possess," Urraca the Shadow crooned. "And you shall see many who have escaped from the jails, and the wretched captives of the Moors wearing the pieces of iron with which they were enchained. But as the prophet said, 'In vain the cleaner cleansed, for the stain and urine did not come out.' "

"And you will see, madam, assembling in this town, people from diverse provinces and kingdoms, speaking foreign tongues, wearing garments of all shapes and sorts, trading in every goods imaginable, and knowledgeable in many trades and arts," I replied.

The candlelight revealed a cat with a human face watching me from atop one of Santa María de Regla's ruined walls. When it saw that I returned its gaze, it glared defiantly into my eyes. Sancho Saborejo threw a stone at it, but it didn't budge.

"That's the devil's cat," Froila affirmed. "Since al-Mansur destroyed León, it appears there every night. It's best not to look at it. At dawn it will vanish."

VISION XXV

The more they heard about the terrors of the end of time, the more people feared their own deaths.

"The less we feel the end of the world, the better," Froila said to Fronilde, a Leonese maiden.

"The more estranged we are from our own death, the better it will be, for then universal death will not grieve us," said Fronilde to Froila.

From the rooms of the bishop's inn and in other houses where Christian men and women from Castile and al-Andalus and lands even more distant were lodged, issued moans and panting of couples indulging in corporeal pleasures. And old men and maidens, beldams and boys, tender girls and strapping fellows grappled anxiously beneath the city walls and among the riverbank poplars.

Confronted with the omens of the high assize, people were even less willing to abstain from gluttony and lust. The threat of damnation and eternal fire did not intimidate them; they burned with another, more urgent fire, the fire of desires never satisfied in their lifetimes.

After all, Antichrist already walked the earth, judging the quick and the dead, sending the righteous to hell, and nothing had happened. God's creatures, Isidoro had said, would not survive Antichrist's pursuit or his rule. But for many the problem lay in finding tasty dishes and bodies in which to lose themselves, as these forms of perdition were reserved for the chosen few.

For several nights in a row, Jimena came to visit me in the scriptorium. She fondled me, and I fornicated with her, as if to live and die in her midst had become natural for both of us. As if I could have saved myself from physical and spiritual death by taking refuge inside her and, immersed in her alien darkness, have hidden from my worst enemy, I myself, my brother.

The more my desire was satisfied, the more I wanted to become one with Jimena, to exist in her. No matter that she carried in her belly the body of my child, the Child of God, heralded by the angels in heaven.

That Sunday toward midnight I covered her face with a death's-head mask I had painted on parchment. With a desperation very like the final agony, I held her body beneath my body. On the brink of the supreme delight, I breathed such a deep sigh onto her sealed lips that I felt that I was dying inside her.

"Let us not assign a date to darkness," Urraca the Shadow cautioned me later, "for death has no calendars. There are many visionaries, just as there are charlatans who claim God has revealed to them the imminence of the Day of Wrath. No one knows when it is, not even the Son. Dates for the end of the world have been set many times, but we have awoken easy in mind, and the dates have passed. When it happens, we won't have time to think that the world is coming to an end around us, because we will have come to an end as well."

"This fear, which preceded the year 1000 and will persist after it, is fear of life, fear of history, fear of death, fear of Satan, fear of ourselves, fear of everything," Jonás ibn Gabirol said to me.

Gradually the sky was suffused with blue, and the earth brightened. The mountains revealed their rugged silhouettes, the trees their contours, the city its walls and towers. Sister Froila appeared on the road holding García Cabezón by the hand, no one knowing where they had spent the night but everyone knowing they had spent it together.

Today, Monday, could be the last day of the world. Perhaps tomorrow, Tuesday, the Virgin without sin would appear in the firmament. And perhaps the day after tomorrow, the radiant dawn of the new millennium would shine over the world. Each day the miracle we had never seen could happen, the miracle we hoped would happen on earth each day during the last thousand years. As I stood there, García Cabezón ordered the ram's horn blown so that knights, clerics, cotters and all others who wanted to do battle with the emissary of the Evil One might come to join us.

"Friends, believe that before the year passes, you will receive considerable help from Saint James the Apostle, believe that in the battle of the millennium we will not be vanquished," he proclaimed, with Froila at his side.

VISION XXVI

I sidoro, the Messiah of the Poor, was imprisoned and chained in a tower, his feet cramped into heavy irons and his legs restrained by shackles. The door of the cell was barred with a thick plank with a millstone against it, so that no one could remove it. Four armed knights stood guard, with instructions to kill anyone who approached who did not work in the prison. The door of the tower was secured with an iron bar that fit into holes in the wall. To it was affixed an iron hasp with an enormous padlock. Outside the jail three ferocious dogs followed the movements of any suspicious-looking people.

At the stillest hour of night, when the dreamy strands linking yesterday and tomorrow are still unsevered, Isidoro was sleeping his sleep of stones and chains.

"What are you doing there, you wretch, you living corpse?" a figure wrapped in a black cloak suddenly asked him.

"What else can I do except cry over my captivity, for my enemies weary me with shadows and torment me with thirst and hunger. The fetters chafe my feet terribly," Isidoro replied.

"Why not run away?" the presence asked. "You can withdraw from yourself whenever you wish."

"My only escape is into death, inasmuch as I am lying here with my legs trapped in irons, and I cannot straighten out my body. My tormentors have weighed down my fingers; I can't extract them from the pincers without breaking them. And supposing I did get loose, the door, the millstone and the armed knights would thwart my escape. After that, the other door, which is bolted closed, and the barking dogs would block my passage," Isidoro answered.

"Don't be afraid to flee. If you only try, you'll succeed in slipping your body out of the irons; the ancient evil will aid you. Concentrate on thinking bad thoughts, and you'll free yourself from your prison. Once you're outside, take to the streets and make your way to my church and say that you're the Second Jesus who has come to redeem the wicked from having sinned by passing for righteous. Say the devil sends you, and preach these things."

Isidoro stood up and found himself on his feet, the chains having unloosed themselves from his limbs. He pushed at the door, shoving aside the millstone and the thick plank, and went out. He was right in front of the knights, but they took no notice of him, as though he were invisible.

The street door sprang open of its own accord, the iron bolt and the enormous padlock fell to the ground. The watchdogs, overcome by sleep, were snoring.

"Go into the world and don't be afraid of the knights or the hounds or the men who imprisoned you. Don't be afraid of your own fear, and know that there is no one on earth who can harm you except me."

With that, the scarlet figure who was guiding him went some distance away, but then returned and said to him, "I have spoken in the ancient language, made of lies, only for you, because you are lying itself. My name is Ahriman."

His heart churning, Isidoro hurried away from the jail, tiptoeing past armed knights and vigilant canines. Suddenly, behind him, the shackles and irons jangled as if they had been thrown from the top of the tower, the doors of the jail flapped, the knights began to stir, and the dogs barked.

At that moment, the monks from the monastery of San Salvador were on their way to celebrate Lauds. The sexton opened the door to let someone in, but this someone was so dark that no one imagined who it could be. This someone, having reached the altar, prostrated himself on the slab until the morning office was over. Then he vanished.

Meanwhile, Sacul lay in chains in a different prison. During the night, when the sky was serene and the frost severe, the false apostle had been dragged out of doors by his jailers, his legs fettered, his arms bound behind his back. His bare soles pressed against the biting ice of the bare earth.

The bailiff Diego Bamba tortured him by throwing cold water over his head until the water froze on his flesh. When he could stand no more, they led him to the fire, rubbed his hands and body, and took him outside again.

To mislead them, Sacul said, "As I am nearing death, I request that my body be carried to the church of Santa María de Regla. Once I am dead, I would have the night vigils kept, as is the custom. To that effect, I beg you to give me the cross that will be placed upon my deceased body, according to usage. Once that is done, lay it thus upon my chest, so I may squeeze it between my stiffening fingers."

They gave him the cross and, feigning madness, he grabbed it and ran off, wielding it as a weapon. He took it to where Isidoro was summoning him, all without a word.

Nauj and Noel were laid naked on beds of sharp shards in a pair of short, shallow caskets. Large stones were piled on top of the caskets, and crosses were put on the stones. Both false apostles were unable to move, stretch their legs or shift their bodies, and their chests were cramped. Day and night they were kept thus, without bread or water, although from time to time they were taken out to be hung by the genitals and thumbs, and forced to enjoy the tightening and loosening of the hempen and flaxen cords, until Isidoro came, undetected by all, to release them.

With red-hot pincers Socram's chipped and jagged teeth were wrenched from his jaws; not all at once, but one each day, so that when today's tooth was torn out his mouth would still be aching from yesterday's and the day before yesterday's.

"Abjure the devil, in whose power you believed. Abjure the devil, under whose power you fell." Diego Bamba belabored him.

"I will abjure before the holy water in the church of San Salvador. Lead me to it," Socram implored.

"Try to think how and in what way I may help you, for by my soul, I am willing to help you however I can," the bailiff said to him.

"Release me, and I will confess my horrible sins," Socram pleaded.

"Released you are, brother," Diego Bamba replied.

"May the devil reward you!" the toothless Socram cried, scrambling as fast as he could toward the city walls.

Around noon, Isidoro's disciples, who usually came to post themselves outside the jail to hear news of their messiah, found the doors wide open, and they shouted, "Long live King Isidoro the First." Before long they appeared at Bishop Froilán's house, whistling and yelling, carrying a doll on their backs, an image of the messiah. Unaware of everything, the bishop asked Sampiro and myself the reason for such an uproar.

Sampiro answered that, if his ears did not betray him, the noise issued from the tower where the heretic Isidoro was imprisoned. Don Froilán replied that he thought something peculiar was happening to the prisoners, although they should be chained and closely guarded in their cells.

At that, two messengers from Isidoro's faithful came to inform us that the mother of the Messiah of the Poor would be presented in the village as the Nigriv. Henceforward, she would be called Airam. Airam Aneladgam would be her repentant companion. The ceremony of consecration would take place that midnight before the ratla in the ruins of the hcruhc fo Yram.

"In this, our city, we shall make you our bishop so you may share the honor with Don Naliorf and live among us vilely, rejoicing over the corpses of our enemies," one of the messengers said to the bishop.

"If you accept our counsel, we can promise you concord and the affection of the Haissem," said another one, his eyes belying the hope they expressed.

"It is neither seemly nor sound for me to share the duties of the bishopric, removing the virtuous monks and giving to thieves and robbers that which belongs to God. You know all too well the nature and magnitude of the affronts Isidoro has visited upon the church of León, a church almost destroyed and reduced to dust by the Saracens. You know full well the iniquities and cruelties which Isidoro's coming occasioned, and though he is fugitive, he will be captured and punished by God's justice, which overlooks no one," Don Froilán answered angrily.

"Enough of these blasphemous arguments. Get out of here," I said in turn.

Bishop Froilán rose from his chair and ended the messengers' visit. Together we went to the church of Santa María de Regla, where before the assembled monks and faithful he pronounced the following sentence:

"Froilán, by the grace of God bishop of León, by election of the holy Church of Rome, to Isidoro and his disciples, major and minor: If they choose to obey, health! I admonish you to present yourselves immediately before the seat of justice of León and to submit to our judgment. Should you delay because you do not wish to obey our admonishments, from this day forward you shall be subject to excommunication, the which we have already determined with all the bishops and synods of León. No Christian may have intercourse or participate with you, either in speaking, eating, drinking or prayer, and no one may buy any goods from you or sell to you, because you are subject to excommunication for that you did blaspheme the sanctuary of the living God and subjected it to mortal man. And even your clerics, the which, disdaining our command, should presume to celebrate masses, are subjected by us to excommunication and accursedness until you and said clerics duly and worthily give satisfaction to God and to the martyrs of Jesus Christ and to us. Should you be obedient in the aforesaid, you will benefit by it and achieve salvation."

It is unpleasant and unnecessary to record all the insults to our Lord Jesus Christ and all the scurrilities aimed at the Virgin Mary that flew from their loathsome lips no sooner had the sentence been read.

Meanwhile, Isidoro had fled naked down the roads of León. Catching up with him, Socram furnished him with clothes and a mount he had stolen. Sacul gave him the sustenance he hungrily sought, which he had snatched away from peasants who were about to eat it themselves. He thrust into Isidoro's hand the cross he had carried away with him, and together they smeared it with black until the painted body of Lord Christ disappeared. Noel and Nauj brought him weapons.

But Isidoro dared not stop anywhere to sleep or eat. Panting like a mad dog, he roamed hither and thither without repose. Finally, he reached San Juan de Lairones, where the clemency of evil protected him, providing him with the persons necessary to ensure his safety.

A former monk from Toledo by the name of Gaufredo, who had apostasized, was living there. He gave them all lodging, revealing to them the great antipathy and wrath he felt on their behalf toward King Alfonso and Bishop Froilán, whom he publicly and privately abhorred.

Isidoro replied that, because of their good works, something bad was going to happen to Alfonso and Froilán, and that his enemies in the kingdom of León would lose their souls in the pursuit of truth. "Falsehoods and deceit ripple off our tongue, and thus shall we win over the peasants and lesser folk," he concluded.

"Had we been innocent of the transgressions they impute to us, it would have been fair to clap us into jail, but, being guilty, we find that injustice has been fairly done," Socram opined.

"Despondency and dread tired us during the brief span of our torment, and so much hunger famished us," Noel and Nauj complained. "However, divine pitilessness was a consolation to us, and all the goodly wicked condoled with our despair and cursed the friars for our imprisonment, although this neither afforded nor gave us help. And it fretted us that if we remained there overlong, with each day our ruthlessness and perversity would dwindle, and it could come to pass that we would pardon, without death or damage, those guilty of our tribulation. But our protector did not allow us to find peace, and so here we are with you, ready to return to the century that will be fatal to us."

"Isidoro the First, unreceive your unwords with unjoy," Sacul interrupted them.

"You will carry to the king of León the following letter sealed with the seal of the yloh haissem," Nauj bade Noel.

"It must read thusly," Socram dictated: ' "Isidoro the First, messiah of the messiahs of Ahriman, to the unbeloved children of Niac, sickness and apostolic accursedness . . . You and your vassals, who are now in the disfavor and disprotection of the Millenary King, must most loyally place yourselves at the service of his person; and inasmuch as we have heard that you raised your head high against the prophet and his disciples, stealing and destroying their material and spiritual goods, and you have violated the ancient laws and traditions of the year 1000, offering us all manner of insults, which are difficult for us to overlook, we command that you and your vassals make restitution of all that rightly belongs and does not belong to my church, and of lands and vineyards and orchards which had been mine and others'. Furthermore, you must discard and burn in the fire the new laws and practices you have made. And once all dominion has been taken away and removed from you, you shall be subject to my apostles as their vassals and must be content to live according to the laws and practices that shall be established in the time of Isidoro the First. Otherwise, you will incur the rage, indignation and vengeance of my divine wickedness. Signed by your Lord, Isidoro the First.' "

"You will deliver this letter to the king himself, who upon receiving it must swear on this book, in which the four gospels of Isidoro the First will afterward be written—to wit, the Third Testament of our faith," Nauj told Noel. "And once the king has read the letter, I order that it be recited in the churches and read aloud in the squares."

"From this day hence, we no longer wish to be subjects of the king or queen, or of any other mortal. We wish to live under the protection of Abd Allah of Córdoba, the Black Rider, and under his dominion, so as to evade the sentence of excommunication which, I perceive, Bishop Froilán has made public throughout the kingdom of León," Isidoro declared.

After Noel's departure, Gaufredo set four guards to watch the road and lay down with his wife, bedding her with considerable moaning and noise, as though they were alone in the inn.

"My lord Ahriman appeared to me this morning and said to me: 'Isidoro, make ready all that is necessary and take the road to Rome that pleases and suits you, for upon the death of Gerbert, wrongly called Sylvester II, you will be pope of the year 1000. From the unholy city you will rule the church of the devil during the next millennium. Abd Allah of Córdoba, the Black Rider, will be Emperor of the World instead of Otto III," Isidoro announced, gazing toward where he believed the pontifical city was.

"Before midwinter we shall cross over the Pyrenees, and once past the great mountains, we shall reach Rome,'' said Airam, her eyes clouded with dreams of magnificence. Socram and Sacul then prostrated themselves to kiss the feet of the future holy father.

"When they have heard about the destruction to be wreaked on earth by the Saracens under command of Abd Allah of Córdoba, the Black Rider, and the manner in which the king and the bishop have undone this ill-starred kingdom, the abbesses and sisters will curse their virginity and maidenhood and come flocking to implore the fornicators to lie with them on the altars of their churches and on their spindly-legged beds,'' said Airam Aneladgam.

"We shall remain in León to turn the young servants and peasants, tanners and blacksmiths, makers of shields and painters of chairs, wood-choppers in the forests, and those who toil at their trades in cellars against their lords and betters, against the abbots and churchwardens. I will call on all of them to take up bows and arrows, knives and lances, and go smash and set fire to the palaces of kings, the houses of knights, the churches of bishops, the monasteries and estates of abbots. Our disloyal troops will steal the fruits from the trees, the shoots from the vines, hacking, cutting down and sullying the bounty of the earth before it reaches ripeness, so that there will be hunger and death throughout these kingdoms,'' Socram gloated.

"And let our men go into the marketplaces and towns proclaiming our rebellion,'' Sacul added.

"Should anyone reprehend the outrages we, the principal evildoers, commit, let him be damned,'' Socram continued.

"Should anyone utter a word in condemnation of these things, we will chop off his head and smash it on the stones,'' Socram warned.

"We will not allow the gluttonous abbots and monks to eat and drink as long as the chosen of our lord Ahriman perish of hunger,'' Airam declared. "In truth, my tongue cannot express all the harm and hardships I wish on those people.''

"With my lord, I shall follow the twisted roads that will lead him to Rome,'' Airam Aneladgam affirmed. "I shall cast to the ground the caskets containing the relics of the dark saints, and rummaging through their bones and limbs I shall find gold and silver amid their skeletons. The mules will not turn back once they take the first step toward the desecration of the pontiff. The pontiff Gerbert, not Saint Isidoro.''

"The city of your coronation is close by and groveling at your feet, my son, for the emperor Otto and the pope are already embarked on the path of mortal flesh,'' Airam said to Isidoro.

"First we must make a great leap, like lions bounding from a cave, and then, one by one, we will ravage the towns with iron and blood, hunger and death, robbing them of all substance. Whatever we cannot carry away we shall throw into the fire, so no one can make use of it. We will take from them bread, wine, beasts and cattle, and all the fruits and herbs nourishing to man,'' said Sacul, warming as he spoke.

"Oh, execrable, swindling, sullied, shameful, sanctimonious rogues, slanderous and notorious forswearers, it behooves you to know that, having made an enemy of the messiah Isidoro the First, once you are defeated by him, you will depart this life blasted and bewildered. But if you follow my advice and throw yourselves most humbly at my feet, begging my pardon for all the past, present and future wrongs you have done me, peradventure I shall have mercy on you and permit you to enter the kingdom of my heavens,'' Isidoro thundered at an invisible throng.

"We have no wish to contend with you, for you have given evidence of sufficient strength on your messianic road, and ample injustice has been done you here in León. We need no displays of your divine might to know that you are a god,'' said Gaufredo's wife.

The words were still in her mouth when Diego Bamba, who had come in through the back door, lunged at Isidoro's legs, grabbed him around the knees and toppled him. A stout peasant who accompanied him threw blankets over Isidoro's face, drubbed him and kicked him. Then he lay down on his chest so that the messiah was unable to move.

The bailiff, Diego Bamba, afraid that Isidoro would break away from their clutches, crawled over him, biting him and yanking out his hair.

"Keep hold of him even if he dies of it,'' he exhorted his accomplice.

The stout peasant tried to pacify the messiah by smacking him repeatedly with the hilt of a dagger until he nearly drove his soul out through his jaws.

Meanwhile, a number of horsemen crowded into the house and pounced upon Noel, who had just returned, and upon Socram, Sacul and Nauj, Airam, Airam Aneladgam, Gaufredo, his lady and the guards, using their weapons and bodies to immobilize them. A pack of dogs, which appeared out of nowhere, nipped at the fugitives' arms and legs. Before they left, the horsemen put ropes, chains and shackles on each of Isidoro's followers, and youths and dogs stood guard over the house, for Diego Bamba feared the disciples still lurking in the vicinity.

"Death to the devil's spawn, death!" the stout peasant exclaimed. "Today you shall be hanged for a thief, blasphemer and traitor."

"Don't you dare touch the found messiah, or abbesses and nuns, bailiffs and monks, the enemies of my person, will lose their heads," Socram screeched, wriggling out of the grasp of a horseman in whose hands he left his clothing. To make a speedier escape, he tumbled a man off his horse, seized his lance and furrowed his flesh with it from head to toe. Then, naked and wounded, he fled on the man's steed, loudly shouting words backward.

"Give us back our messiah and pope and then we'll go," Sacul cried as Diego Bamba and the peasants pushed and prodded his body.

"Te igitur," said Isidoro, on his feet, attempting to recover his lost dignity, anticipating his own demise in the others' imminent deaths.

"After your execution, you will leave us your ill-gotten riches and earthly misteachings; you who have instilled in us the value of discord will not die in peace, that is your fate," Airam Aneladgam reassured him.

The Christian horsemen dragged away Isidoro, who clung to the ground, becoming heavier by the moment. Finally, they splashed holy water on his face and chest to make him let go of the clods of earth onto which he had fastened.

After night fell, Bishop Froilán's emissaries traveled as far as they were able, with the prisoners firmly chained and guarded, fearful that the disciples would attack them on the way, or that once in León they would try to free all the captives from jail.

"Reward, my lord, give me a reward, for God is on our side," cried Diego Bamba as he burst into the bishop's house full of the good tidings.

Once Don Froilán had been informed of the capture, he ordered his people to make a puppet resembling Isidoro from straw and rags, to be propped in a window of one of the city towers, to fool his followers into believing that he was free and unharmed.

"Not a monk was wounded, not a peasant killed, not a virgin debauched, not a female dishonored; that sewer of an Isidoro was flushed out, that latrine of an Airam was emptied, and that strumpet called Airam Aneladgam was sprinkled with holy water," Diego Bamba reported to the king.

"We found four human heads, peeling and putrefied, buried beneath the manger in Gaufredo's house," the stout peasant revealed.

"Doubtless the wretches' clamoring and the sinners' blasphemies reached the ears of the most high," Bishop Froilán said.

The next day, before sunup, Isidoro the First's time came: The silver sword reserved for the devil's spawn sliced him in half.

Such was the downfall and death of this so-called Christ.

As he died excommunicate, the bishop forbade burying his mortal remains in the cemetery of the monastery of San Juan or in any other graveyard attached to a monastery in León. His carcass was tossed onto the dunghill for the beasts of the field to gorge on. The celestial letter certifying him as the son of God was burned.

Noel and Nauj were condemned to the stake, to which they came laughing, claiming that, as they were saints, the flames would not harm them. But the fire turned them into human torches, into hot bones and ashes.

Two days later, Socram, mistakenly believing that no one would look for him in the same place where he had been found once before, was ambushed by King Alfonso's knights in Gaufredo's house in San Juan de Lairones. As they were about to seize him, he escaped through a window, leaving behind his lance, apparel and belongings. He crawled away on all fours over the rooftops until he slipped, fell and was captured. The bishop bade Diego Bamba to gouge out his eyes and send him blind to roam the earth deprived of the light shared by all.

"Behold, you who are beholding, know, you who would know, that I have been cast out of this city without eyes and without any of the things I owned and possessed, save these two coins which I take with me," Socram cried for all to hear as he was expelled from the city through the Count's Gate.

"Thus may the enemies of the messiah perish and die!" Sacul yelled.

On the verge of being executed, he broke free and flung himself into a well so deep that no one heard him strike the bottom at the end of his fall.

Two accounts are given of Airam and Airam Aneladgam: One, that when they went to fetch them to take them to the gallows, they had disappeared from the jail, rescued by the fiend; the other, that they were confined to cells in the monastery of Santiago, where the abbess Sinduara and the sisters strove in vain to save their souls until at the end of a year both had withered into living skeletons.

The day after the death of Isidoro's body, several of his most violent followers were arrested, put to torture and then quartered after confessing to countless crimes, sacrileges and blasphemies, including the repeated invocation of the unintelligible name of a god who would come to save them from their tribulations, and of having tried to use the divine powers granted them by the Messiah of the Poor.

Six faithful of low estate each had a hand and foot amputated to advertise their infamy. Branded in this fashion, they dispersed among the villages, hurling insults and threats against the king, the bishop, the stout peasant and Diego Bamba, until, vexed by hunger and poverty, they came to beg mercy from Froilán II, acknowledging that they had done wrong in letting themselves be duped by a son of the devil.

Upon learning of Isidoro the First's death, other fools fanned out over the land and became murderers and highwaymen. Until their last breath, they clung to their belief in the divinity of the false messiah. Very few returned to the true faith.

"Lord Christ will not forgive us if we allow these affronts he has endured in his bodily and spiritual image to pass in silence," I remarked to García Cabezón.

"Let us pray to Lord Christ to deliver us henceforth from these diabolical creatures and to succor our Church in this time of untallied dangers and evils," the bishop exhorted the faithful.

"Let us give thanks to God that the ancient error did not flourish, that the image of Jesus did not suffer grievous harm, and that the honor of his Glorious Mother was stained only for a single season," Urraca the Shadow added. "Now, let us ready ourselves for the final battle."

VISION XXVII

At the first flush of dawn the cocks awoke, and the Moors played their drums, horns and trumpets while they swarmed over plains and hills, confident that soon they would have us in their grasp. Seated on his armored horse, wearing a coat of mail and a helmet turbaned with a red cloth, al-Mansur observed the movements of Christians and Moors from a hilltop. Perched on his right arm was a raven, whose black plumage shimmered in the sunlight. He was surrounded by armed princes and by Berber, Leonese, Castilian and Navarrese soldiers. Behind them ranged the pitched tents and the grazing horses.

When dawn had spread, the valley was filled with Christian warriors mounted without stirrups on lean horses, wearing leather tunics and small bucklers on their arms. They held their spears erect, broadswords at the ready. Helmeted, their hoods were painted with signs.

On a knoll, in the shade of a tree, the child king Don Alfonso was preparing to witness the battle. By his side, the queen, Doña Elvira, mounted on a sturdily saddled mule, directed the guards and clerics to search the surroundings with vigilant eyes. Sampiro, the royal notary and priest, examined me unblinkingly, while the King's armor-bearer displayed the royal insignia, which had been blessed.

Bishop Froilán made his appearance armed, not with the gold Visigothic cross or the pastoral crozier, but with sword, spear and shield. Abbot Andrés was also armed, but with Saint Romuald's treatise *On the Battle Against Demons*. The monks from the monastery of San Lucas carried relics: Saint Genadio's bones, three hairs from Saint Eulogius's beard, a link from Saint Peter's chain, a thread from Lord Christ's shroud. The peasant Spernicius, who was with them, brought the nearly entire skeleton—a foot and a hand were missing—of Saint Fósforo, in the belief that the bigger the relic, the greater its power and the more protection it afforded against death. Spernicius claimed that, if night overtook the struggle, Saint Fósforo's body would glow in the dark and frighten off the Saracens, those same Saracens who upon their death would be transmogrified into demons, as Sampiro was wont to say.

Since early morning, other warriors had tucked relics beneath their clothing and armor, convinced that these miraculous souvenirs could protect them from wounds and death. The renegade Christians scoffed at them, saying the bones and hair came from mules and pigs, not saints. Martín Meñique tried to comfort the most frightened; he told them that it didn't matter if they were killed, because the army of the dead was more powerful than the army of the living, because all the generations of humans who had ever been in the world were enrolled in its ranks, and the more deaths we suffered, the more numerous the spectral army would be.

I espied Jimena standing a few steps from the child king, smiling at me. Clothed in light, she had a sun in her belly, the moon beneath her feet. All was ready inside her for the birth of my daughter.

Abd Allah, the Black Rider, captain of our enemies, appeared. His coat of double mail was known as "the one that fends off death." Close-fitting and supple, it sheathed his entire body, stopping short of the ground. An iron clasp closed the opening at the neck. It had a breastplate and a back plate, and the rings were linked two by two. No sword could pierce it.

The hooves of his mare, Black Dawn, struck sparks from the stones.

Almarada rode alongside Abd Allah, pale, wrathful, black-clad, her thick hair rising in snakes. She was riding a white horse, fierce and swift. Two traitorous eunuchs mounted on bony-eyed colts watched over her. Each carried a shield, round or oval; each buckler was made of donkey or cowhide. Both were left-handed and bore a spear of great size, a curved bow and a quiver full of arrows. Bartolomea Rodríguez peered from behind the eunuchs.

Moors from the borders and foreign mercenaries guarded Abd Allah. Five perfidious creatures rode black demons panting with impatience to join in the battle. The creatures had human faces, hair as long as a woman's, and bristly legs protected by pleated greaves tied on with sturdy laces. A metallic casque concealed half their faces, while a nosepiece left exposed their doglike teeth. They made no effort to hide the mark of Antichrist on their foreheads, or the wings sprouting from their backs, or their scorpion's tails. For ornament and for protection, they wore pointed hoods and iron pectorals.

"These are the riders of the Apocalypse; when they attack a man, they puncture his breast with their tail. The man turns black from the poison," said Jonás ibn Gabirol, standing near me with neither horse nor weapon. He was staring into nowhere, at no one, at the vague spot, the exact spot between the two armies, where death, which has no cause, no religion and no language, was waiting for us.

"Don't be afraid, Alfonso de León," Doña Urraca encouraged me, crossing herself. She rode up and down on a mettlesome chestnut, looking handsome in her blue gown. She did not intend to fight; she would follow the particulars of the battle from our camp, and she would invoke the saints and the Glorious Virgin to beg their intervention in our favor.

Sancho Saborejo sat on a skinny roan with a high back and slender hindquarters, a skittish nag with uneven hooves and one ear longer than the other. On this beauty, he felt very much the fighter.

Doña Miguel was going into battle on a quadruped with a breast so bulging it was all that could be seen of it from its flanks. Its hooves were scaly, and it lacked a testicle. When it walked its hocks chafed against each other; its eyes were bloodshot, and at night it stumbled. In addition to being vicious, it was balky and a biter.

García Cabezón, armed to the teeth, pulled on the reins of a sweating, potbellied mare.

"Ward off the spears," I told my white horse, bow slung over my back, crown askew on my head. "If you are not wounded, I will grant you salvation, and if you wish it, I will make you human in the next life."

"Mahomet!" screamed the Saracens, striking fear into our unseasoned men. The horns and trumpets blared, and almost at once the foot soldiers and archers entered our camp, darkening the sky with arrows and causing not only a stampede among the simple peasants, but a great loss of life as well.

"Saint James!" the Christians cried, crossing themselves and invoking the names of Jesus and Mary. One after another, they took up their shields, lowered their lances, bent their heads, whipped their horses and made the ground quake.

Saracens and Christians broke through the opposing ranks, fell upon each other savagely, hypnotized each other with swords and spears, downed each other from ambush, were dragged by horses and mules. The two armies took turns facing the sun, as they had agreed.

Yelling mightily, the Saracens attacked unexpectedly. They avoided frontal encounters, pretended to fall back and charged anew on the flanks and from behind. They cut the harnesses and reins from the horses, they noted where the arrows landed, and they knew precisely when to use sword and spear, when to turn tail and flee. Everywhere their cavalry prevailed.

The Black Rider galloped imperturbably in search of his first victim. His mail coif concealed his head and face, his veiled figure gleamed like amber in the rising sun. Motionless, Almarada watched him set off, awaiting her own moment to enter the fray. The depraved eunuchs, advancing and retreating, remained in front of her. The Black Rider carried a peasant from San Juan de Lairones hooked on his spear, as if the man were running backward, until he left him dead in his tracks.

I commended myself to God and charged on horseback, assailing, attacking Abd Allah's warriors, cleaving them asunder, cutting through their cuirasses. The slashing sword grew heavier in my hand as I dispatched more Moors to hell. Once they were dead, my white horse trampled them. I stabbed my lance into a Moor midway between his breasts; his hauberk and padded tunic gave way. I wounded another so severely in the face that I sheared off the nosepiece from his helmet and half his nostrils. He turned away, and I thrust through the lining of his knotted quilted tunic and into his flesh. A shield broken off at the handle lay at his feet.

And there was yet another, who rode his horse haughtily. I dented his shield, I split open his helmet, and I plunged my lance into his neck. His iron skullcap fell to the ground. Still in the saddle, the Moor began wiping the blood from his eyes and face with his sleeve. Nothing could withstand the blows of my slashing sword. I slit open the fastenings on his back, lopped off his arm, leather strap and all, and beheaded him. Blood streamed down the broad blade of my sword and splashed beneath my elbow. When he lost his head, his hair remained behind, caught in the leather straps and rings.

The Black Rider never let me out of his sight. Unable to draw near each other, we nevertheless strove to do so, for we knew that the outcome of the war depended on our encounter. He hewed his way through our troops, whipping his shield to right and left with amazing speed, the outside always toward his adversary. And when his shield was struck by sword or spear, the fissure sealed immediately, leaving no trace at all. With a sudden movement, he lifted off his iron helm and challenged me with the sight of his naked neck. His head was vulnerable, and his long black hair streamed in the air.

Seeing him off guard, a Leonese petty nobleman sank his ax into the Black Rider's right shoulder. A white bone was shorn, and a gush of blood mantled the murderer's arm and hand. A head fell, gazing up from the ground with bewildered eyes at its own decapitated body.

For an instant I thought I saw my brother sitting headless on his horse. But he did not die. The head on the ground was not his; it belonged to some other Saracen. Abd Allah rode after the Leonese, snatched up the alien head with his left hand, bore down on his assailant, grabbed the ax from the bloody hand and cut off the man's head with his own weapon. The nobleman, dumbfounded by the attack, had not defended himself because he had seen the Black Rider with a cloven neck; he had killed him, but he wasn't dead.

The Black Rider caught up with other Christians and slew them one by one, exhibiting a perverse pleasure in piercing their loins with his lance, in spurring his black mare to kick them. Almarada rode with him on her white horse, brandishing a snake, which bit her enemies.

The beasts of the Apocalypse made deceptive gestures to our men, drawing them into battle. The real warriors surprised them from the rear, or from their flanks, and swiftly unhorsed them, striking the death blow with axes and lances. The Saracen tactic of charging suddenly with yells and howls and abruptly retreating was putting us to rout.

There was one horseman whose ruses had already occasioned many deaths. He was gesticulating deceitfully at Sancho Saborejo when I laid him low. The monster tumbled facedown into the mire, looked up at me with muddy features, and tried to slither away and to sting me with his scorpion's tail. I riveted him to the ground with my lance. Venom oozed from his mouth. From his gaping chest two breasts sprouted like gory flowers.

It began to drizzle. The rain wet my bloody hands. At times it blinded me, preventing me from seeing the Moors I was killing. I kept getting closer to my brother, who was ruthlessly lopping off the arms and legs of Christians. Panic-stricken, friends and enemies fled from us on their armored horses, galloping at breakneck speed toward a brook, seeking to hide their bodies from the weapons of Abd Allah of León and Alfonso de Córdoba. They knew not which was which, nor at whose hands they would find death.

A Leonese ventured into the stream, dismounted, removed his iron helmet, lowered it into the water, pulled it out full and began to drink in great gulps. Abd Allah arrived. Terrified, the Leonese wavered between assailing him with his sword or remounting his horse and escaping. Abd Allah let him doubt, and when the other man had decided in favor of flight, he landed a blow on his neck, taking off a slice of cheek. Thus wounded, the man attempted to mount, but his foot became entangled in straps hanging from the saddletree, and he fell into the water. Abd Allah smote him hard on the head with his sword, so that the tip pierced it and a bit of cloth, some hairs, and a piece of skin adhered to the blade. Swallowing mud, the Leonese tried to crawl away among the stones, but he took such a drubbing on his back that the water turned red.

On the opposite bank of the stream I overtook two Moors in flight. The first I whacked so hard on his iron helmet that helmet, hair and head flew off. The second raised his lance, but to no avail. I buried my sword in his right shoulder down to the hip. He slumped inside his coat of mail, the point of his lance dug into the earth, and the long cloth banner hanging from it crumpled to the ground. To finish him, I carved off a piece of thigh above his knee through the metal leggings intricately wrought from steel rings to look like breeches. The leather helmet he wore was so hard that I could only dent it, tearing the cloth lining and shattering the bones of his cranium.

Thus far the battle had lasted until noon. It continued to rain. From his hilltop, seated on a raised throne, al-Mansur observed the battle's progress and gave orders to the Black Knight and to other captains. The Christians' resistance and the death of so many Saracens caused him considerable irritation. He took off his gold helmet and sat down on the ground. Seeing him in a fury, the captains fought intrepidly and brought in another troop of cavalry. With savage yells, the troop charged the monks from the monastery of San Lucas and massacred them.

Dozens of Berbers on horseback herded dozens of Christians against the walls of León. The Bishop's Gate, opening to admit the pursued, admitted four of the pursuers as well. Luckily, several knights on the other side valiantly dispatched the intruders.

The gate swung shut, although tardily; the Berbers outside attempted to force it with pounding and shouts, clamorously calling on its defenders to unbolt under pain of being stabbed to death. The Leonese turned a deaf ear, but after a time they began to lose heart. A little girl approached the door held closed by so many hands.

"Should you lose the door, we will lose the apple of our eye, and if we lose the apple of our eye, we will lose our soul," she said to the men, and left on horseback through an opening in the arrow-studded gate.

With the Berbers in pursuit, the girl reached the battlefield. One Berber, swift as a courser, was already closing in on her near the stream when I put a halt to his career with my lance. The man from Barbary raised his shield to his chest and wheeled to attack me with his sword. Without a moment's hesitation, I plunged the blade so deep into his belly that my hand felt the bursting of his entrails, which spilled onto the ground. Before seeking another adversary, I made the Berber bite grass and mud; I found and cut off his scorpion's tail.

When he spotted me, another Berber attempted to pick up my horse in his arms, but I chopped off his hands. He tried to hide among the poplars, but García Cabezón speared him through the middle and nailed him to a tree. He was a rider of the Apocalypse in disguise.

Many infantrymen with iron bludgeons, pikes, lances and shields clambered down the left flank of the hill to fight near al-Mansur. Archers whose quivers bristled with arrows penetrated our ranks. Dressed as a warrior and mounted on horseback, the devil was beating the drum on their side.

In our camp small, round bucklers sprang up to rebuff the arrows. Sancho's had been fashioned in Santiago from the rib of a massive fish. Mine had a drawing on it of the earth and the sea. The links of the enemy's mail coifs gradually slackened and separated, and savaging swords punctured their necks, broke their helmets and severed their heads. At that point, Spernicius went over to the other side, after slitting from behind the throat of a young peasant.

A black dog leaped on me from the rear, trying to sink its fangs into my throat, its claws into my waist. Its sharp red tongue pierced my helmet and licked the nape of my neck. I thought I would perish under its attack, so powerful and heavy was this animal from hell.

Doña Miguel slew the black greyhound by stabbing it in the back. But Bartolomea Rodríguez sprang at her with her sword, hacking at her breasts until neither cuirass nor gorget were of any avail. Finally she reached her heart. Then, in an instant, the female dwarf was gone.

"Before cold bones carry me off, I want to confess to one among all my sins, to having deceived everybody by passing myself off as Jimena's mother," Doña Miguel said. "She is neither my daughter nor Abbot Andrés's. She issued from the fornication of a maiden nun named Froila, from the convent of Santiago, with a youth, now a deacon, whose name I shall pass over because he is nearby. Out of Christian charity the chaste abbot and I have borne the shame committed by others,'' she gasped, and breathed out her soul.

Abbot Andrés came to examine her. With Martín Meñique's help, he painfully and laboriously dragged her from the field, lest the horses trample her. He wanted to give her a pious burial.

Large, ungainly black birds cawed in the air. Mail-clad arms and helmeted heads lay on the ground. Lances raised, clutching splintered and rimless shields, their swords flashing, the men slew each other vigorously. The devil beat the drum among the dead.

The evil career of the two remaining riders of the Apocalypse was cut short. The deacon García Cabezón, not knowing whom he was confronting, eviscerated one and decapitated the other. Where they fell, the rain turned black and venomous.

García Cabezón's sword emerged scarlet. When he raised it up, blood slid over the hilt. The horsemen had charged him from the front and side. Believing himself a dead man, he pressed the buckler against his heart. A hood of mail protected his head, half his nose, his trimmed beard. His shoes were heavy with mud and weariness.

When they saw that the horsemen were dead, three of the al-Khurs mutely assailed García Cabezón, eager to carry off his head on a pike. Bellicose as ever, the deacon sliced the first through the waist, cleft the second from head to saddle, and lopped off the third's arm, still hugging a lance. Other mutes, hiding behind a stand of trees, sallied forth to fight, and thrown weapons rained down on him.

García Cabezón shielded his body with the buckler. The mutes battered it with their lances, feet and swords. He saw only their gem-studded helmets, heard only the drums coming toward him. As he fought back in the fading light, the mountains looked dark to him, the plains terrible, the streams lethal; he had no desire to drink the water poisoned by scorpions. The blood of others dripped off his elbow. The rain began to trickle down his face and hands. Twilight was coming on.

In another part of the field, Bishop Froilán and two monks were pursuing Almarada on her white horse. Bent on beheading peasants, the eunuchs had strayed from her side. The three ventured into the enemy camp but quickly turned back, arrows whistling above their heads, stones glancing off their horses' hooves, the bishop's liturgical vestments no proof against his fear.

Transfixed by the spectacle, the Black Rider was surprised and surrounded by Diego Bamba and García Cabezón, who cut off his right hand, which held his sword, before he could attack them.

When I saw this, I raised my lance and rode toward Abd Allah.

"I am the man," my brother exclaimed. "It is I you seek."

Diego Bamba and García Cabezón snipped off his mail coif with their knives, and his neck appeared, reddened and creased by the iron rings, his forehead inscribed by the links. A black stone at the crown of his helmet glittered in the setting sun. He was defenseless.

I stared into his eyes, searching for a lost brotherhood. He scrutinized me disdainfully, defiantly, with the hatred of an eternity. There was no remorse in his face, nor did he beg for mercy.

I slashed at him with my silver sword. The edge slit open his hauberk between his breasts and blood gushed out over his body. He tried to embrace me, to bathe me in his blood. He tried to grasp his sword with his left hand, and he cut his fingers. He attempted to drag me into death with him, pushing me toward the lance of a Saracen who was behind me.

He knelt, blasphemed the Holy Spirit and the Virgin Mary, reviled all the creatures God had created, from the beginning to the end of the world. His eyes were suffused with red, they looked at me brazenly with a loathing that sought to penetrate my soul.

On the verge of beheading him, my sword poised above his neck, I realized that by killing him, I would kill myself. I had begun to feel the pain of his wounds in my body, and the anguish of his death in my soul. Our twin existences were mysteriously joined, in this world and in the other.

In vain I had tried to escape from him during all these years; in vain I had attempted to sever our kinship by putting distance between our bodies. He and I were almost the same person, although our beliefs, our gods, and our acts made us different and disunited us.

He did not separate himself from me. He could not separate himself from me, no matter how much we both might desire it. Enemy brothers since our birth, we were perhaps condemned to die together. The mere thought that his head would roll in the dust as if it were mine paralyzed me.

"Kill him," Urraca the Shadow urged, suddenly beside me. "A moment of your doubt signifies a millennium of terror for the earth. If you let him live, I shall never forgive you for it. One day his accursed spirit will strike you down with your own hand."

"I cannot," I exclaimed.

"Kill him," Urraca insisted, seeing us looking at each other with the same eyes, eyes brimming with tenderness.

"Almarada is coming toward you with her sword drawn," García Cabezón warned. "You haven't much time left to execute him."

I felt I was drowning, my image sinking into his as into a waterless well. I thought that my self was dissolving in his self, that once again we would fuse into a single body, like the one existing previous to our birth. Almarada was now so near that I could hear her breathing.

"Let me go," Abd Allah wheedled in scarcely audible words. "I will part from you for always."

Almarada raised her sword to decapitate me. The blade's deadly sheen dazzled the air. Her head tumbled to the ground, but even without a head, her body remained upright.

Urraca the Shadow's hands were covered with blood. For the first time in her life she had used a weapon, she had killed someone.

In the distance another Almarada was waiting for Almarada. She came toward her. She entered her. Within her they became a double spectral figure.

Abd Allah was not able to depart; I dealt him the fatal stroke. His eyes still open, dragging himself over the ground, clawing the earth, he tried to move me with brotherly love, a love so despairing I couldn't tell if it flowed from him or from me.

His lips parted, his mouth twisted into a grimace, uttered a curse and closed.

His black mail coif, beyond his reach, was kicked by the hooves of a passing Berber's horse galloping by in flight.

In the throes of death, Abd Allah clutched at the muck, the rain. Before he could pick up a lump of mud, seize a few drops of rain, I nailed his remaining hand into the mire.

There his body lay: maimed, inanimate.

Upon seeing him lifeless, the Saracens stopped fighting, laid down their arms and began to flee. They stood gaping from the plains, the brushlands, the knolls. The battle of the end of the millennium had concluded. Satan would be enchained again in the abyss for another thousand years.

They unfastened my helmet, and my face was seen by the victors and the vanquished. My features were wan, like a newly dead man's. A ray of red light struck my forehead. It was the last ray of the setting sun.

Sancho Saborejo looked at me with stupefaction, not knowing which of the two was the living man, which the dead.

"I, Alfonso de León, command every man who has a hauberk, lance, sword, shield, horse or mule to surrender it to the king's men. I, the Messiah of the Second Millennium, command you to take my weapons, which are hanging from the saddletree, to Santa María de Regla and to place them on its ruined altar as a token of mourning for having slain my brother, Abd Allah. I, Abel, who have killed Cain a thousand times over, command you to swathe my horse in black and give him to a common, wretched man to toil the land and bring forth fruits to give to the poor," I said.

Then I commanded them to divest Abd Allah of his armor, to strip off his black garments, and to lay him simply shrouded on a wooden bench; to bury him by night in a coffin nailed closed with cruciform nails in the chapel of our monastery of San Juan el Teólogo, so that there, among spent candles, with a silver cross on his breast and a blessed stone atop the cross, he might await the Day of the Resurrection of the Dead and the Last Judgment.

On the hilltop al-Mansur, who had witnessed the battle in a rage, saw a mounted messenger riding toward him, but before receiving the news of the Saracens' defeat he had already heard it with his own eyes and divined it from the disastrous appearance of the emissary, who had blood on his teeth, in his eyes and on his torn clothing. Moreover, he had seen for himself the dead, the wounded, the stampeding horsemen, the riderless horses.

"I don't care a fig for the news you bring me!" al-Mansur shouted at him, and commenced the retreat.

Behind him, the Saracens began to abandon their positions. Many were the dead, the wounded, the prisoners they left behind, and they had lost princes and captains. Their ruin was general, their garments were torn, their armor crushed, foreheads skinned, arms and legs broken, jaws dislocated. One of Almarada's eunuchs—the other had died—a prodigious murderer, was unable to walk because he had long iron splinters sticking out of his rib cage. Two *muladies* bore him on their backs while he stabbed at them with knives he held in his hand. A black Saracen carried a plucked goshawk; now and then the bird tried to take to the air, but the chain hindered its flight. With blood-smeared fingers, grimly smiling Berbers parceled out stale bread, fumbling for their mouths when they attempted to eat it. On my instructions, none of our men went in pursuit of them, although one Leonese knight, who had not taken part in the battle, had a mind to behead them all.

Al-Mansur descended the hill, pallid, and on a litter borne by six black runners. To his left went the raven, its plumage bloody, beak chipped, wings nicked. With his right hand al-Mansur gathered the cloth of the winding-sheet that his daughters, named after flowers, had woven for him.

The wearied armies followed him in combat order, as did the women, the eunuchs, the slaves. A Saracen, whose clothes were rent and whose hair was shorn, ran alongside him, repeating in Arabic and in Romance, "In Calatañazor Almanzor will lose his tambor; in Calatañazor Almanzor will lose his tambor."

Al-Mansur seemed to be coming toward us when he swerved around a large ilex grove, took the road to Córdoba, crossed a narrow pass and receded down the darkening valley until he was lost to sight.

The Black Rider's forces marched off, skirting the poplars lining the Bernesga River. For a moment I thought they would join al-Mansur's troops, but they took different roads. Her face veiled in black, the dwarf Bartolomea Rodríguez led the defeated hosts. Spernicius accompanied her, transformed into her servant.

"'Twould be better for him if he'd never been born." The Leonese knight spurred his mare, intending to ride after the traitor and capture him.

"It is not advisable to resume the slaughter." García Cabezón restrained him with his sword.

"Making for *Qurtuba,* al-Mansur makes for his death. In a few years the Victorious One of Allah will die racked by hideous pain, merely one more miserable wretch who has trodden this earth on feet of clay," Urraca the Shadow foretold.

"In Córdoba, after his death, crimes will follow upon crimes, uprisings will follow upon uprisings, the buildings of Madinat al-Zahra will be sacked, burned and destroyed; the third caliph of al-Andalus, the weakling Hisham II, will die strangled by a son of the Berbers' *imam.* In Seville his assassins will for some time display another man, a dummy, passing it off as him," Jonás ibn Gabirol continued.

"On the day of his death al-Mansur will be buried in hell," the Leonese knight prophesied.

Immediately the Christians began to divide among themselves the treasures of al-Mansur, the Black Rider and the other Saracens, which they had found in their tents, saddlebags and leather pouches: richly adorned swords and hauberks; goblets, beakers, crucifixes and chalices of gold; boxes and caskets of ivory and wood; phials of ivory, metal and gemstones; diadems, necklaces and earrings of gold and silver; lamps, candelabra, braziers, pitchers and spouts of bronze; silver perfume bottles; silk and linen stuffs; dinars minted in Madinat al-Zahra, bearing the following words in Arabic at the center of each coin: "There is no God but God alone, no one can compare with Him," and on the reverse: "The *imam* al-Hakam, Commander of the Faithful, he who seeks victory in God."

I asked Abbot Andrés, Martín Meñique and the physicians from Puente Castro—the Jews Yusuf ben Guzmán and David ha-Leví—to tend the wounded Christians and Moors. I ordered that the shackles be removed from the captives and vassals of al-Mansur and the Black Rider, that they be given clothing and food and that the bodies of their friends and kinsmen dead in the war be delivered to them, making them take an oath on the Gospels that they would not depart from León until they had given them honorable burial. When they did leave, they took with them the mules, horses, chattels and provisions we had taken from the Mahometans.

"In towns and the wild, we will never fail you, we will always serve you as loyal vassals. In battle we will provide you with bread and water, we will give barley to your horses," several of the free men promised, loath to depart.

"Now it is we who will take slaves and captives," declared Sampiro, showing García Cabezón the white horse that had been Almarada's.

"There's no glory to be gained from beheading Moors; if we sell the Moorish women, we'll be selling our souls to the devil. Better for us to use them as God's creatures," Martín Meñique declared.

"Keep me in your memory, master. At dawn Oro María, Gómez and I will continue on our way to Santiago." Sancho Saborejo bade me farewell. "Give us your blessing."

"Tomorrow your son will speak words you will not want to hear. When you hear him say them, you will wish he were mute again," I told him.

"Well, then, if you so order it, let Gómez live mute in this world and in the other," Sancho Saborejo replied, "for there is no evil in silence."

"The whole world is a temple without walls and without doors, and we can worship God anywhere. Here we shall remain," Oro María said as she joined us.

"I shall go with Froila, mistress mine and nun of the monastery of Santiago de León, to populate the century. Her belly is heavy with my second offspring, conceived in May," García Cabezón declared.

"And what about Jimena?" I asked.

"Before God and man I acknowledge Jimena as my most beloved daughter, and as such, I bless her," he answered. "She, the concubine of the Lord of the Last Days, will soon give birth to his daughter. May the Blessed One absolve you and resurrect you in the life of the kingdom to come."

The First Millennium had ended. That day Doña Urraca and I watched night fall on the plains, on the mountains and in the eyes of those who were there. She and I perceived, as if in our own bodies, the emergence of the era of the Holy Spirit, with its tumult of marvels and horrors, with its multitude of births and deaths. In the depths of our souls we trusted that the ineffable Light would appear the next day, to illuminate not only the sleeping horizon of the world, but the darkness of the human heart as well.

"From today onward, relics of holy men and women will be found in the most unexpected places, in mountains and fields, in glades and caves, where they have remained hidden for centuries awaiting the moment of their resurrection," Martín Meñique announced.

"Although we have bound the Evil One, evils are still to come. A famine such as has never been seen will ravage the earth; an avenging sterility will make men eat carrion and kill and devour one another, in body and spirit," Urraca the Shadow warned.

"Only for one millennium, for afterward the elements will return to their original condition, the fields will be covered with green, and throngs of men and women will gather from the most remote confines of the earth to recapture paradise," Jonás ibn Gabirol predicted.

"I know that an invisible world exists beyond the temporal world, where the spirits are alive, where I will meet Abd Allah again as before our birth," I murmured. "In that world he will keep on dying his death, he will keep on falling into that abyss, which is himself."

My real story begins here. At daybreak I will set out on horseback to roam the chessboard of the morning. On that playing field, the ivory pieces of good and evil will dispute dominion over the new millennium.

Jimena will bring into the world a girl child: the Virgin. Those who see her after her birth will surely swear that her body is made of light, that a radiant crown of sun sits on her head, that her green eyes dazzle whoever contemplates them. She will be the goddess of the millenary kingdom. As of now, I kneel and uncover myself before this human Theotokos.

I, Lord of the Last Days, have made the first move of the chess game. I don't know if I'm playing with the white men or the black. I don't know if I am Alfonso de León or if I am Abd Allah of Córdoba. The deceased man who he was is alive in me. The live man who I am is dead in him. In silence, Urraca the Shadow, Martín Meñique and Jonás ibn Gabirol are watching me depart for the last night of the millennium and for the dawn of my destiny. Thus is it said in the book called *Visions of the Year 1000;*

thus say I, personage and author of the book. At the proper moment, my unnamed daughter will follow me on the road to Revelation, Passion and Resurrection.

I, Lord of the Last Days, will ride to the end of this spiritual era, flying the banner of faith in myself and in the light of day. I, the omniscient.

Today, the first day of January of the year 1001, the Third Testament commences, which records the words and deeds of Alfonso de León.

Here end the visions. Here begins life.

Blessed be God for centuries upon centuries. Amen.

BIBLIOGRAPHY

I am indebted to the following books and authors for the historical documentation of *The Lord of the Last Days: Visions of the Year 1000:*

Actas del simposio para el estudio de los códices del "Comentario al Apocalipsis" de Beato de Liébana. 3 vols. Madrid, 1978.

Al-Andalus: Las artes islámicas en España, ed. Jerrilyn D. Dodds. Madrid-New York, 1992.

Alatorre, Antonio. *Los 1,001 años de la lengua española.* México, 1979.

Alexander, J.J.G. *The Decorated Letter.* New York, 1978.

Alfonso X el Sabio. *Cantigas de Santa María.* Madrid, 1985.

———. *La Gran Conquista de Ultramar,* Madrid, 1877.

———. *Lapidario. Madrid, 1981.*

———. *Libro de ajedrez, dados y tablas de Alfonso X el Sabio.* Madrid, 1987.

————. *Libro de las cruzes.* Madrid-Madison, 1961.

————. *Primera crónica general ó sea estoria de España que mandó componer Alfonso el Sabio.* Madrid, 1906.

————. *Las Siete Partidas, Santiago, 1982.*

The Annals of Fulda, trans. and ed. Timothy Reuter. Manchester and New York, 1992.

The Annals of St.-Bertin, trans. and ed. Janet L. Nelson. Manchester and New York, 1991.

The Apocalypse in the Middle Ages, ed. Richard K. Emmerson and Bernard McGinn. Ithaca and London, 1992.

Arjona Castro, Antonio. *Anales de Córdoba musulmana.* Córdoba, 1982.

Las aves acuáticas en la provincia de León, ed. Joaquín Alegre, Angel Hernández, Tomas Velasco. León, 1991.

El Beato de Valcavado. León, 1991.

Benito, San. *Sancta Regula.* Madrid, 1954.

Berceo, Gonzalo de. *Obra completa.* Madrid, 1992.

Biblia medieval romanceada judío-cristiana, ed. P. José Llamas. Madrid, 1950.

Biblioteca Apostolica Vaticana: Liturgie und Andacht im Mittelalter. Köln, October 9, 1992–January 10, 1993.

Bloch, Marc. *La Société féodale.* 2 vols. Paris, 1939–40.

Bouhdiba, Abdelwahab. *La Sexualité en Islam.* Paris, 1975.

Cantera Montenegro, Enrique. *Instrumentos y técnicas de cultivo en la plena Edad Media europea: siglos X–XIII.* Madrid, 1987.

Carbajo Serrano, María José. *El monasterio de los Santos Cosme y Damián de Abellar: Monacato y sociedad en la época astur-leonesa.* León, 1988.

Carretón Hierro, Dom Eufrasio. *La ermita mozárabe de Santa Cecilia.* Valladolid, 1990.

Cohn, Norman. *Europe's Inner Demons.* London, 1975.

————. *The Pursuit of the Millennium.* London, 1970.

Colbert, E. P. *The Martyrs of Córdoba (850–859): A Study of the Sources.* Washington, D.C., 1962.

Cuadernos de Madinat al-Zahra. Córdoba, 1987.

Delehaye, Hippolyte. *Les Origines du culte des martyrs*. Bruxelles, 1933.

―――. *Sanctus: Essai sur le culte des saints dans l'antiquité*. Bruxelles, 1927.

Del Valle Rodríguez, C. *La Escuela Hebrea de Córdoba: Los orígenes de la Escuela Filológica Hebrea de Córdoba*. Madrid, 1981.

Dozy, Reinhart P. *Histoire des musulmanes d'Espagne*. 3 vols. Leyde, 1932.

―――. *Historia de los musulmanes de España*. 4 vols. Madrid, 1988.

―――. *Recherches sur l'histoire et la littérature de l'Espagne pendant le Moyen Age*. Paris-Leyde, 1881.

Dronke, Peter. *Poetic Individuality in the Middle Ages: New Departures in Poetry 1000–1150*. Oxford, 1970.

―――. *Women Writers of the Middle Ages*. Cambridge, 1984.

Duby, Georges, and Philippe Ariès, eds. *L'An mil*. Paris, 1980.

―――. *La Fin des temps: Terreurs et prophéties au Moyen Age,* préface de . . .

―――. *Historia de las mujeres en Occidente,* bajo la dirección de . . . y Michelle Perrot, vol. 2. Madrid, 1992.

―――. *A History of Private Life: Revelations of the Medieval World*. Cambridge, 1988.

―――. *Hommes et structures du Moyen Age*. Paris, 1973.

―――. *Le Moyen Age, 980–1140*. Genève, 1967.

―――. *Le Temps des cathédrales: L'Art et la societé 980–1420*. París, 1976.

Duckett, Eleanor. *Death and Life in the Tenth Century*. Ann Arbor, Mich., 1967.

―――. *The Gateway to the Middle Ages: Monasticism*. Ann Arbor, Mich., 1938.

Escalada, Marcos de. *San Miguel de Escalada, iglesia mozárabe: siglo X*. León, 1993.

Escalona, Romualdo. *Historia del Real Monasterio de Sahagún*. Madrid, 1782.

Estepa Diez, Carlos. *Estructura social de la ciudad de León (siglos XI–XIII)*. León, 1977.

Eulogio, San. *Obras completas*. Córdoba, 1959.

Farrer, Austin. *A Rebirth of Images: The Making of St. John's Apocalypse*. London, 1949.

Férotin, D. Marius. *Le Liber Mozarabicus Sacramentorum et les Manuscrits Mozarabes*. Paris, 1912.

Fichtenau, Heinrich. *Living in the Tenth Century: Mentalities and Social Orders*. Chicago, 1991.

Fiore, Joachim de. *Expositio in Apocalypsim*. Frankfurt, 1964.

Fita, Fidel. *San Miguel de Escalada: Inscripciones y documentos*. Boletín de la Real Academia de la Historia 31 (1897), 466–516.

Florez, Enrique. *España Sagrada: Theatro geográfico-histórico de la Iglesia de España*. 52 vols. Madrid, 1747–1918.

———. *Memorias de las Reynas Cathólicas: Historia genealógica de la Casa Real de Castilla y de León*. Madrid, 1770.

Floriano Cumbreño, A. *Diplomática española del período astur*. 2 vols. Oviedo, 1960.

Focillon, Henri. *L'An mil*. Paris, 1952.

Frenk Alatorre, Margit. *Las jarchas mozárabes y los comienzos de la lírica románica*. México, 1975.

Friedman, John Block. *The Monstrous Races in Medieval Art and Thought*. Cambridge, Mass., and London, 1981.

García-Aráez Ferrer, Hermenegildo. *La miniatura en los códices de Beato de Liébana*. Madrid, 1992.

García de la Fuente, Olegario. *El latín bíblico y el español medieval hasta el 1300,* vol. 1: *Gonzalo de Berceo*. Logroño, 1992.

García Gallo, Alfonso. *Las instituciones sociales en España en la alta Edad Media (siglos VIII–XII)* y *El hombre y la tierra en la Edad Media leonesa*. Barcelona, 1981.

García Lobo, Vicente. *Las inscripciones de San Miguel de Escalada*. Barcelona, 1982.

Geary, Patrick J. *Furta Sacra: Thefts of Relics in the Central Middle Ages*. Princeton, 1990.

Glaber, Rodulfus. *Historiarum libri quinque*. Oxford, 1989.

Gómez-Moreno, Manuel. *Iglesias mozárabes: Arte español de los siglos IX al XI*. Madrid, 1919.

———. *Provincia de León*. Madrid, 1925.

Grabar, André. *Christian Iconography: A Study of Its Origins*. Princeton, 1968.

———. *Martyrium: Recherches sur le culte des reliques et l'art chrétien antique*. 2 vols. Paris, 1943–46.

————, and Carl Nordenfalk. *Early Medieval Painting from the Fourth to the Eleventh Century.* Geneva, 1957.

Guía del peregrino medieval ("Codex Calixtinus"). Sahagún, 1991.

Gurevich, Aron. *Medieval Popular Culture: Problems of Belief and Perception.* Cambridge, 1988.

Head, Thomas, and Richard Landes. *The Peace of God: Social Violence and Religious Response in France Around the Year 1000.* Ithaca, N.Y., and London, 1992.

Hildegard of Bingen. *Book of Divine Works.* Santa Fe, 1987.

————. *Le Livre des oeuvres divines (Visions),* Paris, 1982.

————. *Louanges.* Paris, 1990.

Hoppin, Richard H. *Medieval Music.* New York-London, 1978.

Ibn Hazm de Córdoba. *El collar de la paloma.* Madrid, 1971.

Ibn Hudhayl. *Gala de caballeros, blasón de paladines.* Madrid, 1977.

Isidoro de Sevilla, San. *Etimologías.* Madrid, 1982.

Jewish Travellers in the Middle Ages: 19 Firsthand Accounts. New York, 1987.

Jungmann, Rev. Joseph. *The Mass of the Roman Rite: Its Origins and Development (Missarum Solemnia).* 2 vols. New York, 1950–55.

Kieckhefer, Richard. *Magic in the Middle Ages.* Cambridge, 1989.

Lambert, Malcolm. *Medieval Heresy.* Oxford, 1977.

Le Goff, Jacques. *L'Imaginaire médiéval.* París, 1985.

León y su historia, vols. 1–IV. León, 1970–84.

Lévi-Provençal, E. *Una crónica anónima de Abd Al-Rahman Al-Nasir* (en colaboración con E. García Gómez). Madrid-Granada, 1950.

————. *L'Espagne musulmane au xème siècle: Institutions et vie sociale.* Paris, 1932.

————. *Histoire de l'Espagne musulmane.* 4 vols. Paris, 1950–53.

Libro de Alejandro, versión de Elena Catena. Madrid, 1985.

El libro de los engaños, ed. John Esten Keller. Valencia, 1959.

Libro de los exemplos por A.B.C., ed. John Esten Keller. Madrid, 1961.

El libro de los Gatos, ed. John Esten Keller. Madrid, 1958.

Libro de viajes de Benjamín de Tudela, trans. José Ramón Magdalena Nom de Déu. Barcelona, 1982.

Linage Conde, Antonio. *Los orígenes del monacato benedictino en la Península Ibérica.* 3 vols. León, 1973.

Liturgia y música mozárabes: Ponencias y comunicaciones presentadas al I Congreso Internacional de Estudios Mozárabes. Toledo, 1975.

Loewe, Raphael. *Ibn Gabirol.* London, 1989.

López Ferreiro, Antonio. *Historia de la Santa A. M. Iglesia de Santiago de Compostela.* 11 vols. Santiago, 1898–1911.

Macer floridus: Edición facsímil del herbario-médico medieval de la Real Colegiata de San Isidoro de León. León, 1990.

McGinn, Bernard. *Visions of the End: Apocalyptic Traditions in the Middle Ages.* New York, 1979.

McNeill, John T., and Helena N. Gamer. *Medieval Handbooks of Penance.* New York and Oxford, 1938, 1990.

Marcus, Jacob R. *The Jew in the Medieval World: A Source Book: 315–1791.* Cincinnati, 1990.

Medieval Europe, a Short Sourcebook, ed. C. Warren Hollister et al. New York, 1987.

The Medieval Health Handbook: Tacuinum Sanitatis. New York, 1976.

Meinardus, Otto F. A. *St. John of Patmos and the Seven Churches of the Apocalypse.* Athens, 1974.

Menéndez Pidal, Ramón. *Crestomatía del español medieval.* 2 vols. Madrid, 1965–66.

———. *La España del Cid.* Buenos Aires, 1929.

———. *Manual de gramática histórica española.* Madrid, 1966.

———. *Orígenes del español: Estado lingüístico de la península ibérica hasta el siglo XI.* Madrid, 1926 and 1950.

———. *Poesía juglaresca y juglares.* Madrid, 1924.

———. *Poesía juglaresca y orígenes de las literaturas románicas.* Madrid, 1957.

———. *De primitiva lírica española y antigua épica.* Madrid, 1951.

———. *Reliquias de la poesía épica española.* Madrid, 1980.

Millares Carlo, Agustín. *Introducción a la historia del libro y de las bibliotecas.* México, 1971.

Millás Vallicrosa, José Ma. *Selomó ibn Gabirol como poeta y filósofo.* Madrid-Barcelona, 1945.

Millet-Gérard, Dominique. *Chrétiens mozarabes et culture islamique dans l'Espagne des VIIIe–IXe siècles.* Paris, 1984.

Mollat, Michel. *Les Pauvres au Moyen Age: Etude sociale.* Paris, 1978.

Moxó, Salvador de. *Repoblación y sociedad en la España cristiana medieval.* Madrid, 1979.

Murray, H.J.R. *A History of Chess.* Oxford, 1913.

Museo de Telas Medievales. Monasterio de Santa María la Real de Huelgas, Burgos. Madrid, 1988.

Mütherich, Florentine, and Joachim E. Gaehde. *Carolingian Painting.* New York, 1976.

Nebrija, Antonio de. *Gramática de la lengua castellana.* Madrid, 1980.

—————. *Vocabulario de Romance en Latín.* Madrid, 1981.

Pasionario hispánico. Barcelona, 1953.

Pelikan, Jaroslav. *The Christian Tradition: A History of the Development of Doctrine,* vols. 1, 2 and 3. Chicago and London, 1971, 1974, 1978.

Peña, Joaquín. *Los marfiles de San Millán de la Cogolla.* Logroño, 1978.

Pérez de Urbel, Fr. Justo. *García Fernández (El conde de las bellas manos).* Burgos, 1979.

—————. *Historia del condado de Castilla.* Madrid, 1945.

—————. *Los monjes españoles en la Edad Media.* Madrid, 1945.

—————. *Sampiro: Su crónica y la monarquía leonesa en el siglo X.* Madrid, 1952.

—————. *San Eulogio de Córdoba o la vida andaluza en el siglo IX.* Madrid, 1942.

Pirenne, Henri. *Medieval Cities: Their Origins and the Revival of Trade.* Princeton, 1925.

—————. *Mohammed and Charlemagne.* New York, 1939.

Poema de Fernán González, ed. Juan Victorio. Madrid, 1984.

Poema de Mio Cid, ed. Ramón Menéndez Pidal. Madrid, 1968.

Rabanal Alonso, Manuel Abilio. *El Camino de Santiago en León.* Ponferrada, 1992.

Reilly, Bernard F. *The Medieval Spains.* Cambridge, 1993.

Riché, Pierre. *Gerbert d'Aurillac, le pape de l'an mil.* Paris, 1987.

Risco, Manuel. *Historia de la ciudad y corte de León y de sus reyes.* Madrid, 1792.

————. *León,* vols. XXXIV, XXXV and XXXVI. Madrid, 1784 and 1787.

Rodríguez Fernández, Celso. *El antifonario visigótico de León: Estudio literario de sus fórmulas sálmicas.* León, 1985.

Rodríguez Fernández, Justiniano. *La judería de la Ciudad de León.* León, 1969.

————. *Sancho I y Ordoño IV, reyes de León.* León, 1987.

Ruiz Asencio, José Manuel. *Colección documental del archivo de la Catedral de León, III (986–1031).* León, 1987.

Sainted Women of the Dark Ages, ed. and trans. Jo Ann McNamara and John E. Halborg with E. Gordon Whatley. Durham and London, 1992.

Sánchez-Albornoz, Claudio. *Una ciudad hispano-cristiana hace un milenio: Estampas de la vida en León en el siglo X.* Buenos Aires, 1958.

————. *La España cristiana de los siglos VIII al XI: El reino astur-leonés.* Madrid, 1980.

————. *La España musulmana, según los autores islamitas y cristianos medievales.* 2 vols. Buenos Aires, 1947.

————. *España y el Islam.* Buenos Aires, 1943.

————. *Estudios sobre las instituciones medievales españolas.* México, 1965.

————. *Miscelánea de estudios históricos.* León, 1970.

Scholem, Gershom. *The Messianic Idea in Judaism and Other Essays.* New York, 1972.

Simonet, Francisco Javier. *Glosario de voces ibéricas y latinas usadas entre los mozárabes, precedido de un estudio sobre el dialecto hispano-mozárabe.* Madrid, 1888.

————. *Historia de los mozárabes de España.* Madrid, 1903.

Sota, Francisco de. *Crónica de los Príncipes de Asturias y Cantabria.* Madrid, 1681.

A Spanish Apocalypse: The Morgan Beatus Manuscript. New York, 1991.

Theotokos (Museo Catedralicio Diocesano). León, 1987.

Viajes de extranjeros por España y Portugal desde los tiempos más remotos hasta fines del siglo XVI, ed. J. García Mercadal. Madrid, 1952.

Visions of Heaven and Hell Before Dante, ed. Eileen Gardiner. New York, 1989.

The Visions of Tondal, ed. Thomas Kren and Roger S. Wieck. Malibu, Calif., 1990.

Vor Dem Jahr 1000: Abendländische Buchkunst zur Zeit der Kaiserin Theophanu. Köln, 1991.

Waddell, Helen. *The Desert Fathers.* Ann Arbor, Mich., 1957.

Wallace-Hadrill, J. M. *The Long-Haired Kings and Other Studies in Frankish History.* London, 1962.

Ward, Benedicta. *Harlots of the Desert.* Kalamazoo, Mich., 1987.

Warner, Marina. *Alone of All Her Sex: The Myth and the Cult of the Virgin Mary.* London and New York, 1976.

Williams, John. *Early Spanish Manuscript Illumination.* New York, 1977.

Woman Defamed and Woman Defended: An Anthology of Medieval Texts, ed. Alcuin Blamires. Oxford, 1992.

Women in Medieval Society, ed. Susan Mosher Stuart. Philadelphia, 1976.

Women's Lives in Medieval Europe: A Sourcebook, ed. Emilie Amt. London and New York, 1993.

Wright, Roger. *Late Latin and Early Romance in Spain and Carolingian France.* Liverpool, 1982.

Yáñez Cifuentes, Ma. del Pilar. *El monasterio de Santiago de León.* León, 1972.

Yepes, Antonio de. *Crónica general de la Orden de San Benito.* 3 vols. Madrid, 1959–60.

Zaleski, Carol. *Otherworld Journeys: Accounts of Near-Death Experience in Medieval and Modern Times.* New York and Oxford, 1987.

I will not attempt to list the numerous articles I consulted in the scholarly journals *Al-Andalus, Anuario de Estudios Medievales, Boletín de la Real Academia de la Historia, Bollettino dell'Istituto Storico Italiano per il Medio Evo, Catholic Historical Review, Cuadernos de Historia de España, English Historical Review, Harvard Theological Review, Hispania, Hispania Sacra, Journal of Medieval History, Journal of Theological Studies, Medieval Studies, Revue Historique, Speculum, Studies in Medieval and Renaissance History, Studi Medievali.*